LEGEND OF THE GALACTIC HEROES

VOLUME 7
TEMPEST

YOSHIKI TANAKA

HAIKA SORU

SAN FRANCISCO

LEGEND OF THE GALACTIC HEROES

OF THE

GALACTIC HEROES

VOLUME 7

TEMPEST

WRITTEN BY
YOSHIKI TANAKA

Translated by Daniel Huddleston

Legend of the Galactic Heroes, Vol. 7: Tempest
GINGA EIYU DENSETSU Vol.7
© 1986 by Yoshiki TANAKA
Cover Illustration © 2008 Yukinobu Hoshino.
All rights reserved.

English translation © 2018 VIZ Media, LLC
Cover and interior design by Fawn Lau and Alice Lewis

HAIKASORU
Published by VIZ Media, LLC
P.O. Box 77010
San Francisco, CA 94107

www.haikasoru.com

Library of Congress Cataloging-in-Publication Data

Names: Tanaka, Yoshiki, 1952- author. | Huddleston, Daniel, translator.
Title: Legend of the galactic heroes / written by Yoshiki Tanaka ; translated
    by Daniel Huddleston and Tyran Grillo
Other titles: Ginga eiyu densetsu
Description: San Francisco : Haikasoru, [2016]
Identifiers: LCCN 2015044444| ISBN 9781421584942 (v. 1: paperback) | ISBN
    9781421584959 (v. 2: paperback) | ISBN 9781421584966 (v. 3: paperback) | ISBN
    9781421584973 (v. 4: paperback) | 9781421584980 (v. 5: paperback) | ISBN
    9781421584997 (v. 6: paperback) | 9781421585291 (v. 7: paperback)
    v. 1. Dawn -- v. 2. Ambition -- v. 3. Endurance -- v. 4 Stratagem -- v. 5 Mobilization --
    v. 6 Flight -- v. 7 Tempest
Subjects: LCSH: Science fiction. | War stories. | BISAC: FICTION / Science
    Fiction / Space Opera. | FICTION / Science Fiction / Military. | FICTION /
    Science Fiction / Adventure.
Classification: LCC PL862.A5343 G5513 2016 | DDC 895.63/5--dc23
LC record available at http://lccn.loc.gov/2015044444

Printed in the U.S.A.
First printing, August 2018

MAJOR CHARACTERS

GALACTIC EMPIRE

REINHARD VON LOHENGRAMM
Kaiser.[1]

PAUL VON OBERSTEIN
Minister of military affairs. Imperial marshal.

WOLFGANG MITTERMEIER
Commander in chief of the Imperial Space Armada. Imperial Marshal. Known as the "Gale Wolf."

OSKAR VON REUENTAHL
Secretary-general of Imperial Military Command Headquarters. Imperial Marshal. The "heterochromatic admiral."

FRITZ JOSEF WITTENFELD
Commander of the *Schwarz Lanzenreiter* fleet. Senior admiral.

ERNEST MECKLINGER
Rear guard commander in chief. Admiral. Known as the "Artist-Admiral."

ULRICH KESSLER
Commissioner of Military police and commander of capital defenses. Senior admiral.

AUGUST SAMUEL WAHLEN
Fleet commander. Senior admiral.

KORNELIAS LUTZ
Fleet commander. Senior admiral.

NEIDHART MÜLLER
Fleet commander. Senior admiral. AKA, "Iron Wall Müller."

ADALBERT FAHRENHEIT
Fleet commander. Senior admiral.

ARTHUR VON STREIT
High deputy to the kaiser. Vice admiral.

HILDEGARD VON MARIENDORF
Chief secretary to the kaiser. Often called "Hilda."

FRANZ VON MARIENDORF
Minister of Domestic Affairs. Hilda's father.

HEIDRICH LANG
Chief of the Domestic Safety Security Bureau.

ANNEROSE VON GRÜNEWALD
Reinhard's elder sister. Archduchess.

JOB TRÜNICHT
The Free Planets Alliance's former head of state.

RUDOLF VON GOLDENBAUM
Founder of the Galactic Empire's Goldenbaum Dynasty.

DECEASED

SIEGFRIED KIRCHEIS
Died living up to the faith Annerose placed in him.

HEINRICH VON KÜMMEL
Hilda's cousin. Failed to assassinate the Kaiser.

HELMUT LENNENKAMP
High Commissioner to the Free Planets Alliance. Destroyed himself over a personal grudge.

FREE PLANETS ALLIANCE

YANG WEN-LI
Commander of Iserlohn Fortress.
Commander of Iserlohn Patrol Fleet.
Marshal (retired).

JULIAN MINTZ
Yang's ward. Sublieutenant.

FREDERICA GREENHILL YANG
Yang's wife and aide. Lieutenant
commander.

ALEX CASELNES
Acting general manager of rear services.
Vice admiral.

WALTER VON SCHÖNKOPF
Commander of Fortress Defenses at
Iselohn Fortress. Vice admiral.

EDWIN FISCHER
Vice commander of the Iserlohn Patrol
Fleet. Master of fleet operations.
Temporarily laid off.

MURAI
Chief of staff. Rear admiral. Temporarily
laid off.

FYODOR PATRICHEV
Vice chief of staff. Commodore.
Temporarily laid off.

DUSTY ATTENBOROUGH
Division commander within the Iserlohn
Patrol Fleet. Yang's underclassman. Rear
admiral (retired).

OLIVIER POPLIN
Captain of the First Spaceborne Squadron
at Iserlohn Fortress. Commander.

ALEXANDOR BUCOCK
Commander in chief of the Space Armada.
Marshal.

LOUIS MACHUNGO
Julian's bodyguard. Ensign.

KATEROSE VON KREUTZER
Corporal. AKA Karin.

WILIABARD JOACHIM MERKATZ
Highly experienced veteran admiral.
Commander of the Yang Fleet's remaining
forces.

BERNHARD VON SCHNEIDER
Merkatz's aide. Commander.

CHUNG WU-CHEN
Chief of staff. Acting commander in chief.
Admiral.

JOÃO LEBELLO
Head of state.

PHEZZAN DOMINION

ADRIAN RUBINSKY
The fifth Landesherr. Known as the "Black
Fox of Phezzan."

NICOLAS BOLTEC
The Empire's proxy governor of Phezzan.

BORIS KONEV
Independent merchant. Old acquaintance of
Yang's. Captain of *Beryozka*.

*Titles and ranks correspond to each
character's status at the end of *Flight*
or their first appearance in *Tempest*.

†First called "Kaiser" by his soldiers
on Phezzan, he officially adopted
the title upon his coronation.

TABLE OF
CONTENTS

"Well now! If it isn't his Excellency, Count Reinhard von Lohengramm! You've ascended to lofty heights, I see. And to have come so far, from a life even a peasant would blush to own…I simply can't imagine the many struggles you must have faced."

"You are far too generous, Marquis. I believe your Excellency is most certainly capable of understanding. After all, my own life's point of departure will be your final destination."

—January 1, I.E. 487 (old Imperial Calendar), from a conversation between Marquis Wilhelm von Littenheim III and Count Reinhard von Lohengramm, at the New Year's celebration held in the Black Pearl Room at Neue Sans Soussi Palace. Two days later, Count von Lohengramm would depart for Iserlohn Fortress, leading a military expedition.

CHAPTER 1:

I

WHEN IMPERIAL MARSHAL Oskar von Reuentahl, secretary-general of Imperial Military Command Headquarters, ducked his tall frame through the door of the room hosting the day's imperial council meeting, two other attendees were already present and seated: Paul von Oberstein, minister of military affairs, and Wolfgang Mittermeier, commander in chief of the Imperial Space Armada. Both were imperial marshals. It was the first reunion of the so-called Three Chiefs of the imperial military in quite a long time.

In appearance alone, they made a remarkable trio: the slender, sallow minister of military affairs, with his white-streaked hair and artificial eyes; the handsome secretary-general of Imperial Military Command Headquarters, with his dark-brown hair, black right eye, and blue left one; and the gray-eyed, somewhat diminutive commander in chief of the Imperial Space Armada, whose golden hair was the shade of honey. The latter pair were not merely colleagues; together, they had faced life and death on the battlefield many times over. All three were young men, in their early thirties.

It was October 9, SE 799. Year 1 of the New Imperial Calendar.

Planet Phezzan's history as home to Reinhard von Lohengramm's imperial headquarters had only just begun. Planet Odin had served as the empire's capital across five centuries, but in September of that year, the twenty-three-year-old emperor had cast it aside and moved his throne to Phezzan, which until the previous year had rejoiced in its independence from the greater Galactic Empire. One hundred days had not yet passed since the crown had come to rest on his head.

After arriving on Phezzan, Kaiser Reinhard had installed his imperial headquarters in the same hotel he had used as a temporary admiralität during Operation Ragnarok, back before the crown had yet to come to him. Now, as well as then, this hotel was neither prestigious nor known for any high-class facilities. It did, however, provide convenient access to both the spaceport and the center of the city. While this was generally considered its only selling point, it was exactly why Reinhard had chosen it. Running alongside this handsome young conqueror's dazzling looks and talent was a spirit of admiration for the pragmatic, and even the prosaic. He had even tried to make do with just a single room for his own private quarters in the hotel.

The room that von Reuentahl had just stepped into was also hardly what one would call luxurious. Spare and simple, its furnishings had likely been costly, but did not seem to have been chosen with any great care. That said, the banner of the Lohengramm Dynasty, just recently approved, was hung on the facing wall, covering it entirely, and it brought a stunning brilliance to a room that was otherwise lacking in character.

Up until recently, the banner had been that of the Goldenbaum Dynasty—a golden, two-headed eagle on a black background. That had been abolished and replaced by the banner of the Lohengramm Dynasty: a crimson flag with golden edgework, the image of a golden lion positioned at its center.

This banner, dubbed the *Goldenlöwe,* was a flag of incomparable majesty. While designwise it was nothing terribly original, the flag gave a powerful impression both at that time and in generations to come, due simply to the fact that it symbolized the golden-haired youth who flew it, and the multitudes that followed him.

The three imperial marshals were representatives of those multitudes. Their positions, achievements, and fame were second only to those of the kaiser himself. With von Oberstein either at command HQ or in the rear guard, and the other two on the front lines, they had taken part in countless battles—and contributed to victories in equal number. Mittermeier and von Reuentahl, known as the "Twin Ramparts" of the imperial military, had won particular praise for their undefeated service records, along with redheaded Siegfried Kircheis, who had departed this world so young.

It was because of his loss that Mittermeier—called the "Gale Wolf"—and the heterochromatic von Reuentahl had been able to reach the highest positions of authority within the Imperial Navy by the young ages of thirty-one and thirty-two, respectively. Others followed behind them, but there were none who ran ahead of them.

The two marshals already present nodded at von Reuentahl, who proceeded to take his seat. He might have liked to enjoy a pleasant chat with Mittermeier alone, but as this was an official setting, he couldn't simply ignore the despised secretary of military affairs. He would have to look for another time and place to catch up with Mittermeier.

"At what time will His Majesty be joining us?" von Reuentahl asked, although the question was a pure formality. Receiving an answer of "Shortly" from his good friend, he proceeded to pose another question to the minister of military affairs: For what purpose had His Majesty called this assembly?

"Could it have something to do with the Lennenkamp affair?" he asked. If so, that would certainly be an important matter.

"That's correct," von Oberstein replied. "There's been a report from Admiral Steinmetz."

"And?"

Von Oberstein's prosthetic eyes locked on the inquisitive von Reuentahl and Mittermeier, who had leaned forward slightly, in equal measure before he gave answer: "Lennenkamp, he informs us, has already passed through the gates of Hades. The body will arrive here shortly."

The name spoken by the minister of military affairs was that of a senior admiral stationed on Planet Urvashi in the Gandharva System—located in the very midst of the Free Planets Alliance. Last July, Senior Admiral Helmut Lennenkamp, serving as High Commissioner to the Free Planets Alliance, had been abducted by malcontent elements of the FPA military, and Steinmetz had been rushed over to negotiate with the criminal group and the FPA government.

"Has he, then?" said von Reuentahl. "Well, I can't say I'm surprised…"

Such an outcome had hardly been unforeseen. From the moment the kidnapping had first been reported, hope for Lennenkamp's safe recovery had been largely abandoned. This was the "sense of smell"—the common sense—of those who chose lives of tumult during tumultuous times.

"And the cause of death?"

"He hanged himself."

The minister of military affairs' reply was the essence of brevity, his voice low and dry, capable of penetrating deeply into the psyches of his listeners. Two famed imperial marshals exchanged a three-colored glance. Mittermeier's vivacious grays tilted slightly as their owner cocked his head.

"Meaning we're in no position to declare Yang Wen-li responsible," he said. Mittermeier hadn't asked the question so much as raised the issue. He needed to know what Kaiser Reinhard and his minister of military affairs intended with regard to coming military decisions and actions.

"Lennenkamp had everything a man could want," said von Oberstein. "There was no reason why he should have killed himself. For driving him to those circumstances, Yang Wen-li clearly does bear a portion of the responsibility. As he has taken flight without attempting to explain his actions, it is, of course, inevitable that he should face questioning in the matter."

Yang Wen-li was not a name to be taken lightly, either in the Alliance Armed Forces or the imperial military. As an admiral in the FPA's navy, he had been reputed to be invincible, but after the Free Planets Alliance had bowed the knee to Reinhard, he had retired from the service and started his life as a pensioner. On two separate occasions, Yang had bested Lennenkamp on the battlefield, though, and Lennenkamp had never managed to forgive or forget those humiliations. After placing Yang under surveillance and plotting to have him arrested without any material evidence to support his suspicions, Lennenkamp had suffered a harsh blowback indeed.

Many things about the circumstances had not yet come to light, and for now could only be guessed at. There was no room for doubt, however, that the regret and frustration arising from his defeats had become a heavy burden clouding the lens of Lennenkamp's better judgment. Hounded by responsibilities that outweighed his talents, he had become a rare example of an error among Kaiser Reinhard's appointments.

Mittermeier folded his arms. "But Lennenkamp was always fair to his men," he said.

"Sadly, Yang Wen-li was not among his subordinates."

When it came to either magnanimity toward his opponents or flexibility of thought, Lennenkamp had been lacking. That was a fact, and there was no choice but to acknowledge it. Von Reuentahl and Mittermeier both mourned the loss of a colleague, but when it came down to it, they also held the abilities of their enemy, Yang Wen-li, in greater esteem than they had those of their unfortunate colleague. As such, their disappointment might have been far greater had things turned out opposite of the way they had. They both acknowledged von Oberstein's point, though the minister of military affairs' own feelings remained somewhat opaque.

At one time, Reinhard had been so impressed by Yang's abilities that he had hoped he might bring the man under his own command. Even now, it wasn't certain whether he'd abandoned the idea completely. When they had learned of their lord's intentions, both Mittermeier and von Reuentahl had inwardly agreed with him, but von Oberstein, it was said, had politely—but strongly and firmly—voiced his objection. "If you must have him in your camp, it behooves you to set certain conditions he must satisfy," he had insisted.

"I've always wondered what exactly you urged His Majesty to make Yang do at that time."

"Are you asking me, Marshal von Reuentahl?"

"No, I can tell without asking."

"Can you, now?"

"Make him regional governor over the territory of the former Free

Planets Alliance, have him rule over the land where he was born, force him to subjugate his own former allies. Surely you intended something along those lines?"

Von Oberstein merely unlaced his fingers, then laced them once more; his facial muscles and vocal cords remained utterly motionless. As von Reuentahl stared at his profile with his sharp, mismatched gaze, one corner of his mouth crept infinitesimally higher.

"That *is* the sort of thing you'd think of. What's more important to you? Gathering talented individuals to serve His Majesty, or setting trials for them to overcome?"

"Gathering talent is important, but is it not also my responsibility to determine whether or not those people can be trusted?"

"So in other words, all who gather at His Majesty's feet must be subjected to your interrogation? That's a quite a job you have—but who makes sure the examiner himself behaves fairly and with loyalty toward His Majesty?"

On the surface, at least, the synthetic-eyed minister of military affairs was calm in the face of this acid sarcasm.

"The two of you are welcome to perform that task."

And what do you mean by that? von Reuentahl probed, not with his voice, but with his mismatched eyes.

"The system itself aside, command of the empire's military is effectively in both of your hands. Should the day come when my impartiality appears lacking, you will surely have the means to dispose of me."

"The minister of military affairs seems somehow mistaken."

Bald-faced hostility was beginning to reach the saturation point in von Reuentahl's voice, and Mittermeier, swallowing down his own angry shout, turned a worried gaze toward his friend. Von Reuentahl was not a man to fly into a rage easily, but as his friend of ten years, Mittermeier was well aware of how his linguistic expression could often become extreme.

"Mistaken?"

"Regarding the one in whom authority over the military is vested. In the Lohengramm Dynasty, all military authority resides with His Majesty, Kaiser Reinhard. Both myself and Commander in Chief Mittermeier are nothing more than His Majesty's representatives. Your words, Minister, seemed to suggest we make that authority our own."

This sort of acrid reasoning was better suited to von Oberstein's use. The artificial eyes of the minister of military affairs would brim with a gelid light whenever he struck at an argument's weak point; when he did so, his opponents were usually silenced, with the subcutaneous flow of blood draining out of their faces. Yet even when put on defense, von Oberstein remained calm.

"You surprise me," he said. "By your own logic, there was never a need for you to concern yourself over my impartiality, or lack thereof, toward His Majesty. After all, who but His Majesty alone can decide whether I am just?"

"An impressive bit of sophistry. However—"

"Will both of you please just *stop!*" Mittermeier rapped the desk once with the back of his left hand, prompting both the minister of military affairs and the secretary-general of Imperial Military Command Headquarters to break off their microscale, yet gravely intense, skirmish. There was the low sound of an exhaled breath, though it was hard to judge from whom it came. After a short moment, von Reuentahl adjusted his position on the sofa to take advantage of the backrest, and von Oberstein rose from his seat and disappeared into the washroom.

Mittermeier scratched his unruly, honey-blond hair with one hand, and in a deliberately teasing voice, said, "I'd thought it was *my* job to fight the war of words with von Oberstein. This time, you kept stealing my limelight."

A hint of a wry smile appeared on von Reuentahl's face in response to his friend's jibe.

"Spare me the sarcasm, Mittermeier; I know I was being childish."

Indeed, von Reuentahl could feel himself cringing inside at the very thought of that aggressive mood that von Oberstein's cool demeanor had provoked in him. For just a moment, it had felt like he'd lost his grip on reason.

Mittermeier started to say something, but then, uncharacteristically, hesitated.

That was when von Oberstein came back into the room. Any emotion he might have had was still concealed behind the pallid drape of his expressionless face, and his presence charged the air with a faint electrical current. The awkward silence did not last long, however. With luxurious golden hair swaying in the soft breeze of the air conditioner, their kaiser appeared, clad in a black and silver uniform.

II

Senior Admiral Ernest Mecklinger, known as the "Artist-Admiral," appraised his young sovereign as follows: "The kaiser expressed himself through his own life and the way he lived it. He was a poet. A poet with no need of language."

That was a sentiment shared equally among the brave admirals serving this youthful conqueror. Though some gave little thought to what distant land the great river of time might be carrying them, even they harbored no doubt that if they followed this young man, they could engrave their names in history.

A number of historians have said, "The Goldenbaum Dynasty stole the universe; the Lohengramm Dynasty conquered it." And while that appraisal might not be an entirely fair one, Rudolf von Goldenbaum's shift from political maneuvering prior to his enthronement to open oppression afterward had reversed the flow of history itself. Compared to that, Reinhard's conquest was one vastly richer in the sort of extravagant spectacle that enflames people's romanticism.

Since his first taste of combat at age fifteen, Reinhard had offered up seven-tenths of his time on Mars's altar. His incomparable successes on and around the battlefield had been won by his own cunning and bravery. Those who had once berated him as an "impudent golden brat" now swore epithets as the goddess of victory showered him with her favor. To Reinhard, however, that goddess was merely following his orders, and producing results commensurate to his talents; never once had he ever fled to her skirts for protection.

By this time, Reinhard had already proven himself to be one of history's outstanding military leaders, but as a ruler, he had yet to face the test of time.

The many political and societal reforms he had enacted as prime minister of the Old Galactic Empire had been worthy of adulation, all but purging it of the corruption and decadence that for five centuries had been percolating in the depths of its history, and banishing its privileged classes to the graveyard of time. No other ruler had ever made such great accomplishments in the brief span of two years.

And yet, the ultimate challenge for any great and wise monarch is to go on being great and wise. Exceedingly rare is the king who begins his reign by ruling wisely, and doesn't end it in foolishness. Before receiving the verdict of history, a monarch must first endure his own declining mental faculties. In the case of a constitutional monarchy, some or even most of the responsibility can be yielded to constitutional law or a parliament, but an autocrat has nothing to lean on except his own talents, abilities, and conscience. Those who lack a lordly sense of responsibility at the outset have an odd way of turning out better. It's the ones who stumble while striving for greatness who often become the worst tyrants.

Reinhard was not the thirty-ninth emperor of the Goldenbaum Dynasty; he was the founder of the Lohengramm Dynasty. Should no successor be born to him, he stood to be its only kaiser. At present, it was through no tradition or institution that his "Neue Reich" towered high amid the rushing waves of history; it was due rather to the personal capability and character of the man who occupied its highest seat. It was generally thought that Paul von Oberstein, the minister of military affairs, viewed this as a fragile foundation, and planned to strengthen and perpetuate it through institutions and bloodlines.

.·. ·
·
· ·

Kaiser Reinhard was already aware of Lennenkamp's death, but after hearing about it a second time in the minister of military affairs ' organized report, he remained silent for quite some time. Sometimes, when this handsome young man was feeling glum, he would take on a still, lifeless appearance—one that brought to mind not a sick or a dead man, but rather one sculpted from crystal.

Then the moment passed, and the statue spoke as life returned to him. "Lennenkamp," said Reinhard, "was never a man of flawless character. Still, his sins were not so great as to deserve being driven to this kind of death. I've done a regrettable thing."

Softly but pointedly, von Reuentahl asked, "Does Your Majesty believe someone should be held criminally accountable?" His intent was not to criticize Reinhard. In his capacity as secretary-general of Imperial Military Command Headquarters, von Reuentahl needed to know who the kaiser thought was to blame so he could prepare an appropriate military response. Should he track down and attack the fugitive Yang Wen-li? Attack the government of the Free Planets Alliance, which in his view was not merely incompetent and ineffectual, but had actively made matters worse by neglecting its obligations under the Baalat Treaty? Or should he take the opposite tack and have the FPA government deal with Yang instead? No matter what was ultimately decided, it was bound to exceed the sphere of purely military action.

And yet at the same time, von Reuentahl personally did not want a mundane reply from his young liege. Even for an intelligent man like himself, this was a difficult psychological element to sort out. Back when the Goldenbaum Dynasty's power structure had still seemed immovable and inviolate, von Reuentahl, together with his best friend, had willingly placed themselves under Reinhard's command. They had placed their futures in the hands of a young man of about twenty with no impressive lineage to speak of. Rightly rewarded for that decision, von Reuentahl was an imperial marshal at the age of thirty-two, and had made the seat of secretary-general at Imperial Military Joint HQ his own. Naturally, he possessed skill and accomplishments worthy of that office. Boasting countless acts of heroism on the battlefield, von Reuentahl had contributed greatly toward establishing the Lohengramm dictatorship and dynastic hegemony.

During that time, he had made achievements off the battlefield as well. At the conclusion of the so-called Lippstadt War two years prior, red-haired Siegfried Kircheis, a man who had been like a brother to Reinhard, had lost his life defending his sworn friend from an assassin's gun, and Reinhard had seemingly lost his mind from shock and grief. Right on the heels of overwhelming victory, the Lohengramm faction had faced its greatest crisis. At that time, it had been von Reuentahl and Mittermeier who had executed the vicious stratagem devised by von Oberstein, leading the team that had carried out the overthrow of the enemy to their rear, Duke Lichtenlade. It was unlikely that the other admirals would have taken action on von Oberstein's insistence alone. It was through their decisiveness and leadership that he and Mittermeier had established themselves as the "Twin Ramparts" of the imperial military—a matched pair of glittering jewels.

Everything they had done, all their courageous deeds, had been to multiply the rays cast by an enormous star named Reinhard von Lohengramm. Von Reuentahl had never harbored any dissatisfaction on this point. What did cause sudden writhing in the subversive corners of his heart were those times when he detected a *dimming* in the rays of that great sun. Perhaps von Reuentahl was looking for perfection in the object of his allegiance.

Pride—and objective self-evaluation as well, most likely—told von Reuentahl that he possessed talents and abilities surpassing those of numerous emperors of the Goldenbaum Dynasty. Should not one who ruled over a man like himself be equipped with even greater talent, broader ability, and richer character?

His good friend Wolfgang Mittermeier had imposed on himself a lifestyle that was steadfast and clear-eyed to the point of being simpleminded. And while he had great respect for his friend's righteous behavior, von Reuentahl didn't think it impossible that he could adopt such ways himself.

Had Reinhard been able to guess at the vast emotions compressed and sealed within that brief question asked by the secretary-general of Imperial Military Command Headquarters? Somewhat affectedly, the young kaiser brushed the hair back from his fair-skinned forehead, and golden light swayed inside the room.

This was, of course, an unconscious action. Not once in his lifetime had he ever brought his good looks to bear as a weapon. No matter how extraordinary his appearance might have been, he himself had contributed nothing toward achieving it. Credit for that achievement belonged to the bloodlines of his hated father and a mother who, compared to his elder sister, had left little impression on him. Therefore, his handsome face was not something he prided himself on. His own wishes aside, though, his comely visage could put a sculpture to shame, and his lithe movements were the very essence of fluid elegance—it was a fact of his life that others couldn't help being moved to praise these qualities.

"Rather than mourn last year's bitter wine," Reinhard said, "let's examine the seeds of the grapes we'll be planting this year. That's the more effective course."

Von Reuentahl had the feeling he'd been parried, but it didn't bother him. Reinhard's outstanding wit and resourcefulness never offended him.

"Instead, I'd like to exploit the rift between Yang Wen-li and his government at this time, and invite that extraordinary genius to come serve under me. How about it, von Oberstein?"

"I think it would be a splendid idea."

Surprise glimmered between the long eyelashes of the young kaiser, and observing that through his artificial eyes, von Oberstein added, "I also believe, though, that such an offer should be made on the condition that Yang Wen-li cut the Free Planets Alliance's lifeline himself."

Reinhard's eyebrows, like fine strokes of a classical painter's brush, twitched just slightly. Mittermeier and von Reuentahl glanced at one another, both looking like they wanted to cluck their tongues. The very idea that the secretary-general of Imperial Military Command Headquarters had criticized just moments before was now brazenly being proposed by the minister of military affairs.

"For Yang Wen-li, becoming your vassal would mean casting aside a state he has served to this day, and denying the reasons he's had for fighting all along. That being the case, it would also be for his own good that he eliminate each and every element that would otherwise remain as an unresolved attachment afterward."

Reinhard regarded him in silence.

"Still," said von Oberstein. "I doubt such a thing is possible for him."

On the sofa, Reinhard crossed his long legs. With one elbow on the armrest, the spearhead of his piercing gaze turned on the minister of military affairs.

"So what you ultimately wish to say is that Yang Wen-li will never become my vassal?"

"Yes, Your Majesty."

With no hesitation, and quite calmly, the minister of military affairs had given an answer that might also be interpreted as, *Your Majesty lacks the ability to make him.* Even the other two marshals, who despised von Oberstein, had to hand it to him when it came to his boldness—or insensitivity.

"I'd further like to ask what position and duties Yang Wen-li will be rewarded with in the event he does bow the knee to Your Majesty. Too small a reward will not satisfy him, but too great a reward will make others uneasy."

Though he didn't say so out loud, von Oberstein had a feeling that once Yang became the kaiser's vassal, he would not long content himself with competing against Mittermeier, von Reuentahl, and the rest. Would he not surpass them, integrate the forces of the former Free Planets Alliance, and come to occupy the seat of number two?

Number twos had to be purged. The rise of the upstart Reinhard, founder of the Lohengramm Dynasty, had come so suddenly that he was better called the "one half" of his name rather than the first, and in his new regime, the relationship between lord and vassal was neither codified nor established in tradition. The existence of a number two capable of replacing the number one could never be tolerated.

Mittermeier and von Reuentahl alike were vassals sworn to Reinhard von Lohengramm personally, and likely had little consciousness as yet of themselves as court vassals of the Lohengramm *Dynasty*. Taken further, if they considered themselves Reinhard's sworn compatriots rather than his vassals, order could not hold in the lord-vassal relationship. It was loyalty, codified and enshrined in tradition, that would secure the Lohengramm Dynasty in perpetuity, so their only proper role was that of "the kaiser's vassals," not "the kaiser's friends."

After a long silence, Reinhard answered. "Very well. We'll set aside the matter of Yang Wen-li for the time being."

Reinhard hadn't said he'd completely given up. Von Oberstein, perhaps reluctant to pursue the matter further, held his peace.

"Still, democratic government must be remarkably shortsighted if an individual like Yang Wen-li can't find a place in one."

Reinhard thought so, and said so. The one who responded was Wolfgang Mittermeier.

"If I may, Your Majesty, the problem is likely not so much the system as the people who are running it. I'd call to your attention a most recent example, in which Your Majesty's own gifts could find no place in the Goldenbaum Dynasty."

"I see. That's certainly true." Reinhard smiled wryly, but the enthusiasm had vanished from his graceful countenance.

With a cynical look, von Reuentahl said, "In that case, Your Majesty, what shall we do? Use Lennenkamp's death as an occasion to annex all of the FPA's territory at once? We've given them something of a reprieve already."

"We *could* send the full might of the imperial military to cut this Gordian knot, and yet it seems a shame to do so with the republicans dancing about so madly. We also have the choice of watching them from the grandstands a little while longer, and letting them dance themselves to exhaustion."

Reinhard's words had been chosen to rein in his own fighting spirit. For the three imperial marshals, this was somewhat unexpected. Had moving imperial headquarters to Phezzan alone been enough to satiate their kaiser's spirit? His white hand was playing with the pendant on his breast.

Above the golden gleam of the handsome young kaiser's hair, a lion of that selfsame color was roaring voicelessly. The three imperial marshals saluted in unison before their new banner and kaiser. Each man's eyes harbored his own deep feelings and expectations. As Reinhard returned their salutes, a thin haze of irritation directed at himself clouded his expression.

Lieutenant Commander Emil von Reckendorf, aide-de-camp to Imperial Marshal von Reuentahl, was standing by outside the meeting room awaiting his senior officer's decisions on two or three clerical matters at Imperial Joint HQ. When the imperial council was adjourned and the young, heterochromatic marshal emerged from the meeting room, he exchanged a simple farewell with his friend of the honey-hued hair, then set off down the hotel's hallway. As he was walking, subordinates handed him documents, and he issued instructions while perusing their contents. The aide-de-camp followed the imperial marshal with his eyes, feeling that something was a little off in his lucid, yet somewhat mechanical tone of voice. There was no way he could have seen through him, though, to plumb the depths of von Reuentahl's inner heart.

Please, kaiser, don't give me an opening to rise up against you. It's you whom I've chosen to steer the rudder of history—you whom I've put forward for that task. I follow your banner with pride. Don't ever make me regret it. You must always walk ahead of me, lighting the way. But how can a light like yours burn if fueled by passivity and stability?

That unparalleled spirit of yours, that capacity for action, that's where your true worth lies…

III

Hildegard von Mariendorf, chief secretary to the kaiser, had naturally followed Reinhard when he'd moved his headquarters to Phezzan. Hilda's father, Count Franz von Mariendorf, was minister of domestic affairs, and had stayed behind on Planet Odin, long the location of the imperial capital. There he was busy attending to affairs of state. The kaiser and his chief cabinet minister were separated by a distance of several thousand light-years, and no matter how much use they made of FTL comm channels, it was hard to expect the nation's business to run smoothly. However, this unorthodox system was a temporary arrangement, and soon enough, the minister of domestic affairs would follow the kaiser to Phezzan. The opposite was impossible. Odin's days as the crux of the empire were already over, never to come again.

Hilda was assisting Reinhard with the processing of government business, while at the same time advancing an analysis of the rapidly—sometimes drastically—changing situation. Thanks to Lennenkamp's going off the rails and the resulting chaos in the Free Planets' government, Yang Wen-li was now on his own, naturally complicating the political and military factors that made up the present situation. They mustn't grow complacent, and dismiss his forces like some bothersome swarm of flies. After all, though the Lohengramm Dynasty and the Free Planets Alliance might both be great rivers, each had started from a single drop of water.

There were many forces at work within the galaxy. Listing them, Hilda wrote down the following:

A: *Neue Reich (Lohengramm Dynasty)*
B: *Present government of the Free Planets Alliance*
C: *Yang Wen-li's autonomous forces*
D: *Former Phezzan forces*
E: *Old Galactic Empire (Goldenbaum Dynasty holdouts)*
F: *El Facil (has declared independence)*
G: *Holdouts from the Church of Terra*

Was it fair to say she was being a little too suspicious here? Hilda threw a glance at a small mirror on the table, closed one eye, and looked at her face, besieged as it was by frown-inducing worries. The expression made the face of the short-haired, boyishly attractive daughter of a count look all the more boyish.

Hilda shrugged her shoulders, stretched her arms high up over her head, and took a deep breath. Every once in a while, even her energetic brain cells needed a rest.

When she thought about it, political conditions long ago were more cut-and-dried. About half a century ago, police and detectives from both the empire and the Free Planets Alliance had cooperated to expose a drug syndicate smuggling thyoxin. Political acrobatics like that were possible if the leaders on both sides could just agree. Although even back then, that kind of coordinated investigation was never attempted a second time. These days, it seemed like each and every cell in the divided human family was trying to preach at its fellows about what was right, all of them brandishing dictionaries tailor-made to their positions.

And the camp with which Hilda was affiliated had surely had a dictionary thicker than any other. Reinhard himself, though, had been too proud to submit gracefully to those gilt-edged pages in the hands of the Boyar nobles. Who was there, in the camps opposing Reinhard now, who could say that that old Reinhard no longer existed?

Hilda once again turned her eyes toward the various forces labeled A through G. Viewed from this perspective, she could see that each of them had large or small weaknesses. D and G had lost their home bases, and possessed no known military forces. B and E suffered from a lack of talented people. F was as powerless as a newborn. And in A and C, everything depended on the personal abilities of their leaders. If the leader of either side were lost, their organizations would crumble. Hilda couldn't help but shudder at the thought of what would have happened if Reinhard, leaving no successor, had died at Yang's hands at Vermillion the previous April.

The enemy meriting the most caution would be an amalgam of B, C, D, and F—a union, in other words, of malcontent elements from the Free Planets Alliance and Phezzan, built around a core of confidence in Yang Wen-li. Were such a combination of military might and economic power to react chemically, it could create the conditions for a faint, poisonous smoke to fell an enormous dragon. Surely not even Yang himself believed he could bring down Reinhard with just his small military force. If that *was* what he was thinking, there would be no need to fear him. That would mean he was nothing more than a sick man, afflicted by the mental illness of heroic narcissism.

Supposing he did bring down the kaiser…*Would Yang Wen-li have any prospects afterward?*

That question was coiling around and around in Hilda's mind. Of course, there was no way her gaze could penetrate all the universe's phenomena, but she had guessed that Yang's flight had not been premeditated; it was better described as an emergency evacuation. She could see that by looking at his conduct during the Vermillion War. As far as he was concerned, the orders of a government elected by the people must have been naturally akin to divine oracles.

There was something very interesting about this man, this Yang Wen-li. In Hilda's view, his abilities were rather spectacularly out of sync with his disposition. While possessed of talents extremely well suited to dispassionate, realistic problem-solving, he personally seemed to despise those abilities. Hilda could picture the man staring at himself in glum dissatisfaction, even though he had become the most important man in his nation at a very young age.

Immediately following the Vermillion War, Yang had been invited to meet with Reinhard on board his beloved warship, *Brünhild*. Based on what Hilda had heard from a few crewmen, including Commodore Günter Kissling, chief of Reinhard's personal guard, he'd looked nothing at all like a man whose résumé was buried in innumerable wartime achievements. The impression Kissling had gotten had not been of a marshal or commander, but of merely a slender, up-and-coming scholar. And yet, Yang had apparently seemed completely undaunted while visiting an enemy warship all alone. That ambiguous point was likely where the true worth of the man named Yang lay.

If that slightly peculiar aspect of Yang Wen-li's character were to cease to exist, then the military power of the Free Planets Alliance and the economic might of Phezzan would lose the catalyst through which they could combine. On the other hand, if that happened, each of the other smaller forces would try to squirm away in whichever direction they saw fit, which would perhaps necessitate squelching them individually. That in itself was bound to be a lot of trouble.

Even Kaiser Reinhard, with his exceedingly clear intellect, had seemed unable these past few weeks to make a clear-cut decision on how to deal with the situation.

"Be that as it may, I wonder what His Majesty is thinking?"

Hilda harbored not half a gram of doubt regarding the young kaiser's talents. Still, one thing did concern her: the threads of Reinhard's psyche were made of tough, highly advanced steel, but intertwined with delicate silver strings. The former were always at work on the battlefield, lending credence to the myth of Reinhard's invincibility, and the same had been true even in the halls of governance. However, was it not the silver threads that wove together to compose the psychological norms of this youth who was on the verge of completing a conquest of a size unknown to history? The flames that burned inside Reinhard were brilliant in their intensity, yet was it not the brightest flame that burned out most quickly? That concern was casting a shadow over the heart of the count's bright daughter.

IV

Kaiser Reinhard's move to Phezzan turned out to be an enthralling stimulant for the technocrats of the Neue Reich. Bruno von Silberberg, a young man doubling as minister of industry and chief secretary of capital construction, was living in a run-down building not far from the imperial headquarters, carrying out difficult assignments day and night. His only time off had been a week's worth of sick leave.

The minister of industry's vice minister, Gluck, a middle-aged bureaucrat-turned-politician, should have been suitably competent, yet despite his best efforts, the office work had fallen behind during von Silberberg's sick leave. When the recuperated minister of industry had returned and dealt with the delinquent matters in practically no time, the vice minister had lost his self-confidence and submitted his resignation to the kaiser.

The vice minister had been bracing himself for an angry rebuke, but the handsome young kaiser had instead given him an unexpected smile.

"The responsibilities of a vice minister are secondary to those of a minister. If your talents surpassed those of von Silberberg, I would have installed you, not him, as minister. You're a modest man who knows his limitations. That's good enough for me."

Per the kaiser's wishes, Gluck had stayed on as vice minister to the minister of industry. Reinhard didn't come out and say so, but it was not his intent to perpetuate the Ministry of Public Works' gigantic organization and vast powers. Once the structure of the state and the framework of society were stabilized, he planned to privatize the departments doing on-site work and shrink the organization. During the establishment and expansion phases, an outstanding talent like von Silberberg was indispensable, but during the periods of downsizing and stabilization, it was the steadfastness of Gluck that was preferable. The kaiser saw that if he used Gluck as a plumb line of sorts, and shaved away the parts that were beyond his ability to manage, what remained would be an organization of appropriate scale and authority.

While mistakes—such as the installment of Senior Admiral Lennen-kamp as chief commissioner to the Free Planets Alliance—could indeed be found among Reinhard's appointments, they were vastly outnumbered by successes rooted in his magnanimity and discerning eye. As for von Silberberg, whom even the kaiser recognized as a rare talent, he was devoting a portion of his vast energies to hashing out a plan to transform Planet Phezzan into the center of all the universe.

As the Lohengramm Dynasty's first minister of industry—or rather, the first in humanity's spacefaring history—he already stood to have his name remembered by future generations. That being the case, he figured, why not really make it stand out, with decorations of lavish gold and crimson? He wanted to make it so that his name would never be forgotten so long as Planet Phezzan existed.

The Phezzanese people, on the other hand, were unable to feel at ease. Thus far, the empire had merely occupied their ancestral planet, but now that they had been swallowed, they were also being digested. "The next stop for us'll be the chamber pot," some were saying, showing just how deep their sense of defeat ran by trying—and failing—to twist it into a crass joke. By taking fullest advantage of their astrographical position between the empire and the Free Planets Alliance, and utilizing their wealth and every trick in Machiavelli's book, they had striven to become the de facto rulers of all the universe, but now all of that had vanished like foam on the seashore.

"The wisdom of the civilized, undone by the strong arm of the bar-barian," some opined, but in the end, this was nothing more than the self-pity that followed on the heels of a forced admission of defeat. In any case, they had been unable to guess that the other side would resort to brute strength.

"Whether I look to the right or look to the left, all I see are ugly mugs of imperials."

"Still, it's hard to believe how much has changed in less than one year."

As regretful and indignant looks were traded among the Phezzanese, the silver and black uniforms of the imperial military increased by the day, until it seemed as though half the atmosphere were being consumed in service of their breathing.

The greater part of the Phezzanese people had no reason to be supportive of Kaiser Reinhard, yet they couldn't seem to help developing a grudging admiration for the sheer grandeur of his plotting, and the speed with which he made decisions and took action. It was true, of course, that a number of impurities were mixed in with those feelings. To curse Reinhard as an incompetent would be to shove themselves into a mire of disgrace for having been outmaneuvered by said incompetent. Economic might that was supposed to have been overwhelming had lain idle in the face of military force, and intelligence that they were supposed to have monopolized had been stolen by the hands of the imperial military without affording Phezzan any benefit whatsoever. It was the clever, scheming people of Phezzan who had been living complacently in the greenhouse of a conservative worldview, not knowing how fragile its glass walls were until that golden-haired youth had come along and shattered them.

In any case, there was no room for doubt that Kaiser Reinhard was in the process of creating history. At the same time, the people of Phezzan could not stave off concern over what kind of role they would be given to play on the magnificent stage of the history now being created.

There were also those who imposed upon themselves positive perspectives and actions. The strong point of the Phezzanese had always been their ability to extract the maximum profit from whatever political circumstances were laid before them. Even in the old days, Phezzan had never been some paradise of universal equality—small and midsize merchants had been left weeping by wealthy tycoons' high-handed abuse of vested rights, and families had been brought to ruin by defeat in the competition for sales. For people such as these, the violent change of the times that Reinhard's conquest brought about was a once-in-a-lifetime opportunity for what might be called a consolation match.

And so, seeking the conqueror's favor, they scrambled to procure supplies needed by the military, to construct housing for soldiers, and to provide information regarding the economy, transportation, geography, and mood of the citizenry. The younger generation in particular harbored an accelerating rebelliousness toward Phezzan's elders, as well as support on an emotional level for their young conqueror, and the imperial government made a deliberate point of treating young Phezzanese well, as they began roller-skating down the road toward coexistence.

∪

It was the first of November when an even more massive upheaval shook the ground under the people's feet.

That day, the funeral of the late senior admiral Helmut Lennenkamp was conducted in secret. Marshal von Oberstein, minister of military affairs, was named chair of the funerary committee, and although Kaiser Reinhard and many high-ranking government and military officials were in attendance, it could have been called a modest affair considering the rank of the deceased. The imperial government had not yet received a decision from the kaiser regarding whether or not to publicize the deaths of high-ranking officials, and furthermore, unlike the case of Admiral Kempf in recent years, the deceased's cause of death this time was a dishonorable one—suicide by hanging—so even the admirals in attendance found it difficult to find much meat in his death to feed their fighting spirits.

Sandy-haired, sandy-eyed Neidhart Müller leaned over and whispered to Mittermeier, seated next to him, "So, Admiral Lennenkamp won't be promoted to imperial marshal?"

"Well, he didn't die in battle, so…"

"He did die in the line of duty. Despite that, he gets no promotion?"

Wordlessly, Mittermeier nodded. As Müller had said, Lennenkamp had indeed perished in the line of duty, but his death had been brought about by guilt rather than achievement. It was likely because he had deviated from his original mission that the new order, based on the Baalat Treaty, was about to be robbed of the time it needed to build itself up and develop. Temporary though it would have been, peace had been on the verge of arriving in this age, and Lennenkamp inevitably received at least part of the blame for grabbing it by the ankles and dragging it back down into the depths.

Just before the funeral, a rear admiral who had been attached to Lennenkamp's fleet approached Mittermeier with a heartfelt request. "I served under His Excellency, Admiral Lennenkamp, for five years. While it's true he was a little set in his ways, he was a good senior officer. Could I ask you, please, to request that His Majesty launch a retaliatory strike on his behalf?"

Mittermeier sympathized with the rear admiral's request. Still, if he had stated his opinion clearly, he would have said that both Lennenkamp and those around him would have been fortunate if he had never been promoted beyond rear or vice admiral. Human beings had a thing called capacity, which was different for everyone in both size and shape. An able fleet commander did not necessarily make an excellent commissioner. Misjudging him had indeed been the kaiser's mistake, but at the same time Mittermeier could not deny that the plunge in Lennenkamp's stock had been all his own doing. Naturally, acting against the kaiser's wishes and marring the authority of his new dynasty had not been considered small crimes either.

Accordingly, Lennenkamp did not deserve promotion to imperial marshal. Kaiser Reinhard, in not bestowing that title on him, might have been thought a harsh man from the standpoint of human sentiment, yet in rational terms, it was the right thing to do. Had Kaiser Reinhard yielded to emotion and given Lennenkamp the rank of imperial marshal, he would have doubled his error, and the second wrong would not have made a right of the first.

Simply giving high ranks to one's vassals didn't make everything right. If there was any point on which Cornelius I, successor to the wise Emperor Maximillian Josef II, had fallen short of greatness, it was not to be found in his talents nor his achievements. It was rather in his propensity to bestow imperial marshalships on his vassals to excess, until even commanders of small fleets were holding marshals' scepters. After Cornelius's attempt to conquer the Free Planets Alliance had ended in failure, he had finally thought better of the practice, and until his dying day had never again bestowed the rank of imperial marshal.

Mittermeier felt himself wanting to change the subject, and turned his gray eyes toward his young colleague. "By the way," he said, "how does it feel, riding on that brand-new flagship of yours?"

Though Müller was concerned about what people around him might think, his face lit up a little at that, and he answered right away: "It's fantastic!"

Percival was the first warship the ordinance factories had completed following the establishment of the Lohengramm Dynasty, and it was he—Senior Admiral Neidhart Müller—who had had the honor of receiving it from the kaiser. For the courageous fighting he had displayed in the Vermillion War—rescuing his lord Reinhard in a critical situation and escaping from sinking ships as many as three times during the chaos of ferocious battle—he had made himself known to both friend and foe as "Müller die eiserne Wand"—Müller the Iron Wall. Even his archenemy Yang Wen-li, whose complete victory over Reinhard Müller had prevented, had praised him as an excellent commander, and Müller's fame as a warrior had risen until it now trailed only that of the Twin Ramparts. In spite of that, he had never grown conceited, and the faithful, sincere attitude he had as the youngest among his colleagues never faltered.

Müller was about to answer Mittermeier further when the reflection of someone new appeared in his sandy eyes. Kaiser Reinhard's assistant deputy was bending down toward the two of them. Theodor von Rücke had been promoted to lieutenant commander. This had been in recognition of his recent act of bravery, when an attempt had been made on the kaiser's life at the estate of Baron von Kümmel, and von Rücke had shot and killed one of the criminals involved. He was the same age as the kaiser, and although it manifested itself in a manner rather different from that of his lord, he had a certain boyishness about him that even now suggested a clueless underclassman at officers' school.

"Would all imperial marshals and senior admirals please gather in the

Granite Room on the sixteenth floor? His Imperial Majesty would like to hear your opinions on a certain matter."

Von Rücke had almost certainly not been told what the matter to be discussed was, so Mittermeier didn't bother asking him. An image was floating around in the back of his mind of the kaiser in the imperial council meeting just a few days ago, seemingly wavering in his decisions and choices.

The Granite Room was wide and spacious, more a salon than a meeting room, and coffee had been prepared for the admirals.

"Will His Majesty lead us into battle again?" Senior Admiral Fritz Josef Wittenfeld murmured to no one in particular. It was clear as day to his colleagues that he was not asking a question but rather expressing his hope. More than any other, Wittenfeld was a man who embodied the militaristic nature of the new dynasty, a fact he himself acknowledged. His light-brown eyes roved across the room's decor disinterestedly.

"His Majesty longs for enemies to fight. Although he was born for battle, the battles have ended too soon…"

Neidhart Müller felt the same way. He was a warrior himself, and not yet of an age to feel the fatigue of battle. Would it be disrespectful to say that pity was mingled with the reverence that his glorious young kaiser inspired in him? Still, he had seen what Reinhard had looked like after Admiral Kircheis had died.

Senior Admiral Ernest Mecklinger, who had stayed behind on Odin in the important post of rear guard commander in chief, had once said to Müller, "It's well and good for His Majesty to move to Phezzan, but I'm a bit uneasy about these reforms to the military. Military power ought to be centralized. If you give military precincts the power to lead and command troops, won't that lead to authority splintering according to territory at the very moment central control weakens?"

Kaiser Reinhard was young and filled with vitality and possibilities, but although he was a genius, and although he was a hero, he was not immortal. The greater his presence, the greater the hole that would be left after he was gone. Mecklinger was worried about that, and while Müller sympathized, he couldn't take his concern quite that far. From the standpoint of age, both Mecklinger and Müller were sure to pass on before the kaiser did; the trials that came afterward were best left to the next generation.

As Müller picked up his coffee cup, the soft tones of the Twin Ramparts' conversation came flowing into his ears.

"By the way," said Mittermeier, "how do you think the FPA government and military are dealing with the present situation?"

"By running around in confusion, and then dropping from exhaustion," von Reuentahl replied.

The chaos and confusion in the FPA military had been particularly awful. Their civilian authorities had yet to release an official statement regarding Commissioner Lennenkamp's dishonorable death or the flight of retired marshal Yang Wen-li. The blame for the former they laid at the feet of the imperial government's policy of secrecy, while with regard to the latter, they obstinately insisted that the government could not be expected to know the movements of a single civilian. The result was that the eggs of unease they had been laying had hatched out chicks of distrust.

Setting his coffee cup back down hard on the table, Wittenfeld joined in the conversation. "All I can see is that the FPA has lost its ability to self-govern. The minute the barrel hoops come loose, boiling soup's going to spill out everywhere, and nothing but chaos will follow. That being the case, shouldn't we pry those hoops off ourselves? We should accept the chaos in the Free Planets' government as a sign from Lord Odin that he's already granted us their territory."

"Even if we did mobilize, our supply chain isn't ready yet," Mittermeier calmly pointed out. "It would turn into a mirror image of Amritsar three years ago—this time we'd be the ones starving."

"Then we should just capture the Free Planets Alliance's supply bases."

"On what legal basis?"

"Legal basis!" Wittenfeld gave a mocking laugh that set his long orange hair swaying. Even when he acted like this, the hawkish admiral had an odd sort of innocence about him; Mittermeier couldn't bring himself to seriously dislike the man. Wittenfeld casually pushed aside his coffee cup.

"Is a legal basis really that important?"

"As long as the FPA government has the will and ability to crush armed forces resisting it, we have no way of moving against Yang Wen-li ourselves. After all, the Baalat Treaty expressly forbids interference in their internal affairs."

"I see. They might have the will, but isn't it obvious that they lack the ability? Where is Yang Wen-li right now? Where did Lennenkamp go? If you ask me, I'd say these questions in essence show exactly where their limitations are." Wittenfeld's words could not have been sharper, and Mittermeier fell silent, a rather wry expression on his face. Truth be told, he had been thinking something similar. Under normal circumstances, it fell to Mecklinger to rein in Wittenfeld's more radical pronouncements, though.

"Ultimately, it may come down to a question of whether our empire or the Free Planets Alliance's government knowingly violated Yang Wen-li's legal rights," Mittermeier said, flashing an ironic glance at von Oberstein, who remained silent with arms folded. Mittermeier harbored a suspicion that Lennenkamp's actions had been due at least in part to von Oberstein's prompting.

Setting that aside, the imperial military's options were not so cut-and-dried. If Yang Wen-li were determined to be a public enemy of the New Galactic Empire, then imperial forces would be able to take direct action to eliminate him. At the same time, though, that might provide an opportunity for miscellaneous, poorly organized anti-empire movements to coalesce around Yang Wen-li as a symbol.

"Even if they're just a disorderly rabble, they could obviously project power greater than their own abilities if they had Yang Wen-li and his clever schemes on their side. On the other hand, if forces opposing us remain splintered as they are now, we'll have to go around squelching them one by one. Sounds like a lot of trouble to me."

"In that case, why not *let* Yang Wen-li rally the anti-kaiser forces and unify them? Then we deal with Yang, and with one attack extinguish the whole chain of volcanoes. No matter how much lava spills out, once it cools, it will be powerless. Don't you agree?"

Though Wittenfeld's opinion sounded crude, as strategic theory it wasn't mistaken. Crushing the core of an organization that had unified organically was more efficient than destroying a large number of smaller, separate organizations individually. Down that path, however, there also lay the danger that a unified force with Yang at its core could grow into something too powerful for even the empire to suppress.

The newborn Lohengramm Dynasty possessed overwhelming power in the military sense, and the young kaiser who stood at its head was a prodigy in the art of war. Military might, however, was not the sole factor determining history or geometrical space; it followed naturally that the parts that had expanded with Phezzan's annexation and the Free Planets' surrender would cause the structure as a whole to lose some of its density. If a rip occurred, who was to say whether it could be mended?

"Yang Wen-li is a concern," Neidhart Müller said, tilting his head, "but what about the rumor that's driven this whole chain of disruptions? Is it true? Is Admiral Merkatz still alive?"

The admirals all glanced at one another. As Müller had said, rumors regarding the status of Admiral Merkatz—whose death in the Vermillion War had been publicly announced—had provided Lennenkamp with the chance to make the Free Planets Alliance's government arrest Yang, and had also led to the panicked reaction of the Free Planets government.

"At this point, we should probably assume he's alive…"

A sharp glint flashed in the pale aqua eyes of Senior Admiral Adalbert Fahrenheit. He and Admiral Merkatz had known each other for many years. Both he and Merkatz had fought against the FPA Armed Forces under Reinhard's command in the Astarte Stellar Region. Then, when Merkatz had been forced into the role of commander in chief of the aristocrats' military forces in the Lippstadt War, it had been he, Fahrenheit, who had become Merkatz's most trusted colleague. As the Lippstadt War had drawn to a close, Merkatz had defected to the Free Planets Alliance on the advice of his aide-de-camp, and the captured Admiral Fahrenheit had been spared criminal prosecution and welcomed into Reinhard's ranks.

"Nowadays, he and I serve under different flags. Incredible, the difference just two or three years can make."

Fahrenheit was not particularly given to deep sentimentality, but when he reflected on the past, then looked toward the future, he couldn't help but feel something. And what kind of conclusion would this upheaval arrive at? *I can't very well die before seeing this through to the end,* Fahrenheit murmured in his heart.

At this time, Reinhard's advisors in the Granite Room consisted of only three imperial marshals and four senior admirals. Of those who had been present immediately following his victory in the Lippstadt War, three of them—Kircheis, Kempf, and Lennenkamp—had gone on to Valhalla, while another four—Mecklinger, Kessler, Steinmetz, and Lutz—had remained at their various posts, and Wahlen was still being treated for his wounds. The living they could eventually meet again, but as it sank in that the number of advisors assisting Reinhard had been halved, even these brave, battle-hardened admirals felt a fleeting instant of quiet stillness.

"It's gotten a bit lonely around here," Wittenfeld said with a casual shake of the head.

The admiral sitting next to him was Senior Admiral Ernst von Eisenach. Von Eisenach was thirty-three years old, and rather slim. His hair was the same shade as copper beginning to oxidize, and though he had combed it back neatly from his face, one small tuft was standing at attention in the back, aimed toward the heavens.

Von Eisenach nodded wordlessly. A man of extremely few words, it was said that even in the presence of Kaiser Reinhard, he never said anything besides *ja* or *nein.* Of course, reputations usually became exaggerated as stories passed from person to person, but one rumor—that his aides and attendants were trained to respond not to their commander's voice but to his gestures and facial expressions—was almost certainly based in fact. When he snapped his fingers three times, for example, an attendant would come running at near-sonic velocity, bringing with him half a cup of coffee with half a lump of sugar. Müller had seen it happen twice.

It was said that while still a student in officers' school, no one had ever seen his mouth open at any time other than breakfast, lunch, or dinner;

that even when he'd been tickled, he had laughed without using his voice; and that when he had muttered "Drat" after dropping a coffee cup on the floor at Zie Addler—a club for high-ranking officers—Mittermeier and Lutz had just stared at him intently from across the table, and had afterward said, "Did he actually *speak*?"

Regardless of what anecdotes might be told about him, though, there was no one who doubted von Eisenach's abilities as a commander. Perhaps his guardian angel was merely incompetent, and that was why he had had so few opportunities to take the stage during spectacular scenes of enormous battles.

Even so, with quite literally not a word of complaint, he had long performed those less glamorous yet still essential duties, such as harrying the enemy's rear guard, blocking the arrival of reinforcements, defending his own side's supply lines, and even executing diversionary tactics and providing landing support. Von Eisenach had served his young lord, and Reinhard, whose expectations he had never betrayed, had bestowed on him the rank of senior admiral, treating him as the equal of courageous admirals with innumerable heroic accomplishments. Even Marshal von Oberstein, the minister of military affairs, who often expressed disagreement when it came to Reinhard's military appointments, had instead rather encouraged the promotion in his case. With neither a frown nor a grimace, von Eisenach had always contributed to his comrades' victories no matter what kind of orders were given him, and even von Oberstein, notorious for his rigorous performance evaluations, rated him highly.

Von Eisenach also had a wife and a newborn child, though how this exceedingly quiet man had ever wooed a woman was a mystery that Mittermeier and the others did in all seriousness wonder about.

Men who had been married were in the minority among Reinhard's highest-ranking executive officers. Among the imperial marshals there was only Mittermeier, and two senior admirals, Wahlen and von Eisenach, brought the total to three. Wahlen's wife had passed away, however, so there were actually only two who were ordinary family men. And while both Müller and Wittenfeld had missed out on chances to wed while going to and from the battlefield, von Eisenach, the "silent admiral," was the only one who had both wife and child. While Mittermeier did have a loving wife, they remained unfortunately childless. As for Mittermeier's best friend, whether on Odin or here on Phezzan, he was never shy about his womanizing, and had ceaselessly creased the brows of moralists during his rise to the high rank of imperial marshal.

When they had departed Odin, Mittermeier had once again tried suggesting marriage to his friend.

"Marriage?"

Reuentahl had responded with a low-pitched laugh. Even though he was grateful for his best friend's concern, laughter had been the only means of maintaining emotional balance he'd been able to find. When that laughter finally subsided, those mismatched eyes that the ladies found so charming had gleamed with an indescribable light.

"I'm neither willing nor worthy to have a proper family. I think you should know that better than anyone."

"Me? I don't know any such thing."

At Mittermeier's less-than-sympathetic reply, an uncharacteristic look of unease had flashed across the face of the famed admiral with mismatched eyes.

"Whoa, that wasn't contrition I just saw now, was it?"

"Is there a reason you should concern yourself with that?"

The two had looked at one another for a moment, then with wry grins let the matter drop.

"By the way, I understand the most recent woman is coming all the way to Phezzan with you. Do you really like her that well?"

"Oh, her? That woman is at my side because she wants to witness my destruction with her own eyes, it seems. A lady of exquisite tastes, I should add."

They spoke of Elfriede von Kohlrausch—she had moved into von Reuentahl's officer's residence, and was the daughter of the niece of Duke Lichtenlade, who had been executed by von Reuentahl. Many concerns had wrapped around Mittermeier like chains about that. He had wondered what von Oberstein would think of the situation. Or what he was thinking of it.

"Von Reuentahl, I don't know what she meant by saying such a thing, but that woman is bad news for you."

"And? What do you want me to do about it?"

"Give her some money and send her away. That's the only thing you can do."

Von Reuentahl did a double take, and looked at his friend with a slightly surprised expression. "That's not the sort of advice I'm used to hearing from you."

"I don't care how you do it—just find an exit and get yourself out of this. All I see is you crawling deeper and deeper into this maze."

"I'm sure it looks that way to you."

"Am I wrong?"

"No. To be honest, I'd be lying if I said that the same thing has never crossed my mind. It's just…"

At that moment, von Reuentahl's piercing blue left eye and deep black right eye seemed to dim to the same color. Presently, von Reuentahl forced a smile and slapped his friend on the shoulder.

"Don't worry, Mittermeier. I'm from a family of warriors. When I die, it will be by the sword. I won't be destroyed by a woman."

By the time Mittermeier found his way out of memory lane, the heterochromatic marshal was straightening his posture and rising to his feet.

The Gale Wolf hurried to do likewise. Kaiser Reinhard had entered the room.

VI

Reinhard was in a foul mood. Ever since Lennenkamp's kidnapping at the hands of Yang Wen-li's faction, he had been paralyzed by indecision. The golden-haired young man was unaccustomed to this state, to say the least.

Now, with the cause of Lennenkamp's unexpected death made clear, should he seek redress by striking the Free Planets Alliance? Or leave the matter to the passage of time for a while, as he had briefly proposed to do earlier, and simply await the enemy's slide into confusion and self-destruction?

It was hardly any wonder that the Three Imperial Chiefs found the kaiser's recent contemplativeness difficult to accept. The kaiser himself was having trouble accepting his own passivity. What had made him like this was a mental state of self-admonition against high-handedly exercising his nigh-unlimited authority. His youthful sense of aesthetics recoiled at the idea of bringing military force to bear against a defeated enemy a scant four or five months after the signing of the Baalat Treaty.

What blew that feeling away was an impassioned speech from Wittenfeld. Asked his opinion by the kaiser, Wittenfeld made the same argument to his young lord that he had just made to Mittermeier. At first the kaiser hadn't seemed terribly moved by it; he clearly considered it all too obvious that Wittenfeld would advocate for more militarism. It was his next words, however, that summed up the situation for him.

"Your Excellency, the reason you've been able to boast of invincibility thus far lies in the fact that you've acted to move history. Are you going to fold your arms now, of all times, and wait for history to move you?"

The effect that that line had on the golden-haired young man was surprising indeed. He looked like a sculpture that had had life breathed into it.

"Well spoken, Wittenfeld."

As the kaiser rose from his sofa, his ice-blue eyes gleamed, filled with a bitter light. Stellar coronas were dancing wildly in those eyes. He had not been moved by Wittenfeld. He had rediscovered what he himself had been looking for.

"I've been overthinking this," he said. "The unification of space is the greatest and highest justification. Yet here I've been, putting various pretexts that scarcely merit consideration ahead of that."

Amid a stillness so complete that the very air seemed to have crystallized, the kaiser's voice stirred rhythmical waves.

"Admiral Wittenfeld!"

"Aye!"

"Here are your orders. As swiftly as possible, take the Schwarz Lanzenreiter fleet and depart for alliance space. Rendezvous with Admiral Steinmetz on Planet Urvashi, and maintain security there until my main force arrives."

"Aye!"

Under his orange hair, the fierce young commander's face flushed red. Everything he had wished for had just been granted. As Reinhard gave the order, he also turned his ice-blue eyes toward his chief secretary, who had accompanied him.

"Fräulein von Mariendorf, I will shortly make public the death of Admiral Lennenkamp, and announce a mobilization seeking redress from the government of the Free Planets Alliance. See to it that a draft speech is on my desk by week's end."

"Yes, Your Majesty."

Overpowered by Reinhard's spirit, not even Hilda was able to caution or dissuade him. In her eyes, too, the kaiser seemed to shine blindingly bright.

"Be that as it may, Your Majesty will lack a permanent dwelling until your palace is completed," said Wittenfeld.

Reinhard, who had started for the door, stopped and turned around, his luxurious mane of golden hair stirring the air. Then, the graceful lips of the young king and conqueror shot back the words which future historians would never fail to reproduce when assaying to write Reinhard's biography.

"I need no palace," he said. "The royal palace of the Galactic Empire is wherever I am. For now, my throne shall be ensconced on the battleship *Brünhild*."

A thrill of exultation that was almost a shudder went shooting through the admirals' central nervous systems. *That* was the kind of spirit which revealed their praiseworthy kaiser's true self. The kaiser did not reside in palaces; he was a man of the battlefield.

Reinhard's spirit aside, however, a central hub for politics, military affairs, and intelligence gathering was indispensable for a vast interstellar empire, and there had been no change in Reinhard's plan to give it one in the form of Phezzan. With Minister of Industry von Silberberg as its head, Imperial Capital Construction Headquarters was becoming ever more lively in its activities, and plans were moving forward for the kaiser's new castle residence—tentatively named Löwenbrunnen, or Lion Fountain. As is widely known, however, construction on this palace did not begin during Reinhard's reign.

Reinhard's elegant figure disappeared behind the door, and the admirals, saluting as he departed, went their separate ways. Each of them could feel their blood temperature rising.

November 10.

On the bridge of *Königstiger*, flagship of the Schwarz Lanzenreiter fleet, Senior Admiral Fritz Josef Wittenfeld stared at the main screen, arms crossed. His line of sight was directed at Phezzan, already on its way to becoming merely the brightest of the many stars there displayed. Although it was a hurried departure, what had been demanded of him had been more a hasty one.

Admiral Halberstadt, the fleet's vice commander; Admiral Gräbner, the chief of staff; and Commodore Dirksen, a senior aide, made up his staff. With strong and courageous expressions on their faces, they stood arrayed around their commander. Moving his gaze across each of their faces, the fierce leader of the Schwarz Lanzenreiter invincibly declared, "Well then, shall we head for Heinessen, and our victory toasts?"

The extravagant colors of the Goldenlöwe blazed from the wall of the bridge. Beneath its new banner, the military forces of a new dynasty commenced their first greedy voyage of conquest. One hundred forty-one days had passed since the golden crown had come to rest on Reinhard von Lohengramm's golden-haired head.

CHAPTER 2:

I

AS THE RULER and armed forces of the Lohengramm Dynasty were going into action to bring history and the universe to heel before the brilliant Goldenlöwe banner, another group of spaceships was wandering the eternal night, with no flag of its own to raise at all.

In times to come, this would often be called the "Yang Independent Fleet," but the man to whom that name referred simply called it the "Irregulars," and his subordinates called it "Yang's Irregulars." Be that as it may, the fleet needed some kind of official name for itself, and its would-be pensioner, driven unwillingly from his cozy greenhouse into the cold, cruel world, had solicited naming suggestions from the crew members themselves. His tacked-on rationale for this was that it would encourage a sense of solidarity and self-awareness among fleet personnel, but in fact, the primary motivating factor had been that coming up with a name himself was a pain in the neck.

The measure was, indeed, effective. While some certainly participated because they had nothing better to do, there is little doubt that it bore fruit in terms of creating a shared awareness of "our fleet." From a brigade's worth of respondents' submissions, Yang selected the least self-consciously eccentric.

One famous leader in the fleet, temporarily away from the main force at the time, would later lament that had he only been present to suggest it, "Studly Olivier Poplin and His Male Supporting Cast" would have surely been the chosen nomenclature—although he lacked even one sympathizer for this claim. In any case, Yang Wen-li did not let them pin any ridiculously overwrought names on their fleet.

Yang was aware that the acid phrase "wandering private navy" had gained currency among those who opposed him. If one ignored everything that had happened thus far and focused only on the present, that evaluation had some surface truth to it. Even with Yang Wen-li as its commander, Wiliabard Joachim Merkatz assisting him, and Walter von Schönkopf, Alex Caselnes, and Dusty Attenborough as staff officers, it still existed entirely divorced from its nation's official sanction. These five officers could likely organize and lead a force on the scale of five million personnel, but in reality, their fleet numbered somewhere above six hundred vessels, with personnel numbering only about sixteen thousand.

They had no political cover and no supply bases. Now that the festive mood from their reunion with Merkatz at Dayan Khan's abandoned base had cooled somewhat, the Irregulars' leadership had to think long and hard about their direction going forward.

Only Dusty Attenborough, running a hand through a tangled head of wooly, iron-gray hair, was moving toward action, rather than thought, first. In appearance, he looked more like some activist student revolutionary than a navy admiral. Yang had always rated his old underclassman from Officers' Academy highly in terms of his skills as tactician and commander, but now freed from the shackles of the FPA military, Attenborough had, to a surprising degree, shown himself to be a man of action as well as organizational skill, surprising others with his hard work and energy as he applied himself to tasks such as reorganizing the fleet, preparing tactical battle plans, and training soldiers. Yang's indolence only made his vitality more apparent.

"How about this, Marshal? We recapture Iserlohn, create a liberation zone extending from the corridor region all the way to El Facil, and then respond to the empire's offensive."

Dusty Attenborough's proposal actually did sound like something a student revolutionary would say. This was evident from his use of terms like "liberation zone." Yang, for his part, felt like puffing a smoky cloud of sarcasm back in his face. *You don't have a problem in the world, do you?* he thought. But he had also discerned strategic value in his old underclassman's proposal.

"If retaking Iserlohn was all we did," Yang said, "we'd just end up being isolated in the middle of the corridor. But if we could secure El Facil as a beachhead, and from there build connections with Tiamat, Astarte, and other nearby systems to establish corridors of liberated space, that might make it easier to respond to whatever changes may come down the line. Still, this isn't the time for that yet."

Yang believed that. Furthermore, thinking ahead in terms of political as opposed to military strategy, he felt it was probably best to go ahead and start setting the stage for a future political settlement. By recognizing the hegemony of Reinhard von Lohengramm and the Neue Reich, and restoring Iserlohn Fortress to him, it might be possible to get El Facil all but freed in exchange, naming it a "free city of the empire" or some similar euphemism, and preserving the faint lamplight of republican democracy. In order to extract such a concession from Kaiser Reinhard, though, a commensurate price would have to be paid.

At present, Yang was giving no thought whatsoever to the possibility of Reinhard reneging on his word. That young man, whose comely visage was like a portrait made with paints infused with the Muse's breath, might conquer, might invade, might purge, and might avenge, but he seemed incapable of breaking a promise once it was made. The one time Yang had met him, he had felt that from the other man's very presence.

So in other words, various things work out better if he does us the favor of staying alive. Yang was the very man who had driven Reinhard to the brink of defeat in the Vermillion War a scant year and a half ago, yet sometimes he still had such thoughts. From the beginning, Yang had never harbored any animus toward Reinhard as a person.

The man known as Yang Wen-li was an organism composed of innumerable contradictions. While detesting the military, he had risen to the rank of marshal; while avoiding battle, he had stacked victory on top of victory; while doubting the significance of his state's continued existence, his contributions to that state had been many; while ignoring the virtue of diligence, he had accumulated incomparable achievements. For that reason, some argue that he had no guiding philosophy—that what did flow consistently through his psyche might perhaps have been the heartfelt wish to be a mere understudy in the great play of history, and a desire to hand off the lead role and find his seat among the spectators as soon as some greater individual took the stage.

Scribbled in an unfinished historical treatise that Yang abandoned writing was the following: "All the universe is a stage, and history a farce with no author." As he was merely restating a very old proverb, it was not the fruit of any particularly creative thought process. Still, it was useful for understanding at least part of where his viewpoint was coming from.

If Yang had been born in the same generation as Ahle Heinessen, founding father of the Free Planets Alliance, his life would have probably been simpler and his choices more clear-cut. Most likely, he would have offered his complete, unconditional loyalty to Heinessen and his ideas, and on the military side of things, worked in a limited advisory capacity, staying one step behind the leader, and supporting him from the background.

Some historians have pointed out Yang's psychological tendency to prefer the role of number two to that of number one. They claim, for example, that when Yang extended his utmost courtesy to his elderly senior, Commander in Chief Alexandor Bucock, he was not doing so based on simple feelings of affection and respect, but out of a deep-seated wish to rise no higher than the number two position.

Those who argue that the strongest lineup for the Free Planets Alliance Armed Forces would have been Bucock as commander in chief and Yang as general chief of staff—and lament the fact that this was ultimately not to be—base their views on such opinions.

Naturally, Yang himself never made any clear answer to these claims. What is certainly factual, though, is that during the span of his own life, Yang was ultimately unable to find any *individual* worthy of his political allegiance. Whether this was a blessing or a curse was likely unclear even to Yang.

II

Immediately following his and his subordinates' escape from the murderous hands of their government, Yang rendezvoused with Merkatz, and learned that the government of the El Facil system had declared independence from the Free Planets Alliance. Attenborough's "liberation strategy" had of course been devised based on this information.

Walter von Schönkopf also encouraged him along similar lines. Yang's impression, though, was more of him waving around a red flag to egg him on. "Go to El Facil right away," von Schönkopf said. "The people over there are passionate, but they don't have any political or military strategy. They'd probably be glad to have you as their top leader."

Even amid such circumstances, though, Yang held to his refusal to become supreme leader of the anti-empire movement.

"The top leader has to be a civilian. There's no such thing as a democracy or a republic ruled by soldiers. I can't be the leader of this."

"You're being too stubborn," von Schönkopf persisted. He and the word "discretion" had fallen out of touch years ago. "You're not a soldier anymore. You're without rank, an out-of-work civilian whose government won't pay out your pension, let alone a salary. What's holding you back?"

"Nothing's holding me back," Yang said, and although it sounded like he was just being argumentative for the sake of it, he had more than one reason for not rushing over to El Facil. What he wanted to say was that things just weren't that easy.

"Marshal, have you ever thought about where it is that you lag behind Kaiser Reinhard?"

"It's our difference in talent."

"No, it isn't," von Schönkopf averred. "It's your difference in spirit."

Yang fell into a gloomy silence at von Schönkopf's words, one hand still on the black beret he was wearing. It was his way of admitting that he couldn't deny the truth in von Schönkopf's assertion.

"If fate were to try and sashay past Kaiser Reinhard without batting an eye at him, he'd grab 'er by the collar and force her to follow him. For better or worse, that's what he's good at. You, on the other hand…"

Contrary to Yang's expectations, von Schönkopf left off criticizing him further, as an expression that defied easy description appeared on his handsome, gentlemanly face. "I think there is something you're after. What are you hoping for, Marshal? At our current stage?"

After a brief hesitation, Yang answered in a small voice: "There's only one thing I'm hoping for. That Chairman Lebello will do a good job smoothing over my absence."

Since escaping from the Free Planets' capital of Heinessen, Yang had been groping his way through a labyrinth of thought and strategy, and had needed a lot of breaks along the way.

Given five years' free rein, Yang might have employed constructive planning and destructive plotting like a knife and fork, slicing and dicing the entire universe to his liking, and flavoring it with something approaching his ideal democratic republic. The hourglass grains that had actually fallen into his palm, however, had amounted to no more than sixty days. Lennenkamp's arbitrary actions and Lebello's overreaction to them had stopped up his hourglass's passageway with the concrete of their obstinacy, and Yang had been driven from his humble nest of hibernation.

The sweet lullaby of his long-dreamt-of pensioner's life had broken off after a scant two months. Yang had been paying a portion of his salary into the pension system for the last twelve years. It was an outrage to get only two months' worth of payments out of it, and he felt like screaming, "At least let me see some return on the investment!" As both a public figure and a private figure, this was the height of disappointment, in both the abstract and concrete reality.

Still, it wasn't as though he had tried to abandon the responsibility he had to participate in the creation of history.

When El Facil had rather recklessly struck the colors of independence, Yang had for a brief time seriously considered rushing to their aid. Attenborough and von Schönkopf hadn't needed to try tempting him. If he had done so, he would have secured both justification and a home base, and El Facil would have acquired able military specialists.

However, Yang had foreseen that such a drama would soon lead to the entrance of a magnificent windstorm by the name of Reinhard von Lohengramm, and until he could determine what direction events would take, he didn't want to drive any permanent wedges between himself and the Free Planets Alliance.

If he were to throw in his lot with El Facil now, it was not inconceivable that a panicked Free Planets government might join hands fully with the Galactic Empire. Local governments in other systems would probably rise up in response to El Facil, but given the scale of Yang's present forces, there was nothing that he could do for them. All he would be able to do was look on from far away as they were crushed beneath the empire's gargantuan body.

Kaiser Reinhard was sure to make a move. On that point, Yang harbored no doubt whatsoever. Within the year, he would come, leading his forces in person. The glittering stars of the Free Planets Alliance he would toss into his golden chalice, and then, like some immense deity out of ancient mythology, he would swallow them whole. In a sense, Yang had a better grasp of Reinhard's true nature than Reinhard did himself. That handsome young man, in appearance like a figure fashioned from solidified crystal light, would never permit the fate of the universe to be decided by someone other than himself. "Sleep, and wait for luck," some people say, but dozing lazily in his canopy bed waiting for good things to come his way did not become that young man in the slightest. On this point, Yang was in full agreement with von Schönkopf's appraisal.

When he turned that thought around and evaluated himself in light of it, Yang had trouble suppressing a wry smirk. His viewpoint differed from von Schönkopf's—he believed he was walking a path he had never been meant for.

In times to come, some would harshly criticize Yang's actions during this period.

"Yang Wen-li had no strategic calculation in mind when he broke away from the Free Planets Alliance. Faced with the threat against his life, he did nothing more than impulsively embark on a course of extremely simpleminded self-preservation. A disappointing move indeed for one so lauded for his brilliance as a commander…"

"If Yang Wen-li had intended to live his life as an ambitious upstart bent on conquest, he should have ignored the government's cease-fire order in the Vermillion War, and with a hail of laser fire put an end to Reinhard von Lohengramm. If, on the other hand, he intended to live his life as a loyal soldier of the Free Planets Alliance, should he not have obeyed the will of his government, even to the point of accepting his own unjust death? But Yang Wen-li was not a perfect example of either philosophy…"

Yang knew very well that he was a far cry from perfection, so it is unlikely that he would have denied these one-sided criticisms. Not that he would have ever simply accepted them like a good little boy either.

．　　　．　　　　●
　　．　　　　．

On the subject of imperfection, Miracle Yang's newlywed wife Frederica Greenhill Yang had been made to realize in all sorts of ways her imperfections as a homemaker. When her umpteenth cooking disaster had transformed her Irish stew into a black mass of carbonized goo, Charlotte Phyllis, daughter of the Caselnes family, which was also on board the flagship, had spoken these words of encouragement: "It's okay, Mrs. Frederica. If you keep trying, you're sure to get good at it."

"Er…thank you, Charlotte."

Naturally, Charlotte Phyllis's father, in charge of the Yang Independent Fleet's resupply and accounting, could not be infinite in his generosity. Every meal Frederica ruined consumed one meal's worth of the soldiers' food stocks. No matter how great a master of desk work Alex Caselnes might have been, not even he could make something out of nothing. Employing a multitude of indirect expressions, he managed to convince her that there were more important things than giving her all to cooking practice.

So, rather than fixating on her domestic position, Frederica decided to make the most of her strong points in the role of aide-de-camp to a young and famous admiral, electing to focus on desk work for a while instead. As to whether her husband and his former upperclassman relievedly toasted this development with paper cups of whiskey, no record remains. In either case, Yang had had no particular expectation that his seven-years-younger wife would be a master of housework.

On the other hand, Frederica's abilities as an aide-de-camp were far above average. Her sharp instinct for understanding exactly what her senior officers wanted, her powers of memory, her decisiveness, and her office skills were all worthy of the showered praise of millions. There was also the fact that in terms of her personal history, she had been Yang's aide for far longer than she had been his wife. Yang as well somehow seemed to prefer talking about strategy with her.

"When Kaiser Reinhard comes in force, there's half a chance that the government will panic and send me a messenger. Yeah, they might even ask me to do double duty as director of joint ops HQ and commander in chief of the Space Armada, and hand me authority over the whole military."

"Would you accept that?"

"Well, when you've got a gift in both of your hands, there's no way to dodge when the knives come out."

Yang, for his part, couldn't help speaking a bit mean-spiritedly. If he, after being feted with countless honors, were to cheerfully, shamelessly step outside for a walk and get assassinated, he would earn the grief of his ancestors and the scorn of future generations. There was also the possibility that the Free Planets' government would seek to secure peace by offering him up as a sacrificial lamb. After all, they'd already tried to have him killed.

Coupled with a considerable dose of melancholy, the solemn face of João Lebello, chairman of the High Council of the Free Planets Alliance, rose up in Yang's mind. Lebello had plotted Yang's murder, but not out of malice or ambition—he had sincerely been conflicted about it, seeking nothing more than the continued existence of the Free Planets Alliance, with its two and a half centuries of history since Ahle Heinessen. If the state could live on, he was even willing to murder Miracle Yang, and let his own name go down in infamy in the annals of history. Even supposing that this was nothing more than a psychological effect associated with narcissism, it wouldn't be an easy thing for Yang to counter if Lebello had at least a subjectively thorough belief and determination.

One other problem was that the wishes of the military and the government that Lebello represented were not necessarily the same, and the greatest factor determining their actions was likely impulse. No matter how superior Yang's powers of insight might be, it was all but impossible to guess the content of an impulse. Even so, he had made one particularly terrible prediction, although he hadn't spoken of it yet even to his wife. If that prediction turned out to be correct, the course he would have to take was already decided. But in order to justify that course, Yang knew that, at least for now, he mustn't go to El Facil.

⁘ ⁘ •

When Dusty Attenborough visited the fleet commander's office bearing a juicy bit of intel, they were heading into the third week since their escape from Heinessen. He called it "intel," although it had nothing to do with military or political matters, and was more along the lines of everyday gossip. Frederica started to get up to leave, but Attenborough motioned for her to stay, and lowered his voice with exaggerated drama.

"Were you aware that Vice Admiral von Schönkopf has an illegitimate child in this fleet?"

Attenborough looked straight into the faces of the Yangs, and a satisfied grin spread out over his face. To leave Miracle Yang dumbfounded was no easy task. This was neither earthshaking news nor anything constructive, and it certainly wasn't lofty conversation, but he had succeeded in surprising Yang.

At his core, Attenborough was a man who preferred the buzz of activity in conflict to the doldrums of peace, though he did understand in his own way when it was and wasn't advisable to leak secrets. Regarding this fact, he had said nothing even to von Schönkopf.

While reading over a list of all the crew in the Irregulars, his memory had tripped on the family name of one Katerose von Kreutzel. It had taken him quite a while to realize that she was the daughter of unknown whereabouts whom von Schönkopf himself had told him about.

"So just now, I snuck down to the pilots' lounge to behold the fair face of Vice Admiral von Schönkopf's young fräulein."

"And? What was she like?" Yang's voice was about to spill over with curiosity.

"Probably fifteen, sixteen years old. Quite a beauty, and it looks like she's still got potential to improve. Maybe just a little bit bossy looking, though."

"Thinking of recanting your bachelorism, Admiral Attenborough?"

At Frederica's question, Attenborough thought about it hard for a moment. To the Yangs, he was looking more than halfway serious, but in the end, he shook his head of tangled, wooly iron-gray hair.

"Nah, not gonna go there. I can't quite see how calling Vice Admiral von Schönkopf 'Father' would ever connect to the blissful future of my dreams."

Yang nodded with complete understanding, and Attenborough smirked.

"In terms of age, she seems like a better match for Julian," said Attenborough.

"Oh no, you don't," Yang said. "He's got Charlotte Phyllis."

Neither Yang nor Attenborough were aware that Yang's ward Julian Mintz had already met Katerose von Kreutzel six months ago, or that they were leaving his wishes entirely out of the conversation.

"...Still, if the daughter of Caselnes and the daughter of von Schönkopf both started fighting over Julian, that'd be a sight to behold! I wonder how those blockhead dads of theirs would compete for the role of father-in-law?"

Frederica, looking slightly aghast at her husband amusing himself so irresponsibly, calmly tossed a stone into the waters: "You're right. No matter which of them won, the Yang family would gain a wonderful new relative."

Yang, when he heard that, fell into some very serious contemplation, and Frederica and Attenborough had to try hard to stifle their laughter.

"Anyway," said Attenborough, "how many months is it now since that kid took off for Earth? Wonder if he's all right..."

"Of course he is. He's *safe*," Yang said with a slight emphasis.

Yang was thirty-one this year, but Julian Mintz, who had already lived for five years as his ward, was seventeen, and had been given the rank of sublieutenant. He had logged military accomplishments four years earlier than his guardian had, although that had of course been a one-off.

Caselnes had predicted, "He might just end up a field officer at twenty, and His Excellency the Admiral at twenty-five. He's a faster runner than you are."

"Do things ever really go that well?" Yang had replied in a grave tone, though his expression had betrayed his voice. "Don't flatter him. He'll get conceited."

Yang had had no intention of making a soldier of Julian, but given Julian's own wishes, he had given the boy military training in both official and unofficial capacities. Strategy and tactics Yang had taught Julian himself, von Schönkopf had taken charge of hand-to-hand combat training, and Olivier Poplin had instructed him in aerial combat. Frederica and Caselnes had coached him on the ins and outs of bureaucracy. Yang's intention had been to discover at the outset what kind of work the boy was naturally suited to. Some observed that the mental pressure this first-class team of instructors exerted on the boy seemed calculated to make him give up his dreams of military life, but those people were overthinking things, most likely.

Julian was, however, blessed with an abundance of natural talent, and showed a wealth of ability in everything he put his hand to. His instructors were pleased, yet at the same time felt a slight hint of concern.

One day Olivier Poplin sat the flaxen-haired youth down for a sermon.

"Julian, you may be *good* at everything, but if you can't rival Yang Wen-li when it comes to strategy and tactics, if you can't hold your own against Walter von Schönkopf in hand-to-hand, and if your aerial combat skills can't hold a candle to those of one Olivier Poplin, you'll end up a textbook example of the jack-of-all-trades who is master of none."

Most of what he had to say was a fine representation of what Yang was feeling, but Poplin being Poplin, he had to go and tack something unnecessary on at the end of this most sensible sermon: "So, Julian, I want you to work hard so you can at least surpass me in the acquisition of nooky."

Of course, to hear Alex Caselnes tell it, neither Poplin's sermon nor

Yang's worrying had much of an effect. After all, when he was better than Poplin at strategy and tactics, better than Yang at hand-to-hand combat, and better than von Schönkopf at aerial combat, what business did any of them have condescending to him?

Still, no matter how they might evaluate Julian with the spoken word, they all held affection for him, and were hoping for his safety and success.

One other reason why Yang wasn't taking action was that he was waiting for the day when Julian would come back to him bearing vital intelligence from Earth. Though he bore little responsibility in the matter, he had been unable to defend the home that Julian was supposed to return to, and had ultimately been forced to flee Heinessen. For that, Yang did feel like he was to blame.

III

Following the escape of Yang Wen-li and his subordinates, pitiful flailing was on display in the Free Planets capital of Heinessen, like that of some herbivorous dinosaur that had wandered into a dried-up swamp.

On the occasion of Yang's escape, gunfire had been exchanged among three parties—Yang's subordinates, the Free Planets' governmental forces, and the imperial troops commanded by the late commissioner Lennenkamp. The people, of course, knew about it. Ever since that day, silent, intangible cracks had been forming in the land and sky of Heinessen.

Though João Lebello, chairman of the High Council of the Free Planets Alliance, was hard at work even now trying to preserve the state's suddenly crumbling contours and leadership, his efforts were producing almost no real effect.

Lebello had concealed from the public the reluctant death of Commissioner Lennenkamp as well as what was, after all, the reluctant departure of Marshal Yang. He had done so because he believed it necessary to protect the honor and safety of the Free Planets' government. The battle that had unfolded in the streets of the capital's uptown area he had dismissed as "an accident not worthy of comment," but by dodging the questions, he had only succeeded in amplifying the people's unease and distrust.

As a later historian would put it, "There is no room for doubting João

Lebello's loyalty and sense of responsibility to the state. But there also exist in this world wasted efforts, and pointless devotion. And that describes perfectly what João Lebello, chairman of the High Council of the Free Planets Alliance, was doing...

"Of course, João Lebello's misfortunes began with his assuming the seat of head of state, following the ignominious flight of Job Trünicht. Had he been outside of government, he would have had no involvement with the shameful attempt made on Yang Wen-li's life, and might well have taken the top seat in Yang's planned Civilian Revolutionary Administration. All possibilities, however, had turned their backs on him..."

Lebello had never been a heavy man, but day after day of hardship and overwork had greedily eaten away at his body until he was now no longer thin so much as pointy. His skin had lost its healthy sheen, and the redness of capillaries was now perceptible only in his eyes.

Concerned, the chief civil cabinet secretary and ministerial secretary had urged him to take some time off, but without even answering, Lebello had rooted himself in his office, broken off personal friendships, and clung tightly to his official duties with only his shadow for company.

"Won't be around much longer..."

That indiscreet but very serious prediction was being whispered back and forth in the office. The subject of that sentence had been rather daringly omitted—was it the name of a man, or the name of a nation?

Job Trünicht, Lebello's predecessor as chairman of the High Council, had been utterly detested by his opponents, who had called him a "silver-tongued, handsome-faced suck-up," but when it came to playing on the emotions of supporters and undecided voters, he had been a master. One reason for that was that his good looks and eloquence stood out from the crowd, but when he had made the leap from Defense Committee chair to chairman of the High Council, he had invited four young boys and girls to his inauguration ceremony.

One had been Kristoff Dickel, a young boy who, after losing both his parents while defecting from the empire with his family, had worked to put himself through school, graduated top of his class, and gone on to Officers' Academy. Another had been a young woman who, despite having been accepted to university, had volunteered to become a military nurse instead, and had saved the lives of three soldiers on the battlefield. One was a young girl who had become a leader in raising funds to help wounded or ill veterans. And the last was a young man who had recovered from drug addiction, gone to work on his father's farm, and taken first place in both a milk cow competition and a debate contest.

Trünicht had introduced these four as "young citizens of the republic," made a show of shaking their hands onstage, and presented each with a "Young People's Medal of Honor" he had come up with. The speech that had followed had been one utterly divorced from shame or objectivity. It had been a deluge of pretty words and phrases, and a waterfall of self-praise. Those who were showered in its spray had been caught up in waves of delusion that spread by the moment. Every attendee had been a holy warrior, battling the empire to protect freedom and democracy. The energy of this illusion had coursed through their veins.

Hugging the shoulders of the four young men and women, Trünicht had sung the national anthem in chorus with everyone, and when he had sung "Oh, we are freedom's people!" the excitement and emotion in the room had become an active volcano that erupted. Attendees had become a wave of human bodies as they rose to their feet and unleashed a downpour of praise on the Free Planets Alliance and Chairman Trünicht.

Among the attendees at the ceremony, there had naturally been critics and opponents of Trünicht, but while the calculated nature of the whole production had inwardly disgusted them, they had nevertheless been unable to withhold applause. Ultimately, an enemy of Trünicht was viewed as an enemy of the state, and that was a danger they had avoided.

"I see—those are four fine young men and women he's got there. But how, exactly, do the things they've accomplished relate to Mister Trünicht's policies and decision-making?"

That question had been hurled at the screen by Iserlohn Fortress's then commander Admiral Yang Wen-li, but as he had been in a place four thousand light-years from the capital, his words had never reached the ears of the authorities. In Yang's estimation, the Free Planets' greatest enemy had not been Reinhard von Lohengramm, but their own head of state.

"Every time I hear that guy getting all Shakespearean in his speeches, my soul just breaks out in hives."

"That's too bad. If it was your skin, you could take paid leave."

This reply had been Julian's, Yang Wen-li's constant companion in conversation, who had been carefully pouring honey into Shillong tea.

Word was going around that Job Trünicht had secured guarantees for his personal safety and fortune, and embarked on a life of self-indulgence on the imperial capital of Odin. Though he was roundly criticized for his abandonment of principle, the people still couldn't help acknowledging that—questions of good and evil aside—he had been a pillar on which their government had rested. Even if he had been falsehood made flesh, Trünicht had drawn people's hearts together and inspired them, while Lebello's efforts, much like the warming of an unfertilized egg, had done nothing but disappoint.

Neither the small number of people who knew the facts about Yang Wen-li's escape nor the majority who knew nothing about it could fail to notice the stench of a rotting foundation rising up from the floorboards of that wooden house known as the Free Planets Alliance. All by himself, Lebello had pinched his nose shut and kept on working inside of that tilting house.

His sense of responsibility and mission didn't always work in a positive direction. The load of duties he was trying to shoulder by himself in truth required over half a dozen shoulders to support it, but he seemed to be trying to solve every issue alone. Even his good friend Huang Rui, having been refused a meeting for want of free time, had shrugged his shoulders and not come again. His friend had always had little mental energy to spare, and once it was depleted, he had no choice but to shut the doors of his invisible shelter.

During this period, the empire had continued to keep its silence, but this was merely the silence of a dormant volcano waiting to erupt, and once it became active again, it would engulf the whole galaxy in boiling lava. Unable to imagine when and how the eruptions would resume, people were already gazing up at thick clouds of volcanic smoke in their minds.

Yang Wen-li's clique had disappeared into the torrents and swells of the stars, continuing their unseen journey like a school of deep-sea fish. Naturally, antennae of reconnaissance had been extended for them in all directions, but with High Commissioner Lennenkamp's unexpected death, Marshal Yang's flight, and of course the order from the imperial high commissioner and the FPA government's scheme—which together had flung Yang bodily into a zero-g vacuum—classified as top secret, the recon orders had hardly been followed with any great attention to detail.

Once Yang's Irregulars had been spotted by FPA naval vessels on patrol, but Marshal Yang—with a face unknown to no one in the FPA Armed Forces—had shown himself on-screen and said, "We're on a top secret mission from the government." The ships' commander, rather moved, had saluted and seen them off without incident. He had used the military's own authoritarianism and the government's own secrecy against them perfectly, but a common understanding that formed among many high-ranking officers later was, "If they'd revealed the facts to us, not only would I not have arrested Yang—I would've switched sides and joined him."

It required no self-deprecation to state the obvious: both soldiers on the front lines and civilians in the rear held Yang Wen-li in far greater esteem and had far greater trust in him than they did the government.

Unable even to warn his good friend, Huang Rui would stare out the window of his study each day, watching one small eddy in the rushing torrent of history.

The fall of the Free Planets Alliance was no longer avoidable. And if it was going to be destroyed anyway, Lebello should have refused Lennenkamp's order to arrest Yang Wen-li, and in so doing demonstrated clearly the significance of a democratic nation's continued existence: No one was arrested without legal grounds. The rights and dignity due to each individual were given precedence over the ever-shifting interests of the state. These were the things that could have chiseled into history the significance of the Free Planets Alliance having existed.

It was too late now, though.

For Huang Rui as well, it was supremely regrettable that a good friend like Lebello had given himself over to the sort of illicit tactics that had been so unlike him, only to fail. Lebello had always been one to pursue the ideal with straightlaced, earnest conviction. The sight of his friend, no longer able to fall on his sword after a lifetime spent free of compromise, had now all but vanished from Huang Rui's field of view. Huang Rui's vision couldn't even penetrate to the bottom of the waves.

IV

Following the retirement of its commander in chief Marshal Alexandor Bucock, the Free Planets Alliance Space Armada had been left without a supreme commander. Its general chief of staff, Admiral Chung Wu-cheng, had remained in his position while serving as deputy commander in chief, although he was now widely known as "a baker's son gone to work for the scrapyard." In fact, all he had done since taking on the duty was oversee the disposal of battleships and mother ships in accordance with the Baalat Treaty. Or to put it more precisely, he was really just doing so on paper; even the man himself was avoiding comment on whether or not the numbers in his statistics were trustworthy.

"How about I take the deputy thing once Yang Wen-li comes back to the military? There's no one else who could work as our commander in chief."

That, followed by an apology, was what Chung Wu-cheng had said to Lebello when he'd been about to appoint him to the position officially.

"He kidnapped High Commissioner Lennenkamp and made the fracture between the Free Planets and the empire irreparable," Lebello had said. "After that, there's no way he's ever coming back."

"If I may say a word, how exactly would you deal with Yang Wen-li if he were overcome with a thirst for personal vengeance, and threw in his lot with Kaiser Reinhard's forces? There's no reason we should cut off *any* chance for reconciliation. We need to prepare an environment where he can jump back in at any time."

Chung said nothing further, although he was already implementing numerous measures to allow Yang to command as effective a fighting force as possible when he returned.

"If you tell me to go fight him, I will," he added. "Not that I'll have any hope of winning. First of all, do you really think the soldiers have any desire to fight that undefeated admiral? The punch line to that would be them running over to join his camp with weapons in hand."

The content of what he was saying had stopped just short of becoming a threat, but Chung Wu-cheng's expression and tone had remained easygoing and nonchalant, so Lebello hadn't realized it. His psychological circuits already overloaded, his ability to project the words and actions of others onto his own consciousness had been starting to break down.

This guy's gonna totally burn out before much longer, Chung Wu-cheng had observed, wondering if that might actually be a blessing for the unfortunate head of state. In fact, the only person living who could speak to Lebello unreservedly or sarcastically was, at present, himself, although naturally he did not put that observation into words.

The voices of journalists were getting steadily louder and more intense as reporters laid siege to the government, saying, "Tell the people the truth!" While they would have to brace for retribution if they criticized the empire, the pen apparently still retained its power when it came to criticizing the Free Planets' government.

Those in the office of the imperial high commissioner would have loved to have made the incident public to expose the lack of leadership in the Free Planets' government, but if the facts of High Commissioner Lennenkamp's kidnapping had indeed come to light, the authority of the imperial government would have suffered no small injury. Furthermore, it would have given direction to anti-imperial sentiments held by the Free Planets' citizens, and that could have ended up making Yang Wen-li a symbol among the anti-imperial resistance efforts. A variety of conditions had forced them to remain silent, but that had lasted only until instructions arrived from the imperial government. Hummel, who had been Lennenkamp's aide, was ensconced in the darkness of the high commissioner's office like some sort of nocturnal beast, busily sharpening his claws and canines.

A certain journalist confronted the government, saying, "There are just two things I'd like to ask. First, where is High Commissioner Lennenkamp? And secondly, where is retired marshal Yang Wen-li? That's all I want to know. Why won't the government answer?"

Those questions, however, were exactly what the government could not answer, and in this way they ultimately lent credence to the proverb "A witness's silence is the mother of rumors."

"…Marshal Yang was kidnapped by Commissioner Lennenkamp. He's being held out of sight in their camp on Planet Urvashi, since it's been put under the empire's direct jurisdiction."

"…No, the government has Admiral Yang hidden away in a mountain cottage in a certain highland region. A rancher who lives in the vicinity caught sight of both Yang and his wife. Apparently, the marshal had his arm around his wife's shoulder, and they were strolling through their garden, with their faces turned down a little."

"…According to a very accurate source, Marshal Yang and Commissioner Lennenkamp both shot each other, and are in a military hospital with serious wounds."

"…All you guys are full of it. Marshal Yang has already shuffled off this mortal coil. He was assassinated by one of the kaiser's men."

Scarcely a word of these rumors even came close to touching a part of the epidermis of a fact, and naturally, the one that became most popular was the one that most strained the limits of exaggeration with regard to Yang's fame and abilities. It claimed Marshal Yang was concocting a thousand-year plan to perpetuate republican democracy, and had chosen his old stomping grounds of El Facil as a stronghold. This whole chain of circumstances was playing out in the palm of Marshal Yang's hand, and the day would soon come when the marshal would reveal his undefeated, gallant figure on El Facil, assume his seat as leader of their revolutionary government, and declare to the whole universe that he was raising an army!

"We are not isolated," said the spokesperson for El Facil's autonomous government. "We will surely answer his call, and then the politics of true republican democracy will be promulgated throughout the universe. From the bottom of our hearts, we will welcome the coming of Marshal Yang, democracy's greatest protector."

With no one to pick up where he left off, however, the spokesman's sense of isolation only deepened. Naturally, his comment drew objections:

"In its words and deeds, the autonomous government of El Facil is turning its back on the good of the Free Planets Alliance as a whole. This is a grave betrayal that threatens the very existence of the republican form of government. It's our hope that you will abandon your self-righteousness, and return to the ideals of our founding father, Ahle Heinessen."

Those words were spoken by Lebello himself, but because he had remained silent on the matter of Yang's life, death, or present whereabouts, it was no surprise that they failed to apply much pressure.

The scenario presented by Chung Wu-cheng—a diagram depicting Yang and Kaiser Reinhard uniting their forces—seemed to shine out like a red signal lamp even in Lebello's extreme tunnel vision.

"You're saying that if we back Yang into too tight a corner, he'll have nowhere else to go and will join hands with Kaiser Reinhard and place himself under imperial command?"

That was exactly what Chung Wu-cheng was pointing out. What other way was there to interpret it?

"Even if he doesn't want to, he could be forced into taking the only option he's got if there's no other way to survive. We mustn't corner him."

"Still, no matter how tight a fix he's in, Yang grew up drinking the water of republican democracy—I can't believe he would ever subordinate himself to a despot."

"Don't forget, Your Excellency, Rudolf von Goldenbaum started out as a leader in a democratic republic and ended up the ruler of a dictatorship that was positively medieval."

"In that case, do we need to deal with Yang before that happens?"

"Kill the snake while it's still in the egg, you mean? Still, we'll need soldiers if we're going to fight Marshal Yang. And that's definitely a tall order."

The imperial forces considered Yang their greatest enemy. The battles at Astarte, Amritsar, the Iserlohn Corridor, and Vermillion had proven that was true. And as for the soldiers of the Free Planets Alliance Armed Forces, they couldn't think of killing Yang as anything other than aiding and abetting the empire.

"I don't believe that fighting Yang means sinking to the status of imperial cat's-paws."

"Chairman, the problem I'm pointing out has to do with the soldiers' emotions, not your opinion."

After firing off that impolite line in a courteous tone of voice, Admiral Chung Wu-cheng took his leave of the agonized head of state. He had other things to do, and could not afford to waste time on grave but fruitless discussions.

What finally pushed Lebello off of his merry-go-round of limitless trepidation was a young man with luxurious golden hair. On November 10 of that year, Reinhard von Lohengramm, kaiser of the Galactic Empire, appeared on FTL comm screens all across the galaxy, standing in front of his new banner.

"Citizens of the Free Planets Alliance, the time has come for you to reconsider whether or not your government is deserving of your support."

Kaiser Reinhard's speech, which began with that introductory remark, was one that shocked both the citizens and the government of the Free Planets Alliance.

He spoke of the imperial high commissioner's—of Senior Admiral Helmut Lennenkamp's—suicide. Of retired marshal Yang Wen-li's escape from the capital. Of the commissioner's office's heavy-handed approach and the FPA government's scheming, which together had formed the seedbed from which these results had sprung. All the things that the people couldn't have learned if they'd wanted to were told to them at that time.

"I freely admit my own ignorance and the imperial government's thoughtlessness. These things are deserving of criticism, and I can't help but grieve for the accomplished man who was lost, and the peace that was shattered. Yet at the same time..."

In the eyes of a people riveted in place by shock, that golden-haired young conqueror was like a gilt idol to the god of vengeance. His ice-blue eyes blazed with a bitter light, searing the retinas of onlookers.

"...At the same time, I cannot overlook the incompetence and faithlessness of the Free Planets' government. It was wrong for the late high commissioner Lennenkamp to demand the arrest of Marshal Yang. The Free Planets' government should have appealed to me regarding this injustice, and safeguarded the lawful rights of your most illustrious citizen, Marshal Yang Wen-li. Instead, they chose to curry favor with the powerful, violating even their own laws in the process. Not only that, when the scheme fell apart, they sought to avoid retaliation by offering the high commissioner up to his enemies!"

The pale form of Lebello, facing impeachment from a distance of several thousand light-years, was doubled over in an underground room at the High Council building, surrounded by his secretaries.

"They sold out your most distinguished citizen for the sake of a temporary benefit to the state. After which they immediately switched sides and sold out my representative. Where did the pride—and the very reason for being—of the republican form of government go? At this present point in time, it has become an injustice to recognize the perpetuation of such a system. The spirit of the Baalat Treaty has already been defiled. There is no way to correct this except through force."

This was the abolition of the treaty and a redeclaration of war. The air of every inhabited world was suffused with a horror-stricken silence. Piercing this silence, soaking into the people's eardrums, was the voice of the kaiser, speaking in a slightly altered tone.

"Marshal Yang is not entirely without blame in this matter, but he was a victim, and merely protecting his own rights. If Marshal Yang will present himself before me, I will receive both him and his followers warmly."

The dignity of the Free Planets' government was dealt a fatal blow by the verbal atom bomb that Reinhard had lobbed their way. That was clear as day even to small children.

Among that government's high-ranking officials, there were some whose faces showed release from their rather weighty responsibilities. They were saying to themselves, "I knew all along things would turn out like this. There was simply no other course I could take. Even the worst outcome was better than no outcome at all." Those who spoke such words probably wanted to live steady, stable lives within a blueprint created for them by some gigantic, overwhelmingly powerful Other. Far fewer in number were those who would joyfully take up brush and easel when presented with a pure white canvas.

A life of subordination, of following someone else's orders, was just easier. This was the psychological soil from which had sprung man's acceptance of dictatorships and absolutism. Five hundred years ago, a majority of citizens in the USG had by their own free will chosen the rule of Rudolf von Goldenbaum.

In any case, there were also those who had no escape from weighty responsibilities. These included João Lebello, isolated in the High Council chairman's seat which nobody even wanted any longer, and the military leadership, which had to face a second imperial invasion while leading a force that, in terms of both spirit and provisions, was a hollowed-out husk of what it had been.

V

Since retiring due to age and poor health, Marshal Alexandor Bucock's requests to return to active duty had been turned down three times. Two days after Kaiser Reinhard had turned the whole galaxy upside down with his renewed declaration of war, Bucock went to visit Space Armada Command HQ.

Lieutenant Commander Soon "Soul" Soulszzcuaritter, who had been serving as Bucock's aide-de-camp at the time of the elderly marshal's retirement, raced over to the front entrance of Space Armada HQ in order to assist the labored steps of the revered old admiral, running so fast that his black beret was blown right off his head. Now, as though it were the most natural thing in the world, he showed Bucock to the commander in chief's office. Since Deputy Commander in Chief Chung Wu-cheng was out at the moment, he tried to get him to sit down at his old desk. If the deputy commander in chief had been present, Soul might well have run him out in order to secure the old admiral his seat. Bucock smiled and waved a hand, though, and instead sank his old frame into the sofa that was for guests.

"Excellency, does the fact that you've come here in uniform mean you're returning to active duty to fight the empire? Will I be under your command again?"

The lieutenant commander's words were far closer to wishes than questions. Bucock calmly nodded.

"Unlike Admiral Yang, I've been on the Free Planets' payroll for more than fifty years. At this point, I can't just look the other way."

The hot-blooded young officer felt the temperature and humidity around his eye sockets skyrocketing. Again he saluted, and in a trembling voice said, "Your Excellency, I'm coming with you."

"How old are you, soldier?"

"Huh? I'm twenty-seven, but…"

"Hmm, that's too bad. This time around, I can't take any of you kids under thirty. This party's gonna be adults only."

"Excellency, please—!"

Realizing the old admiral's true intention, Lieutenant Commander Soul was left dumbstruck. Because he was young and had full prospects for the future, Bucock had no intention of taking him along. The old admiral gave him a smile like that of a naughty child who had unexpectedly aged a whole lifetime.

"Listen here, Soul, I've got an important mission for you, and you mustn't take this lightly."

Soul, tightly bound by invisible chains of tension, listened as the old admiral Bucock pronounced each and every word clearly.

"I want you to go to Admiral Yang Wen-li, and tell him this: 'Take no thought of vengeance for the commander in chief. You've got a task that only you can do.'"

"Excellency…"

"Don't get the wrong idea. I might be wasting your time giving you this kind of message. I don't plan on losing twice to a young pup fifty years younger than me. This is nothing more than a contingency in case things go bad."

Physically, Bucock had grown a bit feeble, his once-muscular frame having atrophied with advancing age, but although the shadow of old age hung over him like a gray fog, the gleam in his eye and the power in his voice had a vitality that could overwhelm a man in his prime. Even if this was all just bluster, he wasn't showing off his zealousness to the young man; he was showing his consideration for him. It was through something other than reason that the lieutenant commander realized that he should follow the order.

The door of the commander in chief's office opened, and the "Baker's Son" appeared. Having probably heard report of his visitors already, no surprise showed on his face as he looked at the old marshal and saluted him with an easygoing smile.

"Welcome back, Your Excellency."

Lieutenant Commander Soul would later remark that he had "never seen such a fine greeting before."

"I understand you've said you can't take along anyone under thirty. Being as I'm thirty-eight, I think I'm qualified to go with you…"

Bucock started to open his mouth, then closed it and shook his gray head. Unlike with Lieutenant Commander Soul, he knew that with Chung, he would be the one to get nowhere by arguing.

"I don't know what I'm gonna do with you, either. This, when Admiral Yang's needing all the talented help he can get."

"Too many old upperclassmen, and the young won't have anything to do. Caselnes is enough for Admiral Yang by himself."

The elderly marshal nodded, turning his gaze toward someplace far beyond the wall. "Kaiser Reinhard could've had us tried as war criminals, but he didn't. I at least owe him personally for that, though I'm not going to reciprocate. There's no need for young folks to be so choosy, but as for me, I've lived in this screwed-up country long enough."

Rubbing a hollow cheek, the old marshal smiled at Lieutenant Commander Soul, who stood rooted to the spot. "Oh yeah, Soul, I'd almost forgotten—in the basement of my house, there's a yellow wooden box with two bottles of very fine brandy inside. Could you take one of them with you when you go, and give it to Yang for me?"

· · ·
·
· ·

The spectacular bolt of lightning that Reinhard had hurled stretched out to the very edges of the vacuum of space. Yang Wen-li heard the news in a room on board the "unsinkable" battleship *Ulysses*, pressed into duty as a temporary flagship for the Irregulars.

The handsome young kaiser and the emblem adorning the crimson banner behind him overlapped and were magnified in the back of Yang's mind. *Goldenlöwe, eh? They should've called it "gorgeous banner that's suited to nobody except that young man."*

The kaiser's announcement that he would "receive Marshal Yang warmly" weighed heavier on Yang's mind than anyone else's. When the feeling surfaced, it only took the form of a bad joke ("Think he'll pay me a contract fee?") that earned him icy stares from his staff officers. Still, it was because they were Irregulars staff officers that they could take the joke as a joke; the government of the Free Planets Alliance had a guilty conscience about its actions, and would have almost certainly viewed that comment as evidence of his going over to the empire.

It wasn't as if Yang had faced no dilemmas up till now. If he had revealed the truth about his unjust arrest and how it had driven him to flee Heinessen, the government's ignominious violation of the law would have been exposed, and people's trust in the fairness of republican democracy would have been undermined. To say "What have I been fighting for?" would have been not just a denial of his own past—it would have been a slight against the dignity of countless people who had fought for the sake of republican government.

He was well aware of how truly naive this was, but even now, he was still counting on the government of the Free Planets to own up to its mistakes, to apologize, to ask him to come back.

Democracy had always been worth counting on. After all, hadn't it been in the denial of states' and power structures' infallibility that democratic government had originally begun? Wasn't the strength of democracy found in its willingness to call its own wrongs wrong, to examine itself, and to purify itself?

However, the barren silence from the government of the Free Planets Alliance had dragged on and on, ultimately letting the empire get away with their preemptive move in the most drastic of manners. After all, what the empire had made public was "factual," so the only way the Free Planets had to resist was through a fiction of even greater truth. As no such thing existed, their silence had continued.

Yang's road back to the government of the Free Planets Alliance was already cut off. Thus far, he had not responded to El Facil's declaration of independence, instead letting the fleet burn through supplies as it continued silently running, but that too had been a wasted effort. Kaiser Reinhard's announcement that he would treat Yang well was most certainly not a falsehood. Even after the Vermillion War, Reinhard had encouraged him to join the imperial military. His indictment of the government's true intentions had had the maximum political effect, completely severing the relationship between the FPA government and Yang. This was what made the golden-haired young man so extraordinary. Yang couldn't help but be impressed.

Was it a deficiency in Yang's own reason or the heart's infinite capacity for caprice that even as he denied autocracy—in particular, "merciful and efficient" benevolent rule—Yang couldn't bring himself to hate Reinhard von Lohengramm as an individual? Yang found that question difficult to answer himself. Either way, Yang had now been robbed of every option but one: to take advantage of the struggle between the empire and the alliance and build a third force.

A third force? All Yang could do was shrug his shoulders. Calling it that depended on the Free Planets Alliance being healthy enough to call a second force. The alliance's collapse was closing in right before his eyes.

"Shall we go back to Iserlohn, then?"

Yang had only murmured the words, but in Frederica's ears, they roared like crashing breakers, stirring something very much like homesickness. Not even a full year had passed since their departure, yet that inorganic, man-made silver planet swelled up in her heart with inexpressible nostalgia. *That* was the homeland of Yang's Irregulars, of the Yang Fleet.

"After that," Yang said, "We take El Facil, and secure the entrance to the corridor. Let's give Attenborough's plan a try, shall we?"

El Facil was just one frontier stellar region, but as a supply base for Yang Wen-li's forces it would more than suffice. And then there was the matter of Julian. Whenever he got back from Earth, the boy was going to need a home to welcome him, and for that he could think of nothing other than the "liberated corridor" linking Iserlohn and El Facil.

Yang's dark eyes began to fill with life and energy. Something lurking deep inside him that was not the historian began to stir. In the back of his mind, a seal of ice broke apart, and a powerful torrent of backed-up ideas began to gush forth.

"Kaiser Reinhard is probably going to order Admiral Lutz to launch an attack from Iserlohn. It'll be Operation Ragnarok all over again. And that's when we'll have our opening…"

As Yang began to murmur enthusiastically, Frederica listened with all her being.

CHAPTER 3:

I

AFTER THAT MOST venerable of crowns had come to rest upon his brow, Reinhard von Lohengramm had moved his imperial headquarters to Planet Phezzan. Not five months had passed since that day, and now a second expedition into Free Planets space was about to commence. Others looked on in amazement at the speed of it all, but during that period the golden-haired young conqueror felt slightly ashamed, as though he were backsliding into a preference for stability over progress, and letting history carry him along on its conveyer belt rather than seizing it in his own two hands.

To outsiders, it must have looked like Senior Admiral Wittenfeld's passionate, even extremist, speech was what had finally roused the kaiser, but from Reinhard's perspective, he had merely ripped open the curtains of an afternoon nap, and found that fierce admiral standing on the other side. Since Wittenfeld's arguments aligned perfectly with both Reinhard's strategic thinking and his fundamental nature, though, it was only natural that his regard for the Schwarz Lanzenreiter's commander was on the rise.

Some historians point to a worsening of the new kaiser's biorhythms during the first few months following his enthronement, and indeed,

Reinhard did experience occasional instability in his physical condition, including loss of appetite and outbreaks of fever. Undeniably, scattered glimpses of a slight passivity could be perceived, which had been absent in his precoronation self. Still, even if it was true that his biorhythms were down, Reinhard's mines yet retained rich veins of spirit and talent. He had dispatched Admiral Wahlen to crush the headquarters of the Church of Terra, and he had moved the imperial headquarters to Phezzan from its home of five centuries on Planet Odin. In the meantime, new systems and organizations were taking shape, talented people were being appointed to key positions, and laws were being reformed and abolished on a daily basis—Reinhard was certainly not idling away his days as a ruler.

Nevertheless, Reinhard himself felt more than anyone else that this brief respite of 141 days had been a waste of time. Reinhard's dearest friend, the late Siegfried Kircheis, had once put it this way: "Lord Reinhard's feet were never made for walking the earth, but for bounding across the sky." Construction projects and the work of setting up a government most likely qualified as "walking the earth" to him. He certainly had no intention of neglecting these things. Still, it was when he was commanding gigantic fleets, when he and enemy forces were blasting away at one another, that he felt deep satisfaction—blazing exhilaration—filling the depths of his soul.

Reinhard housed many contradictions beneath his porcelain skin, albeit in a sense slightly different from that of his battlespace rival Yang Wen-li. On and on he had fought, and on and on he had won. Winning meant reducing the number of his enemies, and if his enemies were reduced, then so too would be his opportunities for battle. It was possible that his vitality itself had ultimately been reduced as a result of this.

Little problems that felt alien to his nature were always cropping up both inside and outside of court. Just the other day, a bureaucrat at the Ministry of Industry had caused an unintentional dustup with a careless remark. The man was a hard worker who had even been assigned to Imperial Capital Construction HQ, but one night he went out drinking with his colleagues, and while trying to emphasize the importance of Phezzan during the course of their conversation, he had wagged his tongue too far.

"Phezzan should be the node that organically ties all of human society together. Even if the Lohengramm Dynasty were to end, Phezzan would still be the most important location in the galaxy."

The latter part of this statement had marred the sanctity of the emperor; it was lèse-majesté, and as such deserving of the ultimate penalty, said the one who had informed on him. With a put-upon expression, the young kaiser delegated judgment in the matter to Hilda. After confirming the background and details of the case, she reprimanded the speaker for his carelessness, but pronounced a heavier sentence on the informant—a one-rank demotion for making a colleague's slip of the tongue out to be a deliberate crime, and for causing a needless uproar. In so doing, he had harmed the kaiser's many vassals and officials, and stained the kaiser's reputation for tolerance and equity.

Several days went by, and Reinhard, suddenly remembering the case, asked Hilda how she had handled it. Hilda reported the facts without embellishment. Satisfied, the young kaiser brushed his long hair back behind his neck. "You're most reasonable, Fräulein von Mariendorf. This will make a fine lesson for anyone who thinks I take pleasure in stool pigeons. Moving forward, it seems I'll be delegating a variety of matters to you."

After thanking him, Hilda had a request of her own for the kaiser, regarding a less-than-desirable trend that was spreading rapidly these days both at court and in the government. While it was a matter of course that people show their respect for the kaiser, some were using this as a tool for achieving unworthy ends.

"What, specifically, do you speak of, Fräulein von Mariendorf?"

"Things like criticizing someone who doesn't say 'Sieg kaiser' when greeting a colleague or sharing a toast, for example, or supervisors making notes of such things in personnel performance records."

"That's absurd."

"As Your Highness says. Which is why I would be grateful if you would make a formal proclamation to that effect, which would go out to all of your vassals. A preemptive strike, if you will, against those who would try to advance their own careers by criticizing and tearing down others."

Reinhard's ivory fingers toyed with a lock of the golden hair that hung down over his brow.

"If you concern yourself with such trifles, Fräulein, your labors will never end, either. Still, it would be best to nip this in the bud. Very well. I'll send out the proclamation by the end of the day."

"Thank you for listening, Your Majesty."

If advancement came not by feats of valor against fierce enemies on the battlefield or by solving difficult problems in national government, but rather through the flattery of absolute authority, then the Lohengramm Dynasty was sure to head straight down the road to decadence. Reinhard understood Hilda's concerns, and had himself always hated the sort that tried to ingratiate themselves to rulers.

In the past, Hilda reflected, it had been the late Seigfried Kircheis who had counseled him, speaking frank words of advice. Now he had people like the straight-arrow Mittermeier and the honest Müller with him, but none of his admirals were in a position to be completely unreserved with the kaiser. For her own part, it would be an outrage to think of herself as having such standing; even so, there *were* things that even Reinhard wouldn't notice unless someone spoke up.

On the day that he redeclared war on the Free Planets Alliance, Reinhard was explaining a number of his tactical theories to Hilda after returning to his office from the FTL room. He knew how highly Mittermeier had appraised her incisive planning; he said it excelled the firepower of a battle fleet.

"Do you see some clever move we can make in this coming invasion, Fräulein von Mariendorf?"

"If Your Highness so wishes it, I can bring the alliance's head of state here before you in less two weeks, with no further fighting."

Reinhard's ice-blue eyes lit up with interest.

"And what would you require, Fräulein, to pluck this fruit from the branch?"

"A single e-gram."

With unconscious elegance, Reinhard's head tilted slightly forward in thought, then after only a moment, he broke out in a smile. "I see—you'll have them feast on one another. Am I right, Fräulein von Mariendorf?"

"Yes, Your Highness."

"If I may say so, this is the sort of suggestion I'd usually expect of Marshal von Oberstein. Great minds, it seems, sometimes do cross the same bridges."

Hilda blinked to hide the surprise in her eyes, and then observed Reinhard closely. Maybe he had spoken to her that way expecting such a reaction, but before she was able to tell, he posed a new question.

"Well then, what are the advantages of this plan?"

"We avoid bringing war to the alliance's capital of Heinessen, and we resolve this without involving noncombatants. We can pin responsibility for the alliance's collapse on the leaders themselves, and shift the citizens' ill will away from us."

"And its disadvantages?"

"In the short term, at least, this will strengthen Marshal Yang Wen-li's faction. With no one but him to turn to, each and every one of Your Highness's enemies will flock to him. Also…"

"Also?"

"Following its success, this plan will likely leave Your Highness with a bitter aftertaste. Since Your Highness's wish is to crush the Free Planets' military in a head-on confrontation."

Reinhard laughed in a loud, clear tone, and a sound like resonating crystal glasses rebounded through the air of the room.

"It would seem Fräulein von Mariendorf has a silver mirror, reflecting the hearts of men," he said. That appraisal was rooted in memories of a fairy tale that his sister Annerose had once told him when he was a child, although naturally the young kaiser didn't say as much.

"Even so," Hilda persisted, "without our resorting to cheap tricks, once they are faced with imminent collapse, the people will grow desperate, and some will surely come to us, peddling the sort of merchandise we couldn't buy now if we tried."

"That *is* a distinct possibility," Reinhard admitted.

Finding himself in reluctant agreement with Hilda's assessment, Reinhard rang a bell on the table. Young Emil von Selle, his personal attendant, appeared, and Reinhard told him to bring coffee.

Even now, whenever Emil came before his dear young kaiser, his joints would all go stiff, just like those of an automated doll.

This served only to deepen the affection Reinhard had toward the lad, who was faithful to a fault. If Emil had grown accustomed to the kaiser's affection and become haughty, however, he would surely have incurred Reinhard's displeasure instead.

As Emil took their orders and briefly exited the room, his actions drew a smile from Hilda.

"He's a fine young man, isn't he?"

"With him here, I've no inconvenience. He'll make a fine doctor. Even if his skills are less than perfect, patients will gladly trust him with their lives…"

At times such as this, the ferocity and bitterness associated with one side of Reinhard disappeared beneath his ivory skin, replaced by characteristics of another side. "It's because I've no younger brothers," he said. With those words, Reinhard had revealed one small corner of his heart. As he himself was forever a woman's younger brother, he seemed to take undiluted joy in reversing that role.

While they were waiting for coffee, Hilda suddenly thought of her own status, and unusually for her, her thoughts ground to a screeching halt. She was this great young conqueror's loyal and capable head secretary. Outside of that, there was no other position she should hope for.

．　　・　　●
　　　・
　．　　　　　・
　　　　　　・

Imperial Marshal von Oberstein, the minister of military affairs, had been named commander of Phezzan Planetary Defense Headquarters, and as such was to be left behind. During the kaiser's absence, military matters would be handled by the minister of military affairs, while civilian government would be managed by the minister of industry. While this was only the most obvious of staffing choices, both Mittermeier and von

Reuentahl were thinking the same thing inside: *With him gone, I feel like I can breathe again.*

Von Oberstein had received his orders with his usual unreadable expression, and now in a room at the building where the Ministry of Military Affairs had been installed, he was getting started on some paperwork. One of his subordinates, Commodore Anton Ferner, however, was experiencing the thrill of poking his "coldhearted, emotionless" superior officer with as blunted a verbal needle as he dared.

"I had believed you were opposed to a second invasion, Minister."

"No, I've no issue with it."

Von Oberstein did not believe this sudden, repeated invasion would prove a panacea, but since the Free Planets' government wouldn't have time to mount an effective defensive strategy anyway, the conditions all balanced out. The important thing was to always keep oneself positioned to create the conditions, and not yield the initiative to the enemy. As high commissioner, Lennenkamp had marked no successes to speak of, yet through his own unfortunate death, he had played a role in driving the Free Planets Alliance onto treacherous ground.

"Also, the kaiser is most in his element when swift and decisive action is required. When you think about it, sitting still and waiting for things to change doesn't suit the kaiser at all."

"There's no doubting that."

While he did agree with von Oberstein's thesis, scattered particles of surprise danced in the look that Ferner gave him.

II

Having passed through the Phezzan Corridor and into the territory of the Free Planets Alliance, Senior Admiral Wittenfeld was advancing rapidly toward a rendezvous with Senior Admiral Steinmetz's forces. At one point along the way, however, a tiny formation of about ten FPA navy vessels had been detected approaching in a provocative manner.

The destructive power of the Schwarz Lanzenreiter could have reduced a weak force like that to so much space dust in the blink of an eye. However, from Senior Admiral Wittenfeld on down, the officers and soldiers of the

"Black Lancers" made it a point of pride to earn their reputations battling *large* enemy forces. With a generosity born of having ships and firepower to spare, the Schwarz Lanzenreiter tried to ignore the little flotilla, but the enemy instead began to follow them, persistently refusing to peel off. After the passage of about an hour, Wittenfeld, who had never been a patient man, could endure his irritation no longer.

"The nerve of these guys. They just don't know when to give up."

Upon receiving their fleet commander's order to "vaporize them with one strike, and take the first blood of this deployment," about one hundred ships closed in on the small fleet, licking their chops like ferocious animals.

Unexpectedly, however, that tiny fleet then revealed that it had not come seeking battle, but rather negotiations. Just as their out-of-order comm system had been about to give rise to the worst circumstances imaginable, it regained functionality. On learning that a special envoy from the Free Planets government was asking to negotiate his withdrawal, Wittenfeld's mouth twisted into a light smirk as he contemplated the matter. At last, he mentally snapped his fingers as an idea struck him.

"In my position, I've no authority to negotiate with you. You'll need to speak with Imperial Marshal Mittermeier instead, who's coming along behind me. I'll guarantee you safe passage."

Wittenfeld ordered one destroyer to act as both guide and escort, and then, accompanied by the Schwarz Lanzenreiter, sped even faster into the black space of the FPA's territory.

After being ignored by Wittenfeld, the special envoy from the FPA government likely figured that Mittermeier would be easier to deal with anyway. Led along by the imperial destroyer, they traveled for another three days, until they at last approached Mittermeier's fleet and requested a conference.

"Wittenfeld, you rat," murmured Mittermeier. "You're just pushing a troublesome guest off on me, so you can get farther ahead while I'm dealing with him."

Mittermeier had seen right through Wittenfeld's prank, but as the Imperial Space Armada's commander in chief, he couldn't just slam the door in the face of somebody claiming to be a special government envoy. Clucking his tongue, he ruffled a hand through his honey-blond hair, and invited this "special envoy" to board his flagship *Beowulf*, and see him in the commander's office.

Special Envoy William Odets had been a solivision commentator prior to becoming a politician. A young man serving on the Defense Committee, Odets' ambition was to employ his gift for eloquent speech, and make a name for himself that would be remembered for generations to come. Not even Lebello, who had sent him, was expecting very much out of this mission, but Odets himself was puffed up like a bullfrog with eagerness to "be the solitary tongue that halted the empire's mighty fleet." Escorted by staff officers on his right and his left, he exchanged a polite greeting with Mittermeier, then puffed out his chest and began speaking in his resonant voice. "Both the sovereignty and the territorial integrity of the Free Planets Alliance are guaranteed under the terms of the Baalat Treaty. In spite of that, however, the Galactic Empire is attempting to overrun our territory by means of entirely lawless violence, in defiance of the both the letter and the spirit of the treaty. Unless you desire hostility in the present, and criticism in the future, you should withdraw your forces immediately, and press your case through diplomatic channels."

As Odets finished speaking, a put-upon-looking Mittermeier made no attempt to reply, but simply touched his honey-blond hair with one hand. The special envoy was just starting to open his mouth again when a powerful reaction hit him not from the front, but from his left.

"Hold it right there! What did you just say?!"

Lifting his lanky form from his seat to deliver this tongue-lashing was Admiral Bayerlein. "Who was it that violated the treaty when they sold out our kaiser's ambassador plenipotentiary, High Commissioner Lennenkamp? That was the Free Planets government, was it not? You've never had any intention of observing the treaty, and as our kaiser views you all as incompetent, he has mobilized his forces in person to bring you to heel. Any of you who have consciences should go and prostrate yourselves before him, so that needless bloodshed can he avoided!"

Though faced with such fervor, Special Envoy Odets did not, on the surface at least, recoil. Instead, he said, "High Commissioner Lennenkamp hanged himself, and it was Yang Wen-li's group that drove him to it."

"Well, in that case, why aren't you doing anything about them?"

"Because you imperials aren't giving our government time enough to deal with them."

That answer brought a cold gleam to Bayerlein's dark-blue eyes, like a meteor flashing across the night sky.

"Time! Given time, Yang Wen-li's group will only grow stronger, while your government does nothing but wilt and wither away. Even if you had ten times the force strength of Yang, I don't think you could beat him."

"That may well be true," Odets said. The special envoy's polite reply was undercut by the venom dripping from his voice. "But in any case, not even Kaiser Reinhard, who has a *hundred* times the force strength of Yang, is doing anything about him. So there's certainly no way an untalented man like myself could oppose him."

A silence that was like vaporized lead filled the room. Even bold Bayerlein, for a brief moment, seemed to have been robbed of his respiratory function. Special Envoy Odets had just stingingly mocked the fact of Reinhard's defeat at Yang's hands in the combat at Vermillion. The silence rapidly reached critical pressure, and when it burst, a torrent of murderous rage came surging forth.

"You *dare* insult His Majesty, alliance scum!"

Angry shouts from Büro and Droisen had rung out almost in unison, and Bayerlein, too, fiercely charged toward Odets, lithely jumping across a desk as he closed in on him. Already, a blaster was gleaming in one hand.

That was when Mittermeier, who had kept his arms crossed and remained silent up till then, barked out a sharp command.

"Hold it right there! You're warriors, all of you, are you not? So just who do you plan on bragging to if you kill a man who walked into the midst of his enemies alone and, moreover, unarmed?"

Bayerlein's fierce outburst came screeching to a halt. The valiant young admiral suddenly went red in the face, saluted his commander, and returned to his seat. To the special envoy, who was trying not to look relieved, Mittermeier casually said: "There's one thing I'd like to ask you. Let's suppose one of the admirals here traveled to the Free Planets' capital as a messenger, and then insulted your head of state. Are there any leaders in your military who would want to make him pay for that indignity with his life?"

Special Envoy William Odets had no reply.

The eloquent messenger had found himself dumbfounded for the first time. Something in Mittermeier's expression was telling him that a slick, vacuous answer was not going to suffice.

"There's no one like that…unfortunately."

"Well then, how about Yang Wen-li's people? They *risked their lives* to rescue their commander."

Again, Odets found himself at a loss to answer.

"The Free Planets' mighty government holds no terror for our kaiser, but Yang Wen-li's rabble he does fear. And you've made the reason for that crystal clear yourself now, haven't you?"

Mittermeier rose to his feet. His unexpectedly small build took Odets by surprise. He had assumed that one of the imperial military's Twin Ramparts would be a giant of a man, with a stature befitting his renowned valor.

"Thank you for your hard work today, but it seems we've run out of things to talk about. If you've anything further you want addressed, you'll need to ask the kaiser directly."

"That will be fine, Your Excellency. Although I would appreciate it, Marshal Mittermeier, if you could refrain from further military activity until I can ask the kaiser to withdraw."

"I'm afraid that won't be possible. Whether or not you go to see the kaiser is up to you, but our fleet operations won't be hindered by that in any way. If an edict comes down from His Highness telling me to withdraw the forces, we will of course obey, but whether or not that happens depends on how eloquent a speaker *you* are—it has nothing to do with us. Until a new edict comes down, we will follow the old one. In other words, we will continue our advance into Free Planets space, eliminating any resistance we may encounter. If you simply must halt our invasion, then don't waste a moment—go before our kaiser. Making full use of your oratory here, I'm afraid, is an exercise in futility."

For Mittermeier, it was an unusually long reply, as if he were making up for the silence he'd maintained thus far. Each and every word became an invisible bullet fired into the heart of Special Envoy Odets. Eloquent speech backed by technique alone was not enough to sway the empire's highest, most powerful admirals.

The special envoy hung his head. It seemed he had burned through all of his courage and ambition. His mission had failed. If he was unable to convince Mittermeier here, there was no way he could talk his master, Kaiser Reinhard, down.

When he had departed the Free Planets' capital of Heinessen, there had been a gaseous mixture of passion, courage, and confidence filling him from the inside; by this point, however, its pressure had dropped to near-vacuum conditions. Even so, he put up a bluff and departed the flagship *Beowulf* with his chest puffed out. When he returned to his own ship, however, he hung his head dismally. The next several hours he spent shut up in his cabin, and when he finally showed himself outside its door, it was to announce in a despairing tone that he was going to go and plead his case directly before Kaiser Reinhard.

A few days passed, and Mittermeier asked Büro, "Whatever happened to that blatherer? He started out so strong, and then just fizzled out." On being told that the Free Planets' special envoy had headed off toward Phezzan to make his case to the kaiser in person, Mittermeier nodded once, and mentally filed the matter under "Things I Can Forget About."

Were he to second-guess himself, he might have thought it better to simply arrest that troublemaker who fancied himself an artist of the tongue. Still, he didn't for a moment think that a traveling orator unable to change his own mind would have any hope of swaying Kaiser Reinhard. There was also the fact that he had no business obstructing someone who wished to take his case directly to the kaiser. Once before, immediately following the Lippstadt War, an assassin had plotted to take Reinhard's life, but as a result had stolen the life of Siegfried Kircheis instead. This time, however, such a danger was hard to imagine. Still, just to be on the safe side, Mittermeier had a message relayed to imperial HQ, warning them about who to be careful of.

While Senior Admiral Wittenfeld was en route to Heinessen, barreling along at top speed through a region of Free Planets space now emptied of military forces, Senior Admiral Karl Robert Steinmetz was on full combat alert in the Gandharva Stellar Region—a territory under the direct control of the Galactic Empire—waiting for allied forces to arrive.

Using the forces the kaiser had given him, it would have been possible for Steinmetz to stage a direct attack on Heinessen right away—however, there were a number of conditions requiring he act with caution. First of all, the whereabouts of Yang Wen-li's party were unknown, and although the odds of a sneak attack were scant, the Gandharva system was to become a base of operations for the imperial military, so he dared not leave it undefended. While work on its facilities had progressed since the signing of the Baalat Treaty, its stage of completion was still a far cry from that of a permanent fortress like Iserlohn, and in order to defend both its status as a military stronghold and its stockpile of supplies, it was essential to keep the fleet's main force stationed there.

Furthermore, over ten thousand civilian and military officers formerly assigned to the late high commissioner Lennenkamp were stationed on the Free Planets' capital of Heinessen, and there was a need to ensure their safety. Naturally, a warning had been sent out already to the Free Planets' government, and not even the alliance was likely to kill or maim people who had the potential to become valuable hostages.

Actually, Steinmetz had at one point been on the verge of heading off to Heinessen by himself in order to demand some accountability of the Free Planets' government; at that time, his vice commander, Admiral Glusenstern, had blanched and opposed this vociferously.

"Going to Heinessen now with only a handful of attendants would be tantamount to suicide. Have you forgotten the unfortunate precedent set by High Commissioner Lennenkamp?

"If it comes to that, just blow Heinessen out of the sky, and me along with it," Steinmetz had replied as though that were a trifling matter. "That would wipe out most of the long-standing chaos with a single stroke."

Accompanied by staff officers including Vice Admiral Bohlen (chief of staff), Rear Admiral Markgraf (deputy chief of staff), Rear Admiral Ritschel (Command HQ general secretary), Commander Serbel (Steinmetz's aide-de-camp), and Commander Lump (captain of the escort fleet), Steinmetz had just left Admiral Glusenstern, his vice commander, behind and set out for the Free Planets' capital. Ultimately, however, the meeting had never come to pass; at the outer edge of the Gandharva system, Steinmetz had turned around and headed back to Planet Urvashi. Steinmetz had been the very first captain of Reinhard's flagship *Brünhilde*, and since that time had performed many acts of valor, primarily on the frontier. Now, like a tautly drawn bow, he waited as the days passed by.

Galactic Empire Launches Second Large-Scale Invasion!

That report had understandably sent shudders racing all across Heinessen, the capital of the Free Planets Alliance. Some self-deprecatingly mocked the situation, saying, "Wow, never dreamed we'd get to see imperial fleets *twice* in the same year!" while others shouted that the resistance must continue until the whole planet was reduced to scorched earth. Others argued that resistance was no longer feasible, so "we should tell them clearly that we wish to make an unconditional surrender." Some advocated evacuating the cities and fleeing to the mountains—when the empire had suddenly invaded prior to the Baalat Treaty's signing, there hadn't even been time to panic; this time, however, the rising tide of destruction was slowly soaking its way up the legs of the people's spirits. A false feeling, as of being prisoners set for execution, took hold of people, and a sense of helplessness closed in on them from all sides. When those feelings reached the saturation point, riots erupted. Citizens clashed with security police in front of the gates of closed spaceports, and fatalities rose to the thousands.

Standing in for the old and infirm Alexandor Bucock, Chung Wu-cheng was making rapid preparations for intercepting the Galactic Imperial Navy; lately, however, he was also being pressed into the job of listening to High Council chairman João Lebello's griping and complaining, a role he was getting sick of. Even the secretaries were avoiding the chairman lately. One day in his office, Lebello posed a depressing question to Chung:

"Are you telling me that Marshal Bucock refuses to fight against Yang Wen-li, but when the opponent is Kaiser Reinhard, he will fight?"

"I don't see what's so surprising about that," Chung Wu-cheng replied in a terribly gentle voice. "Please, think about this: you and Marshal Bucock have been on good terms for many long years now. So why is it that he won't meet with you? Don't you think it might be because he remembers *too well* what you were like in the days before he was made a marshal?"

"Are you trying to say that I've changed?"

"Marshal Bucock hasn't changed. Surely you can acknowledge that."

Lebello turned his lifeless gaze toward Chung Wu-cheng, but it was plain to see he was looking through him, staring at something beyond him that only he could see. His mouth opened and closed slightly, spinning out a low, dry voice. Chung Wu-cheng strained his auditory nerves to their breaking points. Lebello was reciting the criminal charges against the fugitive Yang Wen-li.

"I realize this is impertinent of me to say, Your Excellency, but Yang Wen-li could have killed you, or spirited you off to the edge of the galaxy. The reason he didn't was…"

But Chung Wu-cheng didn't finish his sentence. It was obvious Lebello wasn't listening. The space armada's general chief of staff let out a sigh and rose to his feet. His expression was that of one worrying about the future of a financially troubled bakery. When Chung Wu-cheng left Lebello's office, he started to say something to the chief of the security office, but stopped. He couldn't shake the feeling that spiritually, the chairman had committed suicide already.

Back at Space Armada Command HQ, Chung Wu-cheng was informed in the atrium that he had visitors. After first stopping by his own office, he opened the door to the visitor reception room that had been indicated.

There his three visitors turned to look at the "Baker's Son" who was general chief of staff. They all rose from the sofa, and saluted him with stiff movements and expressions.

Vice Admiral Fischer, who had been vice commander of the Iserlohn Patrol Fleet, Vice Admiral Murai, who had been its chief of staff, and Rear Admiral Patrichev, who had been its deputy chief of staff: those were their names.

When Yang had retired from the military following the signing of the Baalat Treaty, what had been commonly known as the "Yang Fleet" had been dissolved, and each member of this trio had been reassigned to different military bases across various frontier sectors that lay in entirely different directions from one another. Up until just six months ago, they had been leaders in the most powerful armed force in the Free Planets Alliance, but now, after many battles in many sectors, many victories, and many labors, they had clearly come to be viewed as obstacles and interlopers, and had thus been driven from the capital. From a political standpoint, this treatment had not been mistaken. The possibility of the most powerful regiment acting autonomously and transforming itself into a military political faction was one that the central government naturally feared, so it made sense for them to promote the Yang Fleet's dissolution—especially when there was no further value in using it.

Although these three leaders had felt not exactly *uneasy* in their new posts, they had been unable to feel entirely comfortable either. Out on the frontier, they were separated from their comrades, and everything they knew of the situation in the capital consisted of official announcements and uncertain rumors that came trickling down the information pipelines like flat, tasteless water from a stagnant reservoir. They didn't know whether Yang Wen-li—the former commander with whom they had faced life-and-death battles during the three years since the founding of the Thirteenth Fleet—had escaped or been purged. All they knew for sure was that either way, he had been driven out of the ideal life he had dreamed of.

"You all must be exhausted after such a long trip. Please, have a seat." Even as Chung encouraged them to sit, he lowered himself onto the sofa. With an easygoing, relaxed posture, the general chief of staff went over what he knew about his guests in the back of his mind.

Murai was lacking when it came to creativity, but he had a highly organized mind that excelled at solving bureaucratic problems; he was known as "the rare sensible one in the Yang Fleet." Fischer was well-known for his skill in managing the operations of large fleets; it was thanks to his flawless control of the Yang Fleet that it had never once failed while executing operations proposed by Yang. Patrichev looked nothing like a staff officer, and while his hulking build alone was enough to make an impression, he had in fact never once allowed the Yang Fleet's headquarters' operations to fall into arrears, and there was no doubting his sincere devotion to his duties and his commanding officer. Yang Wen-li, the young man who had hired these talented individuals, led them, and never let them fall out of step, was no ordinary soldier, Chung Wu-cheng thought.

From a solemn face, a solemn voice spoke.

"If I might ask the general chief of staff, what sort of purpose do you have in summoning us here all this way from our respective posts?"

The other two guests remained silent, apparently yielding the floor to Vice Admiral Murai.

Briefly, yet without sacrificing accuracy, Chung Wu-cheng explained the situation that had led to Yang and his subordinates fleeing from Heinessen. He looked from face to face as those three faces looked at one another, and then took out the documents he had brought.

"And this brings me to the important thing. I'd like you to find Admiral Yang and hand him this document."

"What is it?"

"A contract of transfer."

The three leaders of the former Yang Fleet made three different kinds of suspicious expressions as they stared at the pages. When they looked up, their expressions of surprise and distrust had only grown more severe. Looking a bit tired and reluctant, Chung Wu-cheng crossed his legs and sat up straighter.

"It's exactly what it looks like. I'm signing over 5,560 of our armada's ships to Yang Wen-li. And I'd like you to deliver the paperwork along with the merchandise itself. The statutory procedures are all taken care of, so there's no need to worry yourselves over that."

Murai made a coughing sound.

"Was there really any need to make this kind of paperwork, though? I have to think even pointless formalities have their limits."

"You don't get it, do you?"

With innocent eyes, Chung Wu-cheng looked back at the three men. Patrichev tilted his muscular neck, Fischer blinked, and Murai couldn't even manage that.

"It's a joke, of course," Chung Wu-cheng said, carefully adjusting the angle of his black beret. Murai sat up even straighter. Perhaps he was thinking, *So, my commander up until six months ago isn't the only troublemaker.* If he was, it didn't show in his face. That said, his tone of voice acquired a keener edge, even though he was speaking with a senior officer.

"A joke, Your Excellency? That's well and good, but if you've whittled your fleet down like this, when the time comes to muster forces, it will be impossible to handle the imperial invasion, don't you think?"

"Even if we muster everything we've got, we won't be able to handle them."

Chung's all-too-clear reply left Vice Admiral Murai speechless. With silver-haired Fischer still making no move to break his silence, it was Patrichev who next opened his mouth after the former chief of staff. "So Your Excellency may say, but…you don't intend to hand the capital over without fighting, do you?"

"That's correct—I have no such intention. Commander in Chief Bucock and I are planning to try a bit of vain struggling."

"But that's an act of suicide, isn't it?" said Patrichev. "What if, instead of that, Your Excellency and Commander in Chief Bucock came with us instead?"

Vice Admiral Murai shifted his line of sight, looking gently at the giant rear admiral. "Watch what you say. To begin with, we haven't decided yet if we're going to go to Yang ourselves."

"I intend to," said Fischer, finally breaking his silence as his silver eyes turned toward the general chief of staff. Chung Wu-cheng crossed his legs again.

"Could you do that for me, Admiral Fischer?"

"Gladly, Your Excellency. Vice Admiral Murai, we don't have time to be tiptoeing around our intentions. Let's follow the best course, without wasting any time."

After a moment's silence, Vice Admiral Murai looked up at the ceiling in indignation, although he had probably acknowledged that the older man, Fischer, had the right of it. At last, he saluted and accepted his orders.

• •
•
•
• •

After the three leaders of the old Yang Fleet had left headquarters carrying the contract of transfer, Chung Wu-cheng reported to Bucock what had happened. Thanking him for his hard work, the old admiral suddenly looked off into the distance. "When I got beaten at Rantemario, I should've died then and there. You convinced me to live on for another six months, but in the end all you accomplished was moving back the date of my death."

"When I look back on that now, maybe I spoke out of turn. Please forgive me."

"No, thanks to you I've been able to do a few nice things for my wife, but...what about your family, soldier?"

"There's no need to worry—I've decided to send them to Yang along with Vice Admiral Murai and the others. I'm being selfish in this matter as well, but I do worry about my family."

"I'm glad to hear it," the old man said as he closed his eyes. He himself had always left his elderly wife at home. His wife had refused to leave the house where they'd lived since their days as newlyweds. That probably meant that, eventually, she would face the end of both herself and the Bucock family in that house.

"Yang Wen-li is a man of many faults," said Chung, "but he does have one point that no one can criticize him on: he sincerely believes in the words we tell the public, that the military of a democratic nation exists to protect the lives of its citizens. And he's acted on that belief more than once."

"Yes," said Bucock. "That's very true."

On Bucock's aged face, there appeared a little smile that was like an expanse of fading light.

"He did so at El Facil. And he did so when he abandoned Iserlohn Fortress. He's never sacrificed a single civilian."

Yang was probably going to go down in history as an artist of warfare rivaling or even surpassing Reinhard von Lohengramm. However, there was something else about him that was even more important to pass on to future generations. Neither Bucock nor Chung Wu-cheng would perform the duty of telling it, though. Everyone had their own job to do.

"I think I understand what you're getting at, Chung," Bucock said at last. "If Yang is defeated, it won't be by the outstanding genius of Reinhard von Lohengramm."

It would be by Yang's fixation on his own ideals. At Vermillion, he should have ignored the government's cease-fire order. Bucock couldn't come out and say so, but for Yang's own good, that was what he should have done.

III

After batting aside the visit of Free Planets Special Envoy Odets, Mittermeier fired his first volley of cannon fire at a Free Planets military target. Because it was somewhat removed from the Imperial Navy's direct course, it had been ignored by Wittenfeld, but strategically speaking, the FPA Armed Forces weapons factory on Planet Lugiarna was not something they could afford to overlook. Given its astrographical position and production capacity, it would only cause trouble down the road if they left it alone.

Mittermeier's swift actions cast no shame on his nickname, "Gale Wolf."

On December 2, the military weapons factory on Planet Lugiarna was utterly destroyed by the Imperial Navy's assault, and its commander, Tech Vice Admiral Bounsgoal, shared the fate of the factory facilities. However, half of its recently completed destroyers and cruisers succeeded in escaping. Under the command of Commodore Desch, they eluded Imperial Navy pursuit and, gathering crew and supplies as they went, finally arrived at El Facil after fifty days, where they threw in their lot with Yang's Irregulars.

The long procession of Imperial Navy vessels formed a vast belt of light that stretched onward far past the rear of Mittermeier's fleet, sweeping across entire sectors of Free Planets space. In contrast to the present strength of the Free Planets Alliance Armed Forces, the Imperial Navy's excessively large numbers were stretching their resupply capacity to the limit. Directly aft of Mittermeier, Lennenkamp's former fleet was divided in two, spreading outward in two wings. When Senior Admiral Lennenkamp had been installed as High Commissioner, the fleet he had commanded had been split apart and reorganized under the command of admirals Alfred Grillparzer and Bruno von Knapfstein. Both were young men in their twenties, blessed with abundant spirit and energy. Furthermore, both had made up their minds to avenge their former commander Lennenkamp.

That said, there were naturally differences in their personalities. Von Knapfstein had been Lennenkamp's loyal and able student, possessed of utterly orthodox tactical skills and a personality that had just a hint of puritanical earnestness. On the other hand, Grillparzer's reputation as a soldier was one that belied his tender age, and in addition, he had made a name for himself as an explorer, and was listed as a member of the Imperial Association of Geography and Natural History. Joining that association required a member's recommendation and a scholarly review of a scientific paper, and he had qualified with a dissertation with the long-winded name of *An Examination of the Distribution of Polar Plant*

Life on the Second Planet of the Armento-Phoubel System, Demonstrating the Mutual Relationship Between Its Orogeny and Continental Drift.

He'd received word of his application's acceptance just as he was about to sit down for the funeral of the late Karl Gustav Kempf, and although he was finely attired in his best formal wear, he had run straight into a toilet stall thus arrayed. After releasing an explosion of joy alone in that private space, he had put on a somber face and gone back out to face the ceremony. Because of his personal history and tastes, one might think that he would hold Senior Admiral Mecklinger, the "artist of the admiralty" in higher regard than he did Lennenkampf, but that of course was no obstacle to his passion for revenge. The competitive spirit that existed between Grillparzer and von Knapfstein was likely raising the temperature of that passion as well.

Forming a line to the aft of them were fleets commanded by Admiral Grotewohl, Admiral Waagenseil, Vice Admiral Kurlich, Vice Admiral Meifocher, and others. Even so influential a figure as Senior Admiral Ernst von Eisenach was making an appearance.

Von Eisenach was relatively fond of alcohol, and even en route to battle a whiskey bottle was never far from his side. Nevertheless, he hadn't had a drop since departing Phezzan. There was a bit of a reason for this. As he was admiralty, it followed that a student from Imperial Military Children's Academy would come with him as an attendant; however, his reputation for being "exceedingly quiet, stern, and difficult to please" clung even to his shadow, and the student had frozen up from the very first moment he had received instructions from von Eisenach's deputy.

"If the admiral snaps his fingers once, you bring him coffee. Make absolutely certain you take no longer than four minutes. If he snaps his fingers twice, that means whiskey. Take care not to get them confused."

The student from Imperial Military Children's Academy had tried desperately to remember his instructions, and given his natural powers of memory, that should have been easy enough for him to do. However, the psychological pressure seemed to have warped the young man's memory circuits just slightly, and after setting out from Phezzan, von Eisenach had one day snapped his fingers twice, only to have two cups of coffee delivered to him three minutes and fifty seconds later.

The "exceedingly quiet, stern, and difficult to please" admiral had taken a quick glance at the boy, and seen him standing there completely rigid. Without saying a word, he had drunk both cups of coffee. Tension had drained from the entire body of the Imperial Military Children's Academy student, and he had breathed out a sigh of relief. In this manner, Ernst von Eisenach had never lacked for single or double cups of coffee on this campaign.

The specks of light trailing off to the aft of von Eisenach made up the fleet commanded by the aquamarine-eyed senior admiral Adalbert Fahrenheit. Fahrenheit had been given the vital task of connecting the fleets arrayed out in front with the fleets making up the rear, which were under the direct command of Reinhard. It was safe to say that the whole operation's smooth and organic execution was resting on his shoulders.

Afterward came Kaiser Reinhard's personal fleet. The top staff officer advising Reinhard was the secretary-general of Imperial Military Command Headquarters, Imperial Marshal Oskar von Reuentahl, and under him was Admiral Hans Eduard Bergengrün, who was responsible for managing fleet operations. The kaiser's chief aide, Vice Admiral Arthur von Streit, was also on the flagship, along with Lieutenant Commander Theodor von Rücke (his deputy assistant) and Hildegard von Mariendorf (his chief secretary).

At the tail end was the fleet commanded by Senior Admiral Neidhart Müller, also known as the "Iron Wall." Müller was not merely acting as rear guard; in the event of some disturbance back toward Phezzan, he would have to reverse course and subjugate the enemy as the spearhead of the entire imperial armada. Securing their rear supply lines was also among his duties.

And so, boasting this deep formation, the Imperial Navy's second invasion grew into an angry wave of energy and supplies that seemed ready to engulf all the lands of the Free Planets Alliance. Unlike this gigantic mobilization, however, a quiet but important mission was about to be executed in another tiny corner of space.

Yang Wen-li was beginning the operation to take back Iserlohn Fortress.

CHAPTER 4:
RELEASE, REVOLUTION, CONSPIRACY, ET CETERA

I

THE ABANDONMENT OF Iserlohn Fortress in SE 799 and its
daring recapture the following year have been referred to as the ultimate
realization of Yang Wen-li's theory of "space control" strategy, made possible by tactical skill raised to the level of an art form. This means not
fixating on tactical victories achieved through dueling with other fleets,
but rather securing the necessary positions at the necessary times to
achieve one's military objectives.

"Yang Wen-li was a master of fleet-to-fleet combat, but his true greatness lay in the fact that he still had a good understanding of his limits,
so he never let his own strengths drown him."

So said one historian, who lavished unreserved praise on Yang, though
on that point, Yang's rival Reinhard von Lohengramm was no different,
and both of them viewed fleet battles as nothing more than localized
displays of technical skill within the execution of their broader strategies.
Prepare a stronger force than your enemy's, run a flawless supply operation, gather lots of information, analyze it accurately, appoint trustworthy
frontline commanders, secure astrographically advantageous positions,
and choose the time to begin the battle. Do these things, and one or two

tactical defeats will not be worthy of criticism. The commander in chief actually just had one duty: to tell his entire force, "Don't get careless."

This second Operation Ragnarok found Reinhard von Lohengramm in a position from which he could have done only that. Nevertheless, going to the front line in person was what made Reinhard the "Golden Lion." It was an act related to his character rather than his ability.

Yang Wen-li, on the other hand, had to find his way out of a difficult situation under extremely unfavorable strategic conditions. It was something Alex Caselnes said that ultimately propelled him toward the decision he made. In a cabin on board the flagship *Ulysses*, Yang's senior from Officers' Academy opened his mouth to amusedly say, "Hey, we're broke, y'know? Make up your mind what we're gonna do."

Among the Yang Fleet's personnel, Caselnes was practically the only one who could understand finance and economics on the scale of nations. Yang's long-term plan to rebuild the FPA military had ended as a phantasm, but in it Yang himself had inserted a bullet point regarding financing, proving he was no ideologue for the supremacy of military power. Still, his thoughts did concern mostly military matters, a fact he had to admit even if he didn't like it. Call it a revolution or call it a war, it cost money to run it either way, and for the time being Yang had no magic lamp in hand.

When Caselnes suggested making use of Yang's friend Boris Konev's connections to borrow funds from Phezzanese merchants, Yang had gotten worried. Borrowed money had to be returned, and at present there was no way to come up with a plan to repay it. First of all, providing money for Yang's wandering Irregulars was a foolish enough bet that it warranted the term "speculation," and he didn't think any Phezzanese would be willing to take him up on it.

"What are you talking about? Once we borrow it, it's ours," Caselnes said. Ruffling his black hair, Yang sank into thought. Caselnes continued: "Phezzanese have a sharp eye for their own interests. If they think we have a chance of bringing down Kaiser Reinhard, they will absolutely invest in their future."

Yang said nothing.

"And once they start investing, they'll have to keep investing, so they won't have spent their money for nothing. The initial investment itself will be the first drop toward broadening and strengthening the connection between both sides."

"I get that, but can we really wheedle money out of business-savvy Phezzanese with nothing but maybes?"

"The success of a badger game is up to the woman's charms."

"The woman's charms…?"

Yang cocked his head, then tossed his black beret up in the air as he burst out laughing. He knew exactly what Caselnes was getting at now.

The Phezzanese spirit had always been one of independence and self-determination. It was true they had yielded before Reinhard von Lohengramm's grand, audacious strategy and the military power supporting it. It was true they had been forced into biding their time until clearer skies returned. But Phezzan's merchants in particular had been singing the praises of economic freedom for generations, so naturally they were especially opposed to the present state of affairs. If it was possible, they would surely want to overthrow the rule of Kaiser Reinhard. They just lacked the military power to do so.

That was why the Phezzanese were likely displaying a false obedience while seeking forces that could make up for what they lacked. They could coexist and cooperate with Yang's group. At the same time, though, they were not philanthropists; they would never waste good money on a weak force that didn't have a prayer of winning. For that reason, a powerful drug would be needed to anesthetize their instinct for self-protection.

If Yang could win a massive tactical victory—if he could *show* them that someone other than Kaiser Reinhard might just seize the reins of the future—then Phezzan's scale should tip far in his direction.

"A beautiful woman, to captivate and bewilder the Phezzanese," Caselnes said.

In other words, Iserlohn Fortress. They would retake Iserlohn, show off the power of the anti-empire forces, and get those investors to loosen their purse strings.

"So, that's also a reason to take back Iserlohn, is it?"

That was how recapturing Iserlohn became the supreme proposition for Yang and his followers. This went beyond a mere military objective. They were also doing this for the political effects and for their economic survival. Yang, combining essential elements from every magic trick known in history, had to successfully return to Iserlohn, then secure the exit point of the Iserlohn Corridor—El Facil—then prepare for the next battle, employing Phezzan's power to organize people and gather intelligence.

That said, this would all be for nothing if their Phezzanese sponsors were permitted to interfere and manipulate acts of revolution for the benefit of speculators. That was where they had their work cut out for them.

From Reinhard's standpoint, however, Iserlohn Fortress was ultimately no more than a pebble in the hinterlands. This wasn't just because Reinhard's indomitable temperament had led him to underestimate that pebble's importance; because he had seized control of the Phezzan Corridor and moved his imperial headquarters to Planet Phezzan, it only followed that the Iserlohn Corridor had lost much of its strategic value. He had left Marshal von Oberstein, minister of military affairs, behind on Phezzan and stationed a powerful military force there, while he had sent Lutz's forces to Iserlohn but emptied out the corridor—as a result proving Yang's hunch to be correct.

Naturally, some historians would later claim that it was arrogance that had made Reinhard pay too little attention to the Iserlohn Corridor, but his contemporary, Yang Wen-li, had a different opinion.

"The hawk and the sparrow have different points of view. One gold coin isn't worth picking up to a billionaire, but to a poor person it can mean the difference between life and death."

Reinhard, as the Galactic Empire's autocratic monarch, already ruled the greater part of inhabited space, and was attempting to conquer what little remained. Yang was trying to lead a wandering band of runaways without so much as a stronghold to call their own, to keep alive the democratic and republican forms of government, and with a lot of luck, lure the goddess of history—now smiling so seductively at the Lohengramm Dynasty—over into their camp. Any way he looked at it, Yang was the one attempting to do something outrageous, and worse, he had to go digging around in the pockets of generous tycoons in order to make it happen.

And so it was that on December 9, SE 799, Yang's Irregulars revealed themselves in the El Facil star system.

Actually, it wasn't Yang's proactive intent to rendezvous with El Facil's independent revolutionary government. Yang felt that what El Facil had done had erupted out of intense passions, and was more akin to rampage than revolution. However, as a first step toward unifying anti-empire republicans, a handshake between the political pioneers and the militarily powerful had become a necessity.

II

The leader of El Facil's self-governing body was a forty-year-old man named Francesicu Romsky who had originally been a doctor. Since ancient times, the doctors, teachers, lawyers, and students had been important sources of revolutionaries, so he, too, could be said to be carrying on the old tradition.

Eleven years before, at the time of the so-called El Facil Escape, he had been one of the civilians cooperating with Sublieutenant Yang Wen-li, the officer in charge of the evacuation, though for Yang any memory of his name or face had sunk into the depths of oblivion, and would not so much as peek above the water's surface for him. In any case, he had even forgotten his present-day wife Frederica until she had reminded him who she was, so there was no way on earth he was going to remember some other bit player.

Frederica, whose powers of memory were vastly more ordered than those of her husband, hadn't forgotten Romsky. He had treated her sickly mother on more than one occasion, and she had treated him to coffee and sandwiches. Romsky also remembered that blond-haired girl with the striking hazel eyes. Smiling from ear to ear, the doctor-turned-revolutionary gripped the hands of Mr. and Mrs. Yang. Yang Wen-li inwardly recoiled; the press corps surrounding Romsky had their cameras lined up like a battery of cannons. On the next day, December 10, El Facil's electronic newspapers were buried in exactly the kind of headlines that Yang had foreseen.

"Yang Wen-li Returns! The Miracle of El Facil Repeats Itself!"

"Here it is," Yang said. "This is why I didn't want to do that."

Yang held his head in his hands, but ultimately had no choice but to play the role of the projected image that his own actions and successes had established. He'd gone from being the hero of a democratic nation to the hero of a democratic revolution—and his reputation as a brilliant, invincible admiral was only going to become even more widely publicized.

As for the revolutionary government of El Facil, having Yang's party join their ranks didn't just mean a quantum leap in the power of their military forces, it meant that they were the ones that the greatest leader of the Free Planets Alliance had acknowledged as a legitimate administration, striving for the tried-and-true politics of republican democracy. Concurrent with their delight, they wanted to use that for all it was worth.

It was obvious why Romsky intended to maintain a close relationship with the journalists, from the standpoint of both the ideals of republican democracy and the revolution's intelligence strategy. Yang, of course, couldn't make public his inner disgust. Public access was a pillar of republican democracy. If it were secrecy and nondisclosure he preferred, he would have been better off siding with the totalitarians; instead, Yang had to wrestle his personal feelings to the ground and smile for the cameras.

That notwithstanding, at the magnificent welcoming ceremony that was held in his honor, Yang managed to finish his address in a scant two seconds: "I'm Yang Wen-li. Nice to meet you."

This disappointed the ten thousand attendees who seemed to have been expecting a moving, passionate speech, but if he produced results, that would eventually make up for such disappointments. When Yang sat back down, Romsky said to him in a low voice, "Admiral Yang, I think our new government needs a name…"

"Yeah, of course…"

"I'd like to announce this formally tomorrow, but what do you think of the 'legitimate government of the free planets alliance'?"

This was followed by a long silence—Yang's psychological equivalent of stumbling for about three paces. He wanted to think that Romsky was joking, but it was obvious he was not. When Yang didn't answer right away, Romsky looked at him again, somewhat uneasily.

"You don't like it?"

"It isn't that. It's just, do you really think it's necessary to quibble over national legitimacy? I think you should emphasize the fact that you're starting out fresh…"

Yang made his case as reservedly as he could. He didn't want it thought that he was forcing his own opinion on Romsky with armed forces in the background.

"That's right," said Dusty Attenborough, who had guessed Yang's state of mind and come to provide reinforcement. "First off, calling yourselves the 'legitimate government' is just bad luck. Remember the recent example of the 'legitimate imperial galactic government'?"

Attenborough, it seemed, had managed to attune himself to Dr. Romsky's psychological wavelength. The revolutionary nodded and said that it certainly was inauspicious, and he would try to come up with something else. Even so, he looked a little disappointed.

"Admiral Yang, please don't get fed up over little things like this," Dusty whispered. "Taller mountains than this one are sure to come up in the future."

"I know that," Yang whispered back, and it was not entirely an empty formality. Even if it had a few—make that a lot—of faults, he couldn't afford to let this tiny, powerless bud of democracy get nipped. If he stood idly by, all of inhabited space would be enveloped in the white palms of a more eminent, more elegant personality. The issue now was not Reinhard's own abilities or conscience. Nor was the favorable impression Yang had of Reinhard personally an issue either. What could not be allowed was the whole universe being ruled by a naive system of government dependent on the talents and qualities of a single individual.

Rather than having the justifications of a solitary, absolute god forced upon them, it was infinitely better to have lots of insignificant people waving about their own petty, foolish justifications and hurting one another. Merge all colors into one, and everything turns black; a chaotic jumble of many colors was preferable to colorless purity. There was nothing inevitable about every human society being united under just one system of government.

In a sense, one could say that these thoughts of Yang's were not entirely devoid of elements opposed to republics and democracies. After all, the majority of democratic republicans no doubt wished for the universe to be united by their ideas, and were praying for an end to autocracy.

Even so, this too could not be more ironic. When the enormous body of the Goldenbaum Dynasty's age-stricken Galactic Empire had collapsed with silent rumblings, the Free Planets Alliance, after two and a half centuries of steadfast resistance, had been hollowed out and eaten up by termites.

"Could it be, then, that the historical significance of the Free Planets Alliance didn't end with its opposition to tyranny, but with its opposition to von Goldenbaum?"

That was something Yang had thought about before, and while things did, in his estimation, pretty much look that way, it would have been bad form on his part to decide it was so. All of the history since their founding father, Ahle Heinessen, had boldly set out on the Long March of 10,000 Light-Years, all the accumulated hopes, passions, ideals, and ambitions of countless people—a two-and-a-half-century stratum of joy and anger and sadness and delight—were these all just things piled atop the corpse of one man, Rudolf von Goldenbaum?

Of course, when one put it that way, even the handsome conqueror Reinhard von Lohengramm might not be any different. He had set out to overcome the Goldenbaum Dynasty, and although he had realized that ambition, had it amounted to nothing more than driving the ghost of Rudolf back beneath his tombstone? Romsky was still going on in a heated tone about a new name, a new flag, and a new anthem for his nation. While nodding at appropriate moments, Yang's thoughts were racing through the darkness of the past, as well as the labyrinth of the future...

This was how the "Irregulars" became the "Revolutionary Reserve." Commander Olivier Poplin would later say of the matter, "Winter clothes in the wintertime, summer clothes in the summertime. Whichever you wear, though, what's inside doesn't change."

The commanding officer was Marshal Yang Wen-li, and his chief of staff was Senior Admiral Wilibard Joachim von Merkatz. Vice Admiral Alex Caselnes became rear service manager. Government Chairman Romsky doubled as military affairs chairman. Yang felt a slight bit of relief. Having only one boss was something to be grateful for.

But Yang's arrival on El Facil was rewarded by an even greater joy—his reunion with Julian Mintz and Olivier Poplin.

III

On December 11, Attenborough went to the spaceport and had just wrapped up a discussion about reorganizing the military-civilian dual-use traffic control system when he spotted Yang's ward. Or to be honest, he caught sight of a smart-looking, slightly out-of-place brunette beauty in a leopard-skin coat, walking among waves of people dressed mostly in work coveralls who were flowing through the vast lobby. While he happened to be scanning her with his line of sight, he spotted a familiar-looking head of flaxen hair.

"Julian! Hey, is that you, Julian?"

Beneath the flaxen head of hair that turned about, lively, youthful eyes lit up with joy when they saw where the voice was coming from. With fast, rhythmical steps, he came near and saluted energetically.

"Vice Admiral Attenborough. It's good to see you again."

Unfaithful, the cargo ship he had traveled in, had just come into port, and its captain, Boris Konev, was still at the office, in the midst of the necessary docking procedures.

"So, where's the rest of your followers, kid?"

"That's awful, Vice Admiral—you shouldn't call them that."

Machungo was hanging back behind Julian, carrying the luggage with both arms and both shoulders; he took up twice as much space as the boy. When Attenborough spotted Olivier Poplin, he was several paces away, pleasantly chatting up three young women who all looked to be somewhere around twenty. Light as feathers, fragments of their conversation came floating to them.

"Commander Poplin!" Julian called out.

"Ah, here we go…" Poplin said, grumbling as he approached. "Don't go interrupting me just when things are getting good. Just a little more time, and I would've been having sweet dreams in a double bed tonight."

He gave a perfunctory salute to Attenborough, who was not so small a man to get his feelings hurt over that degree of rudeness—though it did bring out his sarcasm: "Look at you, hard at work the minute you hit port. You must seduce new women by the minute."

Poplin showed no sign of contrition.

"The human race has forty billion people, and half of them are women. If half of those are either too old or too young, and half of that number I disqualify based on looks, that still leaves me five billion eligible romantic interests. I can't afford to waste even a second."

"You must not be too particular when it comes to intellect and personality."

"Oh, I'll leave the ones with great personalities to you, Admiral Attenborough. The half with bad personalities I'll take off your hands."

"Commander, have you no self-awareness? From the way you talk, I could only assume you're a swindler, and that's putting it nicely."

"Aw, you can cut me this much slack. After all, while we've been working our butts off on some gloomy old planet called Earth, you've all been living it up on Heinessen, doing whatever you wanted."

"Hey, we've been working hard, too."

As he made that childish comment, Attenborough noticed Julian trying not to laugh, and with a self-conscious clearing of the throat, he changed the subject.

"Seriously, though, it's great that you've made it all the way out here. We only got here two days ago."

Julian had of course been trying to get back to Heinessen at first, but the instant they had crossed over from the Phezzan Corridor into FPA space, they had heard Kaiser Reinhard's renewed declaration of war, learned that Yang had fled, and been forced to change directions. After carefully considering various factors, Julian had predicted that, regardless of what happened in the meantime, Yang was sure to plan Iserlohn's recapture eventually, and in some capacity make contact with the independent revolutionary government of El Facil.

"A lot happened along the way," Julian said, "but somehow we managed to make it here safely. At any rate, thank goodness everyone's safe, and we get to meet again. Truly."

Though Julian had said this concisely, they truly had had a lot of things happen along the way. Following the conclusion of Senior Admiral August Samuel Wahlen's mission to crush the Church of Terra, they had followed him to the imperial capital of Odin, where they had toured inside Neue Sans Souci Palace, presently being repurposed as a historical museum. Here Poplin, unsurprisingly, had had his picture taken with a dark-haired girl who had also come to sightsee. For cover, they had passed themselves off as a party of very curious free traders from Phezzan. Although it had been a simple formality, they had also faced questioning by military police. The optical disc they had carried out of the Church of Terra's headquarters under utmost secrecy had been stolen at one point, and they'd had to spend three days searching for it. Poplin, on the verge of sharing a night of passion with an imperial officer's wife, had been discovered by her husband. Thanks to Admiral Wahlen's good favor, though, they had finally been allowed to depart Odin. They had returned by way of Phezzan, where there had been obstacles by the dozen to overcome before they could return to Free Planets space. After all that, they had almost been picked up by one of the Schwarz Lanzenreiter's reconnaissance crafts, but thanks to Boris Konev's piloting, they had in the end made their way to El Facil.

Inside the landcar, four men—Attenborough, Poplin, Julian, and Machungo—were en route to the building that now served as Yang's command center. Due to Machungo's bulk and the large amount of luggage, no one was able to sit straight. With effort, Poplin leaned toward the driver's seat, where Attenborough was sitting.

"Still, that's a pretty bold move, cutting ties with the Free Planets' government. Guess this is what happens when he wakes up and stops lazing around."

Probably thinking he should say something, Attenborough, still facing forward, replied: "Listen here, Commander Poplin—don't get the wrong idea. We're in this sort of revolution to show off and have some fun."

"Much as I'd rather not, I can see that just by looking at all of your faces. I guess the Yang Fleet has only changed its nameplate."

When they arrived at the command center, the four men were freed from their state of near suffocation. Carrying a small mountain of luggage, the giant Louis Machungo went down to a basement-level locker room for the time being, while the other three went in through the lobby and headed for the elevator hall. That was where Olivier Poplin stopped in his tracks. A young junior officer, her black beret resting atop a thick head of hair the color of lightly brewed tea, approached with a rhythmic gait that rivaled Julian's, called out to him, and saluted. Hurried salutes and changes of expression crisscrossed among the four of them, and the elevator door closed with just Julian and Attenborough aboard. A somewhat complicated blend of moods drifted on the air of the twelve-cubic-meter enclosure.

"Julian, do you know her? That girl just now."

"Yes, Commander Poplin introduced us at Dayan Khan Base. How do you know her, Admiral Attenborough?"

"Um, well, she's the daughter of someone I know." The young admiral started fanning his face with his black beret. It seemed their commander's bad influence had rubbed off on him.

"Oh, so you must know Corporal Katerose von Kreutzer quite well, then."

At Julian's casual probing. Attenborough decided to go ahead and cross *that line*.

"All right, I'll tell you. That girl is the daughter of Vice Admiral von Schönkopf."

Bombshells, however, don't necessarily have the desired effect when they burst. Julian blinked three times, cocked his head sideways, and stared at Attenborough. At last, his cognitive circuitry matched language to meaning, and the young man started chuckling.

"I'm sorry, sir—it's just a little hard to believe that Vice Admiral von Schönkopf has a daughter."

Even more so if it was Katerose von Kreutzel, a.k.a. Karin. All Julian could do was shake his head.

"You've sure got that right. Even now, I still can't believe it myself. But think about it. Vice Admiral von Schönkopf's been earning his stripes in that arena, too, since he was about your age. I wouldn't be surprised if he's dropped bastards by the dozen, never mind just one."

For a long moment, Julian said nothing as he scanned through the hall of portraits occupying a portion of his memory. Never mind Karin's light, tea-colored hair and those indigo eyes that shone like the sky in early summer; something about her overall appearance left him with the slightest hint of déjà vu. Could that be because she was von Schönkopf's daughter? Poplin had said there seemed to be some sort of situation regarding her birth…

"Does Vice Admiral von Schönkopf know about this?"

When Attenborough said no, Julian sank into thought once more.

"How about it, Julian?" said Attenborough. "Wanna try using that virtue of yours to mediate a father-daughter reunion?"

"It would never work. She probably doesn't like me."

"Did you do something to be disliked?"

"No, sir, nothing in particular. It's just that, somehow, I was getting that kind of feeling."

Attenborough shot a slightly downturned look at the young man, but was unable to make out anything in his face to draw conclusions from.

"Well anyway, for the time being, we ought to be pouring all our energy into retaking Iserlohn, instead of looking down from the nosebleed section at von Schönkopf's family squabbles."

The elevator door opened, and as the view outside expanded, Attenborough laced his fingers behind his head and signaled Julian with a jerk of his chin. "Come on, Julian—our sloth of a marshal's this way, reluctantly hard at work."

⁘

Even His Excellency, their sloth of a marshal, sometimes had momentary bursts of diligence. That day, too, Yang was at his desk, setting off chained volcanoes of thought. Papers that had been used for taking notes and making calculations were scattered all around him.

"You've got to do your best. If this isn't settled during Your Excellency's generation, Julian's generation is going to have an awfully hard time of it."

So said Lieutenant Commander Frederica G. Yang, his aide at Revolutionary Reserve Command HQ, a mischievous twinkle dancing in her hazel eyes. Her husband let out an indignant sigh, and took a sip of the tea that his wife had brought him.

"When we work hard to progress, remarkable things follow," he opined with a patronizing air.

"I'm honored, Your Excellency."

Laughing, Frederica caught a glimpse of her husband rising to his feet, teacup still in hand. While she was turning toward him, she saw her husband's expression change from surprise to joy within a few tenths of a second.

Julian Mintz was standing there. He was even taller now than when they had parted; already fit to be called a young man rather than a boy. His rounded, handsome face smiled with nostalgia as he took in Yang's and Frederica's looks of welcome.

"Welcome home!"

Yang spoke first, and Frederica followed.

"Julian! You're looking good!"

"I'm feeling good...I just got in." Even Julian's voice rebounded with rhythmic excitement. "It's been too long, Your Excellency. This may be sudden, but materials related to the Church of Terra are recorded on this. I hope that it's helpful, even if just a little."

So speaking, he held out the optical disc. Try though he might to assume a grown-up's attitude as he did so, he still seemed so childlike and innocent. He was not devoid of unease, though what he had was measurable only in microns. What if Yang's family was no longer his home? What if the opening bell had rung for the new Yang family's history, and he was nothing more than a foreign element that had arrived too late?

But all that was just needless concern. He was one piece in the giant jigsaw puzzle that was the Yang family, so of course he fit right into the space where he belonged. The warmth of the Yang household and the free-spirited nature of the Yang Fleet formed the temporal and spatial environment that was most valuable, most worthy of nostalgia in all of Julian's memories. That he could never forget this was a great blessing to Julian, and was later to become a nostalgia that accompanied the pain in his heart.

After at last enjoying a pleasant chat with Attenborough and Poplin also present, Yang explained his plan to them—as had long been his custom. In order to organize and reexamine his plans, Yang had often asked Julian for his opinions, which in turn had provided Julian with incomparably valuable lessons in strategy and tactics.

"We'll finally be able to go back to Iserlohn, won't we?"

"If it goes well, Julian."

"It will. I'm sure. But still, Kaiser Reinhard really does like those large-scale pincer and envelopment strategies, doesn't he?"

"I like 'em, too."

Julian could hear a bit of a wry smile in Yang's voice. If he, as strategist, had a large military force whose size exceeded that of Reinhard's, he would have surely divided it in two and tried to catch the enemy in a pincer movement. If he could lure Reinhard out toward Iserlohn, and use an auxiliary force to cut him off from his forces in the rear…Or without even going that far, if he could use one unit to capture and hold Iserlohn Fortress, the other he could send through the corridor to invade imperial space, attacking their former capital of Odin after a long-distance run through their territory…

Earlier, during Operation Ragnarok, powerful admirals including von Reuentahl, Lennenkamp, and Lutz had been positioned within the Iserlohn Corridor, but now, if he could capture Iserlohn Fortress once Lutz was deployed elsewhere, the Iserlohn Corridor would be an open sea as far as the Yang Fleet was concerned. When Kaiser Reinhard tried to return to imperial space, he would have no option save a long detour through the Phezzan Corridor, and if those who wished to recover their independence rose up at the same time on Phezzan, the young conqueror would lose his way home. Then, for the first time, Yang would be able to throw a white glove at the golden-haired kaiser.

Yang rested one hand on his black beret, and shook his head with a wry grin. Unfortunately, there was not enough time to turn this fantasy into a reality. It wasn't as if he were in communication somehow with Phezzan's independence faction. The reality was that that was the task he had to start working on now. He had to capture Iserlohn Fortress a second time, establish what Attenborough called a "liberated corridor" between Iserlohn and El Facil, and finally say to them, "Send us capital—this investment's a sure thing!" He had to show them promissory notes that contained nothing but uncertainties, and with them secure such cooperation as he could. One misstep, and it would be fraud, pure and simple.

Of course, his next operation was itself tantamount to fraud in any case.

Yang had calculated with near perfection the time and circumstances under which Lutz would deploy from Iserlohn Fortress. Yang didn't think the FPA was capable of mounting an organized resistance to Reinhard's second invasion, which was why these calculations had to be perfect to the minute and to the second. Had he known that Marshal Bucock and Admiral Chung Wu-cheng were pulling together the remnants of the FPA Armed Forces in order to challenge Reinhard, he would have needed to devise a different equation.

Regarding this hypothetical, many historians theorize that "Yang Wen-li would have probably, for the first time in his life, thrown himself into a battle he had no hope of winning," although there are also those who display an extremely harsh opinion of Yang: "If word of Marshal Bucock's mobilization had reached Yang, he would have been forced to make an extremely painful choice: stand by and watch as a beloved superior died, or join in a battle he couldn't possibly win. Suppress his reason, or sacrifice his emotions? It was because Yang *didn't know* that he was able to devote his full attention to the artist's task of retaking Iserlohn. Yang Wen-li was a lucky artist indeed."

The evaluation above reeks of prosecutorial malice, yet it does tell half of the truth. Yang believed that Bucock had retired, was taking care of the infirmities that came with advanced age, and would never go out into public life again. That was why, even when he had fled from Heinessen, he had refrained from involving the old admiral whom he so loved and respected. When he had met Reinhard in person after the Vermillion War,

Reinhard had clearly stated that he would not seek to punish Bucock. He had kept that promise, and Yang had been sure he would continue to do so. On that point, Yang believed him implicitly.

Of course, Yang's prediction was, in the end, completely mistaken.

As one more piece of evidence that Yang was preoccupied with the retaking of Iserlohn, one may point to his delay in inspecting the optical disc that Julian had brought back from Earth. The recapture of Iserlohn Fortress was everything, and Yang viewed the disc as something to examine only after he was on firmer strategic footing. He was already carrying a load greater than he could bear, and if another important matter was added to that, even Yang's brain might overload and start throwing sparks. He most certainly was not taking intelligence on the Church of Terra lightly. Still, the fact remains that he received just a basic report from Julian and Olivier Poplin, and that the reporters themselves were more focused on the work ahead than on a past success. Julian and Poplin had both expressed regret—though the phrasing had differed according to their individual characters—at having missed out on the escape from Heinessen; now neither was about let himself be excluded from the plan to return to their "home sweet home."

In any case, Yang was at this time concocting a plan that in times to come would be praised by many a military scholar—those who disliked Yang would say it was less a tactic than a magic trick, and not helpful for others to learn from.

Naturally, Yang intended to personally command the fleet that would nick Iserlohn Fortress, but the independent government of El Facil did not welcome the idea of his absence. What if a military force from the empire or the Free Planets Alliance were to attack, or an anti-revolutionary uprising were to occur during his absence? When Yang told them he would leave Admiral Merkatz behind to hold the fort, their unease and suspicion had been impossible to conceal, and Yang, infuriated, would have walked out of the meeting without another word if Frederica hadn't pulled on his sleeve.

What drove Yang crazy was that Merkatz, as a defector from the empire, was ostracized because his loyalty and trust were most likely directed toward Yang personally. Excessive trust in Yang Wen-li alone, and great wariness toward those whom Yang led, were strongly characteristic at this time of the civilians in El Facil's independent government, and when it came down to it, they are believed to have been fearful that Yang's party would usurp control and establish a military administration.

In the end, Commander in Chief Yang ended up staying behind on El Facil with Caselnes, Attenborough, Commander Rainer Blumhardt, and Frederica, where he was to take charge of and command the entire operation from the rear. Admiral Merkatz took command of the forward unit, and command of combat operations during the capture of the fortress went to von Schönkopf. The following officers—Rinz, von Schneider, Poplin, Bagdash, and Julian—would also participate in combat. Yang would have liked to have had Julian by his side rather than on the front line, but he couldn't just ignore the young man's wishes. It is possible that a meeting he'd had with Boris Konev earlier had influenced his thinking somewhat.

In times to come, the dominant image of Yang Wen-li would be that of a strategist in the rear commanding his admirals on the front, but this operation to retake the fortress was in fact his first time using that configuration. Up until then, Yang had commanded every operation he had devised from the very front lines, uniting in himself the role of both strategic planner and tactical executor. One reason he so respected his rival, Reinhard von Lohengramm, was the fact that the young, golden-haired dictator always led his forces into battle himself. Yang believed it was those who stood at the top who should brave the greatest dangers, and he had always lived that belief himself.

From now on, however, the situation was going to be a little different. One more responsibility that Yang could not shirk had been pressed upon him. He himself was still a young man, and although he was capable of leading military affairs for decades to come, the need to train the generation that would come after him was urgent, and growing rapidly. For that reason, he also had to ask the seasoned veteran Merkatz to do more supervising than commanding, and to let Attenborough gain experience in overseeing the progress of the battle as a whole.

IƲ

During the preparations for the assault against Iserlohn, Yang called in Boris Konev prior to making personnel decisions, and asked him to negotiate and organize on Phezzan, so that the anti-Imperial faction of merchants there might secretly lend support to El Facil's finances.

"No matter what kind of promissory notes El Facil's government might issue, the odds are very high that they'll never be honored. It might sound funny to hear me say this, but to get the Phezzanese dancing to your tune, you've got to offer conditions attractive enough to make it seem worthwhile."

Boris Konev's words sounded plausible enough, and fundamentally, he had accepted Yang's request. As was his wont, however, he couldn't let things go without first trying to throw back a curveball. "Actually, the seeds of a threat would also work. If the empire controls all of inhabited space, that won't be good for Phezzan. If things look to be headed that way, Yang, they'll have no choice but to support you."

"How about this, then? 'In light of negative effects stemming from the Phezzan people's pursuit of profits, the empire will make it its goal to distribute Phezzan's wealth equally and end the monopolization of the means of production. All industries are to be nationalized.'"

"If that's factual, it's going to be a nightmare. But could it be factual, I wonder?"

"It might become factual. The kaiser hates the monopolization of wealth. How are the empire's Boyar nobles being repaid for that now?"

"I can't imagine you being a fan of monopolies either…" For just an instant, Konev seemed to grin wryly. "Well, if you're gonna pick a fight anyway, the stronger the other guy, the more it's worth doing. Still, I'm not without a question or two." Boris picked up his teacup, but didn't drink from it. "I want to ask you this directly and up front: are you really serious about bringing down Kaiser Reinhard?"

Now Boris Konev had not even a cold smile. The expression plastered on his face went beyond mere seriousness. "So far, Kaiser Reinhard hasn't misgoverned, and he's got talent and military strength enough to unite all of space. Once he's overthrown, Yang, what guarantee is there that things will get better?"

"There is none."

Truth be told, Yang was still trying to think of some way to save democracy without bringing down Reinhard, but thus far had arrived at no breakthrough.

"At least you're honest. In that case, I'll leave that one aside and ask you one more: once republican democracy has grown this weak, there's no guarantee it will ever recover—no matter how hard you may try to make that happen. Even if you do involve Phezzan, you might just get taken advantage of. Even though all of this could end up being for nothing, you're still okay with this?"

"Maybe," Yang said, taking a sip of tea that had cooled completely. "Still, if you don't scatter any grass seed because it's just going to wither eventually, the grass won't ever grow. We can't not eat just because we'll get hungry again. Isn't that right, Boris?"

Boris Konev softly clucked his tongue.

"Your metaphors are lame, but they're also right."

"After Rudolf von Goldenbaum destroyed the old Galactic Federation with his usurpation, two centuries passed before Ahle Heinessen appeared. Once republican democracy is completely uprooted, things get really harsh before it comes back. Even if it's going to take generations, I still want to lighten the next generation's burden just a bit."

"By 'next generation,' you mean Julian?"

"Julian's one of them, certainly."

"Julian's got a lot of potential. Working with him these past few months, I've come to see that very clearly.

As a pleased expression appeared on Yang's face, Konev threw him an ironic glance.

"But, Yang, no matter how great a singing voice Julian might have, at least for now, he can only use it on the stage that is the palm of your hand. Though I think this is something you've known for a long time yourself."

As Yang appeared unwilling to answer, Boris Konev returned his cup of untouched tea to its saucer and crossed his arms. "A student who's too faithful to his master will never surpass him. If things continue along this path, Julian will never be anything more than a reproduction of you on a regressive scale. Although that alone is plenty impressive…"

Boris's critical way of putting it rubbed Yang slightly the wrong way. Though Yang was well aware of what his friend was like, there were still times when he could get his feelings hurt. This was because Boris knew how to poke Yang exactly where it hurt.

"Julian has a lot more potential than I do," said Yang, "so that isn't worth worrying over."

"In that case, let me ask this: what kind of teacher did you study under? No, not just you—Kaiser Reinhard must've raised himself, too. Even if Julian outstrips you in terms of raw potential, it's very possible he'll never come close to you, depending on how he's brought up. Actually, there's something related to that that bothers me a little."

Boris Konev's fingertips pinched his chin as his tea reflected the uncertain outline of his upper body.

Julian had not tried to analyze the optical disc they had obtained on Earth himself. He had brought it to Yang still sealed, intending to yield judgment and analysis to Yang. As an expression of fidelity, this was nothing to complain of, but had it been up to him, Boris would have looked through that disc himself first. Then, even if the disc were lost, he could have become a living record, surpassing those more highly ranked in terms of the set amount of data he had, and raising the value of his own existence.

"Julian ought to be a little more rebellious. After all, rebelliousness is the fountainhead of independence and self-reliance."

"That's a nice line, but have you told him that?"

"How could I? I can't say embarrassing things like that."

After Boris Konev had promised him his best efforts and departed, Yang ill-manneredly threw both of his legs up on the table, and set his beret on top of his face. While it wasn't exactly the fault of Boris Konev, he was feeling no small amount of exhaustion. At any rate, it was the government of El Facil—not him—that should be promoting secret handshakes with Phezzanese merchants.

Yang's political stance at this time would in the future become the object of many a debate.

"…Yang Wen-li, ultimately unable to embrace an individual as the object of his political devotion, was forced instead to look for it in a system. The system of republican democratic government. And systems, when it comes down to it, are formalities. Although he understood all too well that in extreme times, extreme measures and extreme talents are necessary, the reason that he ultimately did not try to become head of the revolutionary government himself was his fixation with the system of civilian control that is republican democratic government. In fact, El Facil's revolutionary government was established due to the military might and personnel resources of Yang Wen-li's faction, and no one could have criticized Yang if he had chosen to stand at its top."

"…The most tragic fact was that only one man existed at the time who had character sufficient to stand above Yang, and he was one who could never be the object of Yang's political devotion: Reinhard von Lohengramm. As a dictator, and as an autocrat, Yang held Reinhard von Lohengramm in utmost esteem. This applied to both his talents and abilities. Beyond that, he even liked and respected him personally. Reinhard, however, due to his truly exceptional gifts, became the greatest enemy of the republican democratic *system*. Within the strict confines of the republican democratic *system*, Reinhard could never have exercised his gifts to their fullest. It was only dictatorship to which his immense genius was suited."

"…Yang understood all this very well. Which was exactly why he could not step beyond the bounds of the republican democratic system. The moment he used the excuse of an 'emergency' to exceed the system's framework and become a dictator in both the political and military spheres, the universe would exist as nothing more than a stage for the standoff between the tyrant Reinhard von Lohengramm and the dictator Yang Wen-li. If that standoff was going to call out for bloodshed, Yang considered it infinitely preferable to offer everything up to Reinhard instead. Even if he had to bet on bloodshed and employ tactical trickery, it was the republican democratic system he had to defend."

"…The critical view of this idea of Yang's, which paints it as a hidebound formalism, can, of course, be established. 'It's not the system, but the spirit; Yang, by fixating excessively on the outward appearance, abandoned his responsibility to defend the inner truth,' they say. However, as a student of history, Yang knew of many wicked dictators who had used that line of reasoning. He also knew that the majority of dictators had appeared *because they were wished for*, and that their source of popular support was not the people's loyalty to a political *system*, but to an individual. He knew that his own subordinates tended to be loyal to him personally more than they were to the republican democratic *system*, and that meant he could never stand at the top. He knew very well that the chaotic combination of supreme military power and utmost popularity produced an illness that was deadly to the republican democratic system. More than anyone else, it was he himself that he feared, should authority become concentrated in his person. Who has the right to call that cowardice…?"

This essay, written with great effort to preserve its neutrality, was penned by Julian Mintz. It was a work he poured both his passion and reason into, but if Boris Konev had read it, he might have thought, "He's got no rebelliousness in him." If Yang himself had read it, he would have certainly scratched his head and looked away. In any case, it was certain that Yang Wen-li, who looked carefree at first glance, had no small number of worries.

CHAPTER 5:

I

THE ASSAULT UNIT commanded by Admiral Merkatz, tasked with the recapture of Iserlohn Fortress, rang in the New Year of SE 800 in a remote corner of the Iserlohn Corridor. No matter how fierce the mission baring its fangs before them, it was simply their style to stick out their tongues and pop champagne corks. As Olivier Poplin put it, "Iserlohn Fortress isn't going to run away, but we can only toast the New Year now."

Unusually for him, Walter von Schönkopf was in agreement. The two of them had been taking turns pouring champagne into Julian's glass when Louis Machungo came by, took Julian's glass from him, and turned toward Poplin. "You're making him drink like he's an elephant," he scolded.

Julian shook his head, trying to rid his body of excess alcohol content. He looked over at von Schönkopf, and the story that Dusty Attenborough—whom they'd left behind on El Facil—had told him came bubbling up from the depths of his consciousness.

"It's not like I was seriously hoping for a quarrel in the von Schönkopf family," Attenborough had said earlier, defending himself from a question Julian hadn't even asked.

Just before the assault unit had mobilized, Attenborough had made it a point to inform von Schönkopf that his daughter was about to head into combat for the first time.

"Vice Admiral, are you aware that a teenaged junior officer named Katerose von Kreutzer is in this unit?"

Contrary to Dusty's unspoken expectation, the aristocratic defector had displayed not a feather's weight of surprise.

"She a looker?"

"Er…why do you ask?"

"If she is, she's my daughter. If she isn't, it's somebody else with the same first and last name."

"She's…a looker," Attenborough had admitted with resignation.

Von Schönkopf had nodded, and proceeded to delete the name of Katerose von Kreutzer from the list of volunteers for the Iserlohn campaign.

Now in the crosshairs of Julian's gaze, the father of Katerose "Karin" von Kreutzer was showing off just how hard a drinker he could be, standing obnoxiously erect in the midst of a crowd of drunks. Raining abuse on Machungo for his whalelike imbibery, Olivier Poplin walked over toward Julian with an empty champagne bottle in one hand. He looked at him in profile with green eyes shining like dancing sunshine, and without even saying a word, tossed him the empty bottle. Julian was surprised, but he managed to catch the bottle in time. Poplin stood next to him and followed Julian's line of sight. His attack commenced swiftly, and was effective:

"Given the look on your face, you must know, too, Julian."

"Know what, Commander?"

"That Karin's dad is a middle-aged delinquent by the name of von Schönkopf."

Julian couldn't deny the young ace's observation, neither with words nor with his expression. Poplin's eyes were brimming with emerald mirth.

"Once things are peaceful—and boring as all get-out—again, I'm thinking of opening up a life-counseling office to advise fine young men and women. Young people seem to put a lot of faith in me, probably on account of me being so darned virtuous."

Which probably meant that Karin had come to him for advice. Julian felt unsorted emotions dance in his breast, and for some reason felt slightly alarmed. "So, what do you think about all of this?" Julian said.

"That it finally settles the question of which of us is superior. After all, I might sow the same wild oats as Mr. von Schönkopf, but I'm not so careless as to let any sprout. Surely you agree, don't you?"

Julian, at a loss to reply, ruffled a hand through his flaxen hair. "It seems we have all sorts of problems here, don't we?"

"If you ask me, the problem isn't that Karin's been unlucky in life—it's just that she *thinks* she has."

"Really?"

"Which is why she avoids meeting him, and still won't even talk to him. I don't like the direction this is heading. I keep telling her, 'Go see the guy—tell him to pay up on your last fifteen years of allowance.'"

The young ace pilot exhaled a mist of alcohol. The look on his face was 51 percent serious.

II

Yang had already explained the plan to recapture Iserlohn Fortress to the leaders of the assault unit. No one except for Julian, who was already familiar with its contents, was exactly feeling blown away with emotion. When von Schönkopf declared it "one whale of a cheat," Poplin had agreed enthusiastically.

It was, however, a cheat their lives were riding on. To begin with, they had only limited military forces, and were going up against an outstanding admiral, superior numbers, and an enormous battle fortress.

Ahead of the actual combat, Captain Bagdash took charge of executing the disinformation campaign; at last he had found an opportunity to put his interests and the skills of his original vocation to work.

"What it comes down to is, he's just a cheater's accomplice," Poplin opined, however.

And so it was that, no sooner had the New Year begun, strange orders began making their way into the comm channels of Iserlohn Fortress, confused though they were by jamming of various kinds.

To be precise, each order was in and of itself utterly ordinary and appropriate, but when placed side by side, their lack of consistency was appalling.

The first order arrived on January 2.

"Relaying orders from Imperial Military Headquarters to Senior Admiral Kornelias Lutz, commander of Iserlohn Fortress and the fleet stationed there. Depart Iserlohn Fortress within the day for Heinessen, and suppress the enemy's rear guard there."

Upon receiving this order, Lutz began making preparations for departure, though he couldn't rule out a hint of suspicion: *Could this be one of Yang Wen-li's tricks?*

On the following day the exact opposite order arrived: "Your duty is to defend Iserlohn Fortress at all costs. Mobilizing would make that impossible. Yang Wen-li often employs tricks and deception. Furthermore, individuals sympathetic to the FPA and Phezzan are hiding inside the fortress. In the event of your departure, they may seize the fortress and seal off the corridor. Repeat: this is an order—do not move from your present position."

Lutz was hardly an incompetent man. Still, he wavered for more than just a moment over which of the two orders to believe. As expected, he couldn't see that the contradictory orders had both sprung from the brain cells of Yang Wen-li.

Then, before Lutz's mental scale could tip one way or the other, a third order arrived.

"Regarding your previous orders: some among your subordinates have committed crimes, and are being used by Phezzan to harm Iserlohn Fortress from within. Investigate immediately."

To be on the safe side, Lutz had no choice but to investigate. And with over a million officers and soldiers present, there was no way he *wasn't* going to find *some* wrongdoers. By the end of it, a squad's worth of miscreants had been carted off by military police, and two squads' worth of scandals had been uncovered. Among these cases, there were indeed individuals who had colluded with Phezzanese merchants, attempting to misappropriate military supplies to sell on the black market.

"I see now: His Majesty's true will is for me to defend the fortress. That's our kaiser. He guessed our situation rightly. I was on the verge of falling for one of Yang Wen-li's tricks. I mustn't move from here."

Lutz's mind was set at ease, and he began releasing the fleet from its departure-ready posture. That was when the fourth order came. This one, too, was of course from Yang.

"Admiral Lutz, why haven't you departed? Leave only a portion of your force behind to defend and maintain the fortress. Make for Heinessen at once with the rest!"

"Hmph—a cheap trick. Does he really think I'm going to fall for that?"

Lutz loyally followed "the kaiser's true orders" and made no move to depart Iserlohn Fortress. It was January 7 when the fifth order, again demanding that he mobilize, was relayed to him.

This fifth order Lutz also ignored. This, however, was the first order to actually come to him from Kaiser Reinhard.

It was only natural for Reinhard to be furious with Lutz, ensconced at Iserlohn like a bear that had gone into hibernation. Since his plan was to have Lutz's forces suppress the enemy's rear guard at Heinessen, he could not implement his strategy fully unless Lutz moved his forces; all Reinhard could do now was press onward, and rely on sheer strength to win the day.

It was during his advance toward Heinessen that Reinhard received the report: "Lutz's force is not moving." In a salon for high-ranking officers on board his flagship *Brünhild*, the young kaiser's eyes flashed ice-blue lightning.

"Why won't Lutz mobilize? Does he think so little of my orders?"

His crystal glass shattered on the floor, and each and every shard reflected the young conqueror's fury, their rainbow-hued gleams seemingly flickering with it. The kaiser's chief aide, Vice Admiral Arthur von Streit, threw a light glance at the ruby-colored droplets scattered near the tips of his shoes, then stated his opinion.

"Your Majesty, it's possible this is the result of some cunning plan of Yang Wen-li's. Is there any reason why he might need to hinder Admiral Lutz?"

"'Some cunning plan'? How could Yang Wen-li possibly benefit if Lutz *doesn't* leave Iserlohn?"

Reinhard's voice was hot with anger. Not even he had achieved absolute transcendence, and as a human being it wasn't possible for him to guess all the plans and tactics born in the hearts of others. For that reason alone, he couldn't stop thin clouds of unease from flitting across the fields of his mind, and that realization only made the winds of his anger blow faster.

After a moment of silence, von Streit replied, "I beg your pardon, Your Majesty. That's a question beyond the scant wisdom of this lowly soldier."

When von Streit fell silent, Fräulein Hildegard von Mariendorf spoke up in his stead.

"Your Highness, Admiral Lutz not leaving Iserlohn certainly does run counter to Marshal Yang Wen-li's best interests. And if that's the case, I wonder if it might make sense to leave him there. If the result works to the advantage of our forces, Admiral Lutz's temporary sin will be hardly worth punishing."

Not answering right away, Reinhard's graceful eyebrows formed a graceful frown. While he did acknowledge Hilda's point, he had no words to describe how disgusting it felt to have an order he had given be ignored.

At this time, not only von Streit, but even Reinhard himself had fallen down a psychological pitfall that Yang had cleverly set for them. Lutz's unit stationed at Iserlohn was not really an essential fighting force as far as Reinhard was concerned. If he had never mobilized Lutz in the first place, the matter would have ended there, but in order to put a check on Yang Wen-li's maneuvering, Reinhard had felt it important to use Lutz's forces as an autonomous unit. In terms of her conclusion, Hilda was correct, but that didn't mean she had guessed the entirety of Yang's trap. Reinhard, uncharacteristically hesitant about how to proceed, sent a half-hearted message urging Lutz once more to mobilize and attack. As for Lutz, once more he ignored it.

That was when yet another false transmission arrived. Its content was so blisteringly intense that the comm operator who received it went pale.

"If you're going to ignore my orders and not mobilize, fine. Do as you wish. Once I've destroyed every last vestige of the Free Planets' military, however, I will without fail mount a full inquiry into your crimes."

Although it didn't show in his face, this disturbed Lutz somewhat.

He understood that the wrath of an absolute monarch was a thing to be feared. Should he mobilize or not? He couldn't decide which of those contradictory orders was real, and which was false.

Lutz fell under Yang's spell because he was trying to discern truth from falsehood based on the consistency of his orders. He assumed that the real orders and the false orders formed neat, straight lines pointing in opposite directions. If a real order told him to move out, a false order would forbid him from doing so. If true orders repeatedly forbade him from moving out, then false orders would repeatedly demand he do so. That was what he thought, but that didn't mean Lutz was simpleminded. If there were anyone able to see through the chaotic tangle of orders that Bagdash, in accordance with Yang's plan, was firing at him, that person would best be described as eccentric rather than gifted.

It was the confusion itself that Yang aiming for. If all he had wanted to do was get Lutz to mobilize, there would have been no need to resort to these tricks. It was in making Lutz realize that he was resorting to tricks that Yang's odds of success improved.

Kornelias Lutz was an orthodox strategist, dependable and lacking neither knowledge nor experience. Off the battlefield, conspiracies, information warfare, and the like had never been his strong suit. It was fleet-to-fleet battle that both his temperament and his thought processes longed for.

But at last, he saw through what was happening.

"Yang Wen-li is trying to lure me away from the fortress so he can steal it while it's emptied out. Come to think of it, he used that trick the first time he took Iserlohn, didn't he?"

With that realization, a monochromatic light overtook the back of his mind.

No matter how outstanding a plot it might have been, if Yang was using the same method twice, that meant his wellspring of clever stratagems must have just about dried up. Lutz's blue eyes took on a faint wisteria tint, as they often did at times when he was excited.

When Lutz's subordinate, Vice Admiral Otto Wöhler, was informed by his senior officer that he intended to mobilize, he did not give an optimistic response.

"But, sir, with our intelligence in such a confused state, it's uncertain which orders are real and which are false. Even if it means incurring Kaiser Reinhard's displeasure for a time, it's my humble opinion that we should defend the fortress, and not go out to fight. If we ensure, at least, that Iserlohn is secure, won't it be possible to coordinate with His Highness's forces, and make incursions into Free Planets space any time we like?"

"Your argument is of course correct," Lutz said with a nod, not showing his anger. "I believe that the order to deploy was a false one sent by Yang Wen-li. 'Draw the fleet away, and steal the fortress during the opening.' Isn't that the sort of trick Yang would play?"

Vice Admiral Wöhler's eyes opened wide. "Then, even knowing that, Your Excellency still intends to mobilize the fleet, and leave the station empty?"

"I do, Vice Admiral. I'm going out with the entire fleet. I'm going to make Yang Wen-li think I've fallen for his plan. We, however, will be the ones who are fooling him."

In a fervent tone, Lutz explained his plan to his subordinate. When Lutz led the whole fleet out to fight, the Yang Fleet, which was probably holding its breath somewhere inside the corridor, would slip through that opening and approach the fortress. When the time was right, Lutz would then turn the fleet around and catch the Yang Fleet between itself and the wall of fire that was the fortress's main gun, Thor's Hammer. Then they would be completely helpless before him.

"The wise are drowned in their own wisdom. Yang Wen-li's calendar doesn't have many days left."

His voice trembled with the desire to avenge Lennenkamp and his other colleagues. The vice admiral saluted, showing his respect for the senior officer.

III

On January 12, leading the entire fleet that was under his command, Lutz departed from Iserlohn Fortress. The fleet was composed of more than 15,000 vessels, and the embarkation of this stately swarm of light flecks was picked up by the Yang Fleet right away—though since this was being done for show, that was only natural.

"Admiral Lutz has left Iserlohn."

On January 13, that report from Bagdash was greeted with cheers and whistles among the crew of the Yang Fleet. Another of "Yang Wen-li's miracles" was on the verge of coming to pass, and it was how well they fought that would determine whether or not it came true. Voices rose up calling for an advance celebration, and in no time bottles of whiskey were passing from hand to hand, each soldier drinking in turn.

In the midst of such a cheerful, fearless crew, not even calm, imperturbable Merkatz—whom some even called "the Yang Fleet's only gentleman"—could maintain the dignified aloofness of his imperial days. Although he just touched his lips to the drink for appearances' sake, when he awkwardly raised aloft a small flask of whiskey, the applause and the cheers grew even louder, and that was when he opened his mouth with something important to say.

"We have Lutz acting in accordance with our plan, but Lutz must also think that he has us acting according to his plan. He is an outstanding tactician, and the fleet he commands is ten times the size of ours. Unless we can gain control of the fortress before he turns around and overwhelms us, our chance for victory will be lost forever. The battle to capture the fortress will commence immediately. Vice Admiral von Schönkopf, I'd like to ask you to command the front line."

"You can rest assured, Admiral. Just leave it to me."

Von Schönkopf saluted, showing not a hint of apprehension. In that year of SE 800, he would turn thirty-six, a graceful gentleman in his prime. Watching him, Julian was remembering Yang's explanation of the plan to capture the fortress.

"…Lutz is a fine admiral. He understands just how important Iserlohn is, so even if the kaiser orders him to mobilize, it's possible that he'll stay put and beg him to reconsider. And even if he departs Iserlohn per the kaiser's command, there's no telling when he might catch on to our plan and turn back. That's why we're letting him know up front what our plan is. If he sits there and doesn't mobilize, there's nothing we can do, but depending on how we leak the intel, we can probably make him think that he's catching us in a trap. And to catch us in that trap, it will be necessary for him to be a certain distance away from the fortress. The farther away he moves, the easier it gets for our plan to succeed. You may think I'm relying too much on cheap tricks, but cheap tricks are what we need… so that Lutz can see through them…"

Lutz fell splendidly into Yang's trap. At that time, the orthodox tactician—who under normal circumstances would have led a large force and an impregnable fortress to crush Yang's group head-on without resorting to stopgap tricks—was 800,000 kilometers from port, watching on the screen of his flagship as the Yang fleet bore down on the fortress.

"They've fallen for it, those wandering bandits."

Kornelias Lutz was hardly what might he called a frivolous man, but just this once, he couldn't contain the joy that was bubbling up inside him. At long last, Yang Wen-li, that living treasure trove of trickery and ingenious plans, was about to become ensnared in his own trap, and the knee of the Imperial Navy would soon weigh heavily against his neck.

His joy, however, was not to be long-lived. Though he waited and waited, the white column of Thor's Hammer—the fortress's main cannon, capable at any moment of erasing those impertinent enemies from the sky at point-blank range—never roared forth. The commanding officer's eyes were locked on the screen, while behind him, his staff officers were exchanging uneasy and suspicious glances.

"Why isn't Thor's Hammer firing?" Lutz shouted. A nervous, agitated sweat dampened the brow of the Imperial Navy's intrepid admiral. His carefully timed, intricately constructed plan was beginning to collapse like a wall of sand.

On the other side of an 800,000-kilometer void, the tension inside Iserlohn Fortress had rapidly grown into worry, followed by panic. Operators flooded the comm channels with a mixture of screams and curses, and their fingers raced vainly across their keyboards as though they were amateur pianists.

"It isn't working!"

"No response!"

"Control is not possible!"

Their cries resounded against one another. Numerous transmissions had been broadcast from the rapidly closing Yang Fleet. One of them that Iserlohn's computers picked up was a string of words no operator could have considered a normal transmission—"For health and beauty, have a cup of tea after every meal"—and in that instant, all defensive systems immediately went down.

Vice Admiral Wöhler, entrusted by Lutz with the vital mission of defending the fortress, could feel something akin to a toothache shooting through his mental circuitry. The sense of victory he had felt up until a moment ago had been purged from his body, replaced by the oppressive weight of a nightmare presaging doom.

"Break off computer control and switch over to manual! Fire Thor's Hammer at all costs!" The orders caught in his throat, and wouldn't easily leave his mouth.

Despair transformed into sound, and leapt from the operator's mouth.

"It's no good, Commander! It's impossible!"

Understanding and terror invaded Vice Admiral Wöhler's right and left lungs, and finding it increasingly hard to breathe, he sat there frozen in the command seat.

That keyword for disabling the fortress defenses had been the seed of Yang Wen-li's magic trick—one he had planted one year ago, when he had fled from the fortress. Even so, what an absurd pass phrase! For his part, Yang felt he had worked very hard to come up with an utterance that carried no risk of being used in Iserlohn's official transmissions during the next few years—although not even he could have put up a strong argument for it in terms of stylishness and taste.

Clearly, there had to be another phrase to unlock the systems, but as a practical problem, discovering it was an impossibility.

When the Imperial Navy had recovered Iserlohn, a large number of ultra-low-frequency bombs had been discovered. It had been believed that the fleeing Free Planets' forces had tried and failed to detonate the fortress. However, when he thought about it now, that had actually been an exceedingly clever feint, designed to divert the Imperial Navy's eyes from the real trap.

"The enemy is about to storm the port!"

"Close the gates! Don't let them inside!"

Although the order was given, the reply was not hard to guess. When he heard the operator's cry that the gates couldn't he closed, Wöhler stood up from the command seat, and gave the order to prepare for hand-to-hand combat. The air inside the fortress vibrated with the sound of alarms.

Up until this point, it had looked as though things would unfold overwhelmingly to the advantage of the Yang fleet. But as Lutz, who had ordered a rapid turnaround, had said to encourage his crew, they were now on just about equal footing.

It was calculated that from the time Lutz's fleet reversed course, more than five hours would pass before they could flood into Iserlohn. Unless through hand-to-hand combat the enemy could seize control of the fortress's defense systems and activate Thor's Hammer in that time, there would be no victory for the Yang Fleet. Moreover, in terms of troop strength, the garrison defending the fortress had far greater numbers. Even with the fortress defense systems paralyzed, they could still defend Iserlohn, deck by deck.

The Imperial Navy forces would be fine as long as they could hold out until their allies arrived, but the Yang Fleet had to secure a total victory before that happened. The goddess of victory was still fretting over whom to bestow her kiss of blessing on.

"Same as always, we've just gotta do it."

However, as Olivier Poplin put it so casually, this kind of difficulty was nothing unusual for the Yang Fleet. During the coup d'état of the Military Congress for the Rescue of the Republic, during repeated offensive and defensive battles inside the Iserlohn Corridor, and in the battle at Vermillion, the Yang Fleet had been locking horns regularly with powerful enemies under what were essentially isolated and friendless conditions. Compared to these precedents, the situation that they had been dropped into this time wasn't so dire.

IV

A blistering assault greeted the Yang Fleet as it stormed the port facilities inside the fortress. Under normal circumstances, charged particle cannons mounted at the gate would have been able to unleash slaughter and destruction at will, but the defensive systems linked to the tactical computers were without exception deep in hibernation. Equipment notwithstanding, the combatants had to travel back to the Stone Age for their tactics. The gaseous explosive known as Seffl particles had been released, so already the use of firearms was no longer possible.

Olivier Poplin, who had opened a boarding hatch and stormed outside, was already leaning forward when he dropped to the floor and rolled once. A bolt made of ultrahard steel, fired from an imperial soldier's crossbow, had shot through the space that his head had occupied an instant before, striking the hull of the ship and ricocheting off it with an unmelodic ring. With an imprudent whistle, Poplin looked ahead, and saw imperial troops charging toward him, tomahawks and combat knives reflecting the illumination.

That was how the "barbarians' bloody battle" began. Outside the fortress, a fleet of battleships on the cutting edge of mechanized civilization was hurtling in a straight line back toward its home port, but inside its thick walls, time had run backward until the days before gunpowder had been made practical, and there a clash of bodies and blades and blunt instruments unfolded.

Metals and nonmetals slammed into one another, and the stench of spraying blood surpassed the ability of the port facilities' air-purification filters. Silver-gray armored suits changed from colorless to colorful every instant, as their surfaces were painted over. Julian, wedged between Olivier Poplin on the left and Louis Machungo on the right, was able to fight only facing forward. He had swatted down bolts fired from enemy crossbows, and taken a third in his helmet. The slash with which he repaid it was fierce, but 'ultimately, a crack in his armored suit seems to have been the most I could do with a tomahawk,' he would later reflect.

"Aw, I really hate this." It was the voice of Poplin, who'd been swinging his tomahawk next to him.

"What is it you hate, Commander?"

"What do you mean, 'what'? Between Earth and here, I've gotten used to fighting with my feet on the ground! What else could be that awful?"

A vicious slash came toward him, but instead of simply blocking, he pushed it back, drove a fatal flash of metal into his enemy, and jumped backward. All the while, he was dodging the crossbow bolts that came flying, and moving quickly to trade blows with his next opponent. Even if he couldn't mass-produce casualties on the level of von Schönkopf, his dexterous, ruthless actions made Poplin a target for imperial hatred. One soldier broke through the line where the two sides were fighting, and tried to circle around on Poplin from behind, but Kasper Rinz came running toward him, and with one flash of his tomahawk laid the soldier low beneath a mist of blood.

"The Rosen Ritter!"

Before they could even hear the cry, a shudder ran through the imperial soldiers. Their reputation for valor was known to everyone in uniform, both friend and foe. Shaken, the imperial soldiers fell back a few paces, though no one could have denounced them as cowards for doing so. This was, however, sufficient to give renewed energy to the Yang Fleet's combatants. In combat, fame and exaggerated reputations had to be used to the fullest. During the silence, von Schönkopf gave orders, and the space that had been opened by one side's retreat was instantly filled by the advance of the other. While the imperial line didn't exactly crumble, it was falling back, slowly but surely, like the short hand on a clock.

At 2320, Poplin, Julian, and Machungo's squads stormed Block AS-28, and occupied auxiliary control room #4.

The imperial forces displayed no particular dismay at this development. After all, it wasn't the central control room that had been occupied, nor were their defenses in danger of imminent collapse. However, the Yang Fleet's true objective had been to take control of this room. Expecting that the central control room would be incredibly difficult to break into, Yang had earlier established a link to the tactical computer in this room, which was off of the route leading from the port facilities to the central command room. Poplin threw aside his bloodstained combat knife, leapt to the console, and inserted the main key.

"Thor's Hammer, unlocked!"

With his eyes turned toward Poplin, Julian stretched his supple fingers toward the console, and typed a string of keywords into the channel: *one cup of russian tea. not with jam, not with marmalade; with honey.*

Poplin's sweat-smeared, blood-fouled face cracked up with laughter. Just like the first one, it was a passphrase utterly divorced from the tension and excitement of the military.

At 2325, on the bridge of a flagship hurtling through the darkness of space, Senior Admiral Lutz let out a groan of defeat.

"It's no good. Retreat!"

He had realized that he wouldn't make it there in time. He knew that the fortress's capabilities had fallen into the enemy's hands. On one point of the giant, glistening silver sphere, a speck of light had welled up that was too bright to look at straight on.

"All ships, turn about! Withdraw out of Thor's Hammer's firing range!"

On-screen, the white light that filled the barrel of Thor's Hammer was still increasing in both luminosity and radius. Feeling a cold sweat and a hot sweat on his back at the same time, Lutz ordered his ranks to scatter even more. The fortress was already stolen; but even thrown into the depths of defeat, he still had a responsibility to limit the damage to the smallest amount possible.

The world was buried in white light. In expectation of what was coming, every ship was dampening the photoflux of their screens. Even so, the torrent of white light was more powerful still. Even as it burned into the retinas of the Imperial Navy's soldiers and officers, it froze their hearts as well.

In the less-than-five-second interval during which its 924,000,000-megawatt energy beam had been fully discharged, Lutz's fleet had forever lost a tenth of its force strength, and another tenth had taken damage. Ships that had taken the hit directly had been vaporized with all their crew, ships positioned along the beam's fringe had exploded, and ships on the outer edge of its circumference had had fires break out inside, their crews gripped with panic as they desperately scrambled to douse the flames.

"Battleship *Luitpold*, contact lost!"

"Battleship *Trittenheim*, not responding…"

As the pants and screams and whispers played their chaotic symphony, Kornelias Lutz was standing motionless, blanched all the way to his fingertips.

Thor's Hammer had crushed not only the morale of Lutz's fleet, but also that of the imperial forces inside Iserlohn Fortress. Cracks had formed in psychological suits of armor that had endured four hours of attrition and bloodshed, and by the time a new and unstoppable blow was struck, their will to resist had already evaporated.

Von Schönkopf and the others occupied each floor almost entirely without bloodshed. The enemy was so dispirited that for every meter the Yang Fleet's forces advanced, the imperial forces fell back two. Before anyone was consciously aware of it, the calendar page had turned, and on January 14, at 0045, the imperial forces' commander, Vice Admiral Wöhler, at last asked leave to abandon the fortress.

"I ask that my subordinates be allowed to leave safely. If that request is not granted, we shall resist with hand-to-hand combat until the last soldier falls, and will not hesitate to self-destruct the fortress with ourselves aboard."

Julian had no issues with that demand, but negotiating technique, Captain Bagdash informed him, precluded giving an immediate answer. Julian promised to wait fifteen minutes before responding.

It was safe to say that combat had already wound down by that point. They knew that the curtain would fall after another fifteen minutes, so there was no further need for killing and hurting one another. Both sides sheathed their weapons, and simply stared at one another across a river of spilled blood.

Seven minutes later, Julian sent a reply saying he would accept those conditions. He sent it because he could not bear to look straight on at the moaning wounded in mires of blood. If he let another eight minutes go by, they might not still be alive. Julian found it in himself to ignore the look on Bagdash's face, which seemed to say, *You're soft.*

I can test my endurance some other time, he thought.

At 0059, the body of Vice Admiral Wöhler was discovered in his office, shot through the head by his own blaster. He was sitting in his chair, face down on his desk, but the sight of a repeatedly folded bed sheet, placed with care to keep his blood from staining the desk, bore witness to the character of the man who had died. For someone with such a strict and dutiful nature, there was probably no choice other than death after failing in his mission. Julian took off his black beret and silently paid his respects to the deceased. Respect for one's enemies was something he had learned from Yang time and time again.

Lutz's eyes still wouldn't budge from the image of Iserlohn Fortress displayed on the main screen of his flagship.

"Excellency, please, take a rest," Lieutenant Commander Gutensohn, his aide, said, knowing it was futile.

As he had expected, Lutz simply stood there unmoving before the screen, not answering, enduring the sense of defeat that was weighing on him.

Trains of defeated soldiers, together numbering ten times the size of the occupying force, were filing toward the port from every quarter of the fortress. Blood-tinged bandages naturally stood out, but those who bore psychological wounds seemed to vastly outnumber those with physical ones, and faces that appeared incredulous at the very notion of defeat were forming rolling waves of exhaustion.

"This really is the proverbial 'devilish plan with godly planning.'"

Looking down from afar at the ranks of the defeated, Bernhard von Schneider's eardrums caught that low murmur from Merkatz. Never mind the courageous fighting of von Schönkopf and others; what words could he use to describe the brilliant strategy of Yang Wen-li, who had managed to conduct it flawlessly from across time and space? Von Schneider could understand what Merkatz, who had only preexisting adjectives to rely on, must be thinking.

He had believed the man was more than just a gifted battlefield tactician, but when it came to the skill and efficiency on display just now in the retaking of Iserlohn, he felt Yang was simply astounding. Even while insisting that fighting large numbers with small numbers was tactically unorthodox, he used that unorthodoxy to extremes, and did so perfectly. Just imagine what he could do if he were only given the time and the forces!

In January of SE 800, Yang Wen-li and his subordinates succeeded in returning to Iserlohn Fortress. One year had passed since they had reluctantly abandoned it.

∪

"Iserlohn Fortress is in the hands of our forces."

When that report arrived from Merkatz, along with the news that there had been no deaths among the leadership, joyful displays of fireworks had been fired off all across the planet of El Facil, and the ceremony that was held in its central sports arena was attended by a hundred thousand people wearing a hundred thousand smiles.

"This marks the first victory of our revolutionary administration. Once again, Marshal Yang Wen-li has worked a miracle. And yet this is still just a small first step—a single frame in a film stretching out toward the infinite future..."

Yang Wen-li was sitting in a guest of honor seat, discontentedly listening as the independent government's VIPs gave speeches that were unrefined compared to those of Job Trünicht. Though necessity had forced his hand this time, Yang still had the feeling he'd resorted too much to stopgap tactics and tricks, and didn't feel much like boasting.

Still, though he hated this kind of thing with a passion, no advertising would also mean no political effect. In order to get the Phezzanese to invest, and in order to get human resources from the former Free Planets to gather here, the victory, and the victor, had to be advertised. Out of obligation, Yang attended the Victory Memorial Rally, but afterwards he avoided people and sequestered himself in his quarters—displaying an attitude that would become a seed for criticism in future generations.

"Since this operation had from the start been conceived in expectation of its political effect, its success, obviously, was a thing to be shouted from the rooftops. The fact that he hated that and locked himself up in his quarters proves that Yang Wen-li was a man of narrow abilities, and one not fully committed to his cause."

In fact, while Yang Wen-li was a shaper of history whose accomplishments in war none could rival, he had mostly himself to blame for the rather mean-spirited evaluations that were made of him. In any case, it is a fact that he was "not fully committed to his cause."

Yang took his first step into the nostalgic central control room of Iserlohn Fortress, and a pleasant wind passed through all five of his senses. On January 22, Yang arrived on Iserlohn from El Facil, and was able to regain the place that could fulfill his longings for home. Or as Walter von Schönkopf put it: "It's just because there are no politicians here—that's what lets him relax."

Ultimately, Yang couldn't help feeling like he just wasn't cut out for life on the ground. He would turn thirty-three this year, and most of his life so far had surely been spent not on the surface of any planet, but in spaceships and man-made heavenly bodies. Also, it was a fact that his life and his lifestyle had been cultivated and woven in these spaces.

It was a shame about the late Helmut Lennenkamp. He'd been an important vassal of a dynasty that had conquered half the galaxy, and as such, had had no small amount of pride. Although he had doubtless ordained weightless space as the place where he should die, he had had to die a miserable death on the ground. It was an impudent thing to ask, but Yang himself also wanted to end his life in space if he could…

This was how the "Liberation Corridor" extending from the El Facil star system all the way to Iserlohn Fortress was completed. It was, however, a thing rapidly established by astrographical advantage and the moral power to unite, and those directly involved knew far better than the onlookers that it would need to experience no small amount of wind and rain before it could lay down roots in the soil of history and grow a thick canopy of leaves. Still, these people who were directly involved had come under a common bad influence, in that the more critical the situation became, the more cheerful they would appear on the surface. For one thing, this was because regardless of what they might say aloud, they retained the utmost faith in their undefeated commander. As Julian Mintz would one day reminisce: "We relied on Yang Wen-li for everything. We took it for granted that he was invincible and even believed he was immortal."

Eventually, they would learn that this was certainly not the case, but for now wine and hummed melodies could still be their companions.

However, close on the heels of the good news that the plan to retake Iserlohn Fortress had succeeded, Yang Wen-li had to face news of a tragedy that instantly turned his elation to ice.

It was the news that Marshal Alexandor Bucock had died in battle.

CHAPTER 6:
THE BATTLE OF MAR ADETTA

I

REINHARD'S OWN INVASION of Free Planets space was taking place virtually in parallel with Yang's operation to recapture Iserlohn. This had created an opening in Kornelias Lutz's judgment and actions that Yang had taken advantage of; from the standpoint of Reinhard, the imperial military, and imperial headquarters, however, Lutz's absence from their ranks, while a cause for displeasure, was hardly a crippling blow. Their advance had been brazen to the point of arrogance, scattering the Alliance Armed Forces—or more accurately, their dregs—and annihilating their military facilities in every quarter.

The Schwarz Lanzenreiter fleet was commanded by Senior Admiral Wittenfeld, who was standing in the vanguard. They had advanced rapidly, blowing away several weak pockets of resistance en route, but the guerilla activities of the Alliance Armed Forces' Commodore Beaufort had temporarily cut their supply line, and while awaiting its restoration, they had, among other things, pursued Beaufort and destroyed his base of operations, incurring a bit of a loss timewise. Beaufort had escaped with little more than his own skin, and though the loss of that prize was frustrating to Wittenfeld, it was more than made up for by the intelligence he obtained from the prisoners they took.

"It would appear that Admiral Wilibard Joachim Merkatz is somehow alive and well, and serving under Yang Wen-li."

Murmurs of "Oh?" rose from the admiralty like bubbles popping as they received this news, signifying not so much shocked surprise as the satisfaction of achieving closure. In the end, the late Helmut Lennenkamp had arrived through his prejudice at the correct answer. It was also confirmed that Yang Wen-li had thrown in his lot with El Facil's autonomous revolutionary government. However:

"A general without an army is like a star with no planets. Its light and heat shine but vainly into the darkness."

This optimistic line of reasoning surprisingly received the lion's share of support among the imperial military's leadership. The Free Planets' military strength and Yang Wen-li's genius had been split apart—just because one powerless frontier world had obtained the latter, that didn't make it worthy of fear, did it? At the very least, no one presently believed that the empire's overwhelmingly advantageous military and political posture was in any danger of being overturned.

"As a tactician, Yang Wen-li's talents and achievements are unparalleled. That, however, offers no guarantee of his success as a politician. With his fame and reputation, it's possible that he'll be able to rally the anti-empire forces to his side; the question, though, is can he keep them there?"

That was the question of Reinhard's advisors, and their answer was that it wouldn't be easy. There were a number of reasons for thinking so. Did El Facil have enough real and potential agricultural and industrial production capacity to nourish a large military? Would other planets that fell behind El Facil accept their lot gracefully? And what of the qualities of Yang himself?

In the Vermillion War, Yang Wen-li had obeyed his government's orders even with victory dangling before his eyes, retracting his cannons with neither condition nor demand. This in spite of actually having Reinhard's flagship *Brünhild* almost within firing range. Had he ignored that order, he could have been free of all governmental restraint, and might well have himself conquered the universe.

That decision, while morally praiseworthy, had at the same time exposed

Yang's limits as a political activist. If he were still steadfast in his reverence for the form of democratic republican politics, then going forward
he would still be unable to act outside that framework. Also, even if his
values evolved later, it was unlikely the goddess of luck would cast her
sultry gaze a second time at someone who had already let the greatest of
opportunities pass him by. Even if Yang Wen-li, political strategist, had
what it took in terms of ability, he would be lacking personalitywise. Yang
Wen-li's resistance to the Free Planets' government and his flight from
Heinessen had been measures taken during an emergency evacuation,
not the fruit of some carefully crafted political plan. He put far too many
restraints on himself to stand in the number one position, but with talent
and fame too great to content himself with the number two position, he
drew stares of jealousy and suspicion from those above him…

Even if he had heard such biting appraisals of himself, Yang could
not have argued. And even supposing that the analysis of the staff officers at imperial headquarters—Fräulein Hildegard von Mariendorf's, in
particular—did not reproduce the facts to perfection, it was infinitely
approaching them like a curve to its asymptote. One could say that the
intellect's activity had cloned the facts. He wanted to be number two
or lower, but had never been blessed with any quality number ones to
follow. His powers of endurance and tolerance extended only so far as
his activities as a soldier; in his mind, the possibility of him living as a
politician existed only far beyond the sea's horizon. While it wasn't as if
Hilda had a perfect understanding of this nature of Yang's, a number of
phenomena representative of it had become apparent during the Vermillion War, and thanks to these, she had been able to grasp his limits with
almost perfect precision.

However, even Hilda's piercing insight didn't allow her to fully apprehend
Yang as a strategist. The ingenious stratagems that he had in seemingly
endless supply were worthy of both admiration and fear. That was why
Hilda had no choice but to try to convince the kaiser to avoid directly
battling Yang in a decisive confrontation.

"In the Free Planets' military and in the various units that have cut ties
with their government, they're all saying the same thing: 'Where Yang

Wen-li is, there is victory.' Turn that around, and it means that where Yang is not, there is no victory. So why not multiply your strategic measures in places where Yang is not—exhaust him by creating so many tasks for him to do he'll be forced to give up on armed resistance?"

The handsome kaiser, brimming with youth and spirit, did not appear pleased upon hearing this advice.

"Fräulein von Mariendorf, you seem set upon keeping me from fighting with Yang Wen-li."

Reinhard looked at Hilda closely. The contessina could tell that the spirit in his ice-blue eyes was picking up wind speed.

"Even with your incomparable wisdom, Fräulein, it seems that you sometimes see illusions. If I am not defeated by Yang Wen-li, do you think I'll stay young and live forever?"

Hilda's cheeks, as well as her spirit, flushed crimson as she lightly stuck out her chin, intent upon raising objections.

"You say such unkind things, Your Majesty."

"Forgive me."

Reinhard smiled, but that was merely the result of observing decorum; the next few words he spoke were proof positive that he had no intention of revising what he had willed.

"Fräulein, last year, I fought with Yang Wen-li in the Vermillion Stellar Region. I was defeated splendidly."

"Highness…"

"I lost that battle."

Reinhard spoke with a clarity and sternness that would brook no argument.

"At the strategic level, I let myself get drawn out by his provocations. At the tactical level, I was one step away from taking a direct hit from his cannons. I avoided the death of the defeated only because you got von Reuentahl and Mittermeier to take action and attack the enemy's capital. The credit is yours, Fräulein. I take none whatsoever."

With the field of red passion over his ivory features, the kaiser's words and breathing grew stronger.

"I truly beg Your Majesty's pardon for saying so, but the achievement of a vassal belongs to the lord who appointed him. Your Highness did not lose that battle."

Reinhard nodded, but his gaze still reflected the powerful winds that were blowing through his heart. After hesitating for an instant, Hilda made up her mind to stand firm in the face of that wind.

"Please, don't think of taking vengeance on a single individual such as Yang Wen-li. The day is not far off when Your Majesty will hold the entire universe in the palm of your hand. Yang Wen-li cannot prevent that from coming to pass. That is because the final victory will be yours. Who is there who will say your victory was stolen?"

"Yang Wen-li will not. His subordinates, however, are certain to make such claims."

There was a boyishness—or a childishness, rather—in the way that he said it. Reinhard's white, supple fingers touched his graceful lips, giving the impression that he was just barely restraining himself from biting his nails. This incomparable youth looked like one whom the gods of war and beauty had staked their honor and passion on in a struggle to possess, and he seemed to fear defeat less than he feared having it said he had been defeated. Hilda was slightly shocked by this, and at the same time felt an ominous breeze blowing through her nerves.

Hilda didn't go so far as to think Reinhard had a death wish. And yet she did wonder: if given a choice between growing old and feeble during long years of idleness after his enemies had all been vanquished, or being defeated in the prime of his life by an outstanding opponent, would Reinhard not unconditionally choose the latter? The reason she intentionally phrased that thought in the interrogative was that even for Hilda, giving a definitive answer would have placed on her the greatest of psychological burdens. Even as a question, it felt suffocating.

Hilda shook her head slightly, and her dark-blond hair reflected the light of the room's illumination. It had never suited her, intentionally choosing the dark turns in the labyrinth of her thoughts. It was already three years ago now, but at the time of the Lippstadt War, she and her father had sided with Reinhard because she had seen in him not the beauty of destruction, but his skyward gaze and the strength in his wings.

Five hundred years ago, political ambition and hatred for those who disrupted the order of society had led the iron giant Rudolf von Goldenbaum, then a military man, to do battle against his enemies, the space pirate cartels. That his authority and the privilege of his descendants were sustained by the sacrifices of the weak was a consequence of his brand of justice. Reinhard had denied the justice of Rudolf, and risen up against it.

Why had that been? Because Annerose, his beautiful and kind elder sister, had been unjustly wrenched away from him by those in power, and for this he had sworn to take vengeance. The boyar nobles' system of rule had endured for five centuries, but from it Reinhard had smelled the stench of decay, and set his heart upon its reform. A private but just fury, and a public and just yearning. Surely these were the wellsprings of that young man's vitality—or perhaps it was that his vitality required the most magnificent and bitter means of expression. Recently, Hilda had sometimes found herself thinking so. And at such times, she had worried: *Isn't it the brightest flame that burns out most quickly?*

II

In SE 799, or year one of the New Imperial Calendar, Reinhard and the imperial military—unable to set off fusion reactions in any more mental nuclei—departed, and the New Year arrived. New Year's festivities consisted of nothing more than a small banquet the kaiser held in the auditorium used for ceremonies on board his flagship *Brünhild*, and the distribution of wine to all soldiers and officers. Speaking via comm screen, the kaiser told them that large-scale celebrations would be held once they had fully occupied the Free Planets' capital of Heinessen, and the soldiers and officers rattled the bulkheads of every vessel with cheers of "Sieg Kaiser Reinhard!" The soldiers' faith in the kaiser and their respect for the admiralty were like a blade without nick or chip, and as for morale, there was no unease whatsoever. Communications between the main fleet and Wittenfeld out in front were frequently jammed so that periods of mutual contact tended to be few and far between, and Lutz for some reason was refusing to come out of Iserlohn Fortress. These factors meant that their present situation fell short of perfection, but as long as Wittenfeld, Lutz, and Steinmetz were not being picked off one by one, there was no reason to be disturbed by these developments.

"We'll likely run into a single organized counterattack. Having resigned themselves to death, they'll come aiming to make a final show of resistance. Once we've crushed it, we will occupy Heinessen, and announce the complete dissolution of the Free Planets Alliance."

With that understanding, Reinhard and his staff officers had constructed their plans, but when January 8 came around, a fleet of ships numbering more than a thousand showed itself ahead of Mittermeier's forces. Skillfully maintaining a constant distance, they swam to and fro, as if inviting an attack.

It looked like they would attempt to cut off Wittenfeld's vanguard from the Imperial Navy's long train. Kaiser Reinhard, along with his staff officers, considered scattering them right away, but instead avoided combat, viewing them as rather a scouting force or vanguard for the Alliance Armed Forces' final, all-out show of resistance. Notifying Müller (in the rear guard) that he should secure the safety of their supply route back toward Phezzan was a measure that displayed von Reuentahl's foresight as secretary-general of Imperial Military Command Headquarters. At the same time, Mittermeier brought his entire force to a full stop, and sent out five hundred destroyers and ten times as many reconnaissance craft, attempting to gather intelligence. During this time, communications with Wittenfeld's vanguard were almost totally cut off; the intensification of the jamming was silent proof that FPA forces were approaching for an attack. Reinhard had von Eisenach, Müller, and the forces under them gather together.

Even for a genuinely enormous force, it was never wise from the standpoint of unified command to form extremely long ranks running fore and aft. The tension among the officers and soldiers skyrocketed.

"Did these people come out here expecting to win? Or are winning and losing completely beside the point to them? Are they here to follow their democratic republic into death as it falls?"

Those questions were coiling round and round in the hearts of the Imperial Navy's admirals. If they had been midranking officers or lower, they could have processed this in terms of mind over matter, thinking, *Anyway, we just have to do our best.* The highest-ranking leaders, however, couldn't afford to make tactical plans using the words "should" and "intend."

"Well, they pulled together the numbers, if nothing else. Of course, it's an open question how many will be left when this is over."

Sneering, Bruno von Knapfstein made this assessment on January 10, at a meeting of top staff officers on board *Brünhild*. By general accounts, it was estimated that the Free Planets' military had prepared a force of somewhere in the neighborhood of twenty thousand ships. This number did indeed exceed the expectations of the Imperial Navy, but there was no way they had very many battleships or carriers, and their firepower should also be inferior.

"That being the case," said the young, energetic Karl Eduard Bayerlein, flushing red, "all we need to do is fight them once here, and that will put an end to them. To make the mistake of hesitating—of losing a chance for victory—doesn't become our forces, who seek to unify the entire universe."

Alfred Grillparzer also leaned forward to make an impassioned speech. "Yang Wen-li's forces are presently miserable vagabonds, but if we sit here wasting time for no reason, that may give him time enough to reconstitute his strength. In the Battle of Rantemario last year, it was due to his maneuvering that our forces lost the chance to utterly wipe out those of the Free Planets. Your Majesty, I beg you, please give us the order—the order to fight them."

Von Reuentahl and Mittermeier, not recalling any past need to incite the kaiser to battle, had remained silent through all of this. The only questions for them were where and how to fight. Even if the FPA had a large force of twenty thousand vessels, it was only a small squadron next to the empire's force, and because FPA firepower was inferior, it would no doubt employ appropriate tactics to try and make up the difference. At any rate, it seemed their commander was Marshal Alexandor Bucock, a seasoned tactician who had fought well at Rantemario last year. Carelessness was not something they could tolerate. This was because on January 13, a report had come in informing them that Bucock had deployed his forces out in front of them. By this time, Iserlohn had already fallen into Yang's hands, although the report of that had still not reached Reinhard.

＊　　＊　　＊

The name of the star was Mar Adetta. It was 6.5 light-years distant from Rantemario, where Bucock had intercepted an imperial fleet last year, and been driven to defeat by the vast size of it.

Compared to Rantemario, the strategic value of Mar Adetta was low, but tactically speaking, it was a vastly more difficult space for the imperial forces to operate in. It was impossible to calculate how many planets it had. Asteroids with radii no greater than 120 kilometers formed a vast belt, and the star itself was extremely unstable, with constant explosions taking place on its surface. This of course disrupted communications, and worse, Mar Adetta's solar wind carried not only heat and energy, but also minuscule grains of rock, conveyed chaotically along in its turbulent flow. The larger the military force, the more difficult command and control would become. That was the intel the imperial forces received. Nearly all their astrographical knowledge of this sort came from materials obtained from Phezzan's space traffic control bureau, and it may be said that simply by acquiring that, Reinhard had made an incomparable military achievement.

"That old man...That's a nasty sector he's gone and picked to fight in."

Not even von Reuentahl and Mittermeier could help swearing under their breath. Those oaths, of course, contained an extremely potent element of admiration. This would very likely be the last battleground for the old admiral, who over the past half century had fought continually against the empire's despotism. Recognizing that embodiment of ingenious tactics and solid backbone, both felt an urge to straighten their collars out of respect.

"Maybe we should praise him for having such courage at his age," murmured Müller. Contained in their feelings of praise for him were particles of military romanticism and sentimentality, though there was neither exaggeration nor falsehood in their hearts. At the same time, they intuited that the old man was trying to inspire the democratic republicans by sacrificing his own life, and couldn't help feeling a chill run down their spines. That chill was, of course, linked inseparably to exultation and satisfaction, and on that point there existed a sort of incorrigibility peculiar to the military spirit.

Like a twisted belt, a single winding corridor extended all the way through to the other side of the asteroid belt. The Free Planets' forces were lurking somewhere within that 920,000-kilometer-long, 40,000-kilometer-wide tunnel-shaped void, waiting for the empire's attack. They were making that fact clear for anyone to see. By their actions, they were showing their intent to challenge them.

On January 14, the Imperial Navy commenced a massive invasion of the Mar Adetta Stellar Region. Ice-blue torches were burning in the eyes of Reinhard, first kaiser of the Lohengramm Dynasty, ruler of the Galactic Empire. To the tips of his capillaries, fighting spirit coursed through those eyes. His tall, elegant form, wrapped in a splendid black and silver uniform, brimmed with the reasons that future generations would say, "a taste for warfare was in his character." When he stood looking like that on the bridge of the flagship *Brünhild*, the soldiers and officers of the Imperial Navy could no longer help but see battle and victory as the same thing.

Mittermeier, one of the Imperial Navy's Twin Ramparts, took command of the port wing from his own flagship *Beowulf*. At Reinhard's side was the secretary-general of Imperial Military Command Headquarters, Oskar von Reuentahl.

Move the fleet, rearrange the formation, attack the enemy, do the maximum damage possible, then pull back out of the battlespace. No one could do that faster than Wolfgang Mittermeier. This was why he'd been crowned with the nom de guerre the "Gale Wolf."

"He's faster than lightning, and has good sense, too," were the words that Oskar von Reuentahl used to praise his colleague's superb handling of forces, and was himself praised by his colleague with these words: "His offense and defense are near perfection. In particular, I can't touch the hem of his garment when it comes to prosecuting a battle while calmly looking across the whole of its vast battlespace."

The imperial forces' starboard wing was commanded by the "silent admiral"—Senior Admiral von Eisenach—with Senior Admiral Müller commanding the rear. Both were great admirals, second only to the Twin Ramparts in achievement and talent, with Müller in particular a man who'd been called "a first-rate commander" by his enemy Yang Wen-li.

"Let's give this lifer of the Free Planets' admiralty a fitting place to die. The age of gray-haired old men going into battle is already over."

Von Reuentahl cautioned the young admirals against such bluster.

"That's easier said than done. See to it you're not the ones who get wrapped around your gray-haired old admiral's little finger."

The honor of commanding the vanguard went to two admirals who had made names for themselves under the command of the late Helmut Lennenkamp: von Knapfstein and Grillparzer. Reinhard wanted these two to follow the fine examples of von Reuentahl and Mittermeier. Of course, it was because their like was nowhere else to be seen that they deserved to be called Twin Ramparts, but at a time when these giants of the military were moving gradually from the front lines to the central hub, there was a need for people who could fill their shoes, even if they were only imitators.

As an additional reserve force, Senior Admiral Fahrenheit had placed his forces on standby near the outer edge of the Mar Adetta system. Depending on the tactics that alliance forces employed, they might have to move a considerable distance and range to respond to an enemy attack on their allies' rear or flank, but it was most important to keep the door open for active operations, such as detouring to the rear of the corridor to cut off the alliance forces' path of retreat, or pressing even deeper into the corridor to coordinate with allies in the vanguard and catch the enemy in a pincer movement. This was what most agreed with Fahrenheit's nature. While he wanted Reinhard to give the order to invade the corridor from the outset, Reinhard knew it was impossible to use a large force to its best advantage inside a narrow corridor, and the chances were very high that the Free Planets' military was laying a trap inside. For these reasons, Reinhard chose to open with orthodox tactics. At which point, the astrographical advantage tilted toward the alliance.

It was, in a number of ways, a battle outside the bounds of common sense, and at such times, somebody had to step up and venture a commonsensical opinion. The kaiser's chief aide, Vice Admiral von Streit, by tacit agreement of his colleagues, took on that duty at this time.

"Surely Your Majesty need not personally meet the enemy head-on in decisive battle. If the main fleet makes straight for Heinessen, a separate force can stay behind, bottling up the enemy, and restraining them from taking any ill-advised actions. That would settle the whole matter. Even if Marshal Bucock is a seasoned tactician and has the confidence of his men, it's ultimately a single battlespace he's betting his life on. I think Your Majesty would do well to just ignore him."

Reinhard had been expecting this advice, so no sign of anger or surprise showed on his face. Ice-blue auroras danced wildly in both his eyes as the young kaiser looked around at all of his staff officers. It was clear that he wanted those besides von Streit to hear his reply as well.

"Your advice is not mistaken. But this is the challenge of an aged admiral forged in countless battles, a challenge he's likely braving death in order to make. To refuse it would be discourteous. And while I'm not without other reasons, for me and my forces, that alone should be reason enough."

Offering no further explanation, Reinhard sealed the lips of von Streit and all the advisors under him. They had never thought that the kaiser might lose. What the kaiser's nature had decided, no further words of advice could alter.

Even though both of them had become imperial marshals, von Reuentahl and Mittermeier's custom of drinking wine together before a battle remained in effect. Following a strategy session aboard the flagship *Brünhild* on January 15, Mittermeier visited von Reuentahl in his private quarters. The cabin's master supplied the wine.

"What do you think? About this battle?"

The marshal with the mismatched eyes didn't answer Mittermeier's question right away. In the dark mirror of his wine, the colors of his left and right eyes became indistinguishable. When the blood-colored wine had spread at last through his veins, he moved his lips and weaved together a reply.

"If this battle has any meaning at all, it's on the emotional level, not the rational level. The old lion and the young lion are both craving this fight. Honor will add some color to the proceedings, but in the end, a sword, once drawn, does not return to its scabbard without first being drenched in blood."

"I never knew till today that you had the soul of a poet."

Von Reuentahl ignored his friend's intention to lighten the mood.

"I understand those two," he said. "And surely you do, as well. History is thirsty when it awakens, just like a human being. The Goldenbaum Dynasty is already finished. The Free Planets Alliance might have survived up until today, but tomorrow it will end. History is craving an enormous draught of blood, Mittermeier. It can't wait to drain the cup dry."

Mittermeier frowned, and unusually for one praised among the empire's most courageous admirals, a thin cloud of unease passed across his face. At last, he assayed an argument, though his voice lacked much in the way of assertiveness.

"Even if that's true," he said, "I think it must surely be sick of the stuff by this point…"

"I wonder. Do you believe that, Mittermeier?"

Von Reuentahl's voice, unable to control his emotions or his reason, made him sound like he was slightly confused and was bouncing that confusion off his friend to see what he would say.

Mittermeier thumped his empty glass hard with his fingertip. "The divided universe will be united by the hands of His Majesty, Kaiser Reinhard, and he will bring peace. If, as you say, the Free Planets Alliance ends tomorrow, the morning on the day after tomorrow will shine bright with the light of peace. If it doesn't, then everything we've worked for, and all of the blood we've spilled, will have been for nothing."

After a long silence, von Reuentahl said, "Exactly."

As he nodded agreement, his face took on a sort of invisible camouflage under the mild effect of the wine. Put another way, the labyrinth of his heart had become visible through his skin.

"Here is what I think, however. Even if history did get sick and tired of swilling human blood, it would only be the amount that was the problem. And as for quality? The nobler the sacrifice, the more that cruel god rejoices…"

"Von Reuentahl!" Mittermeier's sharp voice sent a keen gust of reason and realism blowing through the circuitry of von Reuentahl's nerves, acting like a ventilator's fan. The alcohol and the invisible fog that had lain over his thoughts had been driven from his body, and with one raised hand, he waved away both, remaining silent until his usual lucid intellect had reoccupied his brain cells.

"I…seem to have been acting a part that I'm truly miscast for. After all, I'm no poet or philosopher—I'm just a crude soldier. I should leave this sort of thing to people like Mecklinger."

"Thank goodness you've come to your senses. For the time being, we need to know what the enemy in front of us is planning, rather than the will of some 'god of history' we've never even met."

Von Reuentahl pinched his earlobe. "At any rate, this battle is best called a ceremony. One in which we pay tribute to the Free Planets Alliance's funeral procession. Unless it takes this form, neither the living nor the dead will be able to accept the fact of its destruction."

After pouring the last of the wine into one another's glasses, they looked toward the screen in silence. The crests of long waves of light, made up of countless ships both near and far superimposed upon one another, stretched away into the distance. By tomorrow, a considerable number of them would be erased forever, buried under the black boards of which the universe was composed.

At last, Mittermeier took his leave of *Brünhild* and returned to his own flagship, *Beowulf*.

Marshal Alexandor Bucock, commander in chief of the Free Planets Alliance Space Armada, was in his office on board his flagship, checking over the plan one last time.

His personal feelings aside, it was his duty as commander to do what he could to increase their chances of victory, even if only slightly.

Strictly speaking, it was impossible to determine numerically how large a force the FPA Armed Forces had been able to mobilize for this "final battle of the Free Planets Alliance." Already, Joint Operational Headquarters had lost its ability to lead the military, and much materiel and many records had been disposed of, with only estimates and memories existing to fill the gaps. Even so, it was possible to calculate surprisingly large numbers: between twenty thousand and twenty-two thousand vessels, and between 2.3 million and 2.5 million soldiers and officers.

An extreme argument has been made that "the Battle of Mar Adetta, waged at the beginning of SE 800, was not so much the final battle of the Free Planets Alliance as a personal duel between Kaiser Reinhard and Marshal Bucock." However, Bucock at the very least fought with the alliance's flag raised high, while to the soldiers and officers—having run to the old admiral's camp after abandoning an alliance government that had lost its ability to govern—it was Bucock, rather than the political and military VIPs who had gone into hiding on Heinessen, who was viewed as the symbol of the Free Planets Alliance. This was not something to be argued at the level of good and evil; it was simply a fact. The catastrophe that had followed a mere six months after the signing of the Baalat Treaty had put the FPA military at a terrible disadvantage when it came to planning a long-term strategy, though the fact that they had still been in the midst of scrapping their battleships had ironically worked in their favor.

Admiral Chung "Baker's Son" Wu-cheng's first step toward improving their force strength was to put himself in a self-contradictory position. While he was working to pull together a force big enough to actively deal with Reinhard's invasion, he at the same time had to leave behind forces enough for Yang Wen-li and the rest to lead later on. As the Twin Ramparts had surmised, he viewed himself as a priest conducting funerary rites for the Alliance Armed Forces, and at the same time a midwife trying to assist at the birth of a democratic republican revolutionary military. For that reason, he had sent the former leaders of the Yang Fleet, who ordinarily would have become his able and trustworthy allies, to El Facil.

During this time, the fleets led by Murai, Fischer, and Patrichev had still not managed to reunite with Yang. In order to avoid friction with alliance forces and contact with imperial forces, they had been forced from the start to take a wide detour around the frontier sectors before heading to Iserlohn. Normally, a transit period of one month would have been a reasonable calculation, but this time they had to practically grope their way forward along a frontier route, much of which was heretofore unknown. Contact with them was lost in the Fara system, where a stellar explosion scattered the fleet. When they finally finished reassembling their formation, Fischer—that master of fleet operations—developed a high fever due to overwork, and among the frightened and upset soldiers and officers, some attempted to peel away from the armada. For a time, the fleet was faced with the danger of coming apart at the seams. At that time, Murai scrambled to gain control over the main force, while Patrichev and Soon, leading their best and brightest, put down the mutiny. Even so, that mutiny came within a hair's width of being successful.

Patrichev had always trusted in Yang Wen-li's cribbed philosophy of "When they run, don't pursue," but if he permitted the mutineers to desert in this case, there was a danger that both their objective and position would be compromised. Since they lacked sufficient confidence in handling a fleet-versus-fleet battle, one didn't have to be Murai in order to feel nervous about protecting their secrecy. Even after imprisoning the mutineers, Patrichev continued to be vexed by repeated accidents and plots to rebel. According to Soon's reminiscences, after hard labors "equivalent to one scale off the snake that was the Long March of 10,000 Light-Years," they were able to enter the Iserlohn Corridor and at the end of January SE 800 be reunited with Yang Wen-li and the others. At that time, Yang released the more than four hundred imprisoned mutineers, and paid them their salaries for the first time since they'd left Heinessen. Half of the mutineers departed in shuttles they were given, but the other half stayed on at Iserlohn to fight along with Yang Wen-li.

Alexandor Bucock was supposed to reach his seventy-fourth birthday during the year of SE 800, but he had long since given up on having any chance to test his lung power against a birthday cake bristling with that many candles.

Chief of Staff Chung Wu-cheng entered the room with a face lacking much tension.

"How about getting a little rest, Your Excellency?"

"Hmm, I'd intended to, but in the end, if I'm going to fight, I want to put up one I can be satisfied with."

"Don't worry about that. Kaiser Reinhard isn't going to do anything shocking."

"I hope you're right. Even so, this is going to get a lot of people killed, not to mention me. It isn't like I'm just now realizing it, but this is a sinful thing."

"Why not become a doctor in your next life? That way, you should be able to balance things out."

Bucock looked at the chief of staff with surprise in his eyes. He'd never thought he would hear Chung Wu-cheng using words like "next life." But without saying so, he breathed out a reminiscence as though speaking to himself, while rubbing his tired eyelids with his fingers.

"When I think about it, I'm probably one of the lucky ones. At the end of my life, I was able to meet two incomparably great strategists in Reinhard von Lohengramm and Yang Wen-li. And I was able to do so without ever seeing the sight of either of them getting injured or defeated."

Or the sight of the Free Planets Alliance being utterly undone, Chung

Wu-cheng seemed to hear the old marshal say, not with his sense of hearing, but with his powers of insight.

III

On January 16 of that year, after countless preliminaries, the military forces of the Galactic Empire and the Free Planets Alliance met in a head-on clash.

The empire was using a standard convex formation, albeit one whose vanguard wasn't too far out in front. The imperial forces were grinding forward, intent on overwhelming the enemy with the depth of their thick formation.

"Fire!"

"Fire!"

There was probably not a second's lag between the shouting of those two orders. Tens of thousands of brilliant beams gouged through the boundless darkness, white fangs of energy bit into warships and ripped them asunder, javelins of light blazed, and combat screens on both sides became gardens overrun with wildly blooming blossoms. Each of those shining flowers consumed several hundred lives as they bloomed.

After responding to the initial assault, the ranks of the alliance fleet continued to lay down an orderly stream of cannon fire while already beginning a withdrawal. Grillparzer and von Knapfstein led the imperial vanguard in a furious charge, trading intense fire with the alliance force's rear as they tried to retreat into the narrow corridor. After inflicting considerable damage, Grillparzer successfully stormed into the corridor at 1050.

At 1120, however, a wave of solar wind broadsided the imperial port flank with chaotic turbulence, and their formation began to lose its orderly configuration. Mittermeier, cracking whips of rebuke at discomfited allies, tried to rebuild the formation, but Grillparzer's unit had dived deep into the corridor and was taking fire from alliance forces while in a bunched configuration. Unable to evade the assault in that cramped region of space, they were still trying not to hit each other as a chain of explosions erupted.

"What do you think you're doing?" said Reinhard. "Keep that up, and you'll only erode your own force strength. Retreat, and draw the enemy back out after you!"

It wasn't as though Reinhard's rebuke had reached him, but Grillparzer, realizing the danger of letting a large force become concentrated inside a narrow corridor, began pulling back out. The alliance's focused cannon fire could not have been more blistering, and bluish-white flowers of destruction bloomed all across the front line of Grillparzer's fleet. Although he'd been braced to take some damage, the unleashed energy and the shattered hulls came riding in on the solar wind and bore down on the imperial force's ranks from dead ahead, rubbing salt into their open wounds. Drenching the inside of his uniform with both hot sweat and cold, the young new member of the Imperial Association of Geography and Natural History barely managed to keep his ranks from crumbling, and escaped from the corridor under a rain of beams from wildly firing enemy cannons.

Bucock forbade pursuit. They had only had the advantage because they were fighting inside the narrow passage, and it was clear that if they emerged into the vast zone of navigable space, they would be enveloped by an overwhelmingly larger force. The moment Grillparzer was clear of the corridor, he scattered his formation and prepared for an attack from pursuing enemies, but since that pursuit ultimately failed to materialize, he reorganized his remaining forces and deployed them once more at the corridor's entrance, all the while biting back the shame and remorse of having lost nearly 30 percent of his forces. It was 1210. By this time Reinhard, who had been watching the battle unfold on the screen of *Brünhild's* bridge, was already giving orders to Senior Admiral Adalbert Fahrenheit.

"Take your forces, and flush out that old tiger."

Fahrenheit, a seasoned veteran of many battles, required no tactical instruction more specific than that. With a gleam in his aquamarine eyes, he gave orders to his subordinates to fly through an asteroid-rich danger zone at maximum combat speed and, circling around to the back of the safe corridor, try to land a blow on the alliance force from behind. If struck on their rear, they would move forward, and thus be pushed out, as it were, into the overwhelming cannon fire of the fully arrayed Imperial Navy.

At 1300, von Knapfstein launched an incursion into the corridor in Grillparzer's stead. This was a favored ploy for preventing an enemy from noticing a detour operation. Naturally, his job didn't end with merely drawing the enemy's attention; von Knapfstein also had the vital duties of eroding the enemy's force strength and coordinating with the allies who had circled around to the enemy's rear. This meant that von Knapfstein was going to gain valuable experience as a tactician—provided he survived the fierce combat, of course.

It was understandable when von Reuentahl murmured in his heart, *Now, let's see what he's made of.* Inside the narrow passage, von Knapfstein's fleet had been struck by a concentrated fusillade of precise, targeted strikes, and had quickly found itself with its back to the proverbial wall. Von Knapfstein lacked any astrographical advantage, and the difference in experience between himself and Bucock was great. That he was somehow holding the formation together without it collapsing outright was actually rather remarkable.

Eyes still locked on his battle screen, the commander in chief, Imperial Marshal Mittermeier, directed his voice toward a subordinate displayed on a subscreen. "I hate to have to kill that old man, Bayerlein. He may be an enemy, but he deserves our respect."

"I feel the same way, but even if we advised surrender, he'd never consent to it. If he defeated me, I don't think I'd trade in the flag I follow, either."

Mittermeier nodded, but his eyebrows twitched just slightly. "That you think so is well and good, Bayerlein, but do think twice before saying so out loud."

Former enemies such as Fahrenheit and von Streit had sworn allegiance to Reinhard and gone on to become valuable assets—how they lived their lives was not a thing to be criticized. In their case, they had followed the wrong flag at the outset, and their true lives had begun once their enemy had recognized their ability and character. In any case, the alliance forces were putting up a praiseworthy fight. Based on strategic elements such as force strength and the ability of their frontline commanders, the imperial forces should have had the advantage from the very start, but Bucock had skillfully weakened their fighting potential and used his surroundings well, making up for the difference in numbers.

"So, the Alliance Armed Forces are going to show us a good time, are they?" Reinhard praised them, as though he were singing a verse from a lied. Although he was confident that his would be a complete victory, intricate tactics always pleased him, even when they were executed by the enemy.

Von Reuentahl smirked, although only for a moment. While he, too, had felt an ironic pleasure at the sight of the brave and mighty Imperial Navy fighting an uphill battle against a weak enemy force, it was his duty as the kaiser's top staff officer to calculate the right moment to commit reinforcements and seize control over the entire battlespace. And although he had decided to use von Eisenach's fleet for that purpose, choosing the perfect time to send them in was no easy task in a chaotic, closely matched fight like this one.

IV

It was 1540. Fahrenheit's fleet, having successfully circled around to the tunnel's rear entrance, fired its first volley of cannon fire at the alliance rear. The concentrated fire was directed into the inner reaches of the corridor, but the alliance's return volley was unexpectedly intense. Fahrenheit tried storming his way in by brute force once, but at 1615, he halted his subordinates, who had been about to flood into the narrow corridor's entrance, and began pulling them back. No middling eye for tactics could have accomplished what Fahrenheit's had just done. Predicting that the alliance forces were about to make a massive reverse charge at them, he had pulled his own forces back so as to wipe out the enemy with a point-blank attack the moment they came at him.

To that extent, things went as Fahrenheit had expected, and it looked as if the alliance forces were going to emerge from the corridor's back exit to be mowed down by his waiting forces. But at 1620, alliance forces that had been hiding scattered throughout the asteroid belt formed up into a single arrow of light, and struck Fahrenheit's fleet on the back end of its port flank. Commanding this operation was Admiral Ralph Carlsen, who had fought bravely the year before in the Battle of Rantemario. His attack forced Fahrenheit into a reluctant retreat.

On the bridge of the armada flagship *Brünhild*, Oskar von Reuentahl's widely famous black and blue eyes had narrowed slightly. The deep thoughts of a master tactician were racing through his inner space at the speed of light.

He hadn't been expecting it, but there was something about the alliance force's tactics that they couldn't afford to take lightly. To think the enemy had *expected* imperial forces to detour around to the back of the corridor, and set up an ambush! And next, they would of course come out on the imperial forces' rear, and...

"Von Reuentahl."

"Your Highness?"

"What do you make of this? Von Knapfstein entered the corridor planning to strike an enemy in retreat, but now..."

"It's well and good that he went in—the question now is whether he can make it back out again."

"Your reasoning?"

"If I were the enemy commander, I would have mined its interior to halt the advance of invading enemies."

"I concur. Now that I think about it, that's a tactic we should have used."

Reinhard's voice and expression conveyed not so much a sense of crisis as a glow that brimmed with life. Von Reuentahl looked at him, and found his brilliance dazzling.

"Going forward, one possible tactic I could see the enemy using is to buy time using all their forces in this stellar region to confuse the battle. Then, during the opening they create, a reserve force would circle around to *our* rear. That said, I don't believe the alliance presently has such an enormous reserve force. And even if they did circle to our rear..."

The imperial forces' rear guard was commanded by the "Iron Wall," Senior Admiral Neidhart Müller. If an enemy force of equal—or even 50 percent greater—size were to challenge him, there was no room for doubt that he could maintain his lines for a long time.

Reinhard's elegant eyebrows moved slightly. "But where is Yang Wen-li?"

It truly appeared that for the genius, it was not an option to ignore the magician. Von Reuentahl was surprised at what he felt in his own heart at that. Somehow, it seemed like he felt ever so slightly *jealous* of Yang—of an enemy admiral who could seize hold of the kaiser's consciousness like this, and not let him go.

"Even in the unlikely event that the reserve force's commander is Yang Wen-li, he'll try to divide us and cut off our way back, rather than attacking us head-on, won't he?"

"It is as you say."

Reinhard nodded, and his bountiful hair rippled with waves of gold. Yang Wen-li, a continent in the world of men, was a factor that the Imperial Navy should always take into account when honing its strategies and executing its tactics. However, since he had fled Heinessen, his force strength had been viewed as extremely weak, and as there had been no emergency alerts from Steinmetz, this time people were thinking it safe to discount him.

"In the event that Yang Wen-li did cut us off from our return route to Phezzan, it would simply be a matter of continuing our advance, wiping out the enemies in front of us, attacking Heinessen, and returning to imperial space via the Iserlohn Corridor. There would be nothing to fear whatsoever."

It was a lavish expression of spirit, but at the same time, the fact that Reinhard had said it meant he was still unaware of the fact that Iserlohn had fallen.

Then, at 2010, the battle displayed yet another intense development. At that time, Carlsen's fleet of alliance vessels charged clockwise toward the imperial forces' rear. Neidhart Müller arrayed his entire fleet in a concave formation, and was boldly preparing to intercept them. At the same time, Fahrenheit was moving in on Carlsen's back side like some bird of prey with its wings spread wide, but closing in on Fahrenheit's tail was Bucock's main force. The ring of double—no, triple—pursuit and combat was beginning to take shape.

For this reason, had von Knapfstein clung tightly to Bucock's tail, the situation would have been entirely favorable to imperial forces, but von Knapfstein had taken damage from a swarm of delayed-action mines that Bucock had scattered in the corridor. Even now, he still hadn't made his way out of it.

And so Bucock, having obtained a secure zone for his rear, turned his fleet's course to the nadir, and avoiding the foolishness of pursuing Fahrenheit, slipped beneath Müller's powerful formation and attempted to strike at Reinhard's command headquarters.

"Go! Defend the kaiser!"

Realizing the danger, Müller threw 30 percent of his forces against Bucock's fleet, all the while enduring a withering assault from Carslen's forces, who were all clearly determined to fight to the death. Bucock's advance was slowed, but then a portion of Carlsen's fleet broke through a corner of Müller's now numerically weakened force, and also flew toward the rear of Reinhard's command headquarters. At this, von Reuentahl gave coolheaded orders for their defense, and a torrent of concentrated energy beams vaporized the alliance forces from point-blank range.

Carlsen's forces were then caught in a fore-and-aft pincer attack by their brave opponents Müller and Fahrenheit, and were mowed down by swords of blazing energy and explosives. Ironically, Carlsen's forces managed to evade utter annihilation only because the imperial forces, concerned that at such close range they would shoot one another, had restrained their fierce attack.

At 2118, Senior Admiral von Eisenach's large fleet took a wide detour around the battlespace and appeared on Bucock's tail, sending monsoon rains of beams and missiles against him. In the midst of those pulsating lights, the alliance fleet's vessels were being reduced to their component molecules one after another.

Von Eisenach's assault was extremely effective, and it looked as though the alliance forces were about to meet the same end as a lamb swallowed from behind and digested by a python.

It was 2200. The solar wind changed suddenly yet again, and in the chaotic wells of both natural and artificial energies, a vortex formed on the front end of von Eisenach's port flank, disrupting his orderly ranks of warships. While the commander was trying to reorganize the formation, Bucock, using a powerful cone formation, grazed past the killing field where Müller, Fahrenheit, and Carlsen were still fighting, and bore down on Reinhard's command headquarters once again.

"That old man is *good!*" Mittermeier said, marveling, even as he drove a sharp spear into Bucock's flank and, with three successive blasts of cannon fire, opened up a hole in his formation, plunged his own train of warships into it, and began breaking it up on all sides.

⁜

As Siegbert Seidlitz, captain of the flagship *Brünhild*, was the one who bore the utmost responsibility for the running of this "mobile imperial headquarters," he held the rank of commodore, though only as a formality. He was the only member of the admiralty in the entire Imperial Navy who commanded only one ship. After the first man to captain this ship, Karl Robert Steinmetz, had made full admiral and transferred to a frontier stellar district, Reuschner and Niemeller had succeeded to the post one after another, but their periods as captain had been brief. Seidlitz had commanded Reinhard's flagship the longest of any of them. He was thirty-one years old, and from his brick-red hair (with a few strands of gray) to the tips of his boots, he was what might best be called a "purebred" spacer. The fact that "for six generations, no head of the Seidlitz family has died with his feet on the ground" was a point of pride for him, and it had an overwhelming effect on the trust the crew put in him. The only thing about him that his subordinates found irritating was the fact that any time this normally solemn young officer got drunk, he was sure to start singing a particular song. The human race had written uncounted millions of songs, so out of all of them, why did he have to love singing a gloomy song like "Space Is Our Grave, Our Ship Is Our Coffin"?

Although this was said of him, the "seventh-generation scion of the Seidlitz family" possessed near-perfect abilities as captain of *Brünhild*, the jewel of the Imperial Navy, and had satisfied Reinhard in every campaign and every battle he had participated in. Compared to that accomplishment, his deficiencies as a singer were of little consequence.

Brünhild's surroundings had been taken over by dancing clusters of fireballs and spheres of light. It looked as if some immense deity had overturned a jewel box onto a spread of black velvet. Thanks to Seidlitz's skilled control of the vessel, *Brünhild* appeared to be sitting peaceably amid the scattered gems. For Reinhard, it had been an unpleasant experience to be driven to such a confused and difficult battle in spite of the vast difference in force strengths, but this song, too, was now approaching its finale. *The alliance forces' offense has reached its end point*, Reinhard observed. Now, even if they spasmed with the last of their dying strength, the tiny bursts of energy that they could still manage were no longer enough to propel themselves forward. At 2240, in the instant that the alliance forces' overextended battle lines seemed on the verge of beginning to contract, Reinhard's lips—formed for the purpose of commanding massive fleets—gave orders, and together with Seidlitz's signal, the battleship *Brünhild* thrust a silver-white javelin of shining energy into the ranks of the alliance's forces. Almost simultaneously, a comm operator let out an odd cry, and then, blushing red as Captain Seidlitz glared at him, gave his report: the Schwarz Lanzenreiter fleet had just arrived at the battlespace.

∨

"Is that so? It seems the Black Lancers have hurried over in quite the panic."

Reinhard laughed. Wittenfeld, who had lost communications with the main fleet and been rushing ahead isolated from the rest of the force, had at last arrived in time for the battle. After successfully picking up Steinmetz's transmissions, he had followed the alliance forces that had set out from Heinessen, and in that way made his way back to the main force. When Fahrenheit had confirmed the sudden appearance of a massive swarm of lights, he had been momentarily shocked to think it might be a reserve enemy force. Taking no heed of his colleague's surprise, Wittenfeld had charged right past him, and set about kicking around and scattering the exhausted-looking ranks of the alliance forces.

"Don't charge in there like wild boars, gentlemen," the kaiser's chief staff officer, Imperial Marshal von Reuentahl, cautioned over the comm channel with a hint of irony. "The enemy's commander is an experienced and talented man. He might be preparing some trick you can't even imagine."

Although slight, he did feel an urge to say, *You plan on boasting of personal achievement after reaching the battlespace at a time like this?*

Reinhard, however, pushing back his lustrous golden hair, spoke up for his fierce commander, albeit with a bit of a wry smile: "Let him be. If Wittenfeld were to have an excess of prudence, it would end up sapping the strength of the Schwarz Lanzenreiter."

Von Reuentahl nodded agreement. The kaiser was right, so all he could do was recognize it with a wry smile of his own. Charging in like wild boars was, after all, what the Lancers were good at.

Wittenfeld himself had a rationale to defend. As a fleet commander, he had tasted utter defeat only once: in year 487 of the old Imperial Calendar, when in the Battle of Amritsar he had yielded before Yang Wen-li's point-blank counterattack. His defeat had been among the first fruits of the focused-point firing tactic that had come to be the specialty of both Yang and the Yang Fleet, and for the past three years, ever since experiencing that humiliation, the Schwarz Lanzenreiter had continued, in every battlespace, to deliver blows to the enemy that had exceeded the damage they took. For the highborn nobles' confederated forces, and for the Free Planets Alliance's military as well, a swarm of fearsome black-painted warships was an object of awe.

And now, Wittenfeld struck the alliance forces straight on with all his spirit, steadily mowing them down in a storm of cannon fire. Flecks of light consumed flecks of light, as the domain of a dark god spread out across the battlespace. In what had originally been a fight among individuals, the alliance forces were no match for the Schwarz Lanzenreiter, and now, with their energies depleted, they were destroyed without even being able to resist.

At 2310, Bucock received word that Carlsen had died in battle. By that time, the alliance fleet had already lost 80 percent of its force strength. The destruction and slaughter became a one-way affair, and even ships that were second to none in terms of bravery viewed the winners and losers as completely decided, and began groping about for some means of escape. However, the alliance's command headquarters had still not crumbled. A mere hundred vessels surrounding the flagship persistently continued to wage a battle of resistance, creating a narrow path of retreat for the sake of their allies.

"They're tough, just like that old man's spirit."

Guessing Reinhard's mood from his murmured words, Hilda suggested advising them to surrender one more time. The young conqueror, however, shook his head, making his lustrous golden hair wave back and forth.

"A wasted effort. That old man would only laugh at me for getting too attached. In the first place, what need do I as the victor have to curry the loser's favor?"

The kaiser did not sound displeased, but his words did seem somehow tinged with the pride of an injured boy. Hilda once more begged the kaiser's indulgence, saying that to extend one's hand to a defeated enemy showed a victor's ability; it was the vanquished foe who could not accept who was small-minded. Reinhard nodded, and although he did not advise surrender himself, he did have a representative do it for him.

It was 2330.

"To the enemy commander!"

The voice of Imperial Marshal Mittermeier, commander in chief of the Imperial Space Armada, came borne on the comm signal.

"To the enemy commander: you are under complete envelopment by our forces, and have already lost your path of retreat. Further resistance is meaningless. Idle your engines and stand down now. His Highness Kaiser Reinhard will reward your valiant efforts in battle by treating you with generosity. I'll say it once more: stand down now."

As he'd expected no answer, Mittermeier was actually a little surprised when a comm operator reported a response from the alliance forces. In any case, he had it patched through to the flagship *Brünhild*. The old admiral who appeared on the screen had a leaden complexion due to exhaustion, but his eyes had a quiet but bountiful vitality. The hand with which he saluted the handsome young conqueror didn't even tremble.

"Your Highness, Kaiser Reinhard, I think very highly of your talent and ability. If I had a grandson, I would want him to be someone like you. That said, I will never be your vassal."

Bucock looked over to the side, where his general chief of staff, head wrapped haphazardly in blood-tinged bandages, was holding up a bottle of whiskey and two paper cups. The elderly marshal showed a hint of a smile, then turned back to the screen.

"Yang Wen-li, likewise, would be your friend, but he will never be your vassal either. He isn't here to vouch for that, but I'm sure enough to guarantee it."

Reinhard looked on, speaking not a word, as Bucock's extended hand took hold of one paper cup.

"The reason being, if I may speak so arrogantly, that democracy is a mode of thought that makes friends who are equal—not one that makes masters and servants."

The elderly marshal gestured toward the screen, as if making a toast.

"I want good friends, and I want to be a good friend to somebody else. But I don't think I want a good lord or good vassals. Which is why you and I weren't able to follow the same flag. I appreciate your courtesy, but you've no need of these old bones anymore."

The paper cup tilted where the old man's mouth was.

"To democracy!"

His general chief of staff echoed the sentiment. With destruction and death right before his eyes, he seemed unafraid, and even indifferent, although a rather sheepish expression had appeared on the old man's face. It seemed to say that preaching sermons was generally not his style.

His courtesy rejected, there was nevertheless no anger in Reinhard's heart. If even a little had existed, it would have been overwhelmed by an emotion of a different sort. Quietly, but bountifully, it was soaking into the continent of his spirit. When it came down to it, an outstanding death was the consequence of an outstanding life, and Reinhard didn't think it possible for either to exist in isolation. And hadn't Siegfried Kircheis, the friend to whom he owed his life, been the same way as well? Reinhard wrapped his palm around the silver pendant that hung on his chest.

Imperial Marshal Oskar von Reuentahl, secretary-general of Imperial Military Command Headquarters, turned the gleam in his black and blue eyes on the handsome kaiser's profile. Responding to that, Reinhard lifted up his face and looked squarely at the screen. Together with his nod, shards of ice seemed to shoot from his eyes, piercing the flagship of the alliance forces. Von Reuentahl lifted one hand, and then brought it down.

A fireball exploded in the midst of the screen. More than a dozen beams, focused on that solitary vessel, had been fired. In that instant, the Free Planets Alliance Armed Forces, which had boasted a two-century history, was extinguished, along with its last commander in chief and general chief of staff.

"What does a stranger understand…" Reinhard said to himself, his demigod-like beauty lit by the pulsating light. Even in his low murmur, there was a vague note of horror in his voice. In his own life, it hadn't just been vassals he'd been searching for in the beginning. A friend, his own other half, with whom to share dreams more vast than space itself, and to accompany him on the road toward realizing them—that was what he'd been looking for first. For a time, that request had been granted, but after it was shattered, Reinhard had had to bear his dreams alone. He'd had to walk alone. The old man's words had left no impression on Reinhard so great as that of his resolute bearing. He had reached out his hand, and in accordance with his rightful authority, the old man had rejected it. That was all.

It was 2345 on the same day. Marshal Wolfgang von Mittermeier, commander in chief of the Galactic Imperial Space Armada, relayed orders from Kaiser Reinhard to the entire fleet: "While passing by the battlespace during our departure, all hands are to stand at attention for the enemy commander, and salute him."

There was no need to confirm that the order was carried out. It seemed unlikely that Reinhard would soon forget the figure of the enemy's elderly marshal who had gone to his death unyielding, and even resolute. He must have vanished amid the light and heat, still trading toasts with the chief of staff at this side.

"Marshal von Reuentahl…"

"Yes, Your Highness?"

"It seems that in the near future, I'll once again be conversing in this manner with an enemy admiral."

There was no need to ask the proper noun for whom he spoke of.

"Aye, Your Highness…" von Reuentahl answered. As Reinhard left the bridge to return to his private room, von Reuentahl's eyes followed him, with a gaze that rather lacked simplicity.

Should I place Yang Wen-li under my command, or view him only as an enemy to fight against and destroy? It would be hard to claim that the strings of Reinhard's heart were stretched out in straight lines leading to a conclusion.

Although Reinhard's talk of lord and vassal had been clearly rebuffed in the meeting that had followed the Vermillion War last year, Reinhard's greed for collecting talented individuals was thought to still be bent toward adding the greatest thinker of the Alliance Armed Forces' admiralty to a corner of his collection of talent. Did this, too, qualify as the victor currying favor with the vanquished?

No, it does not, Reinhard thought. He wanted to make Yang Wen-li bend the knee to him, and swear his allegiance. He also thought that if that was the result, he might become disappointed and lose interest, but still, it was a shame that one who was out conquering the entire universe was incapable of conquering one man.

When Reinhard went into his private quarters, his young attendant Emil von Selle came bringing cream coffee. Excitement from the battle had left its afterglow in his eyes. "Thanks to being able to serve Your Highness, I've been able to travel so far, and experience so many things. I'll have plenty to brag about whenever I go back home."

"Hearing you speak that way so deliberately, it sounds like you miss your home. If you'd like, I can grant you leave so you can go back for a visit."

Teased by the great young lord whom he worshipped, not just the face, but the whole body of the kaiser's future chief physician flushed red.

"I couldn't possibly ask that. Wherever Your Highness may go, I will come with you. Even to another galaxy."

After a moment's silence, the young kaiser laughed aloud in a voice that was like a diamond hammer crushing a crystal bell. He caressed the boy's face, and then tousled his hair.

"For a child, your attitude is far too generous. This galaxy is plenty for me. The other galactic nebulae you can conquer."

In this manner, the Battle of Mar Adetta came to a close. For the Free Planets Alliance Armed Forces, this was their final fleet battle, and their final defeat.

Three hours later, Kaiser Reinhard received word that Iserlohn Fortress had fallen. It seemed as though history itself was not content with merely trying to swallow its actors in its violent currents; it was carrying them off toward a waterfall as well. It had seemed that way too when Yang Wen-li, immediately after arriving on Iserlohn Fortress, had received the unfortunate news of Marshal Bucock's passing.

CHAPTER 7:
THE WINTER ROSE GARDEN EDICT

INNUMERABLE CHEERS TRANSFORMED into innumerable disappointments, and victory toasts turned to bitter draughts of defeat that were hurled against the floor. The kaiser's uniform shoes transformed all of their owner's weight into a fury that ground the slivers of his shattered wineglass into ever-smaller pieces, and scattered weakly gleaming grains of light across the floor.

Across many hundreds of light-years of emptiness, Senior Admiral Steinmetz stood half cringing before an FTL screen that had finally been cleared of the effects of alliance jamming. When he thought of Lutz, standing in the background with his head hung low, and the imperial rebuke he'd just incurred, he couldn't help feeling sorry for him. Last year, it had been Steinmetz himself who had been seated in the loser's chair, having also fallen victim to Yang Wen-li's cunning tricks. Lutz's regret was not simply "somebody else's problem."

Reinhard, having diffused a portion of his wrath on the wineglass, had managed to listen to Lutz's report all the way to the end without shouting. Lutz, with a pallor that seeped even into his voice, had described the scene of defeat, and apologized.

Behind Reinhard, who was facing the comm screen, Mittermeier said with a mixture of anger and disgust, "Yet again, that man has made fools of us." Von Reuentahl agreed, though he referred not merely to the tactical-level defeat of having Iserlohn stolen from them. The late marshal Bucock and Yang had divided their roles in a difficult coordinated operation, with the former sacrificing himself to hinder the kaiser's main force, and the latter recapturing Iserlohn. This wasn't merely a matter of Yang defeating Lutz as individuals; if what he suspected was true, hadn't Yang—all by himself—just forced the entire Imperial Navy to sip bitter wine from defeat's chalice?

Of course, this was an overestimation arrived at by working backward from the result, but Reinhard had the same suspicion as the two of them. For a moment, a feeling of black, ashen defeat became so intense that the middle part of his field of vision went dark. It was his chief secretary, Hilda, who made the case that he was overthinking this.

"This is nothing more than the result of two mutually isolated solo operations happening side by side. If it had been a coordinated operation, Bucock would have drawn the duty of taking Iserlohn, while Yang Wen-li himself would have come out to face His Majesty. If the plans were already laid out for the capture of Iserlohn, they could have been executed even without Yang present. But when it came to doing battle with His Majesty, Yang himself would have had to have been here. Now, Marshal Bucock has achieved nothing but a death on the battlespace. This must be a difficult loss for Yang. Sacrificing Bucock while securing his own victory runs against the kind of person Yang is, and if it became widely known that he had done such a thing, he might lose the trust that people place in him. I don't believe Yang would adopt that sort of foolish plan..."

"I see," said Reinhard. "You're most likely correct."

Though he accepted Hilda's opinion, the news of Iserlohn's loss was still a bitter pill to swallow. Reinhard decided to hold off on judging Lutz until after his fury had subsided, and ordered him not to leave his quarters for the time being.

Imperial Marshal Oskar von Reuentahl, secretary-general of Imperial Military Command Headquarters, was standing behind Reinhard, in the angel of silence's embrace. The handsome young kaiser turned toward him, white fingers brushing back lustrous golden hair as he said, "Marshal von Reuentahl, your success unfortunately had a life span of less than a year."

"It's most unfortunate," von Reuentahl said. It was a brief reply, but the famed heterochromatic imperial marshal had not collected his thoughts well enough to form a proper response. It was a fact that Lutz had played right into Yang Wen-li's hands, but neither Kaiser Reinhard nor von Reuentahl himself were entirely without fault in the matter. Reinhard had turned out to have taken too light a view of Iserlohn Fortress's strategic value, and when von Reuentahl had achieved the monumental feat of retaking the fortress last year, he had failed to see through Yang's "evil plan."

"I'd thought he was probably up to something, but to think he was making meticulous preparations so far in advance..."

Kornelias Lutz had been von Reuentahl's vice commander at the time he had retaken the fortress. He had a stable personality and an outstanding talent for commanding operations—had there been no way for him to stand against Yang Wen-li's farsighted schemes and clever strategies?

Driven from Iserlohn Fortress, Kornelias Lutz was also leading a force of ten thousand ships of various sizes, and if he had just had the will to do so, he could have mounted a fierce attack on El Facil, and burned it all in hellish flames. Still, plundering an essentially defenseless world had seemed a graceless way to retaliate for Iserlohn's loss, so making an effort to retain his honor in the midst of defeat, he had withdrawn and headed for the Gandharva system, where his colleague Steinmetz was stationed. Had he known that Yang Wen-li was on El Facil, he might have changed his mind, but Lutz believed that the black-haired magician had spearheaded the attack personally, as he had done in all of his battles up to that point. Lutz was not alone in that; Reinhard and von Reuentahl both thought so as well.

Reinhard, for his part, had nothing to say to Lutz by this point. His was just the latest name on a growing list of top imperial commanders defeated by Yang Wen-li's ingenuity since the previous year. Reinhard left to reorganize his emotions, and shut himself away in his private quarters. The assembled admirals looked at one another, and naturally adjourned.

"Are all of the empire's greatest admirals nothing more than a cast of foils for Yang Wen-li?"

Walking down the hallway, von Reuentahl ejected those words from his voice box with a mixture of irony and disgust, and Mittermeier, dissatisfied, ruffled his honey-blond hair with one hand.

"So basically, we've nothing to fear on a military campaign spanning a hundred thousand light-years except the content of Yang Wen-li's skull. If that man had the same number of troops we do—or more—then it might be him that the fates were winking at."

If anyone other than Mittermeier had said that kind of line, he would have been denounced as a coward, but he knew just as well as his lord how to respect an enemy, and on that point even surpassed him.

Von Reuentahl answered, saying that suppositions were meaningless, at which point a different supposition blossomed in the mind of the famed heterochromatic admiral.

"If Siegfried Kircheis were alive, we might not have lost Iserlohn like this."

Had Siegfried Kircheis been yet among the living, then he, acting as Reinhard's alter ego, would have applied his remarkable talents and skills to commanding a massive force that would likely have hemmed Yang Wen-li in on all sides in some distant corner of space. At the very least, the military windstorm named Yang Wen-li would have surely experienced a drop in speed and pressure. Or maybe, if Kircheis had been living, he would have applied his unparalleled fairness and clarity of thought to the duties of high commissioner—duties too heavy for Helmut Lennenkamp—and encouraged trust and integrity in the Free Planets' government, rather than panic and desperation. Or again, he might have occupied the seat of minister of military of affairs, allowing Kaiser Reinhard to undertake his personal campaign without anxiety for the future, and dispelling the admirals' distrust and dissatisfaction with the present-day Ministry of Military Affairs before it had ever begun.

"That's right. If Kircheis were alive, we wouldn't have had that smug-looking von Oberstein guy lording it over Military Affairs either."

Mittermeier spoke as though that were the point deserving greatest emphasis.

Both imperial marshals felt that, in any case, it was imperative to waste not a day in subduing Heinessen, so as to prevent Yang Wen-li from working his martial sleight of hand in tandem with ongoing political developments. Reinhard, who shared this opinion, was preparing to order the entire fleet to renew its rapid advance right away, but Hilda shook her head and held him back.

"Your Majesty, there's no need to hurry. If we approach Heinessen boldly, that alone will exert pressure enough to shatter the Free Planets' government."

Seeming to forget for a moment his displeasure over the loss of Iserlohn, Reinhard turned to look at the beautiful, boyish contessina, forming an expression that appeared to be in striking distance of becoming a little smile.

"Do you think the Free Planets' government is made of eggshells, Fräulein?"

"Yes, and I think a storm is brewing inside that egg. Most likely, they'll destroy themselves with internal squabbling. It won't be worth troubling Your Majesty's hands with."

"Heh—"

Reinhard's little laugh ended before it had begun. He sank into thought with a rather vague expression, and then, having made up his mind, gave orders to resume the advance. Boldly, as Hilda had said, and without any rush.

Karl Robert Steinmetz had so much firepower at his command that he could have reduced Heinessen to ashes with a single word. The reason he did not—devoting himself instead to deterrence, observation, and the duty of improving the empire's base—was blazingly clear. The young, golden-haired kaiser longed to set foot on Heinessen's soil not as its guest but as its conqueror. That was what Steinmetz believed, and in terms of outcome, his judgment had been sound. There was also a need for Steinmetz to act as a guide for the kaiser, so he was frequently relaying to Reinhard intelligence received from Heinessen. However, as they headed into February, a shocking piece of intelligence suddenly arrived.

It informed him of the surrender of the Free Planets Alliance, and of the death of João Lebello.

II

The record is silent regarding what João Lebello, the Free Planets Alliance's final Head of State, was working on in his office on February 2 of that year. What is certain is that, regardless of his ineffectiveness and lack of results, he never tried to shirk his duties, even in his life's final chapter.

Kaiser Reinhard's declaration, which had exposed both Lennenkamp's death and its cause, had now proven a fatal wound for the alliance. Going by the subjective reasoning of an alliance government that had desperately concealed those facts, this was the equivalent of being stabbed in the back by one's partner in crime. However, it wasn't as if they had ever embraced some vision for what came next after the cover-up. Had Lebello been some wicked schemer, he might have clung relentlessly to his fiction, making Yang out to be a despicable fugitive, and shifting blame for all the chaos onto him.

However, he had not been able to take it that far. Even if he was by nature a bit narrow-minded, he was a man who had walked the righteous path, and after Lennenkamp's death, it seemed his meager talent for "flexible planning" had been exhausted. Afterward, he had lost himself in the narrow range of his duties. When he sensed the emanations of a gruesome intent rolling in on him, he suddenly raised his head, looked around, and perceived that he was surrounded by an armed group that could not possibly have been in that place. His one old acquaintance in the crowd hailed him in a rather emotionless voice. It was Admiral Rockwell, director of Joint Operational Headquarters.

"Director, what business brings you here? I don't remember calling for you all."

"We couldn't care less about your memories, Chairman. The issue here is what we require."

Although Admiral Rockwell might have once been plagued by trepidation and indecisiveness, he now seemed ready to roll straight ahead, crushing his own sense of shame under his wheels. A file was applied to Lebello's dulled emotions, and very suddenly, he realized what kind of situation he was in.

"You...intend to kill me, don't you?"

Rockwell didn't answer.

Silence was another way of saying yes. Lebello breathed a rather apathetic sigh, folded his arms, and surveyed this band of officers, here to force on him a ticket to some place not above the ground.

"May I hear your reasons?"

"We can't trust you."

"How do you mean?"

"If the Imperial Navy demanded Yang-li's head, you'd hand it over right away. If they came demanding mine, you'd do the same. This is nothing more than a means of self-preservation. I don't want your power."

"You have no need to defend yourselves. The Imperial Navy won't ever come for your heads. After all, none of you are Yang Wen-li."

This calmly made point was like a noxious spray that stung at the officers' faces.

"You were the one," said Rockwell, "who taught me how to do things this way, Excellency. Didn't Marshal Yang try to defend himself when you made him a sacrificial lamb? Meeting your end here, now, like this, is what they call 'reaping what you sow.' Blame your own foolishness."

New life welled up in Lebello's eyes. It looked as if his whole, weakened body had received an infusion of the energy that came of intellect and will. He sat up straight and faced the officers, looking free of all fear.

"I see. So I'm reaping what I've sown? Maybe I am, but justifying my death is not the same as justifying your actions. My conscience and your consciences were also given different loads to bear. But that's all right. Shoot me down, and buy your security."

Was there no one to feel pity for Lebello's conscience and unrewarded sense of responsibility? Who in the moments before his death would grant him whatever grace was possible for him? At that moment, the slim figure of the High Council chairman carried not a single weapon, and yet he intimidated the assassins. Admiral Rockwell sensed unrest rising like a heat mirage off the figures surrounding him. It was rising off of him as well—his spirit sublimating, robbing his body of energy, feeling as though it would leave nothing behind except regret and defeat. After no small effort, he opened his mouth, then closed it again. When his scattered thoughts refocused, he saw Lebello's body, pierced through by numerous beams, sliding from his chair to the floor.

Reinhard said nothing on receiving the report; at any rate, this would best be called a bloodless surrender. Reinhard ordered the armada to make straight for Heinessen, and there he was welcomed by Steinmetz, who had already deployed his fleet in orbit around the planet. An imperial force of one hundred thousand ships watched over the armada flagship *Brunhild*, protecting it as it descended.

On February 9, SE 800/NIC 2, Reinhard von Lohengramm became the first Galactic Emperor to set foot on Planet Heinessen.

After arriving at the spaceport, Reinhard, protected by four divisions of armored troops under Steinmetz's command, went to the National Cemetery where João Lebello's body was lying in state. The visit itself was a brief one, and the kaiser offered nothing amounting to an opinion, but Steinmetz was appointed council chairman on the occasion of Lebello's funeral.

"João Lebello's misfortune was not that he became head of state at the worst possible time—it was that he became head of state at all. While Lebello was able to believe in fictions created by others—in the inviolability of the democratic regime, for example—he simply wasn't blessed with the qualities—the charisma, to put it bluntly—necessary to construct a fiction of his own."

Such appraisals do exist, but history's verdict aside, Reinhard, as victor, maintained perfect decorum toward this old enemy. Or to put a more cynical spin on it, maintaining decorum would not cause problems of any sort, though the situation being what it was, there is no need to infer any excess of emotion on his part.

After leaving the cemetery, Reinhard transmitted brief orders to von Reuentahl, Mittermeier, and Müller from the landcar he was sharing with Hilda.

The Goldenlöwe, von Lohengramm's golden lion banner, was rustling from the elevated post where the flag of the former Free Planets Alliance had once flown. That day, Planet Heinessen had clear skies over its government and municipal office district, but with a strong, chilly wind caressing their skins, onlookers cringed from the cold air and unease as they watched the young conqueror's procession go by. Ranks of armed soldiers divided the victors from the vanquished, and from time to time, the citizens' eyes would catch sight of the handsome conqueror's divine beauty. When that happened, the women in particular tended to forget for a moment the cold and unease. Of course that was a mostly superficial reaction, so vastly unlike the worship of the soldiers who had followed him from battle to battle on this campaign as to not even register. If we define a hero as someone that many people would gladly go to the land of the dead for in order to satisfy their greed or the ideals of their subjective reasoning, then Reinhard was certainly a hero. Valhalla was bursting at the seams already with dead men who had perished for him—and their residential block was likely to yet require further expansion.

The landcar came to a halt. It appeared that trouble of some sort had broken out among the crowd. An Imperial Navy armored car drew near, and a high-ranking officer, his tall, muscular frame wrapped in a black and silver uniform, got out and bowed on his knee beside Reinhard's landcar. Together with Steinmetz was Senior Admiral Wittenfeld, commander of the Schwarz Lanzenreiter, to whom Reinhard had delegated responsibility for metropolitan security.

"For the Schwarz Lanzenreiter, there is no retreat."

That boast strengthened their faith, and that faith produced results. Under the former dynasty, Wittenfeld had risen to the admiralty in spite of his nonaristocratic birth, and it was his faith and results that had led to his being discovered by Reinhard. He had what it took to be regarded highly by the young conqueror.

It is said that weak troops don't exist in the service of a fierce general. In the Schwarz Lanzenreiter's case, that was an incontrovertible fact. When their commander charged forward while standing at the head of the whole fleet, his subordinates became a muddy stream of steel following after him, continually exhibiting unparalleled destructive power.

Fritz Josef Wittenfeld was the same age as Yang Wen-li and Oskar von Reuentahl; he would turn thirty-three in SE 800/NIC 2. Others felt that his whole being could be summed up in one word: "ferocious." The man himself, far from denying this, was actually using that word himself boastfully. His daring, his rigid, straight-arrow tactics, and the battlespace feats he had accomplished thus far certainly backed up his reputation for ferocity. Following the Battle of Rantemario, however, he had made an evaluation of the greatest feats performed among his subordinates, and the report he had sent to Reinhard had spoken not of heroes mowing down the enemy like grass, but of the crews of medical vessels treating wounded soldiers in the midst of fierce combat, performing daring rescues, and transporting the wounded to the rear of the fleet.

Reinhard was surprised, and frankly moved, and gave generous rewards not only to the medical ships' crews in Wittenfeld's fleet, but to those of the entire armada as well.

"That Wittenfeld…I wonder if he's making a play for His Majesty's favor."

"Even if he is, it's not a bad thing to reappraise the accomplishments of the medical ships."

"You're certainly right about that. Even if he was currying favor, it was pretty shrewd of him just to think of that…"

At that time, von Reuentahl and Mittermeier acknowledged with wry smiles this unexpected side of their colleague.

•

That same Wittenfeld was now kneeling formally next to the stopped landcar. Hilda glanced at Reinhard's eyes, then opened the landcar's door. The fearsome, orange-haired admiral saluted, donning a coat of tension on top of his uniform.

"My apologies for the disturbance, Your Majesty. Please be gracious, and pardon your vassal's error."

The handsome young kaiser had no interest in the usage of polite language. He clearly wanted only to be told what had happened.

"Yes, there was a republican ideologist in the crowd, who attempted to take outrageous action against Your Majesty's life…"

I thought everyone in this crowd was a republican idealist, Reinhard mused, although he didn't say it aloud.

"And the perpetrator? Was he arrested?"

"When we surrounded him, he killed himself on the spot with a gun. Not that even death can excuse the grave crime of attempted regicide. I'll confirm his identity as quickly as possible, and take appropriate measures."

Reinhard's well-shaped eyebrows, as comely as if painted by an artist's brush, formed an arch of displeasure.

"Do nothing unnecessary or unprofitable. Release the body to his family. And to make myself doubly clear: do not harm his family."

"Yes, Your Majesty…"

"You don't care for that? I do prize your loyalty, but too much of that kind of thing will turn me into another Rudolf."

With that one word, the fierce, orange-haired admiral understood his lord's intent perfectly, and bowed his head with the greatest of humility. The name of Rudolf was reviled not only by Reinhard himself, but by his vassals as well.

The door was closed, as the landcar started moving again. Reinhard sat back in his seat, sank into the forest of his own deep thoughts, and closed his eyes. For some time after, Hilda stared at the shadows that his long eyelashes cast on his pale white skin.

III

Reinhard's generosity toward old enemies did not come without some guiding principles. His last official duty for that day was an interview with João Lebello's assassins. Since the other admirals were attending to municipal security duties and the commandeering of various facilities, the only ranking military officer to accompany him was Senior Admiral Adalbert Fahrenheit.

From the very start of Reinhard's interview with the assassins, he made no effort to hide his contempt for them. Arrogantly, he crossed his long legs, and looking down on the awkwardly kneeling Admiral Rockwell and his ten rebellious officers, spoke in a voice far colder than zero degrees.

"My time is too precious to spare for the likes of you. I'll ask you one question: When you did it, what were you ashamed of?"

Admiral Rockwell just barely managed to raise his face toward the young conqueror, but resisting his ice-blue gaze was no easy task. His expression was somewhere between shock and terror.

"Are you saying we lack shame, Your Majesty?"

"If it sounded any other way, my wording was poor."

"Even Admiral Fahrenheit, who's standing by your side, was once an admiral in the aristocrats' confederated forces. But now, he's changed his goals, and serves Your Majesty. That being the case, I think you should be able to deal with us generously as well."

Reinhard strummed a harp of ice with his cold smile.

"Did you hear that, Fahrenheit? These men say they're the same as you."

After a moment, Fahrenheit said, "I am truly, deeply honored."

As he looked directly at the surrendered conspirators, a wrathful steam was floating in the aquamarine eyes of that admiral, famed across two dynasties for his valor. As an officer in the boyar nobles' confederacy, he had done his utmost, and even after losing faith in its shortsighted and incompetent leader Duke von Braunschweig, he had never dreamed of selling him out to his enemies. There were no words for the disgust he felt at having Lebello's assassins equate themselves with him. Glancing at his face, Reinhard nodded.

"Very well, Fahrenheit—I feel exactly the same. I know how you're usually averse to bloodshed off the battlefield, so I'll give the order especially for you. Dispose of these filthy, two-legged hyenas, and sanitize at least one cranny of this universe."

"Aye!"

While the kaiser was still speaking, the surrendered assassins had lost their color and risen to their feet. Fahrenheit raised one hand, and a human circle moved in, creating a wall of uniforms around the eleven men.

After a moment of silent disbelief, Admiral Rockwell said, "I demand legal protection!"

But the cry he let out was deflected as Fahrenheit barked, "I don't know about its predecessor, but the Lohengramm Dynasty has no law protecting traitors. Cease your useless pleading."

The assassins, marched away by Fahrenheit and the others, faded into the distance, stirring the air as they went with a threefold melody of screams, protests, and pleadings.

When they were gone, Reinhard said, "It's just as you predicted, Fräulein. Those who eat rotten meat judge others by their own tastes." He practically spat out the words, placing a white finger against his white front teeth. Hilda was on the point of vomiting from disgust at all of this; nevertheless, she had soldiered through, and after a small cough, murmured words that might have been an appraisal or might have been self-examination. "I think people are probably capable of doing far more despicable things than they realize. In a perfect world of peace and harmony, we would never have to discover that side of ourselves, but…"

The ice-blue curtains of Reinhard's eyes stirred, and one tiny part of his frail soul, wrapped in its thick, tough hide, touched open air. Replace the word "despicable" with "foolish," and he, too, became a criminal best locked away in purgatory. He himself knew that better than anyone else.

At last, he shook his golden hair and said, "If those men were sewer sludge, then that old man who died at Mar Adetta was newfallen snow." Perhaps saying so was an escape mechanism that he himself was not aware of. But even if that were true, it didn't mean he had spoken any falsehood.

"It's from the *ashes* that the phoenix is reborn. Half-cooked, it can never receive new life. The old man knew that. So I'll punish those men, and make them beg his forgiveness in Valhalla."

With a graceful movement, Reinhard turned to face his cluster of aides. "Bring a glass of white wine, would you, Emil?"

His young chamberlain bowed, and at a speed just shy of a full-tilt run, withdrew briefly from the kaiser's presence. At last, he returned with a crystal glass filled with an almost-clear liquid, and reverently held it out toward his master.

However, Reinhard had not asked for wine so he could drain the glass himself. The young, golden-haired kaiser took the crystal glass from Emil's hand, turned his graceful figure directly toward a window, and flipped his graceful wrist. A curtain of white wine ran down the windowpane, drenching the view of a courtyard half-enveloped in twilight's palms—this was Reinhard's offering to the dead.

The following day, a proclamation went out from the kaiser.

"Families of the Alliance Armed Forces' war dead, as well as sick or injured soldiers—even those who fought as enemies against the Imperial Navy—shall be treated kindly. The time of hatred as the mover of history has ended. Those not satisfied with their treatment and those facing real hardship should not hesitate to come forward."

The shock that this proclamation delivered to the Free Planets' governmental bureaucrats was no small one. A deep-seated fear took hold of them—perhaps it was not themselves who had been defeated by military force, but democratic republican government itself that had been defeated by the ability of one individual. Had Reinhard taken heartless vengeance, they said, a spirit of rebellion against his despotism would have taken hold, but instead, its exact opposite, magnanimity, was like the sunlight that melts the ice, discouraging opposition.

Among the high-ranking government and military officers, people were switching sides one after another. The bitter punishment given Lebello's assassins did make these converts quite cautious, but cooperating out of devotion to their duties was unlikely to stimulate the empire's fastidious side.

Many of those who did not cast aside loyalty to democratic republican government were faceless soldiers and bureaucrats of midlevel status and below. Many of these attempted to resist their conquerors through various acts of minor sabotage, but there were also those who stated their intentions openly. Busias Adora, a counselor working in Heinessen's city government district, flatly refused when ordered by the Imperial Navy to submit a declaration of allegiance to the kaiser.

"Who is this kaiser you speak of? Here in the Free Planets Alliance, we have a head of state chosen by the people, but we don't have any kaiser. I don't have to follow orders from somebody who doesn't exist."

Claude Monteille, treasury section manager at the Finance Committee office, was ordered to turn over a list of all state-owned properties, but he stubbornly refused to accommodate this demand.

"Only citizens of the Free Planets Alliance who have the right to vote in elections, have the right to run in elections, and also pay their taxes have the right to view lists of state-owned properties. Furthermore, governmental and public employees perform their duties only according to the laws of the alliance and their own consciences. I am truly afraid. I don't want to die. But once I became a public servant, I could not shirk my duties, humble though they may be."

Furthermore, on February 11, Graham Ebard-Noel-Baker, a secretary second class at the Supreme Council Secretariat, made the following entry in the public record:

"Today at 10:30, a man by the name of Reinhard von Lohengramm, calling himself 'kaiser of the Galactic Empire,' applied for a tour of the assembly hall without legal standing."

Even when the entry's deletion was requested, he did not cooperate.

All three of them ended up in prison, but when the kaiser eventually learned of it, they were released on his order.

"They're fine men, all of them. The failure to promote that sort beyond the middle ranks is exactly why the alliance ultimately fell. We mustn't harm people like that. For the time being, put only obedient people in charge of governmental administrative functions." Since the handful of courageous individuals who were determined to resist caused no particular impediment to the occupation's administration, perhaps Reinhard had been able to let his emotions—or his sentimentality—manifest itself.

Eventually, it came to light through a number of testimonials and pieces of evidence that High Commissioner Lennenkamp's chief assistant, Udo Dater Fummel, had enticed malcontent elements, including Admiral Rockwell, to assassinate Lebello. A storm cloud hung low over Reinhard's brow when he heard of it. He ordered Müller to go and bring Fummel before him, then questioned him as to why he had committed such a dishonorable act of incitement.

"I was afraid of him causing trouble for Your Highness," Fummel answered.

To which Reinhard jumped to a pointed conclusion. "A praiseworthy endeavor, but if that's the case, you should have restrained Lennenkamp's rash behavior. And now you come here acting so clever, intending to put me in your debt?"

The selfsame day, Reinhard made the decision to dismiss Fummel, and sent him back to the imperial capital of Odin.

IV

On February 20, the "Winter Rose Garden Edict" was promulgated as follows. It was referred to as such because it was issued from a garden of winter roses within the expansive grounds of the National Museum of the Arts, located in a corner of Heinessen's government and municipal office district. Its official name was of course a prosaic one: the "Edict of February 20, New Imperial Calendar Year 2." It was a name impossible to misunderstand, as it did not appeal to people's emotions. It was the common name that lingered long in their memories.

Neidhart Müller, standing behind the kaiser, paying careful attention to security while also watching history unfolding in the present progressive tense, would long remember the gold and crimson standing out against a background steeped in greenish grays. Reinhard, standing still before high-ranking officials of the imperial navy and the FPA government, flanked on both sides by imperial marshals Wolfgang Mittermeier and Oskar von Reuentahl as he received the written edict from Hildegard von Mariendorf, looked like one into whom the brilliance of every constellation had been condensed, and seemed a personification of the royal hellebores growing crimson among the other winter roses. The shades of dusk rapidly deepened, and as the substance of the people merged with the shadows, Reinhard's golden hair alone stood out dazzlingly, as though he had wrapped the sun's last flash of light around his own head.

"I, Reinhard von Lohengramm, kaiser of the Galactic Empire, do hereby proclaim that the Free Planets Alliance is utterly fallen, having lost the substance that would justify its name. From this day forward, there is only one rightful governing body to rule humanity: the Galactic Empire. At the same time, I publicly acknowledge that in past history there existed the Free Planets Alliance, which has long been alienated, and referred to as dishonorable rebel forces."

The corner of von Reuentahl's mouth twisted at micron scale with irony. How much more bitter could the kaiser's declaration be? To at last be recognized by the empire's highest ruling authority, only after being extinguished both in name and in fact. Acknowledged, but only as an artifact of the past—a bouquet of lies to decorate a shroud.

When Reinhard completed the proclamation, his gaze went wandering over the garden. Even if this garden, where generations of past alliance heads of state must have strolled, assembled their supporters, and held garden parties, was a far cry from the ridiculous grandeur of Neue Sans Souci Palace, it was still worthy of appreciation.

Even in the middle of winter, hellebores of crimson, white, and pink formed rainbows on the ground. A modest two-story guesthouse adjoined the garden. *I'll make that my residence while I'm here on Heinessen*, Reinhard thought. Although he was known for elegance when boarding a battleship, and magnificence when leading his forces, his personal lifestyle was more simple, and he even exhibited a sense of revulsion toward luxurious estates. Though he took some enjoyment in gardens, he preferred scenic ones that were close to nature over geometric, man-made beauty. Among the cultural relics of the Free Planets Alliance, this garden of winter roses was one of the few things he liked. And while "interim palace" was too grand a word for it, he nevertheless made up his mind to stay there from that point forward.

Marshal von Reuentahl's aide-de-camp, Lieutenant Commander Emil von Reckendorf, whispered something to his commanding officer, to which the secretary-general of Imperial Military Command Headquarters nodded, and begged the kaiser's leave to return to the hotel that was currently his residence. That night, over one thousand high-ranking officers were supposed to gather for a celebratory banquet, and as it was the middle of winter, it wouldn't do to get all dressed up for a garden party. The kaiser started walking, and more than fifty thousand soldiers stationed around the Winter Rose Garden's perimeter began to cheer. They needed no one's order to do so.

"Sieg kaiser!"

"Sieg mein kaiser!"

"Sieg Kaiser Reinhard!"

The wild enthusiasm of officer and enlisted man alike was a bit disorderly, but it became a powerful chorus that spread out like a canopy over the entire imperial military. The courageous, battle-hardened admirals who were standing around the kaiser at that time also felt it just as strongly: that they had *been here* to see a moment that would be spoken of for generations being carved into history with a golden chisel. With pride, they gazed upon their crimson "royal hellebore."

At last, I've finally made it here, Reinhard murmured in his heart. The old alliance's capital was now nothing more than a territory situated at one end of the vast land that he ruled. Before, when he had walked this land, he had still nominally been a mere court vassal of the Goldenbaum Dynasty. But now he was kaiser. Even without falling back on that "holy and inviolable" nonsense, he had become the most powerful presence in the universe.

And yet, the truth of the matter was, he should have been able to become even more powerful—if one of his unseen wings had not been broken because of his own sin. Trying to shake away the pain, he raised one hand, and the soldiers, looking up at him as they would a sun come down to earth, let their emotions boil over, singing the kaiser's praises again and again.

The next day, February 21, Reinhard summoned his top advisors to a room at the hotel that had become his temporary imperial headquarters, and announced that he would personally lead a force to Iserlohn, and attempt to once again retake the fortress.

"What Lutz has lost, I shall regain," he said.

That his young master had splendid fighting spirit, von Reuentahl acknowledged frankly. However, he couldn't help feeling cautious when it came to the unexpected and brilliant plans of Yang Wen-li. It was possible that Yang had already devised a plan, and was waiting for an infuriated Reinhard to come out and attack him in person. *He shouldn't risk it*, von Reuentahl thought. And he couldn't help thinking: *That's a strange thought coming from me.* The kaiser's defeats and failures would lead directly to his own ascension—he could follow his ambition and watch from the sidelines as Reinhard self-destructed. Nevertheless, he wanted from the bottom of his heart to advise him against rash action at this time.

It goes without saying that the historians of later generations were unable to simplistically evaluate the man known as Oskar von Reuentahl. After all, he himself had perceived a labyrinth that existed within his heart.

"Mein kaiser, in the unlikely event that anything should happen to you, the new dynasty would crumble, and this age would lose its standard-bearer. Please, return to Phezzan for a time, and work on plans to perpetuate what you have built. As for Yang Wen-li, I ask that you task both Mittermeier and myself with subduing him."

Mittermeier supported his friend passionately. "Von Reuentahl is right. Since Your Majesty's campaign has for the time being achieved its goal, please take some time to rest, and leave the hard work on the front line to us."

Reinhard's recent frequent fevers due to overwork concerned him.

"I don't intend to rob you of any military accomplishments," Reinhard said, "but I do want to settle things personally with Yang Wen-li. And that man is likely thinking the same thing."

The one who asked to speak at this time was the kaiser's chief secretary, Fräulein Hildegard "Hilda" von Mariendorf.

"Your Majesty, both of your imperial marshals are right about this. Please, return to Phezzan for a little while. Your Majesty's presence there is what stabilizes Phezzan, and allows its position as your seat of power at the center of the universe to take root."

Reinhard's spirit had apparently been stimulated in a negative direction this time; the ice-blue gleam in his eyes contained needles.

"Fräulein von Mariendorf, when caution knows no bounds, the criticism of weakness and indecisiveness become inevitable. Were I to simply head straight back after losing Iserlohn, anti-imperial forces would believe that Yang Wen-li had prevailed by default against me. They would idolize him, and rally around him."

"Your Majesty, please consider this. If Yang Wen-li takes all possible measures at the tactical level, all he can do is barricade himself inside Iserlohn Fortress and mount a strong defense. That means ceding control over both ends of the corridor to our imperial forces, which has no effect at all at the strategic level."

Reinhard dismissed this with a low laugh.

"You're speaking in a roundabout way. It's most unlike you, Fräulein. Has Yang Wen-li not occupied El Facil already, and seized control of the corridor's exit?"

But Hilda refused to back down. "That is true. However, in this case, satisfying his strategic requirements would demand too much support at the tactical level. To begin with, Yang Wen-li's force strength is barely enough to defend Iserlohn Fortress alone. With such a small force, I have to say it's incredibly difficult to take and hold El Facil as well. Even with his superlative planning, Yang Wen-li's circumstances make it difficult for him to simultaneously solve the problems of both his strategic plan and his tactical limitations. As long as this contradiction remains unresolved, we will have any number of opportunities to strike at Yang Wen-li."

"Yang may resolve them," Reinhard tried to argue. Perhaps unable to deny the rightness of Hilda's reasoning, though, his voice now had little strength to it.

In the end, Reinhard postponed his campaign against Iserlohn. It was merely a temporary delay. But Hilda's advice aside, what made him do so was a dossier that arrived from distant Phezzan.

CHAPTER 8:

I

"GOOD NEWS ONLY comes alone; bad news brings its friends."

This not terribly original thought was a recollection of Alex Caselnes's. Ever since the "prodigals' return" to Iserlohn Fortress at the start of the year, the Yang Fleet's visitors of the solitary sort had all but died out.

The arrival of the fleet led by Murai, Patrichev, Fischer, and Soul was the extent of the good news, and thanks to that, the Yang Fleet's military power and human resource pool had become strikingly more robust. On the other hand, the fact remained that Poplin moaned, "Not that crabby old man again!" the moment he heard Murai's name, and began whistling a strain from a funeral march. Attenborough's view, that "our picnic just turned into a study tour," was also well attested.

When Senior Admiral Wittenfeld of the Imperial Navy had turned back and made for Mar Adetta, some of his subordinates had urged him to strike the capital of Heinessen instead, to which he had answered, "We believe that war is our vocation. We aren't like Yang Wen-li's people, playing at war and revolution only when we have nothing better to do. We act only according to principle."

Although Wittenfeld's characterization was the essence of slander, not one of the Yang Fleet's top leaders could have rebuffed the accusation as groundless. After all, Dusty Attenborough had accepted the charge, and even stated publically that "showing off and having fun" had been the wellspring of their energy. In that he actually prided himself on this view, he was a rather hopeless individual.

There is no evidence of subordinates such as these consciously banding together under Yang; it had simply turned out that birds of a feather truly did flock together, and multiple rotten apples spoiled their barrel that much faster. Since its beginning in SE 796, the Yang Fleet—the strongest fleet in the universe—had developed a spirit all its own.

During a break from the military duties with which they were supposed to be occupied, Attenborough and Poplin shared this indiscreet exchange:

"We need our own version of the Imperial Navy's 'Sieg kaiser,' but 'Viva democracy' is about all I can think of. What do you think?"

"As an appeal to public sentiment, it's missing something. I still think we ought to use our commander's name like they do, but in terms of relative impact, that's missing about five somethings, isn't it?"

But it was only natural that even men who prided themselves on fearlessness and good cheer were driven momentarily into the depths of silence when they received word of Marshal Alexandor Bucock's death.

When Frederica heard the news, several hundred seconds of darkness and silence elapsed before she rose to her feet and looked in the mirror. Finding her complexion strikingly devoid of red corpuscles, she steadied her breathing, lightly applied some makeup, and went to the office of her husband and commander. She stepped inside and stood in front of Yang, who was holding a paper cup of hot tea in one hand while looking over some documents. She waited for his suspicious glance to find her, then, in as steady a voice as she could manage, said, "Commander in Chief Bucock has fallen in battle."

Yang took a sip of his tea. It smelled strongly of brandy. He blinked his eyes twice, then looked away from his aide and wife, staring at an abstract painting by some forgotten artist that was hanging on the wall.

"Excellency…"

"I heard you."

It was a feeble voice—one of which no inscription existed on the pillar of Frederica's outstanding memory.

"That report didn't leave any room for corrections, did it?"

"The transmissions we've picked up are all saying the same thing."

After a long silence, Yang murmured, "I see." The life seemed to have drained out of Yang, giving the impression of a young scholar changed into a sculpture of a young scholar. Suddenly, the fragrance of brandy was strong in Frederica's nostrils, and she gasped. Yang had crushed in his palm the paper cup he'd been holding, drenching one hand in steaming hot tea. Frederica took the cup from her husband, and wiped his scalded hand with her handkerchief. From a drawer in his desk, she retrieved a first aid kit.

"Inform the whole fleet, Frederica. For the next seventy-two hours, Yang's Irregulars will be in mourning."

Yang gave the order, accepting Frederica's treatment as though it had nothing to do with him. His emotions had taken a critical hit, and while at first it seemed that his reason alone was in service to his vocal cords, his psyche unexpectedly reversed its vector, and his voice grew intense.

"'Brilliant admiral,' my eye! A hopeless incompetent's what I am. I knew what the commander in chief was like. That the chances of this happening weren't exactly small. Even so, I couldn't see this coming."

"Darling…"

"I should have brought him with us when we left Heinessen—even if it meant essentially kidnapping him. Isn't that right, Frederica? If I'd only done that…"

Frederica tried desperately to console her husband. If he was going to make "what Marshal Bucock was like" an issue, Bucock would have never approved of the flight from Heinessen in the first place. There was no need for Yang to hold himself responsible for his death. Wasn't feeling responsible like that actually taking little account of Bucock's own wishes and decisions?

"I know," Yang finally said. "You're right, Frederica. I'm sorry I got worked up." But the immensity of the blow was such that an easy recovery seemed unlikely.

Even in a system whose sins of despotism were many, there were always some who would lay down their lives and die with it when destruction came. The Goldenbaum Dynasty had been one example. Moreover, if the Free Planets Alliance, which had supposedly lived by its morals and ideals since the time of its founding father, Ahle Heinessen, were to be extinguished without a single martyr among its high-ranking officials, it would mean that the existence of that democratic state had been worth even less than the Goldenbaum Dynasty. The idea of human lives joining the state in the hour of its destruction was one Yang would have liked to have rejected, but he was in no state of mind to criticize Marshal Bucock's choice.

While that old man had lived, Yang had always looked up to him. He felt the same way now, and in the future was likely to feel even more so.

Thoughts of Bucock's age were no consolation whatsoever. Though he had crossed into advanced age, medically speaking, he had still been more than fifteen years shy of reaching the average life expectancy. Still, it did come as some slight consolation that no one could say his life hadn't been fulfilling. Yang's subordinates came to share his mind on that matter as well.

Von Schönkopf toasted the old man, celebrating his life and wishing him a joyful hereafter. Soon Soul opened up his tear ducts and ran them at full capacity for the first time in fifteen years. Merkatz solemnly straightened his uniform collar. Murai turned toward the distant world of Heinessen and saluted. Half of that gesture had been for Chung Wu-cheng, who had given his life for Bucock. Attenborough joined Murai in so doing, and afterward went to join von Schönkopf.

As for Julian, he felt Yang's grief even more keenly than his own. This brought with it a multiplier effect, and he sank into a world devoid of color.

Even Olivier Poplin, oft praised as a veritable reservoir of good cheer, had become noticeably less talkative. His face had not been made for sullen expressions, but now a winter wind was blowing against it, and the young man who described himself as "a half-breed child of inconstancy and indiscretion"—of whom the likes of Dusty Attenborough said, "If trouble's afoot, he's sure to stick his nose in it, and if it's not, he's out sowing the seeds himself"—was left silently wandering around a fortress that for a time had lost its lively energy.

Alex Caselnes was concerned about everyone's uncharacteristic depression. Once he himself had gotten over the worst of his own disappointment, he turned to his wife, Hortense, shaking his head. "Laziness and sunny dispositions are about all this bunch has going for it. We can't have them down in the dumps like this."

Hortense was just then giving the old oven in their officer's quarters—which had not seen use during the yearlong interval that Iserlohn had been occupied by the empire—a reason for living in its old age.

"Well, not all of them have nerves made of steel cable like you do," she said. "Marshal Bucock was a good man. Everyone's reactions are perfectly proper."

"I'm speaking out of concern for them. Gloom and doom just don't suit those guys at all."

Caselnes was excluding himself from his own criticism. He was also beyond any doubt a member of the Yang Fleet; he simply thought that he alone had his act together.

"You should stick to just worrying about supplies and accounting. Do you think they would've ever defied the government, defied the empire, and started a revolutionary war if they were the type to let something like this devastate them for good? Being a yes-man to the authorities is the easiest way to live, but they consciously volunteered to take on hardship. And that's also why the mood around them is always so festive."

"That's absolutely true, those morons."

"Without even one exception, you know. Whose fault do you think it is that I missed out on being the wife of the general manager of rear services?"

Hortense Caselnes humphed at him, flustering the man who had punted the chair of general manager of rear services.

"You weren't *against* what I did, though! When I got home after throwing down that resignation letter, you had our suitcases packed already…"

"Of course I did," she said, showing no sign of backing down. "If you were the kind of man who'd abandon a friend to protect your position, I'd have divorced you ages ago. As a woman, I'd be ashamed if I had to tell my children that the man I was married to was somebody who only made superficial friendships."

Caselnes's word balloons were getting popped inside his mouth. Hortense transferred a splendidly roasted cream chicken pie from the oven to the table.

"Well, dear, call the Yangs over, would you? The living still have to eat properly—and enjoy it for the departed's sake as well."

Olivier Poplin probably rediscovered as early as Caselnes had that a festival mood was essential to the public square that was the Yang Fleet. Even he, who on the day that the tragic news was received had been as formal and respectful as anyone else, had stripped off his mental sackcloth by the second day after, and now seemed determined to work toward the psychological rebuilding of the Yang Fleet. For that reason, he had caused a large amount of whiskey to emigrate to coffee cups in an effort to cheer everyone up. Because they were in mourning, they couldn't openly drink alcohol.

"Still, I wonder if even our esteemed marshal ever gets that depressed?" Bernhard von Schneider pointedly asked. Von Schneider was not a heartless man, but he had hardly even met Bucock, and had thus required no assistance from Poplin in recovering from the blow. "It seems you all think of your own commander as some kind of rare beast, but…"

Poplin didn't answer directly.

"Marshal Bucock was an amazing old man," he said. "Totally wasted on the FPA military. It's a shame I have to use the past tense, now. But even if mourning him is only natural, it's about time we started thinking about the real way to console the dead."

"By which you mean?"

"Fighting the Imperial Navy, and winning."

"I think it's for the best if you don't breeze right past 'how' on your way to the results…"

"The 'how' is what our esteemed marshal will come up with. It's the only thing he's good for."

In Poplin's disparaging words, von Schneider sensed a variety of things at work in Poplin's mind—pride, respect, teasing, and so on.

"Still, Commander von Schneider, you're not too bright either, now that I think about it. If you'd stayed in the Imperial Navy, you could've really moved up in the world working for Kaiser Reinhard."

Von Schneider just gave a curt laugh, and did not answer the ever-provocative Poplin's question. If he had had brothers or sisters, they might have convinced him to serve the brilliant young kaiser and make the most of his talents and skills, but as for himself, he intended to follow the defeated Admiral Merkatz to the very end. Kaiser Reinhard had numerous loyal vassals serving him. So why shouldn't Merkatz at the very least have him?

II

Even after the Baalat Treaty was finalized in April of SE 799, the violent currents of history still were not calmed. In August of the same year, Yang Wen-li rebelled against his own government's stratagem and fled the capital. In the same month, the Church of Terra's headquarters on Earth was destroyed by Admiral Wahlen of the Imperial Navy. The angry swells and surges continued to roll forward without end.

Still, at the beginning of SE 800, the underground streams seemed to boil to the surface all at once, engulfing everything. It may be that the strange sense of stillness associated with the four prior months—despite their chain of innumerable, small-scale bursts of will and action—was due to the immensity of the heat and light given off by the eruptions that bookended that period. To those who look no deeper than the surfaces of events, it may seem that Reinhard von Lohengramm wasted a number of days between departing Planet Phezzan and arriving at the alliance capital of Heinessen. They might also wonder what Yang Wen-li was doing between his escape from Heinessen and his recapture of Iserlohn Fortress, and afterward as well.

Such people probably think that all the kaiser needed to do was give the order, and a massive force of ten million would mobilize on the same day, with no need to organize fleets or set up supply lines; they likely have no idea how much time it takes to develop the strategic plan needed to prepare an environment suited to executing one's tactics on the battlefield. Because Reinhard's imperial forces were large in scale and Yang Wen-li's revolutionary forces were small, both had problems with establishing their respective supply networks. In the Imperial Navy's case, it was oddly difficult to move such vast amounts of goods across the long supply route from Phezzan. For reasons of both honor and political strategy, plundering was strictly forbidden. In the case of Yang Wen-li, El Facil's production capacity and Iserlohn's stockpiles were sufficient for the time being to keep his forces supplied, but in order to resist the Imperial Navy, he had no choice but to increase the size of his force, and as the number of soldiers grew, the supply effort was bound to exceed capacity. Foreseeing a grave choice between two mutually exclusive options, even Alex Caselnes had had no trouble finding things to give him headaches.

Yang Wen-li was in a difficult position, in which it was difficult to make his strategic plan coexist with the tactical conditions needed to carry it out—it was Kaiser Reinhard's chief secretary, Fräulein Hildegard "Hilda" von Mariendorf, who had deduced that, though in fact political tasks were also piling up on Yang at that time. In addition, he once again found himself struggling to stay a mere specialist in the revolutionary government's combat division, and not be made supreme leader of the revolutionary movement itself.

From the viewpoint of Walter von Schönkopf, Yang's way of doing things seemed so roundabout that he felt like clucking his tongue a dozen times.

"Extraordinary times call for extraordinary measures" summed up his feelings; for the past three years he'd constantly tried to talk Yang into seizing power.

Julian once said, "While he lectured others about convictions being harmful and useless, he held to his own pretty stubbornly. His words and his actions didn't really align." Though Julian was also pretty impressed by von Schönkopf's persistence; it had been three years, and the man still hadn't given up.

When Walter von Schönkopf received the news of Bucock's passing, he thought, *This is why you should have put an end to Reinhard von Lohengramm when you had the chance*, although he did not let that thought clear his tongue. There was likely some degree of error among others' evaluations of von Schönkopf, but the man himself understood that there was a time and a place for his sharp tongue.

What he did say to Julian was his only mention of a plan that had missed its chance to come to fruition:

"If Old Man Bucock were still alive, I could've also seen me recommending him to head up the new administration, with your guardian running military affairs. No use talking about it now, though…"

To Julian, as well, this was a fresh and attractive idea. Though it was hard to imagine the elderly, now-departed marshal agreeing to take the top position.

Eventually, von Schönkopf himself had to face a problem of his own. With an attitude that might best be called "resolute," Corporal Katerose Karin von Kreutzer requested a meeting with her father. In whatever form it might take, she was trying to put an end to the awkwardness that had resulted from avoiding contact these past six months.

•   •   •
•
•   •

When Karin appeared in von Schönkopf's office, she was battle ready, wearing two or three layers of invisible armor. Her salute was stiff, her expression tense, and her bearing solemn. None of these qualities suited a young girl who was to turn sixteen this year, von Schönkopf inwardly appraised.

"Vice Admiral von Schönkopf, I volunteered to fight at the time of the operation to retake Iserlohn Fortress, but Your Excellency, serving as commander of combat operations, removed my name from the roster. This is difficult to accept, and I want to hear the reason."

It was obvious that Karin was reading from an invisible script she had prepared ahead of time. A somewhat ironic smile formed around von Schönkopf's mouth; it had just occurred to him how much his colleague Attenborough would like to be here for this, even if he had to pay admission. The girl's demands for an explanation weren't worth worrying about, though.

"I wanted the operation to come off perfectly," he said, "so I didn't want to include anyone—not just you—who was inexperienced in hand-to-hand combat. That's all it was. What's so strange about that?"

Karin was at a loss to answer. She was still shortsighted in a number of ways, and hadn't thought about how others with no experience in hand-to-hand combat had been treated.

After a moment, von Schönkopf said, "Well, that's my excuse. The truth of the matter is that I didn't want to see a pretty young girl brandishing a tomahawk."

The attitude von Schönkopf copped as he appended that comment was exactly the attitude Karin had been thinking all this time that she didn't want to see.

That of a frivolous, unfaithful womanizer.

She steeled herself, and spoke: "Is that how you were when you seduced my mother, too?"

It was she herself who was the more surprised at her sharply rising tone; her father literally did not raise an eyebrow. He looked up again at the girl standing ramrod straight in front of his desk, and said, "So asking me that is the real point of this meeting?"

His voice, which seemed to be holding back a rebuke, was all the more unnerving to her.

"I'm disappointed. If you want to hold me accountable to my responsibilities as a father, you should say so up front. There's no need to go finding fault with my command decisions."

Karin turned red in the face. The fever that had broken out in her heart had spread to her body, and the cells on her cheeks were burning up.

"You're right, sir. I spoke out of turn. So let me ask it again this way: Did you love my mother, Rosalind Elizabeth von Kreutzer?"

"Life's too short to sleep with women you don't love."

"Is that all you have to say?"

"Life's probably too short to sleep with men you don't love, too."

Karin snapped to attention with such energy that it was a wonder her joints didn't pop.

"Your Excellency, I'm grateful to you for giving me life. But for raising me, I owe you nothing, and can think of no reason why I should respect you. I'm speaking clearly, in accordance with your advice."

Von Schönkopf and Karin stared straight at one another, and in the end it was her father who looked away first. The curtains of his identity as a public official hung over his face, but through their narrow gaps, the moonlight of embarrassment and a bitter smile were slipping through. He had not broken eye contact first because he had flinched, but because he didn't acknowledge the need to construct a confusing labyrinth between themselves through conversation. Karin somehow understood this, though not through reason. She gave a perfect salute, which meant only that she'd been hijacked by formalities, turned around, and, suppressing competing impulses to both turn back around and take off running, she left her father's office.

III

Walter von Schönkopf and Olivier Poplin were both leading members of the Yang Fleet's "Enemies of Conscience and Family Morality." If they were to be asked which of them was worse, both would have likely pointed at the other without hesitation. When at the end of SE 799 the two heroes met again for the first time in six months, Poplin greeted von Schönkopf, saying, "Well now, if it isn't my senior officer of ill repute! There is no greater joy for this humble officer than to see a brother-in-arms still so stubbornly alive and well."

In answer, von Schönkopf said, "Glad you're back, Commander Poplin. When you're not around, my taste in women is not nearly as mature."

The ace pilot, having no intention of being reduced to a foil for von Schönkopf, stared his opponent down from across his office desk, feeling rather confident. The glint in his eye brazenly declared, *I may sow the seeds, but I'm not so careless as to let 'em sprout.*

"Anyway," Poplin said at last, "I have a passing familiarity with the *young lady's* situation, if you'll pardon my saying so."

The special emphasis Poplin placed on the words "young lady" was of course unadulterated sarcasm, but as surely as the outer walls of Iserlohn Fortress defended its interior, so von Schönkopf's expression protected his own inner self. Poplin came around to his side, and said, "Karin's a good girl—nothing at all like her old man. Though not a good woman just yet…"

"Well, I think she's a good girl myself. In any case, she never cost me a dinar in child support."

"Compensation for mental anguish might start getting figured in from here on out, though. I'd brace myself."

Once Poplin was finished raining his blades of cutting sarcasm upon von Schönkopf, though, his face and tone grew more formal.

"Vice Admiral von Schönkopf, if I could get a little serious here, that young girl has too much emotion to handle by herself, and she doesn't know how to express it appropriately, either. Personally, I think somebody older than me needs to show her the way forward. I'm sorry if I'm overstepping my bounds."

Von Schönkopf stared at his colleague, seven years his junior, with an inscrutable gaze. When he finally spoke, it was with a ripple of laughter. "I'm sorry," he said. "It's just that this year really is one to commemorate. As far as I'm aware, that was the first conscientious thing you've ever said."

"I guess so. It'll also be the first year your daughter doesn't bear her father's sins."

For anyone else, that line might have been a finishing blow, but von Schönkopf gave only a calm nod of agreement, to which he impudently appended: "That's certainly true. And if I can add one thing, see to it you don't go soft on her just because she's my daughter."

"Tough paternal love, eh? Will do." The young ace pilot had to admit he'd been put a bit on the defensive. If von Schönkopf could do that even to the great Olivier Poplin, then it was no wonder a greenhorn like Karin had gone down in defeat.

Von Schönkopf said one last thing to Poplin as he was leaving. "It looks like this matter is causing a lot of trouble for you, but there is one thing I'd like to correct."

"What's that?"

"I hear you're going around calling me a middle-aged delinquent. But I'm not middle-aged just yet."

Half an hour later, Poplin's elegant figure appeared before Karin. She was in the military port's observation zone, staring off at the groups of warships with seemingly nothing to do, but she saluted as soon as she spotted the young officer. Several soldiers sitting with her got up and left. Were they deferring to him? Most likely, it was deference grounded in a very specific prejudice. Karin didn't notice, and Poplin didn't care.

"How'd it go? What did you think about meeting your father? You look let down."

"No, not especially. I knew what kind of man he is, so at this point there's no way I'd be disappointed."

"Gotcha." A pensive light shimmered in the young ace's green eyes. "But if I can say one thing, Karin—as far as I know, when it comes to folks in this unit who are blessed with a stable family life, Miss Charlotte Phyllis of the Caselnes family is about it. Everybody else grew up in more or less bad environments."

Meaninglessly, he took his black beret in hand.

"Take Julian Mintz. Were his folks alive and well, he wouldn't have had to grow up in the home of a social misfit like Yang Wen-li. I can't really say he's had it all that much better than you."

"Commander?"

"Yeah?"

"Why are you bringing up Sublieutenant Mintz at a time like this?"

"Yeah, Walter von Schönkopf would've made a better example."

Karin said nothing, waiting for him to continue.

"He was a very young child when his family defected from the empire, and his situation wasn't easy, either—"

Poplin broke off, interrupting his own speech. He seemed to have realized how incredibly absurd it was for him to be pleading von Schönkopf's case.

"At any rate, Karin," he said a moment later, "it runs counter to the spirit of our fleet to make merchandise out of misfortune, and it doesn't look good on you, either. Even if there's someone you can't stand, it's not like they'll be alive forever…"

Breaking off again, Poplin had seemed to have unexpectedly remembered his old war buddy, who had departed the world they used to share.

"Ivan Konev, that lousy sonuva—he went and stabbed me in the back. Made me think he wouldn't die even though they killed him."

Unconsciously, Karin turned her eyes back to Poplin's face, but the blinds were pulled down over the young ace's expression, and her powers of insight still weren't enough to penetrate them. Carefully correcting the angle of his black beret, Poplin rose to his feet.

"Assuming things go well, that middle-aged delinquent is gonna die about twenty years before you do. It doesn't mean anything to make up with a headstone."

Even as flattery, Poplin's tone at the moment he said "middle-aged" could not have been called genuine.

Poplin was sitting in the officers' club, planning a training regimen for after the end of the mourning period, when Julian came by and sat down at the same table. Of the alcohol vapor rising from his coffee cup, he said nothing, but as he knew about Poplin's round of visits with the father and daughter, he said, "You must be worn out from all the PTA conferences."

Poplin lightly poked at the grinning Julian's flaxen hair. Though it looked like Julian, too, had somehow recovered from his mental funk, the fighting ace could tell that he was probably still fighting to get over it.

"You've gotten as awful as Ivan Konev. At this rate, you'll evolve to von Schönkopf class before long. What are we gonna do with you?"

"Sorry."

"Forget about it—as long as you stay honest, there's still hope for you."

"Well? Do you have some kind of prescription for bringing peace to the von Schönkopf family?"

"A general pattern, at least: daughter's life is put in danger, father rescues her personally, daughter opens her heart to father…"

"That certainly is a pattern."

"Scriptwriters for solivision dramas have been using the same pattern for centuries now, and they're not the least bit embarrassed. Fundamentally, the human heart hasn't changed since the Stone Age."

"So you'd have still been an infamous womanizer even if you'd been born in the Stone Age, Commander?"

While Poplin did have a comeback for that, Julian's nervous functions, including those of his auditory nerves, had shifted in another direction.

Julian had remembered hair the color of lightly brewed tea, violet-blue eyes, a face whose expressions overflowed provocatively with energy and life. To a young man, that was no unpleasant thing. Up until now, no girls his age or younger had ever caused this kind of emotional response in him.

However, Julian was still not of a mind to color in the sketch he had made in his heart. Just half a year ago, he had looked on with some pain as Frederica Greenhill had married Yang; it felt superficial to him to just immediately pour his feelings into a new vessel. And to begin with, he wasn't even confident Karin liked him.

IV

Internal emotion notwithstanding, at the end of the three-day mourning period, Yang Wen-li became once again capable of sitting up straight and keeping his head up while walking. As Caselnes asked, "Could this mean that it's finally dawned on him that he's the one standing at the top?"

In fact, Yang had not been spending all of that time lamenting the beauty of a sunset's afterglow. A new sun, even more powerful and intense, was rising on the opposite horizon, and he couldn't afford to stand idly by waiting for its blistering heat to arrive. Now that the firm embankment that was Marshal Bucock had collapsed, Kaiser Reinhard's conquering spirit had become a blazing, violent swell that had swallowed the whole alliance, and dissolved the old system.

At the same time that the mourning ended, Yang also removed the bandage from his left hand. Electron therapy had energized the cells of his damaged skin, and Yang's brain cells, as if inspired by this process, had also leapt out of their dark bedroom. Frederica was glad to see that Yang had recovered his powers of intelligent activity, and felt as if Marshal Bucock himself had grabbed him by the collar and dragged him up from his basement of confusion.

Between strategic planning, organizing units, and keeping in touch with El Facil, Yang was extremely busy, but even so, he never sacrificed the time he spent drinking tea. It was what made Yang Yang.

One day, with the aroma of Shillong leaves against his chin, Yang said to his wife: "Frederica, I'm worried. It just hit me that if opportunists in the military try to curry favor with the empire, Chairman Lebello could end up being assassinated."

Frederica was speechless. Her hazel eyes reflected her husband's figure, both his hands playing with his doffed black beret.

"They wouldn't really go that far, would they?"

Frederica was not trying to argue, but to draw a detailed explanation out of her husband. Yang's hands stopped messing around with the beret.

"Chairman Lebello showed them how to do it himself, didn't he? Naturally, he had his own justifications, and it wasn't like he was planning on securing peace for just himself. Still, there are sure to be some people who'll just copy the outward appearance."

Kaiser Reinhard was magnanimous with those who surrendered or were defeated, but if that generosity were mistakenly thought unconditional, people would be lining up to empty their pockets of shame and self-respect, to prepare welcoming gifts, and to try to ingratiate themselves.

Several days went by, and a report arrived from Captain Bagdash of conditions in the capital. Due to the danger of eavesdropping, he had forgone electronic transmissions, instead mobilizing an intelligence-gathering vessel that had departed El Facil and headed toward Heinessen.

"Former Free Planets Alliance head of state João Lebello has been assassinated by elements within the military. The rebel group offered to surrender to imperial forces, and the Imperial Navy successfully occupied Heinessen without resistance."

On receiving that news, Yang made a further prediction to his wife and Julian.

"And with that, those assassins have just signed their own execution orders. There's no way Kaiser Reinhard is going to tolerate an act as brazenly shameless as that."

Two or three days later, there came another report, to the effect that Lebello's assassins had all been executed by firing squad. Yang, however, no longer showed any concern. This was likely because the ideals of the founding father, Ahle Heinessen, had grown weak, and were just about to die. That much had become clear at the time he had fled Heinessen. Also, during the shock he'd experienced at the news of Marshal Bucock's death, he had also come to terms with his emotions regarding the death of the state known as the Free Planets Alliance. Additionally, there were any number of more pressing tasks to attend to.

"I'm going to recognize the right of Kaiser Reinhard and the Lohengramm Dynasty to rule over all the universe. And based on that, we're going to secure for one star system the right to self-governance in its internal affairs. That's how we'll keep democratic republican government alive, and prepare for its future rebirth."

When Yang Wen-li explained that basic plan, the eyes of Dr. Romsky, the head of El Facil's independent government, didn't exactly light up with excitement.

"You mean compromise with the kaiser's autocracy? I can't believe those are really the words of democracy's fighting champion, Yang Wen-li."

"The coexistence of diverse political values is the essence of democracy. Wouldn't you agree?"

Inside, Yang just wanted to sigh at the absurdity of a soldier lecturing a politician about democracy. They were able to converse like this because the Yang Fleet had complete control of the FTL net between Iserlohn and El Facil—not that that guaranteed any fruitful discussions.

Dr. Romsky was working energetically as prime minister of the independent government. It was certain that this revolutionary politician had both a strong conscience and sense of responsibility, but when Walter von Schönkopf had acidly opined, "No matter how high up the ball may go, you still don't score on a foul," Yang had been left with little choice but to nod in agreement. With Heinessen under the empire's complete control and the alliance's final head of state having met an unexpected demise, Romsky's shoes had developed an anxious set of wings. He summoned Yang and spoke emphatically of the danger that the Imperial Navy would invade El Facil.

Yang's tone of voice had included a dash of malicious spice as he said, "I'm sure you've thought ahead and given plenty of consideration to such a scenario."

It looked like they were in a panic now that Kaiser Reinhard's all-out offensive was fast approaching; it took a lot of nerve to be able to shout about "independent government" and "counterrevolution" now. On the other hand, they nonetheless showed reluctance when it came to tolerating Reinhard's rule. They wanted to have their ideals fulfilled without actually facing any danger.

In essence, dreams of Yang defeating Reinhard in battle and of a democratic state uniting the universe were ingredients that they were now trying to get Yang to cook. They themselves were waiting with knife and fork in hand at a table with an embroidered tablecloth. But democracy was not some VIP staying in an expensive hotel called Politics. First, you had to build the log cabin and start the fire yourself.

"When you think about it," said Dr. Romsky, "everything would've gone smoothly if you had destroyed Kaiser Reinhard in the Vermillion War. After all, the alliance government was doomed in any case. If you'd done that, we would have at least avoided the greatest crisis we're facing now. It's a shame you let that moment pass."

That remark hacked Yang off, but he didn't answer him. Even under a thick coating of jocular makeup, it was clear what the unadorned face of Dr. Romsky's comment looked like. Seeing Yang's expression, Romsky unnecessarily said, "I'm kidding!" which only made Yang feel more uncomfortable. But when he shared the anecdote and saw discomfort in the face of an acquaintance as well, Romsky mentioned to him, "Marshal

Yang has less of a sense of humor than I had expected." Yang's mental state could be summed up by the phrase *I've had it with you people!* but it was already too late to reeducate Romsky.

"Yang Wen-li abandoned Lebello of the alliance government and in his place chose Romsky, of El Facil's independent government. Ultimately, we must conclude that Yang was a terrible judge of character."

This verdict, pronounced by some scholars in future generations, was probably lacking in fairness. Yang had very nearly been purged by Lebello; he had never of his own accord cast him by the wayside. To satisfy the minimum requirements of his political thinking and strategic plan, he'd had no choice but to turn to the independent government of El Facil; it wasn't as if he had sworn allegiance to Romsky personally. If Yang had wanted to lead as easy and relaxing a life as he claimed, then he would have likely become a vassal of Reinhard von Lohengramm's, based on the sort of "judge of character" he was. And maybe that decision could have contributed not only to peace in Yang's personal life, but to peace in the universe at large—albeit under a dictatorship, of course. For as long as he lived, Yang would never be free of that deep-seated contradiction and his own self-doubt.

∪

Regarding the matter of that optical disc that Julian Mintz and Olivier Poplin had brought back from Earth, Yang had shoved it back into the innermost reaches of his nest of memories and put a lid on top of it for a time. No sooner had Iserlohn Fortress been successfully retaken than reports of Marshal Bucock's and Lebello's deaths had arrived in swift succession. The chance to inspect it had been lost. In any case, the Church of Terra's headquarters had been destroyed by Admiral Wahlen of the Imperial Navy, and this had become one more reason for the loss of urgency with regard to gathering information about the Church of Terra.

In extreme terms, it can't be denied either that Yang had simply been satisfied with Julian and Poplin's safe return. Nevertheless, a voice of opposition from his mind's hinterlands eventually got through to the center, and Yang took some time out of his busy schedule to examine the optical disc. Seven people—Frederica, von Schönkopf, Julian, Poplin, Boris Konev, Machungo, and Murai—joined in. And when they had learned just a little, they looked at one another with utterly shocked expressions on their faces. What was recorded there was the record of a relationship between the Phezzan Dominion and the Church of Terra going back a full century.

"So what this means is, 'heads' is Phezzan, and 'tails' is the Church of Terra?"

"If that's the case, if we join hands with Phezzan's merchants, we'll be dancing cheek to cheek with that Terraist lot."

Even if Poplin's gaze lacked venom, there were still needles in it as it grazed the face of Boris Konev, wordlessly demanding an explanation.

"You've gotta be joking," Konev said. "I didn't know anything about this. If I have any relationship at all with the Church of Terra, ferrying pilgrims to Earth was the extent of it."

Boris Konev's insistence was only natural; inside the church's headquarters, he himself had worked with Julian and even exchanged gunfire with the fanatics. To suggest he was in league with the Church of Terra just because they lurked in the shadows of Phezzan would be what they call "a bridge too far."

Yang didn't believe that Boris Konev was secretly in league with the Church of Terra. But what about Phezzan's supreme leadership, going back generations? What about the "Black Fox of Phezzan"—Adrian Rubinsky—who was presently believed to be missing? What had he been scheming up until now, and what schemes did he intend to set in motion going forward?

Rubbing his slightly pointed chin, von Schönkopf said, "An obsession that's spanned nine centuries, eh? That is pretty amazing. Still, with things the way they are, this isn't something we can ignore. Have the Terraists really been wiped out? Is their 'Grand Bishop' or whatever he's called confirmed dead?"

On hearing those questions, even the fearless Olivier Poplin frowned and fell silent. It wasn't as if he had actually seen the Grand Bishop's corpse himself; confirming that would have required going back to Earth and digging up tens of billions of tons of rock and dirt.

"All right, send me to Phezzan," said Konev. "Either way, I still have to make contact with the independent traders there. While I'm at it, I'd like to see what I can dig up about that black fox Rubinsky."

"You can't go there, and not come back, Captain Konev." Poplin's tone of voice was controlled, but that did nothing to alleviate Boris Konev's ire when the words themselves were that extreme. For a time, a pair of linguistic cyclones clashed, until at last Yang approved Boris Konev's trip to Phezzan and ended the meeting. For his part, Yang could not feel very positive about this. If Phezzan and the Church of Terra had an abnormally close relationship, blithely joining forces with them might result in an ugly coalition of speculators and fanatics eating the substance of their democracy from the inside out. Jumping into the same boat as Phezzan was unlikely to end with a mere request for economic backing. One of the conditions necessary for Yang's strategy was going to have to undergo some serious revision, it seemed.

The two Yangs and Julian remained in Yang's office. For a while, the three of them were breathing in the fumes left by the optical disc's content and the dregs of heated discussion, but at last Yang sat up straight on the couch, and said, "Julian?"

"Yes?"

"Ultimately, conspiracies and terrorism can't make the flow of history run backward. They can make it stagnate, however. We can't allow the Church of Terra or Adrian Rubinsky to do that."

Julian nodded.

"Especially in the Church of Terra's case, their only goal is to satisfy the ego of a selfish planet. It's not to restore the authority of Planet Earth—it's to justify the past, and drown themselves in the sweet nectar of privilege."

Had the Church of Terra really been destroyed? If holdouts still remained, what were they plotting? Yang wanted to know.

Even so, Yang had to admit he had no time to look for those answers. First of all, Kaiser Reinhard was closing in right before his eyes; that was by far the greater menace. Furthermore, Reinhard was not a threat because of a bad reactionary agenda like the Church of Terra's; he was a threat because he was using a system other than democracy to reform his generation, and succeeding. *Honestly, there's no system more efficient than a dictatorship when you set out to advance reforms. Don't the people always say so, when they're sick of democracy's roundabout system?*

"Give great authority to a great politician, and advance reform!" It's paradoxical, but haven't the people always been looking for a dictator?

And now, are they not on the verge of receiving a dictator of the very best kind? Reinhard von Lohengramm—a hero worthy of their respect and adoration. Compared to the gleam of that golden idol, is democracy nothing more than an idol of faded bronze?

No, that's wrong. Flustered, Yang shook his head back and forth, swinging around his unruly black hair.

"Julian, we're soldiers. And republics and democracies are often grown out of the barrels of guns. But while military power might give birth to democratic government, it can't get away with being proud of that accomplishment. That isn't unfair. That's because the essence of democracy is in the self-restraint of those who hold power. Democracy is the self-restraint of the powerful, codified in law and systematized in its institutions. And if the military doesn't restrain itself, there's no reason anyone else has to, either."

Yang's black eyes burned with mounting passion. If no one else, he wanted Julian to understand this.

"We ourselves fight for a political system that fundamentally rejects what we are. That contradictory structure is something a democracy's military just has to live with. The most that the military should demand from the government is paid leave and a pension. In other words, their rights as workers. Never anything more than that."

Julian reflexively smiled at the word "pension," but Yang hadn't really said that to appeal to his sense of humor. Julian suppressed his smile in about two blinks of the eye, overcorrected and made his expression too serious, and then finally gave voice to something he had been thinking about for a long time.

"But I wanted you to act on your own feelings, and your own desires."

"Julian!"

"And I know I deserve to get dressed down for that, but it really is how I feel."

It's an ironic situation, Julian thought, *when someone with such immense talent can act with greater freedom in a dictatorship than in a democracy.* If Reinhard and Yang's circumstances had been reversed…If Reinhard had been a harmful man of ambition in a democratic government, he might have become the wicked second coming of Rudolf the Great. And it might have been Yang who had ended up with a golden crown.

Julian finished giving voice to these thoughts, and Yang said, "Julian, that's one incredibly bold supposition."

"I know it is, but still…"

"It's not like I've completely eliminated my personal feelings. When we fought at Vermillion, Julian, I *didn't want to kill* Reinhard von Lohengramm. I say that in all seriousness."

Even without Yang pressing the point, Julian understood that.

"Even if his character isn't flawless, he's still the most brilliant mind to appear in four or five centuries of history—I could feel nothing but terror at the thought of my own two hands destroying a man like that. Maybe I used the government's order as an excuse to avoid doing it. Maybe it was loyalty to the government or to myself…*maybe*. But to all those soldiers who died in battle, it may have been an unforgivable breach of faith. There was no reason for them to die for the sake of saving the ruling authorities, or for my sentimentality."

Yang laughed. It was a laugh that seemed to say that all he *could* do was laugh, and whenever Julian saw it, he felt keenly aware of the powerlessness of words, and could do nothing but fall silent.

"I'm always like this. Busy with stuff that never goes anywhere. Well, there's not much time. How about we talk about something more positive?"

Before that, though, it seemed that a little lubricant was necessary. For the first time in what seemed like ages, Julian unveiled his masterful skill, and the fragrance of Arushan tea stained every current in the air of the room.

Frederica reached for the console, and after her white fingers danced across it, a star chart appeared on the screen. After enlarging it two or three times, it displayed the Liberation Corridor connecting Iserlohn and El Facil.

"We've got two strongholds," Yang said. "Iserlohn and El Facil. From the Imperial Navy's standpoint, when there are multiple enemy bases, the obvious tactic is to cut them off from one another. I think the kaiser's personal fleet will most likely target the Iserlohn Corridor in conjunction with a reserve unit launching from imperial space…"

"When do you think that will be?"

"Hmmm…not too far off, I'd say. The kaiser will probably think more of the minuses of taking his time than the pluses."

Yang believed that, above all, that golden-haired youth could not countenance anyone other than himself making history. Taking his time meant giving others the chance to scheme and maneuver. Now that he had dissolved the Free Planets Alliance in fact as well as in name, he would come to wipe out Yang's group with blazing cannons and an enormous, muddy river of warships. Space was about to be flooded by an angry wave of conquering spirit surpassing even that of Rudolf von Goldenbaum long ago.

In the face of that, Yang had to act as a breakwater, using what little strength he possessed, for the sake of a day when the angry swells would depart and the tide receded. He had no idea when that day would come. It would likely be in an age when Yang still existed only in records and recordings.

And so even as he hardened his determination like some "knight of democracy," Yang would also carelessly relativize the position of his opponent. The one represented the shortest road to peace and unity; the other the long road toward mainline democratic government. If a single, supreme God existed in this universe, of which would he approve, when both waged bloody war?

CHAPTER 9:
ON THE EVE OF THE FESTIVAL

I

IN FEBRUARY OF SE 800, and NIC 2, a report was sent from Planet Phezzan to the imperial headquarters on Heinessen which would later become known as the "letter that halted twenty million boots." Had that report's content become public knowledge prior to that time, however, it would surely have been laughed off as a tasteless joke and forgotten. It was little wonder that Fräulein Hildegard "Hilda" von Mariendorf, who received the report first, was left speechless for several seconds, and hesitated to report it to the kaiser.

"There are troubling signs surrounding von Reuentahl," it said.

It would not have come as such a shock to Hilda if Marshal von Oberstein, the minister of military affairs, and Chief Lang, of the Ministry of Domestic Affairs' Domestic Safety Security Bureau, had been the only signatories. This report, however, had come from Minister of Justice Bruckdorf. A man by the name of Odets had begun loudly spreading rumors after arriving on Phezzan. Though he claimed to be an envoy from the Free Planets' government, he had not even met with the kaiser. According to him, Marshal von Reuentahl intended to rebel. Chief Lang of the Ministry of Domestic Affairs' Domestic Safety Security Bureau had jumped on that immediately.

Odets had bet the fate of his nation on the tip of his tongue. Was he now a broken man, ready to die, just trying to spread confusion in the empire? Was he trying to recover—with rather extreme methodology—the confidence he'd had in his eloquence, lost when Mittermeier had brushed him off? Did he want to cause a societal uproar, and did he not care what happened to him? Was he counting on the effectiveness of eloquence coupled with fiction? Did he have psychological tendencies associated with delusions of grandeur? At the time, no one could say for sure. In any case, though, it was safe to say that he had extraordinary creativity and passion. Not even the sharp wit and logic of Kaiser Reinhard or the bravery and cunning of von Reuentahl and Mittermeier could have dreamed that this flippant chatterer could ever do them harm in such a manner. No human being was almighty. Thoughts, in particular, were subject to the restraining influence of temperament. Not even Mittermeier, who had met Odets in person, could remember the names of such small men, so it was certain that neither Reinhard, who had turned him away at the door, nor von Reuentahl, who had been there at his side, had given him even a corner seat in the halls of their memories.

Bruckdorf, the Galactic Empire's minister of justice, was just past forty—a lawyer in early middle age, with an intricate mind and an impartial political stance. That was why he had been chosen by Reinhard while still a lowly public prosecutor, and he was extremely faithful to both his kaiser and his position. At the same time, he was furnished with the ambition and aspiration to be expected of one who had become the first minister of justice in a new dynasty. His weaning foods he had seasoned with ethics and awareness of the public order. As he had grown to adulthood, knowledge of the law had been his wine and clerking for judges his food. It was certainly true that on a personal level he had never thought well of Oskar von Reuentahl's womanizing; nevertheless, his participation in von Reuentahl's impeachment did not arise from any personal animus.

He was, for his part, feeling a need to enforce discipline on high-ranking government officials—certainly not loosely, and of course just strictly enough—and furthermore wanted to establish an advantageous position for the Ministry of Justice in relation to the military. The Lohengramm Dynasty had been under a military kaiser from the beginning, and had a strong tendency toward military dictatorship. That may have been permissible at the time of its founding, but unless the law, the bureaucracy, and the military could all reach a state of equilibrium, there was no way the empire could develop as a healthy nation. That being the case, there was sure to be some value in denouncing the military's most influential figure, Imperial Marshal von Reuentahl, and busting the noses of those military men.

Publically criticizing von Reuentahl's womanizing was in fact not an easy thing to do. Almost without exception, the women had approached him first, and at the end of their one-sided infatuations, been one-sidedly cast aside. In fact, the rumors about von Reuentahl suggested that on the inside he might well be the polar opposite of what his womanizing might seem, in isolation, to imply: a man with a very deep-seated hatred of women. In the absence of any evidence, though, the only one Bruckdorf was aware of who might know the truth was Wolfgang Mittermeier, von Reuentahl's best friend, who had long faced life and death with him. As there was no way Mittermeier was going to speak of such things, the matter had come to rest as gossip, not especially to be trusted.

In any case, Bruckdorf put no stock in rumors. What he believed in were facts that fit circumstances—only therein did evidence exist. For another thing, rather than return to the imperial capital of Odin, which was gradually being abandoned, he perhaps wanted instead to secure a place for himself on Phezzan, the future hub of the entire universe.

With the permission of Minister of Military Affairs von Oberstein and the cooperation of Chief Lang of the Domestic Safety Security Bureau,

Bruckdorf had set up a temporary office on Phezzan, and set about investigating von Reuentahl's background. Then, with an ease that left him slightly dumbfounded, he had found out about the woman named Elfriede von Kohlrausch.

"Imperial Marshal von Reuentahl is hiding a member of the late duke Lichtenlade's family at his private estate. This is clearly in defiance of His Majesty's will, and it's no overstatement to call this a form of high treason."

Lang had tried to hide his excitement, failed at it, and with eyes filled with burst capillaries, incited the minister of justice to act. Bruckdorf felt a bit uncomfortable with this; he also had a conscience as a lawyer, and so he decided to question this Elfriede woman and hear the situation from her directly. Since he had found out about her so easily, he had also wondered if this might all be a setup orchestrated by someone who had it in for von Reuentahl. However, Elfriede had answered his questions without even trying to refuse, and the result had sent Lang into a fit of ecstasy.

"That woman is pregnant with the child of Imperial Marshal von Reuentahl. She testifies that when she informed him, the marshal was congratulatory, and said that for the child's sake, he would set his sights even higher."

In his heart at least, Lang had probably danced a joyful waltz. The next thing he had done was wrest the authority to impeach von Reuentahl from the minister of justice. Von Reuentahl might be in defiance of His Majesty's will, but since he wasn't in violation of any written law, the matter was outside the purview of the Ministry of Justice—that was the reason he had given. Bruckdorf had been furious when he had learned that only his name had been used on the official report, and in the end, he realized what a stupid mistake he had made, getting his foot caught in the law's ultimate trap. The most he could do at that point was withdraw gracefully.

Ernest Mecklinger records the following:

"The man named Paul von Oberstein would frequently resort to clever tricks and merciless stratagems in order to have others purged; moreover, he neither pled his causes nor explained his reasoning, so it's little wonder that he was hated by admirals of a soldierly mind, who love clarity and straightforwardness. That said, he never plotted for personal gain, and at least from his point of view, was offering up selfless devotion to his state and lord. His managerial abilities as minister of military affairs and his devotion to his job were both at an extremely high level. The biggest problem with him was probably his suspicious nature, which had fused to the back of the allegiance he had toward his master. As Imperial Marshal Mittermeier once opined, 'Von Oberstein thinks every important vassal besides himself is a sleeper agent for some rebellion,' and that remark was very much on point. Because of his suspicion, von Oberstein was naturally unable to have faith in trustworthy colleagues, which left him using men like Lang. It's very clear that he did not think highly of Lang's character. Most likely, he thought of him as nothing more than a simple tool. If Lang had been an equal human being, von Oberstein would have mistrusted him, but it was actually because he viewed him as a simple tool that he never even doubted him. However, although that tool might not have had fangs like a wild animal or a beak like a bird of prey, it did have poisonous thorns."

And so, on February 27, Oskar von Reuentahl welcomed Senior Admiral Neidhart Müller into his officer's house. The expression on Müller's face was could not be described as cheerful. The heterochromatic imperial marshal was just finishing his breakfast, and he suggested sharing an after-breakfast coffee with his younger colleague. Although Müller was certainly intelligent enough, the young man simply couldn't act, and with one look at the clouds hanging over his sandy brown eyes, von Reuentahl guessed that whatever he had brought, it wouldn't be good news. After finishing his coffee, von Reuentahl signaled with his black and blue gaze, and Müller, hastily donning a coat of etiquette, requested that he present himself at imperial headquarters.

At nine o'clock on the same morning, Wolfgang Mittermeier went in to work at the old hotel adjoining the spaceport, now designated as the Imperial Space Armada Command Center. There he received the report of von Reuentahl's arrest, instantly driving the sandman's remaining forces from his body. Wordlessly, he turned on his heel, and started to run out his office door.

At that very instant, young Vice Admiral Bayerlein appeared suddenly in the doorway, blocking his path.

"Where are you going, Your Excellency?"

"Isn't it obvious? To see von Reuentahl, of course."

"No, Your Excellency—you mustn't do that. At a time when such facts have come to light, meeting with Marshal von Reuentahl would invite needless suspicion."

Bayerlein's expression was desperate as he tried to prevent Mittermeier's leaving. Mittermeier's eyes flashed with electrical pulses of anger.

"Don't you go getting smart with me. I don't have a single micron of dirt to hide. What's wrong with fellow court vassals—who have been friends for years—meeting with each other? Get out of my way, Bayerlein."

But now, there was someone else preventing him.

"Your Excellency, Admiral Bayerlein is right. You could be completely honest and fair, but if the lens of the people watching you is distorted, the image they see will naturally be distorted as well. Once Marshal von Reuentahl is cleared of this dishonorable suspicion, no one will accuse you, no matter when Your Excellency meets with him. Please, be prudent."

It was General Büro who said that.

Büro was older than Mittermeier, and his words of persuasion were not to be taken lightly. The electric light that had filled the gray eyes of the "Gale Wolf" now weakened, and after standing there silently for a while, he at last sat down at his desk. His sluggish movements were a far cry from his usual speed, and even his voice seemed brittle and lifeless.

"I was given the title of Imperial Marshal by His Majesty, and even a position far above my station, of commander in chief of the Imperial Space Armada. No matter how high my position, if I can't even meet my friend when I want to, doesn't that put me behind even the lowliest peasant?"

His staff officers said nothing, and only watched their respected commander.

"Back then, when His Highness was still Marquis von Lohengramm, he certainly did give orders that the men of the Lichtenlade clan be executed and the women exiled. But he never said that the women had to stay in their places of exile forever. There's no way von Reuentahl has defied His Majesty's will."

It was an extremely clumsy bit of sophistry, one that Mittermeier would never have used to defend himself.

"In any case, Marshal von Reuentahl is an influential figure in the military, and a national hero. His Highness Kaiser Reinhard would never punish him over some irresponsible rumor."

As he responded to Büro with mechanical nodding, Mittermeier was looking out in his solitude over the plains of his heart, upon which raindrops of unease were beginning to fall.

II

The sharp-angled, tightly drawn face of von Reuentahl's staff officer Hans Eduard Bergengrün was filled with concern. Bergengrün had never once lost his strong, silent demeanor while battling powerful enemies, but for the moment even he was powerless in the face of his superior's unexpected crisis.

The year before, when they had recovered Iserlohn Fortress from the alliance military, von Reuentahl had revealed to Bergengrün a part of his less-than-simplistic state of mind with regard to the kaiser. Now, in a room at the National Museum of Art—serving for the time being as imperial headquarters—Bergengrün could only endure the tightness in his chest as he stared from behind at the dark-brown hair of his senior officer, who was sitting with excellent posture in the chair he had taken.

Von Reuentahl's "interrogation" was carried out by Neidhart Müller, but this questioner spoke very politely to his subject, and had allowed Bergengrün to be present with his superior, likely to avoid upsetting von Reuentahl's subordinates and giving the impression of a secret trial.

Von Reuentahl's answers to Müller's questions echoed off the walls.

"If the rumor was that I, Oskar von Reuentahl, was through force or abuse of authority committing acts of plunder or bringing harm to civilians, that—for me—would be the greatest of humiliations. To have it said I intend to rebel and seek the throne for myself is, to a warrior in chaotic times, more of an occasion for pride."

Bergengrün's respiratory organs suddenly ceased functioning at the utter arrogance in those words, while Müller's fingers danced silently across his desktop.

"…However, ever since His Majesty Kaiser Reinhard established his admiralität in the old dynasty, I have every day without exception done my utmost in service of his conquest. On that point, I've not the slightest iota of guilt in my heart."

Maybe Bergengrün's prejudice was eating away at his own field of awareness, but he felt that von Reuentahl's answer was a little too vaguely shaded.

"What's laughable is my slanderer's identity. Who is Chief Lang of the Ministry of Domestic Affairs' Domestic Safety Security Bureau? He's the same misguided individual who last year, without qualification, attended a meeting that was only for officers ranked senior admiral and above and, as if that were not enough, even dared to speak in it. He's likely upset about being ordered from the room, and is making unjust accusations based on his personal feelings. I'd like you to bear in mind the situation at that time."

When the basic questions had been asked and answered, Müller said, "I've heard Your Excellency's case. What would you say to meeting with His Majesty directly, and making your defense to him?"

"I don't care for the word 'defense.'" The corner of von Reuentahl's mouth angled upward just slightly. "Still, if I may meet with His Majesty in person to let him know my mind, my accusers will lose any opening to stab at me. It's a bother, I'm sure, Senior Admiral Müller, but may I ask you to make the necessary arrangements?"

"If the imperial marshal so desires, that won't be a problem. I'll go and inform His Majesty right away."

Reinhard received the report from Müller, and following lunch, interrogated the heterochromatic marshal personally. The venue was a giant gallery in the National Museum of Art, facing the Winter Rose Garden from beyond a grove of cypresses. An exhibition of oil paintings had been on display up until the time of the imperial occupation, and even now, the walls were still lined with those paintings. Mittermeier and other top military leaders whose attendance Reinhard had permitted had with their own hands lined up the folding chairs they now occupied; this displayed a side of the new dynasty that refused to put too much focus on the beauty of forms. As they lined up their chairs and looked on, their golden-haired kaiser—himself a breathing work of art—somewhat reluctantly parted his graceful lips.

"Imperial Marshal von Reuentahl."

"Your Majesty…"

"Is the accusation true that you have a woman of the late duke Lichtenlade's family in your private home?"

As von Reuentahl stood alone in the midst of the wide gallery, his heterochromatic eyes—the deep, sunken black of his right and the sharp, gleaming blue of his left—were fearlessly trained directly on the young kaiser. They were eyes utterly removed from regret and defense.

"It's true, Your Majesty."

What shook the air of the gallery in the next instant was not the voice of von Reuentahl, but that of his dearest friend. Mittermeier had risen from his seat.

"Your Majesty! That woman bears a grudge against von Reuentahl. She's made threats against his life. I speak with full awareness of the impropriety, but please, take into account the situation both before and after. Forgive von Reuentahl's rash behavior."

Mittermeier became aware of someone tugging on his uniform sleeve, and shifted his gaze slightly. Sitting in the seat next to him was the "silent admiral," Senior Admiral von Eisenach. His mouth was still a straight line, and he was looking up at Mittermeier with an expression that was like a piece of ore. Mittermeier understood what he was all but saying, yet even so, he would not stop making his case to the kaiser.

"Your Majesty, mein kaiser, it's Imperial Marshal von Oberstein, the minister of military affairs, and Chief Lang of the Ministry of Domestic Affairs' Domestic Safety Security Bureau whom *I* denounce. At a time when Yang Wen-li's faction has occupied Iserlohn and is openly preparing to oppose the empire, to slander Marshal von Reuentahl—Your Majesty's chief advisor—is to harm the military's unity and cohesion. Is this not in effect tantamount to aiding and abetting the enemy?"

Mittermeier's fervor, it seemed, had melted the kaiser's heart, or at least its outer surface. The graceful line of Reinhard's lips bent slightly into a hint of a smile.

"Mittermeier, that's enough. Your mouth was made for encouraging vast armies—criticizing others suits it poorly."

The youthful face of the Imperial Navy's courageous, highest-ranking admiral reddened, and after steadying his breathing, he sat back down awkwardly. Interrupting an interrogation between the kaiser and his subject was a breach of decorum that ordinarily would have called for the charge of lèse-majesté. Mittermeier had not been trying to impose on the kaiser's kindness; he had been prepared for serious punishments at the sound of the kaiser's shout, but for Reinhard, the Gale Wolf's strong spirit and straightness of heart never aroused displeasure.

"Mein kaiser," von Reuentahl said to his master. This was the tone that would inspire a number of people to later remark, "No one ever pronounced the words 'mein kaiser' more beautifully than Imperial Marshal von Reuentahl." Kaiser Reinhard's physical beauty was as incomparable as his quick wit, but von Reuentahl, too, had a stately, imposing handsomeness, and standing there, ramrod straight before the kaiser, his beauty and dignity excelled even that of the many sculptures the museum had on display.

"Mein kaiser, it was foolish of me to take that woman, Elfriede von Kohlrausch, into my home, knowing that she was a relative of Duke Lichtenlade. I deeply regret my carelessness. But to have that be viewed as a sign of rebelliousness against Your Majesty is undesirable in the extreme, and I swear to you it is no such sign."

"In that case, what of your joy upon learning of her pregnancy, and your statement that for the child's sake, you will aim even higher?"

"That is an utter falsehood. I was unaware that the woman was pregnant. Had I known…"—here an iceberg of self-reproach raised its tip just above the surface of a black and blue sea—"…I would have made her abort it immediately. On that point there is no room for doubt."

"How can you be so sure?"

"Because I am unworthy to be anyone's father, Your Majesty."

There was darkness in von Reuentahl's voice, but no fog of uncertainty, and the silence of those present in the museum's spacious gallery only deepened. Under his uniform, Mittermeier was sweating for his friend's sake.

Regarding that last point, Reinhard asked no questions. Naturally, he was aware that von Reuentahl's personal behavior invited all sorts of unfavorable criticism, but dictator though he was, he was still reluctant to step barefoot into the mental bedrooms of his vassals. The love affairs of others had never held any interest for him anyway. The words that issued forth from between the young kaiser's glacier-white teeth at first seemed unrelated to von Reuentahl's reply. "You pledged your allegiance to me when I had still not succeeded to the name of von Lohengramm…"

That had been on a night five years ago; at the time, Reinhard had been nineteen years old, and merely "Admiral von Müssel." It had been the night that the fleet sent to subjugate Marquis von Klopfstock following the marquis's failed attempt on the emperor's life had returned to Hauptplanet Odin. With peals of thunder rending apart thick curtains of night and rain, von Reuentahl had come alone to see Reinhard and Siegfried Kircheis. Explaining that the life of his friend Mittermeier was in the hands of highborn nobles, he had begged for their aid, and sworn his allegiance to Reinhard thenceforward.

Now, shared memories of that scene were overlapping in the eyes of both the kaiser and the secretary-general of Imperial Military Command Headquarters.

"Do you remember that night, Marshal von Reuentahl?"

"I've never forgotten it, Your Majesty. Not even for a day."

"Very well, then…"

Although a shadow of melancholy had not vanished entirely from Reinhard's face, it did seem as though a shaft of sunlight had broken through the fog.

"I'll decide what to do with you in the coming days. Wait for instructions in your quarters—until then, Senior Admiral Müller will attend to your duties."

A chorus of held breaths, exhaled in relief, stirred the faintest of breezes in the spacious gallery. Von Reuentahl bowed deeply, and after those in attendance had filed out, Reinhard returned to his office—formerly the curator's office—and sought opinions from his inner circle. What to do about von Reuentahl?

His chief aide von Streit looked at his handsome young lord head-on, eyes shining with deep consideration.

"It's known to all that Imperial Marshal von Reuentahl is both an accomplished and valuable vassal to Your Majesty, and a hero to the nation. If you were to treat such a man lightly because you believed a rumor, it would come as a mental shock to others, who would in turn become uneasy about their own standing. Your Majesty, please treat him with fairness informed by your insight."

"Oh? Do I look like I want to judge von Reuentahl?"

As von Streit was answering, Reinhard's eyes turned toward Hilda. The contessina was known for her clever schemes and wise judgment, but unusually for her, she refrained from answering right away in this case. As an ally, von Reuentahl was incomparably reliable, but still, there was something about him that put Hilda on edge.

Last year, at the time of the Vermillion War, Hilda had asked Mittermeier to stage a direct assault on the Free Planets' capital of Heinessen. What she had felt from von Reuentahl at that time Hilda had still not managed to make evaporate.

III

In the office of the secretary-general of Imperial Military Command Headquarters, now bereft of its master, von Reuentahl's advisors were discussing a plan for getting through the coming days.

Lieutenant Commander von Reckendorf leaned forward and said, "Your Excellency, if you'll forgive my impertinence, I think we should have the minister of military affairs hand this von Kohlrausch woman over to us, and make her confront Marshal von Reuentahl in person. By doing so, the fact that she attempted to drag down Marshal von Reuentahl can be clearly established."

At this proposal, Bergengrün cast a glum look around at his colleagues and said, "Things wouldn't go that easily, Lieutenant Commander von Reckendorf. You know as well as I what sort of man the minister of military affairs is. Once that woman is in his hands, he'll make her give whatever kind of deposition suits him, won't he?"

As he felt that the admiral's opinion was correct, the lieutenant commander fell silent. Bergengrün folded his arms.

"Regrettably, we can't yet assume that Marshal von Reuentahl's personal safety is assured. At present, His Majesty seems to trust in his old friendship, and be in a magnanimous mood, but going forward, we don't know which way the scales will tilt…"

He murmured these words as if in warning against his own optimism, and as he was speaking, an officer announced the presence of a visitor.

The visitor was General Volker Axel Büro, a staff officer of Imperial Space Armada commander in chief Mittermeier.

Under the command of redheaded Siegfried Kircheis, Büro and Bergengrün had once competed with one another for fame. During the Battle of Amritsar and the Lippstadt War alike, they had fought with their respective columns side by side. With Kircheis's unexpected death, his flagship *Barbarossa* had lost its honored master and been berthed in the spaceport on the imperial capital, while his team of staff officers had been broken up and reassigned to various scattered posts. But even though the sections they were affiliated with now differed, that did nothing to erode their memories of surviving life-or-death battles together.

Büro met with Bergengrün in a separate room, and encouraged his old friend, informing him that the kaiser would most likely deal generously with von Reuentahl, and that Imperial Marshal Mittermeier had pledged his full cooperation.

"I'm grateful to hear it. Still, Büro…" As he lowered his voice, thunderheads concealing flashes of lightning were scudding across Bergengrün's expression. "It was because of the minister of military affairs' meddling that I lost my senior officer, Admiral Kircheis. He was young, but he truly was a great commander. If I were to lose a second senior officer in the space of two or three years because of that same Marshal von Oberstein, my life would be the epitome of both tragedy and comedy."

"Wait a minute, Bergengrün…."

Before his old friend's eyes, Bergengrün breathed out a heavy, hot breath. "I know what you're going to say, Büro—my duty is to calm Marshal von Reuentahl and see to it he doesn't boil over. And I'll put all my strength into doing that. However, if Marshal von Reuentahl incurs a punishment that greatly exceeds what his crime calls for, I won't be able to let that go."

Even though he knew that no one else was in the room, Büro couldn't help glancing around at their surroundings.

Imperial Marshal von Reuentahl had taken a woman into his private home who was from the family of Count Lichtenlade—that rash action had been the start of all this. But now, at a time when Yang Wen-li and his associates had retaken Iserlohn Fortress and unity and cooperation were needed from the entire imperial military, people were rebuking the secretary-general of Imperial Military Command Headquarters over a blunder in his personal life, and talking about it as if it were directly connected to high treason. Büro could well understand the feelings of hatred his old friend had toward that.

Ever since the unexpected death of Siegfried Kircheis, a little fire of dissatisfaction and hostility toward von Oberstein had been burning away inside Bergengrün, and he had been unable to put it out. On that day, in September of year 488 of the old Imperial Calendar, an assassin's hand cannon had been aimed at Reinhard, and its discharge should have been prevented not by Kircheis's body, but by the barrel of his gun. After all, up until that day, he alone had been permitted to bear arms at Reinhard's side, and his marksmanship had been outstanding.

It had been von Oberstein who had viewed Kircheis's going about armed as an unfair privilege, and advised its revocation. Reinhard had also been at fault for listening to him, but he had regretted what he had done; in contrast to that, von Oberstein was cool and indifferent, and to this very day Kircheis's old subordinates couldn't help feeling indignant toward him.

Back on Planet Phezzan, separated by a sea of stars, Imperial Marshal von Oberstein, the minister of military affairs, was unable to detect the hostility of Bergengrün and his compatriots. Though even if he were to detect it, it was unlikely he would change his attitude or policies in any way.

It was Heidrich Lang who had cultivated mere rumors of von Reuentahl's "rebellious intent" until they had borne the fruit of a personal interrogation by the kaiser. Von Oberstein had been watching in silence as Lang, with depraved relish, had lavished great quantities of water and fertilizer on that irresponsible gossip. Von Oberstein had not encouraged him in this enterprise, nor had he tried to prevent him; rather, he had simply observed, as a teacher might observe the performance of a bumbling disciple. Perhaps he might have said that von Reuetahl's fall would be one acceptable outcome, and if he didn't fall, he simply didn't. Still, simply giving his tacit approval to Lang's actions likely meant he would find no favor with the rest of the admiralty, or with Mittermeier in particular.

Such was the thinking of his subordinate, Anton Ferner. Another possibility was that by concentrating all the admirals' antipathy, hostility, and hatred in himself, the minister of military affairs was serving as a shield for the kaiser. Von Oberstein certainly never let words to that effect slip his tongue, though, so this might have amounted to nothing more than Ferner's interpretation, as it would have been difficult to ascertain in the first place whether von Oberstein had even thought of such considerations. From the outset however, the sight of Lang, who was not even affiliated with the Ministry of Military Affairs, ensconcing himself here on Phezzan while cozying up to von Oberstein like a trusted advisor had hardly been pleasant for Ferner. Nevertheless, it didn't show at all in his attitude. After all, he was not the owner of such a clear and straightforward value system either.

When Lang came to report that Marshal von Oberstein had finally undergone questioning from the kaiser himself, von Oberstein turned the cold light of his artificial eyes toward him. In spite of the joy Lang felt inside, he kept his face downturned, and it seemed as if he were speaking to the desk rather than to von Oberstein's stern face. When he finished his report, von Oberstein spoke for the first time.

"Lang."

"Er, yes…?"

"Do not disappoint me. Your duty is to be vigilant for domestic enemies in order to ensure the peace and security of the dynasty. It would be outrageously disloyal of you to falsely accuse a hero of our nation's founding over a personal grudge, and thereby weaken the dynasty's foundations. Do bear that in mind."

"I'm well aware of that, Your Excellency. Please, set your mind at ease."

Von Oberstein was not furnished with X-ray vision. On Lang's face, bowed so low that he was facing the floor, was a small amount of sweat, and a strange steam of incongruity seemed to hang about him. In a space where not a soul was watching, his face seemed as though it were made up of inorganic pieces of a jigsaw puzzle.

"'…There is no concrete evidence by which we may conclude with confidence that Heidrich Lang was trying to move things along with dangerous intent from the start. It is presently believed, however, that the outlines of his ambition appeared at the beginning of NIC 2, though they were as yet still indistinct. His intent was to stoke conflict between the minister of military affairs, Marshal von Oberstein and the secretary-general of Imperial Military Command Headquarters, Marshal von Reuentahl, and by taking advantage of their struggle, rise to become the chief of all vassals in the empire…' Today, this is considered outrageously farcical thinking, and not even worthy of comment. As everyone knew, Lang was no famous, undefeated admiral with countless achievements to his name like von Reuentahl. Nor was he a capable advisor like von Oberstein, who had long been eliminating the enemies of lord and state by means of intrigues and careful management of the military. Lang was a mere conspirator, and nothing more than the chief of a dishonorable secret police. History, however, instructs us with countless real-life examples of how untalented and narrow-minded conspirators often push individuals of vastly greater talent or nobility than themselves into bottomless mires, sinking not only their opponents but also the very possibilities of their generations…"

The man who would later leave that record, Senior Admiral Ernest Mecklinger, had at this time received orders from Reinhard, and was presently moving the entire force given him as rear guard commander in chief toward Iserlohn. It was his job to restrict both the offensive and defensive activities of Yang Wen-li, who had stolen back Iserlohn Fortress. If Yang invaded imperial space, he was to hold Yang off, and if he headed for what had once been Free Planets Alliance space, he was to attack Yang from the rear. It is fair to say his was a most important mission.

While it appeared as though Reinhard had exploded with anger, and was moving massive military forces based on emotion, his ice-blue gaze was taking stock of the military situation in every quarter of that vast expanse of space. And that was something that Yang Wen-li had already surmised at Iserlohn Fortress.

IV

On the night before he departed the imperial capital, Mecklinger had dinner with two of his colleagues, Kessler and Wahlen.

By this time, Mecklinger's assistant, as it were, Vice Admiral Lefort, the rear guard chief of staff, had already gone up to his orbiting battleship, where he was awaiting Mecklinger's arrival. The empire's military forces were overwhelmingly superior to those of either the Alliance Armed Forces or the Yang Wen-li faction, but from Mecklinger's point of view, that posed a bit of a problem in terms of the distribution of military forces. Kaiser Reinhard had nearly all of his top advisors arrayed across a vast swath of space that stretched from Phezzan into Free Planets space, and at present his subjugation of the alliance appeared to be a complete success. But meanwhile, within the even vaster borders of imperial space, the imperial capital of Odin— seemingly cast aside by the young conqueror—was being defended by Senior Admiral Kessler, and Mecklinger was being deployed to the region of the Iserlohn Corridor. Soon enough, Wahlen would likely also receive orders for his first mobilization since his punitive strike on Earth. In the original territory of the Galactic Empire, it seemed unavoidable that military forces would be spread thin.

Just before their after-dinner coffee, Kessler asked Mecklinger the following question:

"I'm a little bit nervous about this, Admiral Mecklinger. It's well and good for the kaiser to move his imperial headquarters to Phezzan, but what does he intend to do with this planet? There's someone very close to His Majesty here."

"You refer to His Majesty's elder sister, Admiral Kessler?"

Kessler doubled as commissioner of military police and commander of capital defenses, but he was not a fleet commander, and ordinarily would have never been referred to by the title of "Admiral." His colleagues, however, didn't dwell on such formalities, and he himself enjoyed being called such.

"That's right," he said. "Her Majesty the Archduchess von Grünewald. Her."

Senior Admiral August Samuel Wahlen hesitantly posed a question of his own: "The kaiser and the archduchess are brother and sister, but they haven't met with one another since *that* happened, have they?"

That referred to the death of Siegfried Kircheis in September of year 488 of the old Imperial Calendar. That tragedy had been the occasion for then countess Annesrose von Grünewald's move to a mountain villa in Froiden.

A shared concern floated in the air above the table between these three famous admirals.

The kaiser had no heir. There was only one person in the whole universe who shared his blood: Archduchess Annerose von Grünewald. That lady had monopolized the affections of her younger brother the kaiser and the admiration of everyone at court, but now she lived a quiet life at her villa in Froiden, and never used her bloodline as a shield to interfere in affairs of state. The kaiser had asked his sister often to come and live with him at the old imperial palace of Neue Sans Souci, but Annesrose had continued to refuse; all Reinhard had been able to do was send a minimal security detail to ensure her safety.

It was a truly ominous and extremely disrespectful thing to imagine, but in the event that the kaiser departed this world with neither an empress nor an heir, it might be Annerose who would save the Lohengramm Dynasty from dismantlement and collapse. If they followed existing policy and moved the central hub of all of space to Phezzan, Odin would be demoted to just another backwater planet. In such an event, it followed that its security forces would be decreased as well. In order to maintain with greater certainty the security of Archduchess Annerose von Grünewald, it would clearly be best if they could have her move to Phezzan. It would also be better luck than Kessler could have asked for if he himself were able to move closer to the throne in the process.

"Still," said Mecklinger, "that kind of thinking seems to have things backward. First, we should put someone forward to the kaiser to be empress. Then there won't be any issues regarding the dynasty's continued existence."

Mecklinger smiled, but the other two grimaced in reply. That was in fact the biggest problem; though their young lord was possessed of incomparable physical beauty himself, love affairs were, for now at least, alien to him. Had he so desired, he could have buried himself in the kaleidoscopic blossoms of the inner court. Nevertheless, no matter how his vassals might fret, this was a problem that could only be solved by the inclination of Reinhard's own heart.

"I just remembered something!" said Kessler. "Speaking of problems, how about the one with Karl Bracke?" The name was that of a cabinet member occupying the seat of minister of civilian government. Known since the days of the old empire as a crusader for the advancement of knowledge and civilization, he was an aristocrat who had foregone the use of "von" before his surname, and together with Eugen Richter, the present minister of finance, had cooperated all along with Reinhard's reform politics.

"Do you believe Minister Bracke has something against the kaiser?"

"He isn't keeping his dissatisfaction to himself. Just the other day, he apparently vented to his staff, 'Every year, he orders these pointless mobilizations, consumes the national budget on warfare, and swells the ranks of the dead beyond all reason.' Though it does seem he'd had a bit to drink at the time."

"The treasury is still in pretty stable condition, isn't it?"

" 'If he would stop going to war and focus on domestic politics, it would be more stable,' he says. There's truth in that, but to me, it seems problematic if his careless remarks end up aiding anti-kaiser reactionaries."

Wahlen fell into thought, supporting his chin somewhat awkwardly with his artificial left arm, while Mecklinger tapped his fingers on his coffee cup as he might the keys of a piano. "If I were to give free rein to my imagination, I'd say that someone with disquieting intentions might be backstage, putting forward Bracke as his proxy. And while it would be an outrage to comment right away on what to do about him…"

"At any rate," said Kessler, "Minister Bracke is a cabinet member appointed by the kaiser, so there's really nothing we can do about *him*. But backstage…That's right—what if some of those Terraists were slithering around back there?"

Speaking as though the church were a family of serpents, Kessler drew his broad shoulders up in a cringe to display his revulsion.

"When you think about it," Kessler continued "if there are any surviving fanatics from the Church of Terra out there plotting revenge, me and Admiral Wahlen, as enemies of their sect, are sure to have our names on their hit list."

"Well then, does that mean if we go, we'll go together?"

Wahlen had started to laugh off that comment, but not completely succeeding, his face took on a sharp, bitter expression. At the time when he had brought military force to bear against the Church of Terra's headquarters, he had been assaulted by a Terraist assassin, and had forever lost his left arm as a result. For having carried out his mission while enduring unexpected disaster, Wahlen's reputation for fortitude and coolheadedness had only improved, but that appraisal would not make his lost arm grow back.

An old-fashioned clock chimed ten. Along with being a prose poet, a pianist, and a watercolor painter, the master of this estate, Mecklinger, was also a collector of antiques. He was a handsome gentleman with a neatly trimmed mustache, who during the Lippstadt War had immediately raced into art galleries and museums whenever occupying enemy territory, protecting works of fine art from the flames of battle. Kessler had teased him for this.

"That art collector routine of yours has really gotten obnoxious. I can't help but wonder if you're going to start collecting the kaiser's and Yang Wen-li's military histories before long."

Mecklinger had thought about that very seriously.

"Iserlohn Fortress was supposed to be impregnable until Yang Wen-li opened his bag of magic tricks. However, he caused it to change hands as easily as possession of a fly ball does. If that can be called art, then it's surely unsurpassed."

"But still, I don't think there's anyone else who can imitate him."

"He'd never stand for it," said Wahlen. "Still, when you think about it, he is a praiseworthy man, even if he is our enemy. With just that tiny force, he's taking on our empire's entire armada, and is keeping us so busy it's wearing us out."

There was a weighty truth in Wahlen's voice. This was because in the previous year, he himself had been driven to a massive defeat by Yang's ingenious scheming. Naturally, he had an unspoken determination to not let it happen again.

As the evening wore down, Kessler became the first to leave. He had to go and listen to a subordinate report on the movements of Job Trünicht, one of the subjects whom he had under observation.

Kessler's stance toward Trünicht, former head of state of the Free Planets Alliance was, to put it nicely, to politely try to ignore him. Intelligence had come to him through multiple channels that Trünicht had been abhorred by Yang Wen-li, to the point that he found himself sympathizing with an enemy admiral he had still never laid eyes on. In his position, Yang Wen-li had to respect the fundamentals of the majority rule system known as democracy, but Kessler had been able to live free of the sort of ambivalence that Yang had fallen victim to, and because Kessler was in temperament even more rigid than Yang, there was no way Trünicht's sweet words and treachery were ever going to hold any attraction for him. In his eyes, Trünicht was nothing more than a dishonorable thief of a politician. In order to steal authority, he had taken advantage of flaws in the democratic form of government, and in order to steal his own personal security, he had taken advantage of the very decline and fall of the nation itself. After departing for imperial space with his family and fortune, he had left behind ravaged governmental institutions and dumbstruck supporters.

Kaiser Reinhard hated the man as well, and had banned him from holding public office. Trünicht, however, having not yet abandoned earthly desires, had wasted no time in using his abundant capital and unprincipled energy to begin pulling strings in the bureaucracy.

In the back seat of a landcar bound for his own headquarters, Kessler's foul mood continued to take on water. As both commissioner of military police and commander of capital defenses, he had bid his colleagues farewell, and stayed behind on Odin alone. This had been because of the kaiser's orders and Kessler's own clerical skills, which had allowed him to meet those expectations; he had not stayed out of any personal wish of his own. If he had not been so capable when it came to defusing crises or so skilled at managing large organizations, he likely would have avoided crawling around on the ground like this and looking up at the starry sky in dissatisfaction. Kessler did not envy his colleagues' military successes, although he couldn't help feeling a bit jealous about where they had gone. They were heroes, leading fleets numbering in the tens of thousands of vessels and crossing vast seas of blackness filled with swarms of stars. Originally, Ulrich Kessler had been inclined in that direction as well, and had of his own accord chosen for himself the life of an imperial military official.

Nevertheless, the real Ulrich Kessler was tens of thousands of light-years away from that cluster of stars that needed conquering, having to guard a palace that no longer had a master, and entertain the likes of Job Trünicht. If peace and unification were achieved before he headed off to the battlefield, Kessler would celebrate his lord's triumph, but at the same time he'd likely be unable to help feeling tiny, sand-like grains of dissatisfaction.

Around the time that Kessler arrived at headquarters, Wahlen was also on his way home. One month later, these three men would all be separated from each other by distances measured in the thousands of light-years.

V

It was the first of March. The vanguard warmth of the coming spring, inconstant in its cowardice during daylight hours, was wiped out altogether by a chill evening wind, which draped a thick, cold, transparent mantle over a part of Planet Heinessen. At ten o'clock that evening, young Emil von Selle, the kaiser's chamberlain, was told by his master to go on to bed, as he had no further errands for him that night. Emil returned to his room, which was just across the hallway, and changed into his pajamas. He cracked open a window that was fogged a milky white, and the fragrance of winter roses invaded his nostrils, along with a draft of air cold enough to make him shiver. The boy sneezed softly. The sound seemed to echo in the stillness of the night, and soldiers patrolling the spacious garden cast suspicious glances his way. Emil shut the window, stretched once as was his bedtime custom, and was just about to jump onto the mattress. It really did happen at that precise instant. A window-shaped mass of white light gouged its way into the middle of his room. Just as its color seemed to change to orange, an immense wall of sound slammed into Emil. As it dawned on him that something had just exploded, the young boy leapt from his bed.

Sounds of explosions followed one upon another, invading Emil von Selle's auditory canals. He covered his ears unconsciously, only to be tormented by echoes. He tried to run into the kaiser's bedchamber, but instead found Reinhard already standing in front of the door in his nightgown. As imperial guards formed pillars and walls all around him, his golden hair caught undulations of orange light, and glistened.

"Kisling, what's going on?"

The, catlike—or rather, pantherlike—chief of the imperial guards looked at Reinhard and said, "We're investigating now. In any case, Your Majesty, please hurry. I'll escort you to a safe place."

The kaiser nodded. "Emil, help me get changed. If the kaiser were to flee in his nightgown, the rebels would have a new story to laugh about."

Kisling wanted to tell him that this was neither the time nor place for such concerns, but for Emil, any word emanating from the kaiser's mouth was an order. Without hesitation, he followed the kaiser into his room, and assisted the young conqueror in changing into his black and silver uniform. Ignoring the light and shadow and capriccio of explosions unfolding outside the window, Reinhard finished changing, then smiled at the sight of Emil still in his pajamas. He threw his own nightgown around the faithful young chamberlain.

Guided by Kisling, who tried hard not to let his boots so much as squeak with his footfalls, the three of them went outside into the Winter Rose Garden. Already, various officers were gathering here with their troops. Amid wildly dancing stripes of black and orange, the officers advised the kaiser to conceal himself for fear of sniper fire. Taking no notice, however, Reinhard boldly and confidently kept his beautiful, golden-haired head held high. Wrapped in a nightgown too large for him, Emil looked up at him with worshipful eyes.

By the time that the first light of dawn flashed its unsheathed blade across the horizon, the fire had subsided. An investigation into the blaze's cause was commenced first thing that morning. It was, of course, conducted alongside the distribution of money and supplies to those caught up in the disaster, and the cause itself was determined in no time. A Seffl particle generator that the old alliance military had sold off to civilians for mining development had been mistakenly activated while connected to a power source, and some small factory that had been operating late into the night had set off those fireworks.

Ultimately, an accident was to blame for that great fire, which was the illegitimate child of an irresponsible system that had formed during the interval between the alliance government's fall and the establishment of the empire's authority. Almost all of the people of that time viewed it as arson, though. Caught up in the circumstances of that period, it was only natural to view it so. The imperial military wanted to believe that holdouts from the Alliance Armed Forces had started the fire as an act of terrorism, intending to take advantage of the confusion, but in fact there had been no organized uprising. Riots had broken out here and there as people tried to take advantage of the confusion, but each and every one of them had been snuffed out in the early stages. This had been accomplished not only by the levelheaded leadership of Mittermeier and Müller, but also by the good influence of the emergency management manual, wherein von Reuentahl had given thorough consideration to every eventuality. This had allowed imperial forces to mobilize efficiently, seize critical positions, and not get flustered.

"Anyway, we need a criminal to hold responsible for this. Until someone is arrested, the population won't be at ease."

The area lost to the blaze exceeded eighteen million square meters, and the dead and missing numbered over 5,500. Half that number consisted of newly stationed imperial troops unfamiliar with the lay of the land. In addition, many historic buildings had been reduced to ashes, and because the imperial forces had cared nothing for them, there had even been plausible-sounding rumors that the triumphant imperial military had tried to purge them of their hidebound ways with fire. The group that Admiral Brentano, vice commissioner of military police, plucked from among several "criminal candidates" was a group of holdouts from the Patriotic Knights, a domestic pro-war group that had run rampant during the waning days of the former FPA.

The imperial military had indeed considered the danger that cracking down on the Patriotic Knights might turn them into a symbol of heroic resistance against the empire, but by the end of the investigation, it had been learned that from SE 796 to 799, a relationship involving funds and personnel had existed between the Patriotic Knights and the Church of Terra. From that point onward, the empire acknowledged no further need for restraint. A lot of people felt certain anyway that the Patriotic Knights had started the fire, regardless of the lack of evidence. There was also the fact that following the failed attempt on the kaiser's life the previous summer, it was an unwritten rule in the imperial government and military that evidence was no longer needed to crack down on groups associated with Terra.

Twenty-four thousand and six hundred people who had relationships with the Patriotic Knights and the Church of Terra became temporarily subject to arrest, although the number actually arrested failed to reach twenty thousand. This was because 5,200 resisted and were shot dead, and another thousand fled and eluded capture. Weapons were impounded from many of their hideouts, providing evidence that ironically justified the crackdown in the end.

Bretano, as one who had been entrusted with public security, was in this manner able to save face, leaving the reconstruction of a city reduced to ashes as a critical task for the coming days.

On March 19, the imperial military's top leaders gathered at the Winter Rose Garden's temporary imperial headquarters. That was the day on which Imperial Marshal von Reuentahl's punishment was to be announced by the kaiser. Von Reuentahl deserved a lot of the credit for having minimized the chaos accompanying the recent fire, and it was expected that his punishment would just be a slap on the wrist. The kaiser's proclamation, however, covered its listeners' hearts in frost for just an instant.

"Imperial Marshal von Reuentahl, I release you from your duties as secretary-general of Imperial Military Command Headquarters."

A voiceless stir ascended rapidly, but just as it was about to cross the audible threshold, Reinhard's voice, in continuation of his initial proclamation, dashed the attendees' fears from every corner of the Winter Rose Garden.

"Instead, I order you to remain here on Heinessen as governor of our empire's Neue Land, and manage all political and military matters in the territory of the former Free Planets Alliance. The rank and treatment of the Neue Land governor shall be equivalent to that of a ministry head, and he shall be responsible only to the kaiser."

Von Reuentahl's head was bowed respectfully, but blood was rising up into his graceful countenance. This was *not* some slap on the wrist; kneeling low before him now was glory whose like had existed only beyond the horizons of his imagination. He shifted the angle of his mismatched eyes slightly, and his best friend's figure was reflected in his black and blue irises. Mittereier looked as joyful as if this honor had come to him.

Von Reuentahl was given the fleet he had commanded prior to becoming secretary-general of Imperial Military Command Headquarters, and the fleets of admirals von Knapfstein and Grillparzer were also placed under his command. As a result, he became the leader of a force of 35,800 vessels and 5,226,400 officers and soldiers. This was the second most powerful armed force in the Galactic Empire, second only to that of Kaiser

Reinhard. In addition, his position of governor had been declared equal to that of a cabinet minister by the kaiser himself, meaning that as far as the organizational chart was concerned, von Reuentahl had reached equal footing with Imperial Marshal von Oberstein, the minister of military affairs. Of course, in terms of combat ability, he had greatly surpassed von Oberstein already.

Reinhard's decision didn't affect only von Reuentahl; organizational and HR changes that accompanied this appointment were also announced at this time.

"I will take personal charge of Imperial Military Command Headquarters. To assist me, there will be a staff commissioner. To this position, I name Senior Admiral Steinmetz. As the office of the Neue Land governor has now been established, Steinmetz, you may consider the mission for which you were stationed in the Gandharva system to be completed."

In fact, Reinhard had initially prepared this seat for Hilda, but she had declined, instead deferring to the admiralty, as she had never commanded a single soldier before in her life.

"However, these appointments shall only take effect *after* you compel Yang Wen-li and his associates, presently sheltered in Iserlohn Fortress, to surrender."

Reinhard's voice, as though dusted with powdered gold, wrapped invisible threads around the civil and military court officials in attendance, filling them with a tension that was akin to a thrill running down their spines.

"Before his forces and other assets can make any rash moves, I will strike Yang Wen-li and his followers. To lend him time would not only make his force strength more powerful—it would also let it be declared of myself and the military I'm so proud of that fear of one individual's clever designs made us neglect our duty to unify the universe. So I hereby declare: until I have made Yang Wen-li bow down before me, I will not return to Phezzan, let alone Odin…"

Reinhard's voice had become a symphony without instruments that harmonized perfectly with the fighting spirit of the admirals. It was unclear who was the first to cry out, but both the fragrance and icy purity of the wintry air in the Winter Rose Garden was split apart and crushed beneath a hot cascade of passionate voices.

"Sieg Kaiser Reinhard!"

Reinhard announced furthermore that he was removing Senior Admiral Lutz from the front lines and appointing him commander of Phezzan's security forces, as well as summoning Senior Admiral Wahlen from Odin to have him join in their ranks for the battle. Afterward, he returned for a while to the salon at his official residence.

After sitting down in the small but comfortable salon overlooking the Winter Rose Garden, Emil came bringing coffee. Reinhard had just set his coffee cup back down in its coaster when Hilda raised a completely unexpected matter.

"Your Majesty, what will you do about *her*?"

It seemed that for a moment, that pronoun had failed to jog Reinhard's memory in regard to whom it was referring, so Hilda had to append the following:

"That woman from the Lichtenlade family who was at Imperial Marshal von Reuentahl's private estate."

"Ah, yes…"

As Reinhard nodded, apathy and confusion shimmered faintly in his eyes. The truth of the matter was that the woman named Elfriede von Kohlrausch had already vanished from Reinhard's mind.

Still, just to answer the question, he said, "I've heard that she's pregnant, but that should be no problem if she's made to abort."

"She's already in her seventh month. An abortion at this point would be too dangerous for the mother."

"Well, what do you think I should do?"

"By your leave, I'll answer. Although I'm not truly confident that this is the best option, how about moving her from Imperial Marshal von Reuentahl's estate to a medical facility elsewhere, and then putting the baby up for adoption after she's given birth?"

"I wonder if we can't just get her off Phezzan right away, and move her back to her original place of exile."

Hilda was against that, however. She argued that they should take into account the deleterious effects of warp travel on an unborn baby at this point in gestation. If those effects were to result in a miscarriage or stillbirth, Hilda thought, yet another new seed of tragedy and hatred would have been sowed, though von Reuentahl himself likely had a different opinion.

After a moment, Reinhard said, "Understood, Fräulein. I'll leave it to you."

Just like that, Reinhard had delegated the matter to her. His mind had started off down a long road that passed through oceans of stars on the way to conquest; he had no wish to do something so needless as turn his eyes on the modest fate of a single woman. Hilda understood that very well. Reinhard was not without mercy. He had offered up his bountiful, immense sensitivity to the universe and to one other person. Had he been heartless, he would have ordered Elfriede's death, and thereby snipped a thread that might one day become even more tangled. Naturally, there were those who viewed this as soft, however…

"Once you have defeated Yang Wen-li and completely unified the universe, you can return to Odin and meet your sister, can't you?"

Hilda found herself regretting those words just before she finished speaking them. A hint of winter crept into the kaiser's voice as he said, "Remember your place, Fräulein. That's none of your concern."

After a long moment, Hilda obediently apologized. "Yes, Your Majesty. Please forgive me."

When she thought about it, Reinhard had by his own wish sent Hilda as a personal envoy to his sister at her mountain villa in Froiden. Surely he shouldn't brush her off now, saying this had nothing to do with her.

Nevertheless, the whims of that boyish heart remained well within the limits of what Hilda would accept.

VI

Deep beneath the surface of Planet Phezzan was a single room completely shut off from the outside world. Those who had occupied that room for the past year were now secretly moving to the mountainous region of Okanagan, located about five hundred kilometers from the nearest city. Nestled deep in its evergreen forest was a stately mansion that no one else knew about. Fifty or so of those named on the Imperial Navy's "unfriendlies" list were under the control of one man.

That man, Adrian Rubinsky, was in a salon furnished with a fireplace, in which two layers of curtains were pulled shut during the daytime. Back when Phezzan had called itself a domain and possessed sovereignty over its internal affairs, he had been its landesherr. When Reinhard had so boldly occupied the planet, he had been driven from his seat of power, and had gone literally underground just before he would have otherwise fallen into the hands of the Imperial Navy. If current governor and imperial puppet Boltec were to learn of this, he would no doubt lick his lips and have his former master served up on the plate of judgment. For a little bit longer, Rubinsky would have to endure being a forest hermit.

On the sofa facing him, a woman holding a wineglass in one hand opened her mouth.

"It appears the crack between Kaiser Reinhard and von Reuentahl has been repaired. Not only did he not purge him, he's installed him as governor over the entire territory of the former Free Planets Alliance! I suppose your maneuvering has had far too much the opposite effect?"

"It certainly does look like it's been repaired. At least that's what Minister of Military Affairs von Oberstein will think. But the rift is merely hidden—it most certainly hasn't vanished."

"And you're going to make it wider, aren't you?"

The woman who had scornfully tossed that remark like a fishing net at him was Rubinski's lover, the former singer Dominique Saint-Pierre. Rubinsky continued, his powerfully built body absorbing the radiated waves of scorn. "One other thing: the kaiser's weakness is that beautiful sister of his. If anything were to happen to the Archduchess von Grünewald, the kaiser would go into a frenzy. The hero…the great monarch would vanish, leaving only a brat full with raging emotion."

"And you believe he'd be easier to control if that happened?"

"At least more so than before the frenzy." The expression with which Rubinsky responded wasn't so much cool and composed as it was devoid of emotion altogether. He raised his whiskey glass to his lips.

"But will the hit be successful, I wonder?"

"It doesn't have to be. Even if it's just attempted, the simple fact that such an act of violence was planned against her will have all the effect I need. Even the golden brat will finally realize that his life isn't only about advancement and ascendance. As his power expands, it's also becoming hollow. He's standing atop an inflating balloon."

Adrian Rubinsky proceeded to take a drink of liquefied conspiracy from his whiskey glass. As it absorbed into his stomach lining, becoming energy for him, he looked like some inhuman beast.

"If assassins are after his sister, Kaiser Reinhard will set aside his 'Neue Land' and go back to Odin to see her. When that happens, an opening will appear between the kaiser and Imperial Marshal von Reuentahl. I wonder—in the kaiser's absence, will he be able to resist the temptation to become a fallen angel?"

"You're going to be egging him on in any case." Dominique gave him the same sort of response she had given moments before. Using a mocking tone with Rubinsky, it seemed, was becoming second nature to her. "After all, before you even start to speak of necessity, you're enjoying spreading oil around wherever there's the slightest flame. Is it possible that even the great fire of Planet Heinessen was something you set in motion?"

"I'm pleased that you think so highly of me, but that was a coincidence. Spread the fire too much and in too many places, and you'll get burned to death yourself before you can put it out. However, that only goes for fires that have started already. These things I like to use efficiently whenever possible."

"You're a genius when it comes to using old junk."

The Galactic Empire's young emperor, Erwin Josef II, Count Alfred von Lansberg, and former Imperial Navy Captain Leopold Schumacher… those and countless other proper names were packed inside Rubinsky's toolbox. They included names of leaders in the Church of Terra, and former sovereigns of Phezzan's underbelly, as well.

"Still, I wonder if the Terraist movement has really died out…" said Dominique.

"So I was thinking…" Rubinsky began.

Because he did not continue right away, Dominique wanted to think that meant something, but when Rubinsky's response finally surfaced, it was with a splash from a completely unexpected direction. The Black Fox of Phezzan stroked his lover's eardrums with a voice that lacked all emotion.

"How about it, Dominique? Want to have a baby with me?"

The moment of silence that followed carried a stench like that of old cheese.

"Just so he'll be killed by you? No thanks."

Even if that remark had cut like an invisible knife slashing him across the chest, it didn't show in Rubinsky's expression. Once, he had killed a young man, Rupert Kesselring, who had tried to steal his power. That young man had been Rubinsky's son, and Dominique had been the partner in crime who had helped the father kill the son.

The eyes of Phezzan's former landesherr were like bogs in the dry season as he watched his lover leaving the room. Trailing behind her was the fragrance of a perfume called bitterness.

"That isn't it, Dominique," he said. "It's to have him kill me."

Those words, however, were spoken too softly to reach Dominique's back.

VII

In a corner of the Winter Rose Garden, Reinhard von Lohengramm was sitting down in the grass, looking on at the winter roses' deaths as they went down to defeat before the invasion of a haughty spring. Fahrenheit and Wittenfeld were already en route to Iserlohn with their fleets, while Mittermeier, von Reuentahl, Müller, and von Eisenach were making flawless preparations to move forward and join in this great campaign. They were going to pass through the Phezzan Corridor, cut across the domain of the old FPA, charge into the Iserlohn Corridor, and finally return to imperial space. In terms of planning and execution, it was a magnificently grand operation that no one save Reinhard could have made happen.

"Perhaps I've been cursed from birth," the kaiser said, his low voice striking drooping petals.

Standing alone by his master, Emil von Selle radiated waves of surprise into space.

"I prefer war above. I can no longer have color in my life except through bloodshed. Even though some other way might have been possible."

On behalf of his master, Emil fervently answered, "But isn't that because Your Majesty wishes for unity throughout the universe? If there is unity, peace will naturally follow. And if you get bored with that, can't you just go to another galaxy altogether?"

He was right. Unity would beget peace. But what would come after that? The glow of vitality that Reinhard gave off shone so brilliantly because there were enemies there to catch its light. Should he do as this boy wildly imagined, and head off to another galaxy?

Reinhard stretched out and stroked the young boy's hair with a hand so well-formed that only an artist could have imagined it.

"You're a kind lad. You think often of me. I want…I want to make those who think of me happy, but…"

As it was self-evident that he was talking to himself, Emil shyly looked on, not speaking, at the kaiser's impossibly beautiful profile as it smoldered in a fog of sorrow. Reinhard could no longer believe, as he had in former days, that his affection and passion guaranteed the happiness of those off of whom it was reflected. He sometimes even wondered if he had in effect become a god of doom and misfortune to those he loved the most. Still, he had never forgotten the vow he had made long ago, nor had he ever thought of being remiss in his duty to see that vow through to the end.

●　　●
　●
●

Heading into March, steadily increasing numbers of civilian vessels and warships of the former FPA Armed Forces continued to arrive from the direction of Heinessen, having slipped through the fingers of imperial patrols before pouring into the Liberation Corridor. As the footsteps of April drew near, the information they brought showed the degree of danger spiking sharply.

Kaiser Reinhard declared he would wipe out the Yang faction, and ordered senior admirals Wittenfeld and Fahrenheit to spearhead the assault. Planet Heinessen was already in the process of transforming into the Galactic Empire's largest military base. Suddenly, the time was growing ripe for war.

Guessing at Reinhard's grand intent, Yang had peeled out of his winter garment of indolence, turned out the pockets of all of his brain cells, and set to the task of designing a plan for engaging him. In order to realize his plan in an advantageous fashion, he couldn't afford to abandon the method of military resistance. His subordinates, as well, were making preparations to obey their commander's plan, and "show off and have fun" in earnest. Even the gigantic fortress of Iserlohn seem to have reached a state of saturation with all of the human energy filling its interior, and this "night before the festival" of life and death was one that Julian Mintz would remember in great detail later.

Frederica wiped away sweat from Yang's cheeks as he stared motion-lessly at the schematic of his operational plan. Like a knight about to joust, von Schönkopf was cleaning and oiling his armored suit. Poplin was naming his newly reorganized spartanian squadrons after various alcoholic beverages. Murai was solemnly organizing paperwork, Fischer was quietly inspecting the fleet, and Merkatz, with von Schneider in tow, was calming the mood among the soldiers and officers simply by being there. Attenborough was drawing up patterns of fleet movements, all the while never letting a notebook titled "A Memoir of the Revolutionary War" leave his hands. Finally, there was the flushed face of Katerose "Karin" von Kreutzel, facing her first combat mission.

Even though they knew the kinds of farewells and the measure of bloodshed awaiting them, the Iserlohn Corridor was, to the Yang Fleet, a festival pavilion. That being the case, why not enjoy it to the fullest, with all the good cheer and bustle that they alone were capable of?

It was March of SE 800 and NIC 2. Reinhard von Lohengramm and Yang Wen-li were about to exchange fire in person for the first time since the Vermillion War, over control of the Liberation Corridor standing from Iserlohn Fortress to the El Facil system. They could not yet guess, how-ever, that this clash would bring about the greatest shock yet for both of them.

ABOUT THE AUTHOR

Yoshiki Tanaka was born in 1952 in Kumamoto Prefecture and completed a doctorate in literature at Gakushuin University. Tanaka won the Gen'eijo (a mystery magazine) New Writer Award with his debut story "Midori no Sogen ni..." (On the green field...) in 1978, then started his career as a science fiction and fantasy writer. Legend of the Galactic Heroes, which translates the European wars of the nineteenth century to an interstellar setting, won the Seiun Award for best science fiction novel in 1987. Tanaka's other works include the fantasy series The Heroic Legend of Arslan and many other science fiction, fantasy, historical, and mystery novels and stories.